# LIP SERVICE

M. J. Rose

# LIP SERVICE

LADY
CHATTERLEY'S
LIBRARY

Copyright © 1998 by M. J. Rose
All rights reserved, including the right to reproduce
this book or portions thereof in any form whatsoever.

ISBN: 0-7394-0504-7

Lady Chatterley's Library
PO Box 1633 Greenwich, CT 06830
Printed in the U.S.A.

To D.P.S.

~

*who,*

*in all his silent ways,*

*has taught me*

*to have faith*

*in love.*

# Acknowledgments

Special thanks to Mara Gleckel and Joan Sanger for their support; to Mickey Surasky for her creativity, Chuck Clayman, Bob Tishenckel, and D. DeLyon for their help; to Roger Cooper and Erika Tsang for opening so many doors; to Linda Marrow and Amy Pierpont for giving this book a home; to Loretta Barrett, who deserves to get the last laugh; and in memory of the original J. Rose.

*Every blade of grass*

*has its Angel*

*that bends over it*

*and whispers,*

*"Grow, grow."*

THE TALMUD

# LIP SERVICE

# Part One

# Prologue

*October 26, 1996*

Lying on my bed—the same bed my husband and I slept in each night—I shut my eyes against the intrusion of everyday objects surrounding me: the silver-framed family photographs on the dresser, Paul's stained silk tie coiled on the chair waiting to be sent to the cleaners, and the still-unread morning newspapers. I concentrated on the man on the other end of the phone who expected me to create an illusion with words so he could climb out of his mind.

"Do you have a fantasy you want to explore today?" I asked, feeling the slow build of excitement I expected at the beginning of each call. How far I'd come since I'd trembled and tripped over those words the first time I'd spoken them.

"Yes." His voice was refined, cultured. Cautious.

"Tell me," I whispered, seeing the dark inside of my eyes.

"Not yet. First . . . describe what you're wearing."

Almost every man started off this way. They called for verbal stimulation but wanted a visual appetizer first. Some men asked me to describe my hair, my eyes, the shape of my lips, the color of my nipples—one man had asked me to describe my knees. Both of Arthur's previous calls—each a week apart—had begun this same way.

"I'm wearing a silk blouse. Buttoned all the way up to my neck."

"That's all?"

"Yes."

"No pants? Skirt? No underwear?" He sounded pleased.

"Nothing. I'm naked underneath the shirt." And it was true. I'd found, on the phone, it was easier to tell as much of the truth as I could. The blouse I was wearing had a designer label sewn into the neck. I used to wear it with a certain olive green suit I had, or with plain black slacks. But since I'd started to dress—or rather un-dress—for my calls, this particular blouse had become one of my fa-vorite outfits. The washed silk felt like breath on my skin, and when I became aroused, my nipples pushed out against the cloth and I liked how it looked.

"Naked," he repeated slowly, as if he were tasting the word. "For me? You knew you would be talking to me?"

"Yes," I said, knowing it was what he wanted to hear.

"Rub the silk against your skin. Tell me what you feel."

"I'm rubbing it against my breasts. Slowly. Against my nipples now. Against my stomach. Between my thighs."

"Does that excite you—to rub it between your thighs?" he asked.

"Uh-huh."

"Say the words," he insisted. "Spell it out. Turn me on."

"It makes me excited to feel the fabric on my thighs because I know I'm getting closer and closer to coming and it's going to feel exquisite when I get there."

And it did.

That was my secret.

There I was. A thirty-eight-year-old woman. Married for four-teen years. With a decent career. Attractive. Devoted to my stepson. Loyal to my friends. On good terms with my parents. Committed to charitable endeavors. Exactly who I appeared to be. And yet there were these new secret things about me—my indecent hunger, my fearlessness—no one I knew would have even guessed.

"Tell me what it feels like. When you're excited. Go slowly. Be explicit." His voice had dropped into a lower register.

Sometimes I pictured the men I spoke to as colors. Arthur was dark crimson. A hidden color. Leaking, spreading out, staining.

"It starts deep inside my stomach. Flutterings. Opening, closing. Pressures building. And then there are sparks on my skin. Like lightning skimming the surface. Right now, I'm imagining that the silk between my legs is your tongue."

"Do you like that?" He sounded genuinely curious.

"Yes, I do. I love it," I answered.

"You're disgusting!"

His sudden anger threw me.

Nervously, I thought back to the other conversations we'd had for a clue as to what I'd said wrong. This was the third time Arthur had called, and each time there'd been something disturbing about our conversation. Everything would be fine until he'd ask me some seemingly harmless question, then he'd react violently to my answer, doubting me, challenging me. He craved knowing how my pleasure felt but then was furious that I could be pleasured.

During our initial call, I'd tried three approaches before he finally responded to being dominated. I'd never done domination before and that first time I was too insecure to improvise so I used a script. He came when I was on the second page, as soon as I ordered him to undress. During the second call, I got as far as the fourth page. He held off climaxing only because I ordered him to.

"Arthur, am I going to have to tell you what to do?" I asked, assuming the same role I'd used with him before.

"No. Not today. Today, I'm going to—" He broke off.

"Do you have another idea?" I asked, wondering where he would lead me and how I'd respond to being there. But he was silent. "Tell me," I insisted, encouraging him to begin the adventure.

"Can I trust you?" He sounded reluctant.

"Yes."

"Can I? You swear?" His voice was uneven. Erratic. For a moment I grew fearful and then reminded myself I was safe in my own bedroom. How could he harm me?

"Who are you really?" he continued. "You're what—a phone number? A voice? Your name probably isn't even real."

"It's exactly because you don't know me that you can trust me. We have no past. No responsibility to each other except for right now on this phone. I can be anyone you want, Arthur. Just tell me—who is it you want me to be?"

"I can't do it. Not like this. I'll have to decide before I call up: I can't stand to hear your sugary cunt voice begging me. Next time, maybe. This time, you tell me. Make me do what you want. Make me the whore you're buying."

It only took a second or two for me to slip into character. The power I wielded—telling him what to do, ordering him around and having him obey—though still foreign to me, was intensely erotic.

"All right, Arthur. I want you to undress for me. Undress now. But don't come yet. Not until I tell you to. Not until I give you permission."

"Yes." His voice lowered again. His breathing quickened.

"Take off your shirt, Arthur."

Rhythmic breathing.

"Now unbuckle your belt. Unbutton your pants. Unzip your fly. Step out of your slacks. I want to see the bulge in your shorts."

"Yes," he said, entering the fictive dream.

The call was going well. Relaxed, I repositioned myself against my pillows. "Face me. Look at me looking at your erection. Touch yourself where you're hard. Rub your cock for me."

His breathing quickened even more and became labored. The sounds encouraged me and I continued.

"Walk toward me so I can touch you. Closer. Now, take off your shorts. I want to see your penis. I want to see how big it is."

"Hmm," he murmured. I imagined a jaguar rolling over on his back in tall grass.

"Walk closer. I want to watch your cock sticking out in front of you—"

"No," he said, interrupting me.

"Yes. Do it. Do as I say."

"Why?" He panted the word, angry again.

"Because I say so. Now, do it."

"No."

If I was understanding the game correctly, he was asserting himself to test me. I raised my voice. "Do as I say, Arthur, or I will have to punish you. Is that clear? Now, walk to me. And stroke yourself while you do it."

"Can you punish me? Now that's an idea. Can you? Can a sweet little girl like you get mean? Make me sting? Smart? Suffer? Can you make me pain, you little bitch? Can you?" he taunted.

His words crawled on my skin like lice.

For the first time on the phone, I was truly frightened. I'd never talked to a man who'd wanted me to inflict pain—and I wasn't certain I could continue.

On the other end of the phone, he sensed my hesitation. "I thought you were a brave slut," he said, baiting me; his voice still viral, infected.

"I am."

Why hadn't I just hung up? Was I challenged by the call? Was it some kind of proof of how much I was changing?

"Then do it," he continued spewing. "Hurt me. Give me the fucking pain. Pull me to you. Yeah, pull me to you by my balls," he repeated the words, spacing them out.

"All right, Arthur. I walk up to you and reach out and cup your balls in my hand, first softly, sweetly, caressing them, fooling you into thinking I'm going to be gentle. And then I grab hold of them. Squeezing them hard. Pull your whole body to me by your balls."

He moaned a tortured, ugly, but satisfied noise. "Hurt me more. Make me feel the pain. Searing. Shocking. Talk to me, bitch. Make me scream," he begged.

Before this call, other conversations had opened me up to

dreams. This man was dragging me toward a nightmare and I was advancing, though at its edges my thrill was becoming a cold-sweat panic.

I was scared. Nauseated. Repulsed by what he'd asked for and disgusted by what I'd dredged up from my unconscious to give him. I wanted to hang up. To give up. To turn back. Instead, shaking with misgivings at what I had been an accomplice to, I listened to him gurgle through his orgasm.

# 1

*September 23, 1996*

Five weeks earlier

Like most visitors to the New York Botanical Garden, I'd always seen them during the day in sunshine when the colors of the flowers and foliage were bright and their groomed perfection was obvious. But that evening, as we rode up the winding road that led through the gardens, the brilliance of the gardens was concealed by the encroaching twilight. Rather than the cultivated postcard I was familiar with, I found I preferred the mystery that loomed before me now as the shadows deepened. What was hiding in the old branches of the tall elm? In the twisted limbs of the maple? What was it that made the needles of the spruce quiver? Why did the forest seem more spirited in this dusky light? Then we rounded a turn and the illuminated conservatory blossomed out of the darker greenery surrounding it.

Our car pulled to a stop. Photographers waiting in front of the building started shooting as soon as the chauffeur opened the limo door. I have a grainy photo of us clipped from that weekend's *New*

*York Times* roundup of charitable events. Judging from the composition of the shot, the photographers were obviously favoring my husband, who was charming them with his wide smile and sparkling eyes. The wind had blown his thick hair—black, streaked with gray—and he boyishly reached up to brush it back. He was so good at performing for the camera, he did it effortlessly.

There is much that is telling about the photograph. At first it seems no more than a snapshot for the society pages. The caption: "Dr. Paul Sterling, director of FIT, and his wife, Julia, arriving at Thursday night's fete with the honoree, basketball coach Bob Wilcox." But Bob, who should have been featured (he was, after all, the celebrity and guest of honor), is slightly out of focus and to Paul's left.

I am behind my husband, in his shadow.

All of us are well dressed; the two tall men in tuxedos, I in a floor-length, pale gray, long-sleeved column of crepe de chine by Armani. A ghost in the background—which was how I often felt at my husband's fund-raising events.

That night, my straight blond hair was pulled back and twisted into a slick chignon, a style Paul preferred. Earlier, he'd been looking at himself in the hallway mirror, removing a speck of dust off his lapel, when I came out of the bedroom. He nodded his approval. "You look elegant. The gray of the dress is the same color as your eyes," he said to my image in the mirror. It occurred to me his polished voice was too smooth. My husband, who long before had abandoned his Jewish, middle-class background and Long Island accent, appreciated style more than beauty, believing it to be one of the few indications of true class. He turned to me and touched my hand lightly with his. Not sexually, but as if I were a touchstone.

Now, as I look at the photograph from that night, I seem absent. Smoke about to evaporate in the much more vibrant presence of my husband. His eyes are engaged. Mine are vacant. His smile seems genuine; mine seems pasted on for the cameras. He is there in mind and body, I only in body. And not for long at that.

He had been looking forward to the event; I had been looking forward to its being over. I had no sense that the evening would be a pivotal one, setting certain events in motion that we would be powerless to reverse. There are moments like that—impossible to sense when they are upon us—their importance conceivable only in hindsight.

Even if we weren't aware of it, Paul and I, and to a lesser degree our son, Max, were ready for what was to come. We had already changed directions. The time had come to acknowledge it. Was that why I had such a strong desire to be somewhere—anywhere—else that night? Or was it just that playing hostess to Paul's host at charity dinners was wearing on me? Disliking the fawning status seekers, the celebrity mongers, the socialites, and the small talk, I was unnerved by my role. I survived evenings like that by putting on a mask and becoming a gracious character, agreeable and amiable.

Paul and Bob Wilcox walked ahead of me, up toward the elaborate gingerbread conservatory where the party was under way. Around us were miles of late summer gardens that looked so much more inviting than the crowds. How much would anyone miss me if I disappeared and went off exploring the tended paths I knew so well?

"Julia?" Paul's voice implored me as if I were a recalcitrant child. He'd stopped about twenty feet ahead and was waiting for me, his fingers drumming against his thigh—the only outward manifestation of his impatience.

"It's just so lush at this time of year," I offered as a way of explanation. "It's almost a shame to go inside."

"She's right," Bob said in his Southwest drawl. "Let's all play hooky—have ourselves a picnic in the woods." Well over six feet tall, he looked down and out past the party at the gardens darkened but not yet diminished by the twilight.

"Oh no, I'm not going to lose both of you to the wilds of the Botanical Garden. C'mon, Julia, don't tempt the guest of honor." My husband sounded perfectly affable but his fingers were still drumming.

A renowned psychiatrist, Paul had closed his practice four years earlier to become the director of FIT (an acronym for a nonprofit agency called Fathers in Trouble). Now, he navigated the politics of the New York City government as well as the upper echelons of society in his never-ending quest for operating funds. Convincing, seducing, impressing, he catapulted his agency (and himself) into the limelight. FIT had become the charity of the moment.

I rejoined the two men and together we walked up the steps toward the glass building. As usual, I was aware of how much attention Paul attracted. Certainly, a fair share of guests acknowledged Bob, but they stared at Paul, their eyes lingering. There's something hypnotic about my husband's looks; he has the charismatic gleam of either a politician or an actor.

And in a way, he's both.

The first time I saw Paul Sterling—at a party my father was giving in our home for some of his associates in the psychiatric community—I was leaning against a wall sipping a glass of something ice-cold, not knowing what to do with myself. The only thing I had in common with any of these people was that I was in therapy and they were all therapists. Hearing some laughter, I searched for its source and saw Paul at the center of a group. He stood out. His hair was blacker than anyone else's, his eyes bluer. It was as if there were a spotlight on him. As I thought about edging closer to discover what it was about him that could hold those people so enthralled, he looked up, caught my eye, and grinned.

"You look lost," he said, when he finally managed to get through the crowd and over to me. "Can I help you find the bar, some food, a bathroom?"

"No," I laughed, already half in love with his easy confidence. "I live here." But that wasn't what I wanted to say. I wanted to tell him that I really was lost and ask him how he'd known it. I never would have guessed he was lost too.

We had just exchanged names and only begun to talk when someone walked over, interrupting, wanting to speak to Paul. And then someone else. Until, soon, he was in the center of another crowd and I just slipped away.

"You got lost again," he said, when he found me a few minutes later. His hand was determined as it surrounded mine and pulled me over to the piano. "Sit next to me, Julia. There's only room for the two of us here," he said. He began to improvise a jazz riff. I was alone beside him only a moment before a new crowd gathered. Paul always drew an audience. It wasn't his mastery of the piano. It was his assuredness, his attractiveness, his ease.

I slid as close to him as I could without our bodies touching. He must have sensed my shifting, because he turned to me—his fingers poised above the ivory and black keys—and looked at me, searching my face to see if I was all right, if I was enjoying this as much as he was. And then he smiled—that intimate, engaging smile. Around us, people were watching, noting our silent exchange, but I didn't care, and when his fingers came down again, the sounds of his music went through me, conducted up my spine at the same time the others only heard it.

A star, he shined on me. And I wanted to remain in the gleam of his cool blue light forever.

That night, at the Botanical Garden, I was still in my husband's light. But it no longer burned quite so bright.

Inside the Enid A. Haupt Conservatory's cultivated jungle, the huge fronds of green oversize palms hung down in graceful arcs that led the way through the entrance. Giant elephant ears and fragile ferns, four and five feet across, flanked the steps.

I breathed in deeply. The smell was dark and fresh, a combination of earth and humidity, a scent I knew well but usually associated with my own most peaceful moments. Yet there I was, amidst a throng of guests for whom I was supposed to play hostess.

Following Paul and Bob, I stopped at the bar, where Bob's wife, Lanni, who had come ahead, was waiting. A public relations guru who handled both her husband's press as well as FIT's, Lanni was responsible for the guest list that night. Lanni, in navy sequins, also by Armani, caught my eye and winked. When we'd first met, I hadn't trusted her. Used to cosmopolitan New Yorkers, I found Lanni too amicable, too Texas-friendly. As I got to know her, I discovered behind the drawl was a sensitive, supportive woman I had come to admire.

Immediately, we were surrounded by people, and the evening's work on behalf of FIT began.

Certainly, FIT is a worthwhile program. A revolutionary idea created by Paul and a businessman named Mike Menken, the agency's goal is to train and then find work for the many thousands of jobless divorced and unmarried fathers delinquent in their child support payments.

By training these men and getting them work, FIT is responsible for removing thousands of women and children from welfare rolls. The New York City program is so successful, there are now branches in eight other major cities in the country.

Becoming the agency's director fit my husband's image of himself: powerful, successful, and recognized. He mixed and mingled with the top levels of the city's political infrastructure as well as the city's social strata. Paul had mastered the art of garnering attention for his charity and himself; events like this evening's was a perfect example.

In fact, making Bob Wilcox FIT's spokesperson had added a new dimension to the charity's prominence. For one thing, Paul now had a supply of front-row tickets to any home game played in Madison Square Garden. He offered those seats to the charity's major donors, who never seemed to tire of seeing themselves on the eleven o'clock news, seated beside the likes of JFK Jr., John McEnroe, or Spike Lee.

Bob's involvement with FIT also enhanced my husband's wardrobe. An ambassador for Giorgio Armani, Bob was part of an exclusive group of highly visible people given free access to the designer's Madison Avenue boutique. Through Bob, Paul was offered a twenty-five-thousand-dollar-a-year clothes budget, which he shared with me.

At first, it was awkward to go into the Armani boutique, be fussed over, fitted, and then not given a bill. But the simplicity of the designer's style had always appealed to me. The deceptively austere clothes are secretly seductive. Wearing Armani, my need for complicated accessories or flamboyant jewels disappears. But that night I looked underdressed compared with some of the women whose gowns and jewels were so extravagant, they seemed to be competing with the flowers.

I shook hands, kissed cheeks, complimented women on their clothes and their hair, remembered children's names and spouses' job descriptions and recent ailments. Too soon, the vodka I had been sipping was gone. I wanted another but allowed myself only one cocktail before dinner and one glass of wine with dinner; relaxing was not as important as remaining aware of conversational nuances.

A few feet away from me, Paul was talking to a group who were all listening intently to him. My husband's posture, including the position of his arms, was calculated to put people at ease. He'd taught me to mimic these movements. "Sending the wrong signals can cost money. A mistaken inflection can create a bad impression," he'd instructed.

I couldn't be myself at Paul's events, couldn't take a chance of saying or doing the wrong thing. Everyone there was either a donor, a potential donor, a city politician who needed to be coddled, or a celebrity whose status raised the status of the charity.

My concerns weren't due to my own anxiety—I had almost lost a major donor the year before.

~

We'd been at a small anniversary dinner for friends at an East Side restaurant when, halfway through our meal, Paul noticed Dominick Gray, a donor, and his wife, Sally, seated across the room. For several months Paul had been unsuccessfully trying to woo the Grays, but each time dinner plans had been made the Grays canceled them. In fact, we were supposed to have been taking them out the next evening, but that morning Dominick Gray had called Paul and said Sally was having some stitches removed and dinner might be too much for her.

At Paul's urging, I followed him across the restaurant to say hello to the Grays.

"I'm so sorry you won't be able to join us tomorrow," I said to Sally.

"So am I, but I have this thing with the doctor and Dominick thinks I should take it easy."

"Well, I'm sure you'll be fine. I hope we can reschedule soon," I answered.

An ordinary conversation.

Except it wasn't.

Dominick called Paul the next morning and demanded an apology. How dare I insinuate his wife would be fine? How did I know her visit to the doctor wasn't a serious problem? How could I be so flip?

Paul explained I'd only used a figure of speech, that I was an optimist, sometimes overzealous in my positivity. Eventually he placated Gray, but when Paul came home that night, he used the incident to prove a point.

"I defended you, Julia. But now you understand why I warn you to be so careful. Even the most innocent comment can be misconstrued."

And so I was careful. Probably to the point that many of Paul's associates must have thought at times that I was too quiet—boring, even. I learned to ask questions and interview the people seated on either side of me at dinner parties. I censored my thoughts so that telling smiles or smirks never gave me away. I would go home at night with my face frozen into a mask like the masks I collected and hung on my bedroom walls. Features forever pasted in one position—a sincere smile and intelligent gaze. Composed. Interested. Not curious. Not flirting. Not judgmental. Not any of the things I was.

Finally escaping the cocktail crowd, I made my way to the ladies' room. Inside a stall, I lit a cigarette and reminded myself that this too would pass.

I have gotten through too many situations saying that. *This too shall pass.* My mother used to repeat it to me when I was a child and scared of something. *This too shall pass,* she would say and hug me close, and I would smell her Shalimar perfume and feel, for the moment, so very safe. And she was right; whatever it was I was apprehensive about eventually did pass. After I had my nervous breakdown in college, I found myself chanting it like a mantra. *This too shall pass. This too shall pass.* And except for a few scars, it did.

I dropped the cigarette butt in the toilet, flushed, then walked outside. Normally I don't smoke, but I gave myself a treat whenever my presence was required at one of Paul's fund-raisers: a cigarette for being good, for behaving.

I stood at the mirrored vanity and reapplied my lipstick, inspecting my face for smudges, for stray eyelashes, for anything that didn't belong there, including the look I always feared seeing: the wanton, dissatisfied look. The bad Julia's face. It never appeared, but still, I apprehensively watched for its unwelcome return.

Coming out of the ladies' room, I found myself caught up in the throng of people moving through the greenhouse. Could I be the only one looking up at the elaborate domed ceiling? At the flowers? The plants? No one else seemed aware of their surroundings as they chatted to each other and moved about.

No matter how often I went there—to take gardening classes or wander around the grounds—I always found myself inside this building, staring up and out the glass roof, into the sky. This conservatory had become one of my refuges; I resented having it disrupted.

Continuing to follow the crowd, I reached the dining room. The air was redolent with the scent of roses so heavy, full, and fat their voluptuousness embarrassed me. Just as it had been so hard for me to refrain from leaving the party to roam the gardens outside, it was difficult for me to refrain from burying my face in the roses, to keep my fingers from touching their silken petals, to avoid the lure of engaging in some kind of communion with them.

Finally, I found our table in the middle of the room. Bob and Lanni Wilcox were already there talking to Mike Menken and his wife, Georgia, who was on the board of the Botanical Garden.

As I tried to make my way over to Lanni, Paul sidetracked me. "Julia, come meet the Foleys."

I had been briefed in the limousine ride: Tom and Jill Foley—he was in publishing—were involved in a half-dozen causes and had recently decided to consolidate their philanthropic efforts to one or two charities. Paul was campaigning for FIT.

Tom and Jill looked alike in that way a married couple can. Both of them were tall, angular, and stoic and resembled a sophisticated version of Grant Wood's *American Gothic.*

I was polite, interested, and flattering, making good eye contact during the short conversation we had while we waited for the rest of the table to arrive. And then we all went to find our seats.

Tom Foley was on my right. Sam Butterfield was on my left.

"Good evening, Julia," Sam said, his round eyes twinkling, his full lips curving in a smile. A short, compact man in his sixties, his silver hair fell in waves to his shoulders, longer than was currently popular. Instead of a formal white shirt, he wore a rebellious faded blue chambray work shirt with his tuxedo.

As had happened the few other times we had met, I took a slight step backward—leery of getting too close.

After Paul made the introductions around the table, Sam's gaze came to rest on me, his dark blue eyes searching mine as if he were trying to unearth me.

"You don't look anything like the Julia who I used to see at the institute," Sam said. His voice was rough, as if it had been rubbed with sandpaper.

The month before I had done a small freelance job, writing a four-page brochure about the institute for Sam and his wife, Nina. I hadn't gotten to know Sam well, but I'd liked and was impressed by Nina. Since she'd moved up to Harvard to teach for the fall semester, she couldn't be at the fund-raiser that night and I was sorry. She would have made the evening more palatable.

"No, I suppose not," I said. "But how could I work dressed up like this?"

"Hell, I don't mean your clothes." He gestured with his hands, his thick fingers moving in the air. "It's your whole damn persona."

"Does every psychiatrist feel it's acceptable to unabashedly delve into other people's lives?" I asked.

"You tell me." He laughed, and all his features dissolved into each other.

"Well, my father—who's a shrink—does, and my husband does . . . all his associates do."

"I hate to be lumped in with all his associates," Sam teased.

From the right, a waiter served warm mushroom tarts and I used the distraction to attend to Tom Foley.

"So Julia, are you involved in your husband's endeavor?" Tom eventually asked.

"Just as a hostess," I said.

"Demanding job. I see Jill doing it and feel pity for her. Not too rewarding, is it?"

"Actually, I think it is." I had my mask on.

"Bullshit," Sam whispered on my other side and then joined in our conversation. "C'mon. How rewarding can it be for you to meet and greet and make polite conversation with strangers night after night?" Devil's advocate was a role he was well suited to.

"I get to know them, and then they're not strangers; they become our friends." It wasn't the answer I wanted to give but the one I was required to give.

"Look around this room and tell me honestly how many people here are your friends," Sam demanded, but before I could even come up with an answer, he answered for me. "Four. If you're lucky."

He turned back to his tart and I checked on Tom, who was now engaged with the woman to his right.

"You're good at this—being someone you're not, aren't you?" Sam asked.

"I don't know what you mean," I said, hedging.

"Bullshit. You know exactly what I mean. I'm talking about inventing a persona and hiding behind it. Don't bother to refute me. I know the signs; I've studied people my whole life."

Rather than continue the discussion, I glanced past Sam to Jill Foley, who was staring off into space, and drew her into a conversation. For a few minutes, everything went smoothly until Sam made a reference to the institute.

"What institute is that?" Jill Foley asked.

"My wife and I run the Butterfield Institute," Sam said.

"The sex clinic?" Jill frowned.

"Yes. Have you heard of it?" Sam asked.

"It's hard not to. Every time I open a magazine, it seems you or your wife are being quoted. It's impossible to avoid your radical theories." From her tone, she obviously disapproved.

Sam examined her pinched face for a long moment before responding. "We need air to breathe, food to eat, a roof over our heads. And we need sex. It's a primal urge, not an intellectual decision, although our Judeo-Christian ethic has done everything in its power to make it one, screwing up people along the way." He shook his head for emphasis and his white hair flew around him like a lion's mane. "Someone has to undo some of that damage. That's what the institute's for."

Jill Foley clasped her hands together as if she were praying. "We're already far too open as a society," she argued.

Sam enjoyed defending his position. "We're not open at all. We may allow movies, television, and books to depict explicit sex, but shit, as human beings, we're still uptight and puritanical."

"I can't agree. We're much too permissive and altogether too tolerant of deviant behavior. Our whole value system is corrupt." Jill was adamant.

"C'mon, is it deviant or dangerous when two animals mate? Of course not. It's the church, in its effort to control people, that has created these arbitrary boundaries and rules to corral our sexual appetites. They've made us ashamed and guilty about our genitalia because they're too close to the part of the body that produces waste. In our culture, we're fucked by the time we're toilet trained."

"Do you mean to imply other cultures with a different relationship to sex are better off?" she asked contemptuously.

It was well past the time for me to interrupt and change the subject. Jill had become belligerent and Sam, argumentative, but I was too curious. I wanted to hear Sam's response.

"Well, yes. Certain eastern cultures see sexuality not as a fall from grace but as a way to ascend to a state of grace, to a state of self-realization. Achieving transcendental knowledge is their goal; their means is through the body." Even though he'd been answering Jill's question, Sam had been looking at me. So now Jill was insulted as well as indignant.

Across the table, Paul noticed no one was talking to Tom Foley and, excusing himself from Georgia Menken, he walked around to our side.

Not knowing what had transpired, Paul couldn't have avoided what followed.

"Jill, Tom, I wanted to make sure you two got a chance to talk to Sam Butterfield. He's one of our most fervent supporters. Over the last three years, he's employed several of our graduates."

Jill remained aloof, but Tom was interested.

"In fact, we just promoted one of your graduates to be our assistant librarian," Sam said.

"There's great satisfaction in active participation," Tom said. "Anyone can just write a check. What kind of company do you have, Sam?"

Assuming Tom and his wife shared similar prejudices, I tried to warn Paul to intervene, but my husband wasn't paying attention to me—he was absorbed in getting the two men to bond.

"Sam is the founder of the Butterfield Institute," Paul boasted, adding, "In the psychiatric community, it's considered the finest clinic of its kind."

"The Butterfield Institute? Sorry, I don't think I'm aware of it," Tom said.

"It's that progressive sex clinic, Tom," Jill said, as if she'd just eaten spoiled food.

Immediately, Paul changed the subject back to FIT and they continued conversing about the charity until the waiter interrupted with the next course.

"Oh well, I suppose that will put an end to Paul's trotting me out to impress new devotees for a while," Sam said to me in a low voice once Paul had returned to his seat. Jill had turned her full attention to the man on her left and Tom was busy with the dinner partner on his right.

"Perhaps we should play it safe and talk about something innocuous in case anyone's eavesdropping," I joked.

"All right. What do you know about poetry?" Sam asked.

"Sorry—I haven't read any since college."

"Did you ever hear of the poet Robert Herrick?"

I sipped some wine and tried to remember. "I think so. Was he a nineteenth-century English poet?"

"Seventeenth. He had a mistress to whom he wrote reams of poetry." Sam paused. "Her name was Julia. One of the better-known poems is called "Upon Julia's Clothes." Do you know it?"

"No."

Sam shut his eyes and let his head fall back a bit. Slightly too suggestive for the time and place. I looked over at Paul, but he was engrossed in conversation.

"'Whenas in silks my Julia goes, / Then, then (methinks) how sweetly flows / That liquefaction of her clothes. / Next when I cast mine eyes, and see / That brave vibration each way free, / O how that glittering taketh me!'" Sam opened his eyes and looked at me, awaiting a response.

"That was beautiful," I whispered, half enthralled, half embarrassed by his expansiveness.

"You mean you never had a lover read that to you?"

I shook my head no.

"Fucking shame. It was written over three hundred years ago, but it fits you—especially tonight. There's a beautiful tradition in quoting love poetry. It's a powerful and underrated aphrodisiac."

The setting for Sam's sentiment was perfect. Victorian conservatories had often been used as trysting places where lovers met and read poetry to express emotions both were too shy to speak directly. But considering the occasion, Sam's comments were inappropriate.

Because I was on my best behavior, I was able to appear composed. But his flirting had unnerved me.

I reminded myself that a good therapist has the ability to instantly connect to a patient. It was a gift I'd seen firsthand with my father, with Dr. Maggie Stone, who was my therapist, and with my husband. Now, I tried to convince myself that that was all Sam had done with me. But when he'd recited those lines I'd become aware of the thin fabric of my dress against my body. I'd felt my skin flush; my nipples harden. How long had it been since a man had made me aware of myself?

As the waiter refilled our wineglasses, I realized that while we'd been talking, I'd finished my wine. Usually I was able to make one glass last all evening.

It was time to turn my attention to Tom Foley, so it wasn't until after the main course that I spoke with Sam again.

"I've been watching you, Julia. You're damn good at deflecting questions. Too many secrets?" he asked, as the waiter cleared our plates.

"No. None at all," I said.

"How sad," he said, feigning a sorrowful smile. Obviously he didn't believe me.

I wanted to turn his question back on him, trade him one of my secrets for one of his, but he didn't give me a chance.

"I've been thinking that all those radical things we're doing at the institute deserve to be written up in a big, fat book. Would you be interested?" Sam asked.

"Yes, I'd love to read it," I answered.

"Fuck no. I want to know if you'd be interested in writing it."

While I listened in dazed silence, Sam went into more detail including what he'd expect to pay me if I agreed to take on the project. Before I got a chance to respond, Paul, circulating again, came up behind me. Sam wasn't shy about telling Paul how much he was enjoying my company.

"Yes, Julia's very special," Paul said, as if I weren't there. "I'm very proud of her."

"Please, Paul," I said, blushing. "You're embarrassing me."

Ignoring me, my husband continued. "When I first told her I'd been offered the directorship of FIT, I warned her my working for a nonprofit would mean us making sacrifices, but Julia never complained. She rolled up her sleeves and started taking as many freelance jobs as she could get to make up the difference and she hasn't slowed down since."

"Well, she's done a damn good job for us and I'm hoping our association will continue with a book I've been thinking about. I think we both could get a lot out of it."

Beside me I saw Tom Foley's head swing around. Paul noticed it too.

"A book?" Tom asked. "I thought I heard someone talking about a book. Who's writing this book?"

For reasons I didn't understand until later, Paul deflected the question and got Tom talking about his publishing company's newest offerings.

~

"Is Paul supportive?" Sam asked, once my husband had returned to his seat.

"You heard him bragging."

"Yeah, but he was saying what he wanted me to hear. What I'm asking you is how he really treats you."

"Why would you think he wasn't being straight with you?" I asked.

"You didn't answer my question," he said.

"What was your question?" I'd used the therapist's old trick of answering a question with a question and hoped Sam would be polite enough to back off, but he didn't. The truth was, Paul supported my efforts when it suited his purposes; the rest of the time, he worried I pushed myself too hard.

"You should know better than to try that with me," Sam said.

"And you should know better than to pry." We both laughed.

Across the table, Paul was deep in conversation with Georgia Menken, leaning close to her, listening intently, a smile poised on his mouth for the moment it would be appropriate. Unconditional attention. Nonjudgmental responses. It was his good-father role, his sales spiel, practiced so often it was second nature to him by now.

Well coached by Paul not to reveal anything personal or controversial with his business associates or donors, I changed the subject as the waiter poured coffee. "Sam, how is Nina liking Harvard?" I asked.

"She's having a ball, but that's typical. She loves new situations. At heart she's an adventuress."

"You must . . ." I fumbled over my words and started again. "It must be exciting to be married to someone like that."

"Exciting and at times dangerous."

"What makes it dangerous?" I asked.

"Well, Nina and I are both explorers, so sometimes we wind up in uncharted territory."

"Explorers of what?"

"We really believe all that stuff we spout at the institute. We believe that in order for people to survive in a relationship, they have to open themselves up to each other without fearing the outcome or the ramifications. They need to explore their sexual selves with each other, without holding back or worrying how things will look to anyone outside the union."

"You've really managed that?" I asked.

"Your question leads me to believe you haven't," Sam said as the waiter put a dessert plate down in front of me. I inspected the hard chocolate shell filled with ruffles of chocolate mousse, and rather than respond to Sam's question, I spooned some of the mousse into my mouth, letting the chocolate dissolve on my tongue, concentrating on the bittersweet taste.

Suddenly, Sam had ceased to be interesting or eccentric. Probing too deeply, getting too near those parts of myself that I'd long ago closed off, he had become intimidating.

# 2

Paul and I and Bob and Lanni Wilcox shared the limo back into Manhattan, so my husband didn't have a chance to talk to me on the way home. As we headed south on Fifth Avenue, he directed the driver to turn east on 84th Street and then to pull over to the curb a quarter of the way down the block.

Three East 84th Street was a small Art Deco building far more exclusive than Paul and I could have afforded on our own. But the apartment, like the Armani clothes, wasn't really ours.

Apartment 10B belonged to the mother of one of Paul's patients, who'd offered it to Paul as a thank-you for helping her youngest son after a bad psychotic break. Paul could afford the maintenance when he was in private practice, but not when he became director of FIT. We would have had to move if Paul hadn't convinced the agency's board to pay the rent as part of his employment package.

The doorman opened the glass-and-iron door for us, and Paul and I walked across the marble lobby and into the wood-paneled elevator. Paul couldn't wait to deliver his pronouncement and started as soon as we stepped into the hall and out of the elevator man's earshot. "After considering the situation, Julia, I don't think you should take on Sam Butterfield's book."

Paul opened the front door with his key and preceded me inside.

"Why not?" I asked, as I walked past him. Behind me, Paul locked the front door. It was dark in our foyer, but neither of us bothered to turn on the light. We continued down the hall and into the bedroom, which, like the rest of the apartment, was done in shades of pale beige.

"I don't think you're up to it," Paul said, while he carefully removed the pearl studs from his shirt.

I looked away from his face and looked up at the wall above the bed at my collection of masks. There were almost two dozen: porcelain, wood, some made of plaster. Focusing on a Venetian carnival mask, I remembered when Paul had given it to me.

We'd been on vacation in Venice. He'd gone out jogging at sunset and surprised me with the mask when he came back. We drank some wine and made love in a room that had no air-conditioning. Afterward, we'd thrown all the windows open and laughed at the singing gondoliers. How long ago had that been? Eleven years ago? Twelve?

Turning my back on the mask, I unzipped my dress and walked to the closet to hang it up. I still hadn't responded to what Paul had said.

After undressing, I pulled a white cotton nightshirt over my head, went into the bathroom to remove my makeup, and then walked to the bed. Once I climbed in, I pulled the quilt up, covering me to my neck. "What do you mean, I'm not up to doing the book?" I asked.

"It would be too much pressure for you to take on a project like that now." Paul took off his shirt.

"Emotional pressure?"

"Yes, of course." He continued undressing.

"You can't be serious?" I asked.

"Why not?" Paul asked rhetorically, and walked off toward the bathroom.

A few minutes later, wearing only boxer shorts, Paul checked to see if the air conditioner was on and then got into his side of the bed. The room could never be cold enough for him.

"Is this about Tom and Jill Foley's reaction to Sam's clinic?" I asked. "Are you afraid of offending them and losing them as potential donors if they find out I'm writing a book with Sam?"

"That has nothing to do with my decision—"

"Wait," I interrupted. "It's not your decision. Sam asked me to write this book, not you. And I don't want to turn him down. Do you realize how long I've been trying to get an opportunity like this? I'll finally be able to establish myself as a writer. Not to mention what it could do for our finances."

"I appreciate your efforts to supplement our income, Julia, but not at the expense of your mental health."

All during our marriage, Paul had kept psychological tabs on my psyche and talked to me like I was one of his patients. More and more, it ate away at me when he did it.

"Bullshit. My mental health is not the issue here unless you want to talk about the ramifications of my turning down my first shot at a book. And then there's the money. We could use it."

Paul clicked on the television and channel-surfed. "Julia, I couldn't live with myself if I allowed you to risk your health for a few thousand dollars."

"A few thousand dollars? I'd be getting twenty thousand up front and a royalty. That's almost a year of Max's tuition."

"Please, Julia, don't fight me. Call Sam tomorrow and tell him you've decided not to do the book."

The garish television light flickered across my husband's impassive face.

I sat up. "I can't believe this, Paul. A month ago I didn't want to do the Butterfield brochure because I didn't want the pressure of working for your donors. But you said they might be insulted if I turned them down and you couldn't chance it. What's going on?"

"That was a small brochure. This is a book, and in my opinion, a book would be too taxing for you. You're not psychologically equipped for it," Paul said. "Be a good girl, okay?" He smiled and then continued. "Call Sam tomorrow and explain it to him."

Growing up, I'd always been a good girl—doing exactly what my parents expected of me and basking in their approval until I went off to the Ivy League college we'd all chosen together. Suddenly, my parents weren't there to approve or disapprove anymore and I had to look for acknowledgment from other sources: I struggled to get A's to please my professors, I did the most dangerous drugs to make me popular with my friends, and I slept with almost any boy who was interested just to prove I was desirable. Looking back, I can see myself only as a reflection in other people's eyes.

The wilder I was, the emptier I felt, but there was no one to turn to, no one who noticed; it was the late 1970s and there were no rules, no curfews.

And then, just before the end of my second semester of my sophomore year, I crashed and had a full-blown nervous breakdown.

Rather than accept the blame, I split myself in half and blamed the bad girl, the promiscuous wild child who had suddenly emerged. And I—the good Julia—was off the hook.

I didn't return to college that fall; I went into therapy instead. And that's where I still was four years later when I met Paul.

I'd heard so many accolades for Paul from my father, who'd been his supervisor, I was predisposed to like him. I knew that he was an up-and-coming therapist. That he'd married his childhood sweetheart, that they'd had a son. And that when the little boy was two, Paul's wife had tragically died.

By the time we met at my parent's party, I'd romanticized Paul's story, imagining the emptiness in his heart where his love for her had been. It would be a palpable need I'd discern in his eyes, I thought. What I didn't know until years later was that Paul had also been disposed to find me interesting—not only because I was his mentor's daughter but also because over the years, my father had shared much of my psychological history with Paul, almost setting him up to be one of my caretakers.

We started dating and quickly discovered how well matched we were. It seemed quite natural when, after knowing each other only a few weeks, Paul invited me to go ice skating with him and his four-year-old son on a Saturday afternoon.

Max was a silent, wide-eyed child who was shy with me at first. Only after we all got our skates on and set off for the ice did he relax and became a typically joyous, rambunctious little boy. We were at the Wollman Rink in the middle of Central Park and it was one of those crisp, cold days with a gray sky that threatened snow. Paul took both Max and me by the arm and, linked together, we set off, gliding to the rhythm of the music. Like his father, Max was a natural athlete, and I was impressed with his ability to navigate the ice in time to the music.

Finally, it began to snow. Max was enchanted and opened his mouth to catch the flakes on his tongue. Soon the snow was falling heavily and skaters began leaving. Max insisted we stay so we could be the last to leave. And when we were the last ones there, he was so excited about having the whole rink to himself, he decided we should have a race.

Paul looked at me inquisitively. "You up for it?" he asked.

After experiencing the afternoon through Max's delight, racing across the empty rink suddenly seemed compulsory.

We all got ready, Paul shouted go, and we took off across the glassy surface. Skates slashed the ice, the cold wind hit my face, snowflakes fell in my eyes, and the next thing I knew, Paul and Max were standing over me, both looking much more alarmed than I thought they should have been.

"Are you all right, Julia?" Paul crouched down beside me and touched my hand with his, as if he were checking that I was really still there.

Mimicking his father's movements, Max did the same.

I was falling for a four-year-old.

"I'm fine," I said, as I struggled to stand.

"Let me help you." Paul took one arm. Max took the other. Once I was standing, Paul moved his arm around my waist, Max took my hand, and the two of them skated me over to a bench.

"I'm fine. It was nothing." I really felt all right. Actually, I felt better than all right. Paul's concern wrapped around my shivering shoulders like a warm blanket.

For the first time in several years, I could imagine quitting therapy and getting on with my life.

I didn't realize then that all I'd been seduced by was Paul's bedside manner. He'd treated me with the same studied concern he showed his patients. But to me, at that time of my life, with my nightmarish breakdown still so fresh in my memory, Paul's protection and caring, beyond anything else—beyond passion or even love—were the greatest gifts he could have given me.

"You slipped and fell. You might be hurt. I want you to sit down for a while and rest," Paul said.

"When I fall, I can get right back up, but you have to be careful," Max told me.

"How come you can get right back up and I can't?" I asked, laughing.

Max cocked his head and looked at me for half a minute before he answered. "Because I'm tough, like Daddy. But you might break like—" His lower lip started to tremble and Paul knelt down so that he was at eye level with his son.

"Hey, why don't you go out there and do a few more spins for us, and when you're done, we'll all go and find a place to have hot chocolate."

While the snow continued to fall, dusting our clothes and our hair, Max dipped in and out of elaborate figure eights. While we watched the tiny boy all alone on the giant rink, Paul told me about the horseback riding accident that had killed his wife and left Max without a mother.

I saw snowflakes catch in Paul's black eyelashes and melt on his cheeks and didn't know what to say.

That was when he turned to me and kissed me lightly with lips wet from the snow.

What I remember about the first time we touched was how very cold his lips were and how my lips couldn't warm them.

A few months later, Paul asked me to marry him and I accepted. My therapist was the only person who didn't seem pleased. Dr. Stone was too much of a professional to come right out and say so, but I knew her well enough to sense her concern and disapproval.

It was only a few weeks before the wedding when I announced that I wanted to stop seeing her.

"Why do you want to leave now?" she asked, as she leaned forward in her chair so she could be closer to me on the couch.

"I'm ready," I said up to the ceiling, staring at those three cracks that had always looked like a woman's profile to me. "I want to get on with my life. Don't you think after four years I'm ready?" I twisted my head so I could just see her out of the corner of my eye.

"Do you?" Dr. Stone asked.

"Don't do that. Don't answer me with another question." I looked back up at the ceiling.

"Julia," she said calmly, "I want you to think about why you want to leave now. So suddenly. There are rough spots and adjustments in every marriage. Don't you think you might need some help with them?"

"I'll be fine," I answered. "I'm in love with Paul. And with his son. You should see them together. The way Paul takes care of Max . . . how they rely on each other. They need me, Dr. Stone."

"Let's compromise," she suggested. "Stay in therapy until after the wedding . . . then decide."

I promised her I would, but I didn't. Not only was I confident about marrying Paul and becoming Max's stepmother, but my parents were as well. And even though I was an adult, their approval still carried far too much weight with me. My father was especially proud I was marrying a doctor he trained. He was turning me over to a more than competent man, he'd said. It wasn't until many years had passed that I remembered the comment and realized he'd been talking about me as if I were his patient, not his daughter.

Marrying Paul was the first thing I had done in a long time that required no effort on my part. Therapy had been arduous. Every minute of every hour I was there was a struggle. Paul's world was already worked out and there was nothing required of me but moving in. He had a successful practice, a wonderful son, a beautiful apartment. And at the center of it all was an empty space just waiting to be filled. In exchange for my fitting in so exactly, Paul promised his devotion and care. I was finally relieved of my burdens. Around Paul and Max I was safe and felt loved and never feared that the troubling wild side of me would show its face.

I was sitting up in bed, staring at Paul as he continued to diagnose me, explaining how much tension and pressure I'd be under if I collaborated with Sam. "You've always been fragile, Julia—you know that, don't you?" he asked. "Of course you do," he said, answering his own question before I had a chance to.

Armed with my history, and ever the psychiatrist, he knew how to present his case. As usual, I felt myself about to buckle.

I had left the mirrored closet door open, and while he was advising me, Paul was looking at himself. It struck me how much time had passed since Paul had been that young doctor I'd first met. Now, he was an overly confident middle-aged luminary studying his own image while I continued to act like a twenty-three-year-old who was still desperate for his approval, needy of his protection.

"What reason can I give him for not doing the book so he's not insulted?" I asked.

"The real reason. That you're not sure you're strong enough to emotionally sustain the pressure of the assignment. That since your son has left for college you've been depressed and—"

"But I'm not depressed. Sure, I miss Max, but that's normal. Don't you miss him?"

"Julia, you're not the doctor."

"I'm not the patient, either. I'm your wife," I answered quietly.

Trying for compassion, Paul took my hand, but he held it the way doctors do when they're dealing with someone emotionally overwrought.

"Do you really think my being involved with Sam's book could hurt your fund-raising efforts for FIT?" I asked.

Perhaps, if my husband had been truthful that night, everything might be different now, but he hadn't been.

"My fund-raising? Absolutely not. My only concern is for you. In my opinion, you're too delicate, too susceptible to stress to take on a project of that magnitude. All right?"

*No!* I wanted to shout, but as he examined my face, waiting for my response, I lost my nerve.

"Yes . . . ," I whispered, waiting for and then seeing the smile curve his lips and the look of appreciation appear in his eyes. Yes, there I was, reflected in his gaze: Paul Sterling's good wife.

Leaning over, he kissed me on the forehead as if he were putting a period on the end of the sentence. "Good night, Julia. Try to get some sleep," he said, and started flicking through the channels.

His concern still made me feel so cherished. And so disappointed in myself.

Using the remote, Paul continued to search for something that would appeal to him. For all his intelligence, he was addicted to bad television, claiming the exploitation shows and melodramas taught him things about our culture and his clients. But I saw him watch those made-for-television movies and the equally violent entertainment-type news shows, and he wasn't an observing scientist—he was engrossed in the fights, the battles, the crashes, the blood, and the murders.

While Paul watched a Steven Seagal movie, I rolled over on my side and tried to fall asleep, but I kept hearing Sam's scratchy voice describing how he made his marriage work.

Reaching out, I found my husband's hand.

Perfunctorily he patted me, then extricated his arm with a perceptible shift of his body away from me. I sat up, and leaning on one elbow, kissed him on the lips. He didn't respond, but I didn't let up. Instead, I increased the pressure of my lips on his, kissing him so hard I could feel my teeth grinding into his.

What was I doing? Asking him to give me something in exchange for what he had taken away?

"Make love to me," I whispered. "Let me make love to you—"

Gently, he pushed me off. "That's not you talking, Julia. It was a trying night for you; you're acting out."

"No, I'm not."

"I know the signs, Julia . . . please." He sighed in annoyance.

Rejected, I moved back to my side of the bed and while Paul continued watching the movie, I seethed. "You make me feel as if I'm putting pressure on you. But we're married. It's not so strange that once in a while I'd like us to make love." I'd had this conversation with Paul before. So why was I invoking it again? I knew where it would end. I was only setting myself up.

"You have unrealistic expectations of what a long-term relationship is like, Julia."

"No, I don't."

"Speaking as a professional, I don't agree."

"Then don't speak as a professional, damn it. We're in bed. Speak as a husband."

"Julia, it's late and you're upset. Let me get you something to help you fall asleep."

He was out of bed and in the bathroom before I could answer. He returned carrying a glass of water and a pill, which I took obediently. The easy way out.

In the beginning of our marriage, Paul's sexual disinterest suited me. Sex was still an unpleasant reminder to me of how much control I'd lost in college. Besides, it was easy to ignore how infrequent our lovemaking was when Max, who couldn't get enough attention, came into the bedroom almost every night to sleep between us.

But as the years passed and my breakdown drifted further into the past, I began to heal and to crave some kind of physical relationship with my husband. Then I discovered Paul wasn't interested. I wondered why a forty-year-old man would choose to be practically celibate when he had a wife ready and available. I blamed myself and set out to seduce him, but for the most part he rebuffed my overtures. Didn't he have physical needs too? Didn't he need some kind of gratification?

And then, one morning I woke up much earlier than usual, and while I floated between sleep and wakefulness, I became aware of a certain rhythm, a rocking I felt through my whole body.

Beside me in bed, Paul was masturbating.

I lay still while he slowly worked himself up and over the edge.

I didn't say anything; it was an isolated incident.

Until it happened again.

I began waking up early every day. Lying still with my eyes shut, I feigned sleep as I waited for my husband to masturbate. One morning I pretended I was only half awake and rolled closer to him, letting my hand rest on his, moving in time to his movements, trying to become part of his secret ritual. But Paul froze. He shut me out. My husband didn't want me involved in his sexual release; he didn't want to be intimate with me.

Several times I had seriously considered leaving my husband. Once I even got so far as to make an appointment with a divorce lawyer. It was a few days before my scheduled meeting when Max, who was about eight, came home from school, rushed by me without any greeting, and locked himself in his room. It took me a half hour, sitting outside his door, cross-legged on the floor, talking through the wood, but I finally convinced him to come out.

With rivers of tears running down his cheeks, he sat down across from me and bravely hiccuped his way through his story. On their way home, Charlie, a school friend of Max's, had started a fight. Instead of standing up to him, Max had chickened out and run away.

When he finally got it all out, he was exhausted. Lying down, he dropped his head in my lap, shut his eyes tightly against his shame, and let me comfort him.

How could I leave? How could I abandon Max?

But Max had grown up and was off at college. Max had been the one to leave.

"Maybe we should see someone, Paul," I said, after I'd swallowed the pill and put the water glass on the bedside table. It had been years since I complained about our physical relationship, because in many ways my life was exactly how I wanted it to be. But something had irrevocably shifted that night. I'd never cared about the financial sacrifices Paul asked me to make, but I could no longer tolerate the emotional ones.

Without turning away from the television, Paul said: "I am someone, Julia. We don't need outside help. You just have to trust I know what's best for you."

I let Paul go back to the world inside the television screen where he was lost to me. While I waited for the sleeping pill to work, I turned on my side so that my back was to him and tried to count how many nights I'd gone to bed without being touched and wondered how many more were ahead of me. How many more nights would I take the pill my husband offered me instead of himself and allow myself to be silenced, pretending that there was nothing wrong with our marriage?

# 3

How therapists use sexual role-playing and how couples can use it by themselves was the subject of the book Sam wanted me to coauthor. That was the book I was on my way to tell Sam I was turning down.

On 65th Street, between Park and Madison Avenues, sat a lovely limestone mansionette built sometime in the early 1900s. Once it had been someone's home, but now, according to the plaque beside the door, it housed the Butterfield Institute. Nothing about the building's elegant façade or classic lines suggested that past the Ionic columns and through the wrought-iron door was the most progressive sex clinic in the country.

Inside the marble-floored foyer, a glittering chandelier cast a soft light on the reception area. The elegant woman behind an ornate desk complete with ormolu corners and lion's claw feet nodded discreetly and offered me a seat.

If I hadn't known this was a sex clinic, the decor would not have given any indicaton. I might have been in the waiting room of an embassy or an art gallery.

Opposite me, curtained French doors led to what must have been the parlor when the house was first built, and through the partially open doors I could glimpse a marble fireplace, heavy gilt molding around the perimeter of the ceiling, and another chandelier.

There were two other women in the waiting room with me—one quite young, maybe in her early twenties, the other about fifty. Mother and daughter? Aunt and niece? Or were they lovers there to discuss problems in their relationship? I was well on my way to inventing their history when the receptionist told them Dr. Lennox was ready for them. The older woman went first, the younger lagged a few steps behind, looking down at the floor as she passed me.

A few minutes later, the receptionist told me to go on up to Dr. Butterfield's office.

I walked up the marble staircase to the first landing and turned left. In an alcove, Sam's secretary sat at her desk. I had met Elaine when I'd been here last month doing the brochure, and after we exchanged greetings, she told me that Sam would be a few more minutes but that I could have a seat inside.

"Actually, I have a bill to drop off—is there enough time for me to go upstairs and do that?" I asked.

"Sure, Sam's up there in a meeting. It wouldn't be a bad idea to walk by the main conference room on your way to accounting so he sees you and remembers you're waiting."

Taking the stairs, I climbed past the third floor—filled with therapists' offices—then past the fourth floor, which housed one of the most complete libraries on the subject of sexuality anywhere in the United States. I'd done most of the previous month's work on the brochure there, sitting at a reading table looking down on the institute's small but well-tended garden.

Finally I arrived at the fifth floor, jokingly referred to as the Bank by Butterfield's employees—and not because the accounting offices were here. The institute ran its most profitable business from this rooftop extension. The Butterfield catalogue included everything from sexual self-help books and audiotapes to how-to videos for better sexual functioning. Not part of the original building, the fifth floor's ceilings were only eight feet high, and there was no molding, no antiques, no old wooden floors. Here were clean white linoleum floors, stainless steel desks, and state-of-the-art computer equipment.

After dropping off my bill, I backtracked past a glassed-in conference room. Seeing me, Sam motioned he'd be only another minute. I nodded and continued down the hall.

I must have taken a wrong turn, because suddenly I was lost in a mazelike confusion of hallways that not only looked alike but had identical unmarked doors. Hearing a voice emanating from behind one of the closed doors, I stopped and put my hand up to knock, figuring I'd ask whomever was inside to point me in the right direction.

But what if I was interrupting someone? What if these were therapists' offices up here? I stood for a moment listening . . .

"I flash my lights and you pull over to the side of the road. When I get out of my car, you seem surprised I'm a woman. You look me over, but I don't mind. It's part of what thrills me about my job."

There was a moment of silence and then the woman's sultry voice continued. I knew I should walk away, but something about the conversation intrigued me.

"I know, nobody wants a ticket. But you were going much too fast. I clocked you at eighty-five miles an hour."

During the next pause I wondered why I couldn't hear anyone respond.

"I'm sorry if it's going to screw up your license, but what else can I do? As I wait for you to answer, I look down and catch sight of your crotch. You're hard, aren't you?"

Another pause. She must be talking to someone on the phone.

"You see me looking. But that's okay. I'm not ashamed of being interested. 'Maybe it would be easier for us to work this out if you get into my car,' I say. So with this big erection in your pants, you get out of your car and follow me. The whole time we're walking, I keep glancing over at your crotch. You keep looking at me looking, but neither of us says anything. I get into the patrol car and open the passenger door and you slide in.

"It's really hot inside the car from the air-conditioning's having been off for a couple of minutes. Do you want me to turn it on or do you like the heat?"

She paused again, obviously to hear the response. I knew I should leave and find my way downstairs. What if Sam suddenly came out of his meeting and found me there eavesdropping? How would I explain what I was doing? Except I didn't leave; I waited, wanting to hear more.

I'd never been stimulated by pornographic movies. I found the people unattractive, the acting obvious, the sound effects forced. But listening on the other side of that door—imagining a man on a phone somewhere growing more and more excited by the story the woman was telling him—was arousing me.

"It's so damn hot inside the car. I unbutton the top two buttons of my uniform and that gives you a perfect view of the rise of my breasts. You can touch them if you want, just reach over and touch them. That's right. Slip your hands down inside my shirt, rub my nipples. It's so hot, I'm sweating. My skin is so slippery, your fingers are sliding all around." Another pause.

"I know how much you want me to touch you, but you have to wait."

Pause.

"No, don't worry, I'll help you."

What was he saying to her—the man on the other end of the phone? What did his voice sound like? What was he doing while he talked to her? Was he touching himself?

I was fixated on the man's desire. I'd forgotten about the eroticism of lust. Had Paul and I ever lusted after each other? What did it feel like for that woman to know the effect her voice was having? Did it turn her on?

From having written the brochure on the institute, I knew there were many different therapies the Butterfields used in the process of sexual refunctioning—helping people to realize their full sexual potential. In the brochure, I'd written: "Sexual role-playing therapy is a new concept that enables therapists to use fantasy to help their patients solve sexual problems." But this was the first time I really understood what that entailed.

"You wouldn't mind if I unzipped your pants now, would you? Just so I can see your cock . . . maybe touch it . . . maybe put my lips around it and suck on it for a while, but only if you promise not to come right away."

I was leaning against the wall, mesmerized by the woman's voice, feeling like a visitor who'd stumbled on this place by accident and didn't quite belong.

Somewhere a door opened and shut and footsteps came closer.

"Is something wrong?" Sam asked, after he rounded the corner and saw me. "Are you all right? You look flushed."

"I got lost, that's all. And it's hot up here." I cringed at my inadvertent slip.

Sam just smiled. "Well, then I'm glad I found you. Sorry I kept you waiting. My secretary said you called early this morning for an appointment. What's up?" He navigated us out of the hallway and toward the stairs.

"Sam, this role-playing therapy you want to write the book about—is it phone sex?" I asked, as we descended the stairs.

"We don't like to call it that. Typical phone sex is a couple of minutes of down and dirty, fast and often prerecorded sex talk that comes from a factory where twenty or thirty operators work out of cubbyholes—everyone talking and moaning at once.

"What we do on the phone here is really therapy—working with male patients who have problems like premature ejaculation or impotence and with female patients who are preorgasmic."

We reached the fourth floor and he stopped, asking me if I'd mind coming with him while he picked up some books from the library. Waiting for the librarian to come up from the stacks, I asked Sam why role-playing over the phone worked better than surrogates.

"Well, they're similar in that they're both behavioral techniques. But in surrogate work there's a lot of embarrassment to overcome. There's so much fucking freedom that comes with the anonymity of the telephone."

"Does all this go on from here—from those offices upstairs?" I asked.

"No. Generally we prefer the therapist to work from home and record the calls so we can monitor the client's progress."

"Why from home?"

"There's more privacy, less chance for a patient to overhear another call, and more chance for the therapist to get involved," Sam explained.

"Why would a therapist get more involved from home?" I was confused.

"Some of them enjoy the sessions as much as their patients, and being home affords them the privacy to do that."

The librarian handed Sam a pile of books and tear sheets from magazines, and while he checked them over I wondered whether I was really surprised by what he'd said. Hadn't the woman I'd been listening to upstairs sounded as if she were totally involved in the fantasy she was inventing? Wasn't her intensity and her obvious pleasure part of what had so transfixed me?

"Are there other services like this?" I asked Sam as we continued downstairs to his office.

"Only one other that I know of. It's out on the West Coast, and they copied us."

"How much money does a session cost?" I asked.

"The same as a session with any of our other therapists, a hundred fifty dollars an hour."

"So the session is conducted by a real therapist?"

We reached the third-floor landing. Sam stopped, leaned on the balustrade, and faced me.

"What's a real therapist, Julia? I think it's someone who has the tools to help someone else work through their problems. So much of what people need is human contact. Just being able to connect. To have someone listen and respond—even if it's to your demons. Don't you talk to your friends about your problems? Don't they help you?"

"So the therapists downstairs don't actually do the role-playing on the phone?" I asked.

"No, but it's prescribed and monitored by them as an adjunct to therapy."

"Then who does the calls?" I wanted to ask who the woman was on the other side of the door.

"We have one woman who is just finishing up her master's at the New York School of Social Work. Another is a young musician who's earning enough here part time to pursue her music career.

"One is finishing up her undergraduate degree in archaeology. Another is a fifty-five-year-old divorcée who needed to go back to work but felt an office job would be too time intensive. We call them phone therapists."

"So how do these people become phone therapists?" I asked, as we started back down the stairs.

"We have a supervised training program."

"Do the phone therapists train with the institute's patients?"

"No," Sam answered. "In addition to our patients, we have a fairly significant number of regular, routine clients—people who aren't in therapy but want to use our phone services. Our trainees handle those callers."

"Where do those clients come from?" I asked.

"Well, some men and women who start out as patients stay on after their therapy is over and become clients. Then there are referrals—friends who tell friends—plus we get a lot of calls from the advertising we do."

"You advertise? Where?" I was amazed.

"In the personal columns of very upscale magazines," he said.

We had reached the second-floor landing, where the staircase increased in width and swirled down below us, a waterfall of snowy marble.

"Sam, is the phone sex service very successful?"

He hesitated a minute. "Well, as a therapeutic tool, we've used it with over a hundred seventy-five patients so far and we're getting better results than with anything else we've ever tried." He smiled before continuing.

"As a business, it's now completely funding the institute's research studies," he said proudly, and started walking toward his office. "We're grossing over two and one half million dollars a year and our client base has grown to almost three thousand people."

It was an astonishing sum, I thought as I followed Sam through the door he held open for me. "I had no idea," I said. He laughed softly.

Inside what must have been the library when the house had first been built, the wood gleamed in the light of green-glass lamps and books overflowed the carved floor-to-ceiling shelves. "Didn't you ever wonder how we could afford to be such philanthropists?" he asked, as he sat down.

Crossing the room, my feet sunk into the thick green carpet. "I never . . . no. So many donors seem unlikely," I answered as I sat down opposite Sam at the round table that served as both his desk and a meeting table.

On the far end of the room was a therapist's couch with a comfortable leather chair beside it. I'd been in this office before, but for the first time I thought about what would happen if I lay down on the couch instead of sitting at the table. What would Sam see inside my mind? What would I be brave enough to show him?

"So you're here to turn me down on the book offer, aren't you?" he asked.

Had Paul already called him? I was infuriated. "What makes you think that?"

"Because you're acting as if you don't belong here."

It was as if he'd read my thoughts. Or was he baiting me?

"I think the institute is . . . what you're doing is fascinating. . . . I'm just not sure . . . the book is . . ." I knew what I was supposed to say. So why couldn't I say it?

While Sam watched me, waiting for me to continue, I could hear Paul feeding me the lines: *I'm not prepared to take on a project of such magnitude. Since my son left for college, I've been depressed.* But I could also hear the woman upstairs, whispering her fantasy into the phone.

All I'd known about the book until that morning was that it would explore the institute's success with its newest form of therapy. I hadn't asked about the content—I'd been too caught up in the idea of coauthoring a book. Not a four-page article or twelve-page brochure but a hardcover three-hundred-page book.

*Tell Sam you're turning down the book,* Paul Sterling's good wife urged.

And yet, I couldn't. Something had happened while I'd stood outside that closed door on the fifth floor. An abandoned part of me, dormant for so long, had stirred.

*Tell him that you can't handle the pressure.*

*No, not now that this thing in you has finally sprung back to life!* yelled some wild part of me I almost didn't recognize.

"Look, instead of writing another analytic treatise on your new therapy from the third-person point of view, which is always slightly removed anyway, why not write the book from the first-person viewpoint?" What was I saying? "Let a phone-sex therapist speak directly to your reader, Sam, exactly the way she speaks to clients and patients. In alternating chapters, you can explain the therapy and how it works. She can show the reader how to take ad-vantage of it."

"That's a fucking great idea." He slammed his hand down on the table. He was excited, and then suddenly perplexed, frowning slightly. "So I was wrong? You do want to work on the book?"

"Of course. Except I have a condition. I want you to train me to be a phone therapist so I can do the research firsthand and really get to understand the process."

He stared at me intensely. Had I stunned him? He was trying to read my face. Allowing his scrutiny, almost enjoying his confusion, I watched him struggle to find a clue to the puzzle he had encoun-tered.

If he'd asked why I wanted to do it, I would have told him. *So I can be like the woman upstairs,* I would have said. *So I can become someone who feels good about her sexuality. So I can be someone who belongs in her own life,* I would have explained. *Someone who isn't just a bystander.*

# 4

⌐

**W**alking home from the institute, I vacillated between excitement and nervousness. My reflection seemed to hesitate, then hurry, in the plateglass windows. After Sam and I had talked about the book for a while longer, he'd asked me to write up a proposal. It would give me some time to make certain I wanted to go forward with the training and actually do the phone therapy myself.

Except I didn't need any time to think it over. I knew it was what I wanted from the first moment I had told Sam my idea. I didn't know why, but I was determined. Was it to show Paul I could? To show myself? Or was it because I so badly wanted to explore a world I'd never inhabited, where elusive secrets would be revealed, mysteries uncovered?

Suddenly the thick, humid air was making me perspire, or maybe it was thinking about what I was going to tell Paul. It took me only another block to decide I would avoid telling him until I'd done the proposal and Sam had accepted it.

I felt like I had during my first few days of college, overstimulated and anxious about confronting a new landscape. But this time

I would be different, I reassured myself. I was equipped to handle the stress now. And as I walked the last block home, I knew no matter what obstacles Paul threw my way, I wouldn't capitulate.

"Good afternoon, Mrs. Sterling," the doorman said, as he opened the door for me.

I always wanted to turn around and look for Paul's mother when someone addressed me like that. Especially that afternoon. It was a salutation for a complacent middle-aged matron, not the restless woman who could barely catch her breath.

The door clicked shut behind me, and inside the air-conditioned lobby, it was colder and darker than on the street; the air blew against my skin like a cooling breath.

Upstairs, I dropped my bag on the bench in the foyer and went into the kitchen to make a cup of tea. As soon as the water boiled, I poured it in a mug, dropped in a peppermint tea bag, cut a wedge of lemon, and squeezed its juice in. Then, stirring the tea with my finger, I walked out of the kitchen and into the room beside it—my room—the greenhouse where I grew orchids.

When I'd first moved in, the small greenhouse that cantilevered over the east wall of the building was used only as a dusty storage space. Then one day Max, who was eight at the time, brought home a science project involving planting seeds and keeping a journal of their growth.

Together, he and I cleared out part of the greenhouse and set up the experiment. Every morning, before he went off to school, we examined the plants and Max took detailed notes of their progress.

Until then, nature had only been a backdrop to incidents in my life. But suddenly I was fascinated by watching the spiky green shoots grow. Soon, I'd gotten estimates on restoring the greenhouse and hired a contractor.

From the sidewalk, on the opposite side of 84th Street, you can see it if you look up—an English folly incongruous with the 1930s building. Its Victorian design, all glass with wrought-iron ribs peaking in a pointed roof, sticks out. I think it appealed to me because it didn't fit in with the building or with our sleek apartment. Here, I thought, I would have my own private sliver of space. Paul had been so involved in decorating the apartment that his presence possessed every room. Even my collection of masks—which I'd started when I was a child—had become a joint project.

I appropriated nothing from the rest of the apartment for the conservatory. Instead, I bought a slipper chair covered in a faded lilac-blossom fabric and a small distressed bamboo desk. I had a phone installed and bought a good-quality but undersize stereo system. And there I sat, enclosed in my glass room watching as the sky changed color, clouds rolled by, and birds flew overhead. At night, I could look up at the sparkle of the far-off stars. When it rained, the sound of the water hitting the glass was sharp and rhythmic. In the winter, layers of snow created a white cocoon.

Months had passed and I still hadn't filled the greenhouse with any plants. Then one night, I was sitting at my desk working when Paul came in to talk to me. Standing on the threshold, he looked around but didn't step inside.

"Julia, why did you restore this space to a working greenhouse if you aren't going to use it that way?" he asked.

"I'm just not sure yet what I want to grow."

"Max mentioned he's been helping you," Paul said.

"Yeah," I said, and smiled. "We're having fun going to nurseries and hothouses, taking books from the library. So far we've considered and rejected bonsai, hothouse roses, and African violets."

"This quest might be getting obsessional, Julia." In the dim light, he appeared so concerned.

"No, I don't think so."

"Are you sleeping all right?" he asked.

We'd been married four years and his professional attention was as comforting as always, but since I'd enrolled in the Columbia University School of Journalism, it had begun to seem constricting. The closer I go to my degree, the more Paul fixated on my mental state.

"I'm sleeping fine," I assured him.

"I don't know. It seems you're doing a lot: taking classes, taking care of Max, being involved with his school. Are you sure the pressure isn't building up?"

"Paul, look at me; I'm fine." I don't think I'd yet realized this was the only kind of attention he was capable of giving.

"There's a new antidepressant on the market. I want you to try it," Paul said.

It had been years since I'd taken any medication and I had no interest in enduring that semidrugged state again. Besides, I wasn't depressed. Certainly the fear of breaking apart never completely abated, so I took smaller steps than other people. But I didn't fumble; my progress was steady.

"I don't want to take any medication. I don't need any," I insisted.

"Sometimes during the night, I wake up to find you fighting in your sleep—punching the air with your fists."

"Something's unresolved in my unconscious," I offered.

"Please, you're not equipped to self-diagnose. I want you to try these new pills. See if they don't make you feel better."

To keep peace, I agreed, still believing it was more important to please Paul than to tell him the truth.

~

My first lie to my husband was about taking the little white pills. Since then, there have been many others.

Sitting in my greenhouse, ten years later, I was prepared to tell yet one more.

~

It was Max who finally decided what I should grow in my greenhouse. A few months after my conversation with Paul, Max brought me an orchid for Mother's Day; a pale violet flower with a deeper magenta center and broad waxy leaves that fanned out from the clay pot.

He'd gone on a class trip to the Botanical Garden, had seen the orchid there, and had begged his teacher to let him borrow enough money to buy it for me.

"It's not as breakable as it looks," he told me, as he put the flowerpot in my lap. In the glass window I could see our reflections: a robust little boy; a thin woman; and a trembling, fragile flower. "The man said even though they look delicate, they're not. Orchids are survivors. They live on air. And their roots are so powerful they can grow on the side of rocky cliffs."

~

I picked a withered leaf off one of the many orchid plants that now crowded the greenhouse, and as I dropped it in the small wicker trash basket underneath the desk, the phone rang. Picking up the receiver, I glanced at my watch—two o'clock. It was probably Jack back from lunch, calling me before he got back to work.

Jack Griffin and I had met my third week at college in the kitchen of his apartment at four-thirty in the morning. I'd gotten out of his roommate's bed to get something cold to drink and there he was, sitting at the kitchen table, writing. Even though I was wearing only a sheet, he barely seemed to notice me. Challenged, I sat down and started asking him questions. When I found out he was the editor of the school paper, I told him I'd been the editor of my high school paper and was planning on majoring in journalism. He yawned and told me to stop by the paper if I was interested, he was two reporters short.

A tall, gangly boy, Jack had unruly golden brown hair that often obscured his soft brown eyes. Jack was so thin his cheekbones, collarbones, shoulder blades, elbows, and even wrist bones jutted out dangerously. You could scratch yourself if you passed too close to him. He wasn't typically good looking or seductive, but when he focused his intensity on you, you felt everything you said was of critical importance—that no one else mattered to him.

"I called earlier," Jack said from his office in Florida.

"Why didn't you leave a message?" I asked.

"Dealing with too many machines in one day makes me crazy; besides, I always worry Paul will get the message."

"But I have a separate phone line and machine. I told you that. Besides, he knows you call me; he knows we're friends."

"If I were your husband, I'd be jealous."

"Wouldn't you trust me?" I looked up as a pair of birds flew by.

"More than anyone I know," he said. "But I'm human. If some guy called you all the time, I'd need reassurance every once in a while."

I paused. "I can't remember Paul's ever being jealous."

"Fool," Jack said. After so many years of talking over the phone, his deep voice and its nuances were more familiar to me than his face. He never rushed his words and he paused often to think before he spoke.

~

At college, Jack had stood out from other young men because he didn't seem interested in me except for what I could bring to the newspaper.

At first it didn't matter that he was immune to my flirtations. I was moving too fast to care that one man was uninterested. But as I got to know him better, as he turned his intensity on me and I grew to admire his talents, it bothered me that Jack didn't find me attractive. I began to covet him and set out to catch him. He was the only boy I ever had to woo.

I didn't know it then, but Jack was holding out on purpose.

Years after he'd graduated, Jack had a short story published. It was about me. He wrote that he'd wanted me from the first time he saw me—it was the light that shone off my skin, my hair, in my eyes—he wanted to touch my light with his fingers.

Except he was afraid I'd treat him like all the other guys I slept with and discard him too, once I'd made the conquest. So he acted as if he weren't interested. But it backfired because by the time he decided he'd made me wait long enough, I was unraveling. In fact, it was Jack who found me during finals week, under my desk in my dorm room, crouched in fear, unable to stop crying. He wrapped me in his sweater, took me downstairs to his car, put me in the front seat, and drove all night to get me back to my parents in New York City by morning.

During the next few years, while I studied myself in therapy,

Jack studied journalism and, after college, moved around a lot as he worked his way up from cub reporter in Providence, Rhode Island, to editor in Miami, Florida.

We never lost touch, and our long-distance friendship flourished to the point where we spoke several times during the week. Jack usually called from his office, the timing set up when he was first living with Gail, who was jealous of how much time he spent talking to me.

~

"So, where were you all morning?" Jack asked.

I told him about the book and going to the institute to talk about to Sam about it. "But it's probably too ambitious a project for me to even attempt," I finished up. "Maybe I should just give up and settle for writing a column in a gardening magazine."

"If that would make you happy, why don't you?" he asked, without showing a trace of the impatience he must have felt. Jack had heard this self-effacing argument before every career step I'd taken.

"Let's not have this conversation. You must be bored with it by now," I said.

"You never bore me, Julia."

"Maybe I should just come up with ideas for articles and hire other people to write them," I continued self-indulgently, despite myself.

"You mean do what I do for a living?" he asked.

"Yeah. We'll switch. You come here and live my life and I'll go there and live yours."

"Your garden is too small," he said, referring to my greenhouse.

"And yours is too big," I countered. Jack lived in a small house surrounded by two acres overplanted with fruit trees and flowering plants. I hadn't been there, but he often sent me crates of fruit: Key limes, mangoes, tangerines, guavas, oranges, hand-picked and hand-packed. They arrived unexpectedly, the labels addressed to me in his spidery handwriting. As I washed the fruit and then ate it, I would think of him balancing on the ladder, a scarecrow reaching up to the sky to pick what he had grown.

"On second thought, maybe we could switch," he said. "Then you could deal with my estranged wife when the article runs this weekend."

Six months earlier, one of Jack's writers, investigating a corrupt city district commissioner, turned up a connection between the politician and Jack's father-in-law, a prominent Miami realtor. Jack called his wife—they were separated at the time—to prepare her. Despite her pleas, he told her he wouldn't do anything to compromise the piece.

"So, you are running it, despite Gail's threats?" I knew he had too much integrity to do otherwise, but I asked anyway.

"This will only speed up the divorce. There's never been any question of Gail and me getting back together. The marriage was doomed from the start."

"You've never said that before. Why was it doomed?" I asked.

"She wasn't you," he answered.

Jack often said things like that. I rarely wondered how serious he was, but that afternoon I did.

"Sometimes I wish I could be eighteen again like Max. Just starting out at college with everything ahead of me."

"He'll make his mistakes too. It's inevitable," Jack said.

"That's sad."

"Who do you know who hasn't made mistakes, Julia?"

I was silent.

"You're really sitting there trying to think of someone who hasn't made any mistakes, aren't you?" he asked.

"Yeah, I was."

Jack laughed.

Looking out my window, I watched the workmen on the construction site about fifty feet away. "Jack, they've started on the exterior walls."

"How long till they get to your floor?" he asked.

"Maybe six weeks. And then the light will be gone."

A new apartment building going up halfway down the street was going to block my greenhouse from all direct morning sun. After so many years of light, I dreaded the shadow that was coming.

"With Max gone and the sun gone, everything will feel so different around here," I said.

"It can't be easy having Max away. You spent a lot of time together. This book of Butterfield's sounds like perfect timing."

"Oh, I want to do it. You know I do. The only thing is that sometimes Sam makes me uneasy . . . like last night—" I broke off, not wanting to remember how Sam had made me feel, not now that I'd admitted how much I wanted to write his book.

"What?" Jack asked.

"Nothing."

"Nothing? There is no such thing as nothing with you. Every syllable uttered has a purpose, if only to arouse my curiosity. What happened last night, Julia?"

"Well, I guess he scared me."

"Why?"

"I don't know. He recited a poem to me."

"Suddenly I have a rival. What poem?" Jack asked.

"Upon Julia's Clothes," I answered.

"By Robert Herrick. I know. I read that to you when we were in school."

"You did?" I said, and then felt bad. Jack remembered so much of our past that was lost to me. "I wish I remembered." I didn't want him to be insulted I'd forgotten.

"Julia, stop it. I hate that plaintive thing in your voice. We wouldn't have been any good then. You would have gotten tired of me as quickly as you got tired of all those other guys and I would have gotten angry at you. We never would have become friends. And then who the hell would I call all the time? Now, tell me more about the subject of this book."

I recounted how I'd gotten lost on the fifth floor of the institute, what I'd heard, and how it led to the proposal I'd made to Sam.

"So they're selling pornography and running phone sex lines out of one of the most prestigious scientific institutes in the country? This could be a big story, Julia."

"No, it's a new form of therapy." I was defending the institute, now that I was—almost—a member.

"Maybe for the patients, but for the rest of the people who call, the clients, as you refer to them, it's phone sex. Plain and simple."

"You're making it sound sleazy," I said.

"Isn't it?"

"No, it's nothing like those 900 numbers that advertise on television. For one thing, it costs a hundred fifty dollars an hour."

"Sort of like the difference between a streetwalker and a high-class call girl?" he asked.

"No, it's more than that. At the institute, the women who take the calls are trained therapists," I insisted.

"Does that make the calls medical deductions?" he joked.

"Jack, this is a serious business."

"I have no doubt. The truth is, I'm impressed at how Butterfield has capitalized on a questionable field in a completely unquestionable way. How much do you think he takes in?"

I reached over and turned a pot so that the flower faced the light. "Two and a half million dollars, Sam said." I moved the pot a little more to the left. The flower trembled.

Jack let out an amazed whistle.

"It's not illegal, is it?" I asked him.

"No, so far as I know, phone sex isn't illegal."

"It's not phone sex, it's—"

Jack interrupted me. "Julia, he can call it a new form of therapy or anything he wants, but it's still phone sex."

"I know . . . but . . . you should have heard her. Maybe it was crude, but it was also kind of erotic."

"Did you hear her whole conversation?" he asked.

"Most of it." I paused. "Jack, does the idea of phone sex turn you on?"

"I'm not sure," he said. "I don't think some stranger could excite me over the phone. But you could."

Certain he was teasing, I laughed. "Yeah, right."

"Julia?" he asked.

"Yes?"

"What are you wearing?"

"What?" I hoped he was still joking.

"Isn't this how phone sex starts? I ask what you're wearing and you tell me nothing, or an open robe, or whatever lascivious thing you can think of."

"C'mon, Jack . . ." I was laughing again. "I've got to go. I'll talk to you tomorrow, okay?"

"Good-bye," he said, surprising me by how softly he spoke and how quickly he hung up.

# 5

From a distance, everything about Paul typified a certain success: the gracious host in his stylish home, wearing perfectly tailored clothes and a charming smile. Except I knew how studied every part of the picture was. All fashioned to create a certain impression. Disturbed by the affectation, I escaped to the kitchen to put the last touches on dinner. Even entertaining friends in my home was an effort for me, but never, it seemed, for my husband. When I discussed it with Paul, he was, as always, the understanding therapist, reminding me of how far I'd come, admonishing me not to be so tough on myself.

"Have you told Paul about the book yet?" my friend Olivia asked, as I added pepper to the broccoli soup simmering on the stove. Leaving the other guests in the living room, she had followed me into the kitchen.

It had been five days since I'd met with Sam. "It seemed pointless to tell him until Sam had at least read my proposal—"

"But you said he read it and accepted it yesterday?"

"Yeah, but Paul was in Boston till this afternoon," I offered feebly.

"You didn't speak to him on the phone while he was gone?" she asked, with feigned innocence. Only 5'2", Olivia had mischievous brown eyes and curly black hair that framed her face. She was quite beautiful, but more important, she was my friend.

I looked away from her impish smile and stirred the soup. "I'm not going to tell Paul. Not yet, anyway. I have all that training ahead of me. Who knows, I may not even make it through."

"C'mon Julia, you're only postponing the inevitable." She took a clean spoon and dipped it in the soup.

"By the time I tell him, I want it to be too late for him to stop me."

Olivia looked me straight in the eye. "Good for you. You've been going so slow and steady for so long, I was wondering when you'd finally run out of patience."

"With my work?" I asked. "Or with Paul?"

"You tell me."

"Do you think I'm doing the wrong thing?" I asked.

"Not the wrong thing, no. But you're doing it in a dangerous way."

"Maybe . . ." I faltered.

"Hey—" It was her shorthand with me, a familiar warning that I was giving in to old fears. "I know you can write this book. Sam obviously knows it. Now *you* just have to believe you can do it."

"You're right. No more second-guessing myself. It's time. I'm ready," I said. If I could convince Olivia, maybe I could convince myself.

"Just one thing, Julia—you have to promise to let me listen in on some of your calls."

"Great. You on one extension, Jack on the other. My two best friends eavesdropping."

We were standing there like teenagers when Miranda, the woman I hired to help out with dinner parties, came through the kitchen door with an empty hors d'oeuvres tray. "How soon do you want to serve dinner, Mrs. Sterling?"

"In about fifteen minutes," I answered.

When Paul became FIT's director, the charity, in addition to his

salary and the rent stipend, gave him an expense account. On nights
we entertained, that expense account paid for both the food and Miranda's help.

I stirred the soup once more, covered it, and then Olivia and I
rejoined the guests.

"It looks like a set for the quintessential New York dinner
party," Olivia whispered as we entered the living room.

I tried to look at it through her eyes. Through mine, I was too
aware of just how much I'd capitulated to Paul's taste rather than
create tension. I thought the pale beige room was too stark and simple. There was too much glass and not enough wood. Paisley Etro
throws should drape the arms of the plain eggshell couches. Green
Chinese Art Deco area rugs should break up the barren wool sisal.
Colorful paintings should interrupt the cold black-and-white photographs of architectural elements. And instead of all indirect lighting, lamps should sit on the end tables, casting shadows, creating
reflections.

The only visible signs of color were my orchid plants, one on
the glass coffee table, others on the windowsills. Like sculptures,
their delicate lavender flowers arced and broad emerald leaves
bowed.

By one of those windows, Paul was talking to Olivia's husband.
Larry Vernon, as light as Olivia was dark, had easygoing good looks.
A professional tennis player, he'd quit at twenty to go to college and
study architecture. Olivia was a year ahead of Larry at the Cornell
University College of Architecture. After he graduated, they got
married, and as soon as they both finished their apprenticeships,
they opened their own architecture firm. They had become very successful. Two years ago, they had donated their time and talents to design FIT's New York training center.

Adam Bullock, the chairman of the advertising agency that was
doing Paul's pro bono ad campaign for FIT, and his girlfriend du
jour, Tina, were sitting on one couch. Opposite them sat Dennis
Tyler and his wife, Lee Carpenter. He was an investment banker; she
was a mayoral appointee in charge of the housing authority.

Everyone sipped at drinks and munched on curried peanuts and fried baby artichoke hearts. Honey made the peanuts slightly sticky. I served them because when people ate them, they had to lick their fingers. The finger-licking seemed to relax everyone and reduce some of the inevitable stiffness at the start of any party.

After glancing at my watch, I asked Paul to invite everyone in to dinner.

That night I'd made the broccoli soup, a main course of shrimp on a bed of couscous with raisins and nuts, followed by a mixed green salad, and for dessert, a flourless chocolate cake.

Paul beamed as I acknowledged several compliments on the soup, which was creamy and just peppery enough.

"She didn't know how to cook like this before she married me, but I encouraged her to take it up. I knew she'd be a quick study." He lifted his spoon to his mouth.

From across the table, Olivia caught my eye and winked. I shrugged off my husband's ego and joined in the conversation around me.

When everyone finished, Miranda and I cleared the soup bowls and then served the shrimp. By the time I sat down again, Adam Bullock was defending his position that cigarette advertising should not be banned. "What are we? A country of mindless fools who can be completely manipulated by a photograph and a headline in a magazine?"

"Yes, unfortunately," Larry answered.

"No advertising is so powerful that it can force someone to do something they don't want to do," Adam insisted.

"I hope that's not what you tell your clients!" Olivia said. We all laughed except for Lee and Paul, who had been talking between themselves for a long time. As host, it was unlike Paul to allow any one guest to monopolize his attention, but I didn't want to interrupt and draw attention to his faux pas.

It was finally Lee's husband, Dennis, who made a joke, asking Paul if he was ready to declare his intentions. Rather than be amused, Paul seemed irritated but recovered quickly.

"Well, it wouldn't be the first time a married woman succumbed to an attentive man," Olivia said, and then segued into a description of a book she was reading that claimed over thirty percent of married women had affairs.

"The thesis," Olivia continued, "is that while American men want their girlfriends sexually wanton, they want their wives above reproach. They can't reconcile the image of a sexually exciting woman with the mother of their children. And so we women, wanting to hold tight to our husbands and being well trained to please, sublimate our desires and become good girls.

"Then along comes some other man who's not married to her, who responds to her as a sexually active woman, and bam!"

"That means . . ."—Larry paused and looked around the table, his eyes stopping on each of the four women seated there—". . . that at least one of you is having an affair."

"No," Tina said, "I'm not married; I don't count."

"She's still allowed to be sexually wanton," Adam joked.

"What's your opinion, Doctor?" I asked Paul, who hadn't commented at all.

He smiled at me benignly, as if I were one of his patients. "It's quite common." He waved his hand addressing the whole table. "Freud called it the whore/mother syndrome. Once a woman—regardless of how desirable you found her before you married her— becomes your wife and the mother of your child, you identify her with your own mother for whom you had to repress your sexual feelings. To put it bluntly, either you accept your mother as a whore or you stop sleeping with your wife."

Although no one at the table knew it but me, my husband had just diagnosed his own neurosis. I wondered if even he knew how close he'd just come to describing his own problem and the main reason why he and I didn't have a healthy sex life.

If I followed Freud's logic, when we had married and I had become his son's surrogate mother, Paul's desire for me had dried up.

Using the excuse of having to clear the table for dessert, I got up. Inappropriate as it was, I'd received my husband's confession at my own dinner table, not in a marriage counselor's office or during a fight or in the privacy of our bedroom.

My hands trembled. As I carried the dishes into the kitchen, they clattered against each other.

"Do you need help, Julia? That china is quite fragile," I heard Paul say as I pushed back on the swinging door and disappeared into the kitchen.

I was edgy for the rest of the night and glad when our last guests left at eleven. After helping Miranda clean up, I gave her taxi fare home and said good night.

On my way into the bedroom I heard the television in Paul's study. I stood in the hall, not knowing whether I should go in and talk to him. Peering in, I saw him sitting at his desk, turned away from both the television and the door. He was facing the window, looking out at the darkness and talking on the phone.

I tried to catch a few words, but the hallway light must have illuminated my reflection in the window, because without turning, Paul waved me away with the back of his hand.

"Is it Max?" I asked. "Is everything all right?"

"It's not Max," Paul answered, and returned to his conversation.

I woke up in the middle of the night, aware that Paul wasn't beside me in bed. Getting up, I pulled on my robe and went looking for him. He was still in the den sitting at his desk, facing out the window. Wearing his shirt and suit pants, he had draped his jacket and tie on the back of his chair.

"Paul, what's wrong?" I asked.

"Go back to sleep. I'll tell you in the morning." He half turned so I could see only his profile.

"No. Something's obviously wrong, I want to know what it is."

"I've been talking to Mike for hours. I'm exhausted. Please, Julia, let it wait until morning."

Since Mike was the chairman of the FIT board, the problem was obviously with work. Back in bed, I lay alone listening to the silence and wondering what might be wrong. Paul's professional life had been without incident. A therapist isn't a businessman. Yes, some years were busier than others, but there were no great losses or gains, no bad productivity or poor employee performance to contend with. No kickback schemes, no skimming off the top, no underhanded employees. But now Paul was the director of a charity that had nine branches and a working budget of over twenty million dollars a year. Anything could go wrong.

After another restless hour, I got up and went to the kitchen. The remains of the chocolate cake I'd made for dessert was on the kitchen counter under an old-fashioned glass cake cover. I cut myself a slice—a large slice—and slid it onto a plate. Pouring a glass of cold milk, I stood alone in my kitchen, eating cake in the middle of the night while my husband sat in his study, preferring his own solitude to my company.

From the kitchen, I heard Paul opening then closing the bathroom door. According to the clock on the stove, it was four in the morning. It was unusual for me to be up at this hour, but there had been so many shifts and changes in our lives since the end of August when Paul and I returned from taking Max to Princeton. The rhythm of our house had altered and we hadn't yet found a new one. Without my stepson around, I didn't know my husband. I longed for Max to come home so everything would return to normal. His presence would eradicate our silence and separateness and distract me from noticing how little Paul and I shared. The only thing we had in common anymore was our love for Max. Wanting the heady taste of the chocolate to fill up the emptiness inside of me, I pressed the fork down on the crumbs and licked them off.

There was a slight noise and I looked up; Paul was standing in the kitchen door.

"Do you want some cake?" I asked.

"No, but do you think you could make me some coffee?"

"No problem."

His classic features were distorted with exhaustion and I felt a pang of pity for him. "Go back to your study. I'll bring it to you when it's ready."

After the coffee perked, I filled two mugs and carried them both to his den. "Here." I held out a mug and he took it.

"Thank you," he said formally. I knew he wanted me to leave.

"Paul, what's happened?" I asked.

"I told you before——"

"I know you said you'd tell me in the morning, but it's morning now."

My heart thumped loudly in my chest and sweat collected under my arms. I was picking up his fears, making his anxiety mine.

Paul realized I wasn't going anywhere, so he motioned for me to sit beside him on the couch, but as soon as I did, he moved to his desk chair and sat facing me.

"At dinner, Lee told me she'd heard some scuttlebutt about the IRS's investigating several nonprofit charities. She's seen a preliminary list—we're included." His voice was as smooth as glass. "I've been on the phone with Mike discussing the long- and short-term ramifications of being investigated."

"What will they investigate you for?"

"Misuse of our nonprofit status," he said, still without any inflection.

"Paul, you haven't done anything illegal, have you?"

"No. But if they're intent on finding something, they will." His neck muscles tensed; a vein twitched under his skin.

"How could they find something if you haven't done anything?" I insisted.

"No matter what happens, I refuse to resign." Suddenly, he focused on me. "I shouldn't have told you. With your history, the last thing you need is added stress. I'm sorry, honey. Look—you're biting your lip, tying and retying that ribbon on your robe. Listen carefully, Julia. There's no reason for you to be worried about what's going to happen."

If there was any chance left for us, I had to stop him from seeing me in the pathetic role of a frail and frightened patient. It was time to show Paul I was there for him. That he could lean on me now.

"Paul, I'm not worried. Not at all. I have complete faith in you.

Besides, what's the worst thing that would happen if you did resign from FIT? You'd just go back into private practice."

"And destroy my reputation?" His voice wavered.

"It wouldn't matter to the people who care about you. Not to Max. Or me."

Paul ran his fingers through his thick black hair, which sprang right back into place. For a moment he shut his eyes. In repose, the handsome symmetry of his face was even more pronounced.

"Paul, I want you to understand I'm perfectly calm. I'm not upset about the idea of an investigation or its ramifications. You don't have to worry about me—not this time, not anymore—all right?"

"But that's my job as your husband, Julia. To take care of you. Now . . . ," he ordered, "please go back to bed. There's no need for you to suffer from sleep deprivation too."

⌒

I thought if I stepped out of the needy role Paul had long ago assigned to me—and I had, back then, gladly assumed—and stood beside him on equal footing, we could reinvent our relationship. It never occurred to me that once I changed the balance we might not find a new equilibrium—that if we didn't remain in the roles we'd created for ourselves and our relationship, there might not be anyone else for us to become.

# 6

*~*

**D**espite how little sleep I'd gotten and how wasted I felt, I didn't cancel the appointment I'd scheduled for the next afternoon at the Butterfield Institute. Ready to leave, I checked the mirror, wondering if my usual outfit of tailored trousers and washed-silk blouse was too formal for my first session. But even after changing into jeans, a T-shirt, and loafers, I still felt awkward. What should I be wearing? A short skirt? Stilettos? Almost laughing out loud at the image of myself dressed like that, I threw a pale yellow sweater over my shoulders, grabbed my bag, and hurried out of the apartment.

If anything, the strain of the night before with Paul had made me even more determined to begin training. Despite my resolve, as I walked up the institute's solid stone steps, apprehension overwhelmed me. The sweat on my hand made my grip slippery. I struggled to get a strong enough hold on the heavy glass-and-iron door but was unable to open it. My panic wound around me. I tried to take a deep breath, but nervousness stuck in my throat.

Resolute, I pulled even harder, concentrating not on the girth of the door but on the anger I felt at these demons who'd shown themselves again.

Inside, the receptionist was on the phone. While I waited, I fought my spiraling anxiety. I wouldn't prove Paul right. He'd only talked about my fragility. What of my strengths? Hadn't I spent half my adult life fighting to control these tides of emotions that rose in me without warning? Didn't I understand the ebbs and flows of my neurosis and know the tricks to break the cycle?

First, focus. Get hold of something concrete.

Shoving my hand inside my bag, my fingers closed around the spine of my notebook. I pulled it out and along with it came my journalist's mask. At last, I took a deeper breath. And then a deeper one. The grip around my chest loosened; my heart slowed to a normal rate. And by the time I met Candy Lucas in her small, efficient fifth-floor office, I was just another writer about to begin a new project.

In her early thirties, Candy looked ironically boyish. Her skin was scrubbed clean, her reddish brown hair was cut short, and she wore chinos, a man-tailored shirt, sneakers, and no jewelry. But her voice was low-pitched and profoundly seductive, just shy of being a caricature. She offered me espresso from the machine on her windowsill, and when she stopped talking to make the coffee, I was sorry. I'd wanted to go on listening to her.

"Has Sam told you I want to go through the training exactly the way any trainee would?" I asked.

"Yes," she said as she handed me a small china cup. "You'll begin with a two-week orientation. After that, you'll start to take routine calls."

As she described the training period in more detail, I noticed that her phone was hooked up to a high-tech recording system.

"Any questions so far?" she asked after she finished.

"No."

"Okay, let's get started." She popped a cassette into the recorder and pressed the play button.

There was a spasm of static and then a woman's voice I recognized immediately as hers was followed by a man's voice. She was playing the part of a baby-sitter and he was the older brother who'd come home early from a disappointing date. The conversation started off tame but grew in intensity as it became more explicit.

How was I ever going to hold on to a phone and say those words to a stranger? Christ, I couldn't even ask my husband to make love to me without turning him off. Taking on Sam's book was a mistake. My approach to it was a mistake. All an overreaction to Max's leaving home and Paul's insistence that I was still unhealthy.

As the tape ended, I became conscious of my body language. My arms were crossed over my chest, my legs twisted together. I opened my notebook and uncapped my pen. It was only posing for work that relaxed me.

"It's pretty heavy the first time, for everyone. You're listening to this hot talk with me sitting next to you. But you'll get over it." She paused. "Or you won't."

She'd made me smile. "Why do clients prefer the phone to watching a video?" I asked.

"With a video all the work is done for the viewer. All he—usually, our callers are men—can do is watch. But the phone makes him an active participant."

"But isn't that what those 900 numbers do?"

"Yes, but that's all they do. We offer therapists trained to solve problems. Remember, patients aren't the only ones who need help. Basically, every client you'll be talking to is calling because he's somehow troubled or frustrated. Either his fantasies are unacceptable to him or his partner and he needs help coming to terms with them, or he's calling because he has no partner. Or because he has a psychological problem that manifests itself in some kind of sexual fetish."

Through Candy's office window I looked across rooftops, some empty and unused, others elaborately landscaped.

"We have some rules to go over. Before you talk to a client, we've gotten his driver's license number, a credit card, home or office phone number; screened him; and informed him we routinely tape random calls to monitor our therapists."

It was a dull gray day, and against the monotone sky, the green rooftop trees stood out like beacons. I suddenly remembered Jack's suspicions.

"Despite all our efforts, there still are some calls that get past our screening process. You have the right to refuse any call that might freak you out."

"How often does that happen?"

Candy picked up a fossilized rock that sat on her desk and moved it to another spot. "I think we've only turned down three or four calls this year. We don't usually attract men or women who are into extreme fetishes. Our reputation is pretty traditional."

"If this is traditional . . . ," I said, and she smiled as she took a black binder from the bookshelf behind her desk and handed it to me.

"These are transcripts of calls. Read them and familiarize yourself with them. We'll start practicing tomorrow."

I flipped open the cover and scanned the first page.

*Phone Therapist:* I've been waiting for you to call.
*Caller:* For how long?
*Phone Therapist:* About an hour. Do you want me to tell you what I've been doing while I've been waiting?
*Caller:* Uh-huh.
*Phone Therapist:* I've been touching myself, getting myself ready, rubbing my breasts, my nipples, my pussy.

Seeing the words typed out so plainly didn't lessen their impact.

"So that's it for today. We'll meet here every day for the next couple of weeks. How's ten in the morning?"

"Fine," I said, shutting the binder and looking back at her.

"The way this works is after two hours with me, the trainee meets for an hour with his or her supervising therapist, who in your case is Sam. Let's call and see if he's ready for you."

Without any time to dwell on my meeting with Candy, I walked downstairs for my first session with Sam, who started off by explaining some of the reasons a therapist would suggest phone therapy for a male patient.

"Let's go over a recent case. As a young man, Mitch met a sexually active woman named Lois. He found her both attractive and desirable and was able to thoroughly enjoy having sex with her. Their relationship progressed; they married and had a child.

"About a year after his daughter was born, Mitch came to us complaining he had become impotent.

"First, we worked on his problem in a traditional therapeutic way, but though we were successful at getting Mitch to articulate the problem and even intellectually to understand its roots, we had no luck restoring his sex drive.

"So we tried sexual role-playing over the phone. Mitch was unusually responsive to 'pickup' fantasies with young, unmarried, childless women. Using that information, our phone therapist spent several weeks bonding with Mitch, arousing him and bringing him to orgasm. Then, gradually, she altered the fantasy. The single woman who picked Mitch up and seduced him changed to a married woman. And after Mitch accepted that change and could reach orgasm easily with a married woman, we changed the fantasy again. The married woman revealed she had children."

We weren't talking about sex but about an impressive therapeutic process. I was at ease; I'd been conversing in psychobabble my whole life.

"Is anything about this illegal?" I asked.

"No." Sam examined my face for longer than was comfortable. "Why do you ask?"

"Because I'm curious about where the lines get drawn. People call up and someone talks them to orgasm. Isn't that really the same thing as having sex?"

"No, because it's happening over the phone. Not face-to-face. Julia, do you think there's anything morally wrong with what we're doing?"

"Why are you asking me that?"

Sam leaned on the table. "Because we need to discuss your take on this. You can't do this job if you have doubts about it." As he talked, he pushed up the sleeves of his rust-colored suede shirt. "After meeting with Candy, you have a better idea of what this all entails. Do you still want to go forward?" he asked.

"Would you be asking any trainee that question at this point?"

"Absolutely."

"And do many trainees have second thoughts?"

"About fifty percent drop out during the first two weeks. If a trainee makes it past that point, usually they make it all the way."

I wrote the percentage down in my notebook. "Why do you think people are attracted to this job?" I asked.

"Some because they think it's easy or kinky or illicit or because there's sexual frustration in their own life."

I kept scribbling in my notebook, hardly conscious of the words I was writing.

"But most," he continued, "do it because they can make so much fucking money in so little time." He laughed, but then grew serious. "Julia, I have to ask you a question." His thick fingers were splayed on the table. I studied the spaces between them.

"Not if you're going to ask me how I feel," I said.

He laughed again. "You've been around too many therapists."

"Well, for a second there, you were sounding an awful lot like one."

"I fall into that damn therapeutic tone even when I don't mean to. Most of us do. Occupational hazard. It happens even between Nina and me," Sam said, apologizing.

"With Paul and me too. Too often." Saying Paul's name reminded me there was something I had to tell Sam. "Listen, I don't want to put you or Nina on the spot, but I've decided not to tell Paul about what I'm doing yet."

"Why?" It had slipped out before he could stop it. And before I could answer, he apologized again. "Sorry. That's none of my damn business, is it?"

"I guess not, but since you know Paul, I think you deserve an answer."

"No, I don't. If you were any other writer, or one of our trainees, I wouldn't know anything about your personal life, right? Let's leave it at that. We're great with secrets around here. In fact, everyone who works at the institute in any capacity is bound by the doctor–patient privilege." He glanced down at his wristwatch the way I had seen my father, my husband, and my own therapist do a thousand times. "And now I have a patient," he said, as I knew he would.

I closed my notebook and capped my pen. "What a familiar phrase," I said. "Once I called up and made a double appointment at Paul's office under an assumed name just so I could spend more than forty-five minutes with him without his saying that."

Sam grinned. "Great. What happened when you showed up?"

I was suddenly trapped into revealing more than I wanted to.

"He focused on the lost hour and a half he could have given to someone who needed it."

*But you needed it—I needed it*—hung unspoken in the air. A knock on Sam's door conveniently brought the moment to a close.

Sam's secretary put her head in the doorway.

"Your last patient just called. He's stuck in a meeting and can't get away. I rescheduled him for tomorrow." She left and Sam grinned at me.

"So now I have an extra hour to spend with someone who needs it. Come on, Julia, let's go have a cold martini."

"Why?"

"Why should we have a martini?"

I nodded.

"Because you're interested in the subject I have devoted my life to. That's both flattering to me and fascinating. And because you drink in my words and have reminded me, several times already, why I do what I do. Also, because you're a nervous wreck about what you've undertaken and a drink would do you good. Okay?"

"Yeah." I laughed, but the sound was mixed with the fear that had bubbled up to the surface as soon as Sam had exposed it.

~

We walked to a French bistro half a block away from the institute on Madison and 64th. Inside were wood-paneled walls, white table-cloths, and grand bouquets of flowers.

After we were seated, a waiter with an apron tied around his waist came over and asked what we wanted to drink. Sam looked over at me, I nodded, and he ordered two martinis with just a whisper of vermouth.

When they arrived, the glasses were slightly frosted. I took a decadent sip.

"Paul's damn lucky to be married to someone who enjoys his profession so much," Sam said.

"Actually, Paul doesn't like talking therapy, but my father does, and during my breakdown—" I stopped.

"You don't have to tell me. This is a bar, not a confessional," Sam said.

"No, it's okay. I had a breakdown in college. My friend Jack found me in my room, sitting under my desk, crying. I'd been crying for almost two days. Jack brought me home and my father put me into therapy, where I stayed for almost four years. When I finally went back to school a few years ago, I flirted with majoring in psychology."

"Why didn't you?" Sam fished the olive out of his glass and popped it in his mouth, his full lips closing around it. I took another sip of my drink.

"Well, journalism was just as inquisitive a field, but less introspective, and that suited me."

"Was Paul disappointed you didn't join him in his profession?" Sam asked.

"No, quite the opposite. He was relieved."

"Yes, I can see that," Sam mused.

"What can you see?"

"Sorry, Julia; sometimes I can't refrain from trying to piece the puzzle together."

"My father's like that; so's my son," I said and took another sip of my drink.

"Tell me about your son," he asked.

"Max is a freshman at Princeton."

Sam was mentally calculating the years.

"Paul's first wife died when Max was two. I met Max when he was only four—I feel as if he's mine."

"No other kids?"

I moved the vase of flowers closer to me and bent to smell the freesia. "I didn't think about having other children until Max went to high school . . . but then Paul became FIT's director . . ." I shrugged. "Do you have children?" I asked, before Sam could respond to what I'd said.

He looked at me shrewdly. "Okay, you win," he said, acknowledging my manipulation of the conversation. "I've been married twice. I have two sons and a daughter from my first marriage. Nina and I have been married for eight years, but have no children together. She has a son from her previous marriage. Next question, doctor?"

"Was your divorce very difficult?" I asked.

"Look at the information you just surrendered," Sam said slyly. "I never mentioned divorce. All I offered was that I was married twice. Why do you assume my marriage ended in divorce? Perhaps my wife died."

Embarrassed, I remained silent.

"But my previous marriage did end in divorce. And no, surprisingly, it was not that painful or traumatic. I believe in change, Julia. It keeps the soul refreshed. The women I've been with—those I've married and those I haven't—have understood that belief. Shared it. There's always been sadness when my relationships ended. But never acrimony. I like women . . . especially the women I marry . . . too much for that."

Rather than remaining silent, I asked another biographical question. "So how did you and Nina meet?"

"A cliché. I was at a psychoanalytic conference in Arizona delivering an address. She was in the audience and asked the first question. The best question, too. Now ask me what you really want to know."

"What question is that?"

"I'll give you the answer—how's that? Nina and I have a good relationship, we love each other, and we share a vision, but it's not tunnel vision. We both believe you have to love someone for who they are. Not despite who they are. Not excuse their faults. You have to find someone whose faults you can live with."

I was hearing every word amplified.

"What we do may not work for us in the long run, but at least we understand who we are. That is the single most important thing I have learned in my life and my career: you cannot become someone you're not. Your true self will out in the end. Either you make peace with it, or you fight it your whole damn life and live a miserable lie. Which is a lousy waste."

I wasn't even seeing his face, just hearing each word and storing it away—for another time—to deal with when I could.

How did Sam know what to say to me that afternoon? It was, I came to believe, his magic, the reason he was such an exemplary therapist. Unlike my husband, who worked only with his intellect, Sam used his instincts and his guts. Like an emotional Geiger counter, he was able to pick up a feeling even when barely a trace of it was present.

"I'd like to add a postscript by Andrew Marvell. You know the poem called 'To His Coy Mistress'?"

I shook my head no.

> Now let us sport us while we may;
> And now, like amorous birds of prey,
> Rather at once our Time devour,
> Than languish in his slow-chapt power.
> Let us roll all our strength, and all
> Our sweetness, up into one ball:
> And tear our pleasures with rough strife

Through the iron gates of life.
Thus, though we cannot make our Sun
Stand still, yet we will make him run.

The lamplight shone in Sam's dark blue eyes, illuminating them, and I glimpsed silver sparks. His voice was gruff. A mad scientist who recited poetry to make his point. I knew that no matter how frightened I was, I was going to keep working with this man and that he was going to take me somewhere I had never been.

I usually stayed away from men, even the husbands of friends. Usually I was silent and kept hidden. Yet there I was in a bar with Sam Butterfield and it had taken only a half hour for the other Julia to stick her head out and wonder where the hell she'd been for so long.

*I should be home,* I thought, *in my greenhouse with my orchids, writing innocuous collateral material that won't bring me into contact with dangerous men.* Draining the last of my martini, I felt the liquid slide down my throat.

Sam paid the check and we walked outside. The clouds had lifted and a late afternoon sun was shining. We both blinked while our eyes adjusted to the light.

"Headed home?" he asked.

"Yeah."

He said he was going uptown too. We could walk together through the park.

Suddenly we had left the city and the buses and the noise and entered a bucolic landscape with the sounds of children playing, dogs barking, and birds chirping. The first few autumn leaves crackled under our feet. The farther we walked into the park, the cooler and quieter it was. After going up a hill and then down some steps and around a bend, we arrived at the sailboat pond.

Twilight was approaching. Only one lone boat cruised the waters. We stopped to watch the young captain bring her in, pick her up, and lovingly wipe her off.

"Did you bring Max here when he was small?" Sam asked.

"All the time. Paul gave him a boat for his ninth birthday. Max named it *The Mystic,* which disappointed Paul. It bothered him Max was into wizardry and magic. But Max refused to consider any other name. No one is more stubborn than Paul . . . except his son."

We continued walking. "So it was a standoff?" Sam asked.

"Yeah, until Paul backed down."

"He identified with Max and excused his son for his faults because they were his own." Sam offered a diagnosis.

"Exactly." I was stunned.

We'd arrived at the foot of the bronze statue of Alice in Wonderland. Sam stopped to examine her. "You look a lot like Alice, you know?" he asked.

It had been years since anyone had mentioned the resemblance, but when I was a child people had always told me I looked like Lewis Carroll's creation. I too had long blond hair, pale skin, and blue-gray eyes. Alice was my favorite character to dress up as for Halloween; I'd wear a blue dress, a white pinafore, Mary Jane shoes, and a blue ribbon in my hair.

"And you're curious too, just like Alice," he mused.

Thinking of the story, I shivered.

"Cold?" he asked.

"No."

"What kind of woman do you think Alice in Wonderland became?" Sam asked me as we walked away from the statue.

"She got married and had children and was probably quite content. She never thought about the rabbit hole or the queen's garden, but sometimes she did have nightmares about how it had felt to be too tall or too small. When she woke up, she was always thankful that as an adult she invariably fit in."

"When I taught psychology, Alice was one of our case studies. What course of treatment to follow with her was part of the final exam. Who Alice might become, on the basis of analysis of the book, was another part."

"So how did my answer compare to your students'?"

"They ran the gamut from her becoming an alcoholic nympho-maniac to a sexually repressed spinster. Everyone interpreted that rabbit hole symbolism the same way."

"And what was your prognosis?" I asked.

"She probably wound up like you. Quite lovely. With blond hair just a little shorter than long. And big eyes that still open wide with wonder. She'd have some ambivalence about her fantasies. Repressing most of them. She'd choose a profession where her curiosity would be an asset. But . . ."—he stopped to look at me—". . . I think she'd be bored to death by always fitting in."

Relieved we'd reached the park's exit, I said good-bye and, clutching my book of transcripts tightly to my chest, walked away from Sam. And from Alice.

# 7

As soon as I got home, I undressed, took a long, hot shower, and then dried myself off with a big bath sheet. I'd stayed under the water too long, had rubbed too hard with the towel, and my skin felt raw. I wasn't sure what to put on and rummaged around in my closet until I found a sand-colored cashmere robe Olivia had given me for my birthday the year before. I pulled it tight against my body and tied the belt in a double knot. The cashmere caressed the whole length of me; I felt held. I rubbed the buttery wool against my stomach, my calves, behind my knees. It was such an extravagant gift, I'd been saving it—afraid to wear it out—but suddenly it seemed foolish not to enjoy it.

Ensconced in my greenhouse with my homework and a cup of tea, I opened the black binder. Reading through the first transcript, I tried to imagine speaking those sentences, saying those words. I couldn't. Forcing myself, I read the second transcript out loud, at first whispering so softly the words were indistinguishable even to me.

I want to make you come.

Let me suck you.

Touch me and feel how wet I am.

What kind of woman could say these things to a stranger and not be embarrassed?

I shut my eyes and pictured her. She was the graduate student Sam had described when I'd asked him who the typical job applicant was. She was independent. Intelligent. Sexually uninhibited. She wouldn't be scared of enjoying herself or having all her fantasies.

Had anyone asked me at the time, I would have said she wasn't me . . . wasn't anyone I have ever known . . . she was an effigy I have summoned up to help me do this job.

Once I found her, I put on her persona like a coat against the cold. I didn't have as much trouble reading the next transcript out loud and experimenting with my new voice.

And then the phone rang.

"Hello?" I said.

"Julia?"

"Yeah, Jack. Of course."

"That's so strange—I wasn't sure it was you," he said.

I was tempted to tell him it wasn't. "No, it's me."

"I called earlier. Were you at the institute?"

"I started the training, Jack. It's fascinating."

"I thought we'd given up *fascinating*." A writer, Jack often teased me about my using certain words too often.

"Sorry. I slipped."

"So long as you don't write *fascinating* in any sentence, you may occasionally use it when you speak."

"Why doesn't it bother me when you say things like that? I would be furious with anyone else who criticized my vocabulary. Why do I let you get away with it?"

"Because you know that deep in my heart, I'm your most ardent admirer. And as such, I have certain privileges. Don't I?"

"Yeah, right."

"All right, now, that is settled. I was just in the bookstore and saw a book about Venetian masks written by . . . wait, I have it written down . . . here: Nick Santorello. Have you seen it?"

"No. Tell me his name again. I'll see if I can find it."

"Forget it," he said. "I'll send it to you."

I uncurled the phone wire and watched it curl back. "Don't be silly. I can get it."

"Why won't you let me do something for you?"

"Jack, you do. You talk to me."

"And talk and talk and talk . . ." He laughed.

"Do you mind?" I teased.

"Mind? Julia, I enjoy talking to you and listening to you more than anyone else."

I stretched out the cord again and held it straight. "So, do you want to know what happened today?"

"What happened today?" he asked.

I let go of the cord, kicked off my slippers, tucked one foot under me, then described the afternoon to Jack.

"So he's quoting Marvell to you now, huh?" Jack said after I'd finished.

"He makes his own rules, and today when I was with him, talking to him, his rules made a lot more sense than mine did."

"What exactly does that mean?" he asked. Even though Jack was at work, he never seemed preoccupied when we talked, never distracted.

"I can't explain it, except he seems more in touch with everything around him . . . more alive than most people. Does that make sense?"

"I guess." Jack sounded wary. He changed the subject. "So how long will it be until you make your first call?"

"About two weeks."

My fingers fanned out of my lap and settled into the fabric. "That is, if I even get through the training."

"Well, if you don't, you can always do your research the old-fashioned way, by interviewing people." His tone was slightly sarcastic and I didn't understand why.

"Jack, do you think what I'm doing is a mistake?"

"Not if you can handle it," he said.

"Do you think I can handle it?"

"The Julia I know can."

Which caused me to wonder—not just then but for days and weeks to come—which Julia it was that he knew.

"But what are you going to do about Sam?" Jack asked.

"What about him?"

"Well, he's coming on to you."

"Why do you think that?"

"Because I know the things I'd be thinking if I were in a bar with you after work."

"He wasn't coming on to me," I insisted.

"How do you know he wasn't? You might miss the signals. You're out of practice."

"Okay, so what if he was?" I asked.

"I just want to be prepared in case I have competition."

Although I was used to his saying things like that to me, for some reason I suddenly didn't know how to respond. After a few seconds of silence, Jack asked what was wrong.

What *was* wrong?

I had come to expect Jack's attention. Counted on it. He always made me feel better. Made me feel necessary. Not in a way that was threatening to my safely solid life but in a disembodied way over a phone wire. There had never been heavy sentiment weighing down Jack's words; they came from him easily, without prompting.

So what had changed?

We'd always pretended, the two of us, that we were connected only by optic fibers crisscrossing the country. We breathed in each other's words and fed off of them without ever admitting how much sustenance we gave each other.

We'd been light about things that might have been dark. Passionless about passion. We'd never before questioned the way we were together, but now I wondered if perhaps we should.

I switched the phone to my other ear and curled my other leg under me. A corner of the robe fell open, exposing my thigh, and I felt the air on my skin. I asked Jack about the woman he'd been dating off and on for the last few months, an illustrator who'd done a cover for the Sunday magazine he edited. Divorced, with two children, she seemed eager for Jack to take on parenting responsibilities with her daughters.

"It's over as of last night. She was annoyed with me. Told me I wasn't making the right moves in the right directions."

"Sexual dysfunction? I could get Dr. Butterfield to do a phone thing with you."

"Or you could get Dr. Butterfield to show you how to do a phone thing with me."

Even though we were joking, I lost a beat. For the second time during the call he had reached that nether part of me usually so hard to find. I felt a clench inside me and a throb. A flash of wanting something. Then it was over.

"Where are you now?" Jack's voice was never heavy with emotion—sarcasm sometimes, yes—but I'd never heard him choke on a word or stumble over a phrase. Yet that evening every word seemed packed with emotion. His affection passed through the phone wire and settled on me. I rubbed my hand over my hip and the cashmere brushed my skin.

"I'm in the greenhouse."

"What's the light like?" Jack often asked me to describe where I was, the sounds, the colors, and the smells, so he could imagine it while we spoke.

"It's a yellowish twilight."

"I bet you're not wearing shoes. It's the first thing you do when you sit down. You take off your shoes and tuck one foot under your tush."

I looked down at my bare feet. "How do you know that?"

"I know more about you than you realize. I remember everything. I still remember how your lips taste." His voice was so deep, so suggestive.

My blood rushed faster. I felt another clench and then a release deep inside me. What was happening?

I laughed and Jack, taking his cue, laughed too. We said good-bye soon after that, but I didn't hang up the phone. I pressed down the button to disconnect the call but held on to the receiver. A piece of plastic. Wires. A microphone. A receiver. A transmitter. The phone was white. A two-line system with separate buttons for conference calls, redial, and hold. I talked on that phone to several people almost religiously. Jack. Olivia. To Max at school. To my parents in Arizona, who always needed to know that everything with me was all right, in place, steady.

Until that evening, I'd always thought the phone could bring people together, but after ending my conversation with Jack, I understood how it could also keep people apart.

I twisted around in my chair, cashmere rubbing my skin, and while I looked at the orchids—three were just coming into bloom—I averted my eyes from the steel construction out the window.

How many other people, whose windows faced east like mine, were watching this new building's progress? In New York, any sky you can see from your windows is a precious commodity; the more view, the higher priced the apartment. This new building would have a wonderful view, but at a cost to my garden and me. Soon I'd have to outfit the whole conservatory with special lights. Orchids deprived of sunlight develop serious problems; their leaves yellow or get brown spots and ugly black burns.

An orchid requires so few things—water, bark chips, sunlight—but if any one is withheld, the plant will not survive.

Picking up one of the blooming flowers, I carried it into the living room and exchanged it with the one now past bloom on the coffee table.

It was six-thirty. Time for Max to come home, throw his books on the foyer bench, and ransack the kitchen. I'd sit down with him at the table and listen to his stories about the day. He was a wonderful raconteur, probably because, like any therapist's child, he had been encouraged to express himself.

But Max was away at school. Walking through the apartment by myself, it suddenly seemed too big.

At seven I found myself looking at my watch again. I still hadn't heard from Paul and didn't know whether he was coming home for dinner or not. Finally at eight, he called to tell me he was working late. I told him I'd wait to have dinner with him, but he said I shouldn't. He didn't know when he'd get home and didn't want to worry about keeping me up late. His concern should have sounded thoughtful. Instead, it reminded me of how often Paul used my supposed fragility as an excuse.

After getting off the phone, I put a casserole of ziti and four cheeses in the oven, made a salad, opened a bottle of cold Chardonnay, and then went into Paul's study to see if he had any books written by Sam Butterfield.

Sipping my wine, I found *Human Sexuality: Function and Dysfunction as a Result of Social Pressure.*

I ate and read. Devouring my salad, I finished the introduction and started on the first chapter. After putting my salad plate in the sink, I scooped out a portion of the bubbling pasta and cheese, poured myself another glass of wine, and continued reading.

The second chapter was about a popular exercise Sam used at the institute. Under supervision, couples would tell each other their sexual dreams and discuss which parts they'd feel comfortable acting out and why they wouldn't feel right acting out other parts. They were then supposed to go home and try to reenact the dreams.

Of the three case histories he related, two had been successful and one hadn't.

How ironic that the wife, in the couple that had failed, was a psychiatrist.

When Paul finally got home, it was almost midnight and he was too tired to talk. He only grunted answers to my questions as he undressed, yet somehow, despite his exhaustion, he managed to carefully hang up his clothes.

All I was able to learn was that he had been with a lawyer all evening.

"A lawyer? Is this about the investigation? Is it that bad?" I asked.

"Everything will be fine," he said, and disappeared into the bathroom. When he came out, I asked him if he'd told the board of directors.

He sat down next to me on the bed and took my hand.

"Yes, and everybody on the board has given me their support."

His hand was very large and covered mine completely. For a moment, I felt reassured—until he disengaged his hand, stood up, walked around to his side of the bed, and slid in.

"Listen, Julia, I don't want you to tell Max about the possibility of an investigation."

"Why not?"

"I don't want him to worry about what's going on here while he's at school," he said.

"But what if the investigation makes the newspapers?" I asked.

"If and when that happens, I'll deal with it."

"You can't protect him from finding out."

"He won't read the New York papers at Princeton."

"You don't know that. Paul—it's dangerous to keep secrets." I heard the words echo in my head. I was keeping secrets. Was I putting myself in danger?

"There's nothing to tell yet. The investigation is still a rumor. We've hired a lawyer only because Mike thinks we should be prepared. The guy's a prestigious tax attorney. Starting tomorrow, he wants to begin reviewing every single expenditure the agency has made. There are going to be a lot of late nights."

Paul found the remote, turned on the television, and scanned the channels. "You know, I spoke to Max just today," he said, some of the tension easing from his face.

"How is he?"

"Great. A little homesick, but nothing out of the ordinary."

"Maybe we should take a drive there this weekend and see him. Take him out to dinner," I suggested, hoping Paul would agree.

"No, he really needs to get acclimated. It's important for him to find out he can be on his own, even if it's tough going. He needs to realize how capable he is."

What he was saying applied to me too. Maybe this would be a good time to tell Paul about the book. Maybe he'd even understand if I put it in the same terms he'd just used—that I needed to know I was capable of writing a book and earning serious money.

The panic began in the dead center of my stomach and rose up my chest. The rush of anxiety was so great I wanted to hide from it. God, I had spent so many hours in analysis working through these attacks and yet still they came without warning. Literally taking my breath away. There was sweat on the back of my neck, under my arms, down my back. I was suddenly nervous, but not about what I'd undertaken. I was worried that when Paul did find out, he'd insist I quit.

*Don't give up, not now that you're finally getting closer.*

It was the same voice who'd spoken to me in Sam's office, who'd helped me read the transcripts. A voice I hadn't heard in so long I'd forgotten how she sounded.

*Closer to what?* I asked her, but she didn't answer.

Beside me, Paul, having no idea of my internal crisis, had escaped into a B movie.

I shut the light off on my side of the bed and rolled over, away from Paul, away from the noise, and closed my eyes.

Could I ever share my fantasies with Paul?

Can people really change?

And if they can't, then what would it be like to spend the rest of my life exactly like this?

On the television, a shot rang out and someone screamed.

It was Jack I thought of just before I fell asleep. Jack remembering how my lips tasted even though we'd shared only one kiss. Jack intimating that we have phone sex.

What would have happened if I'd accepted? Could he be that

open and use the words that actions make unnecessary when two people are together? Could I? Unsuccessfully, I tried to remember that one time we touched, but my memories had disappeared, stolen by that other self, the bad Julia who after so many long years was just now opening her eyes and coming awake.

# 8

Sam and I were driving in his car, a black two-door Mercedes that smelled of leather and wood. It seemed like an ordinary ride until I realized he was in the passenger seat and the car was driving itself. From the backseat, I pleaded with Sam to take over the wheel, but he insisted that everything was under control, that he knew what he was doing and I should trust him.

Terrified, I looked through the windshield as we sped up Avenue of the Americas and waited for the inevitable accident. "Isn't this exciting?" he asked, and smiled as we glided through traffic.

"No! You're trying to kill me!" I shouted.

I woke up alone, sweating and feeling my pulse race with fear. As usual, Paul had left to go jogging while I was still asleep, and his showering afterward had been my alarm clock. Listening to the water hitting the tiles, I relived the nightmare.

I'd had this same dream almost every night since I'd first started training at the institute. That was two weeks ago. I still didn't understand its symbolism. Lying in bed, I went over the dream once more. As Paul emerged from the bathroom, it occurred to me that it wasn't Sam who was endangering me. It was me.

While Paul dressed, I tried to talk to him about the pending investigation that we knew by now was a certainty. Nothing I said convinced him to confide in me. He continued to tell me only the bare minimum and tried to keep his mounting anxiety hidden. Except I could see his tension in the tight-fisted stance he held all the time now and the deep circles that had settled under his eyes. I felt hurt that he refused both my comfort and counsel. Hurt, angry, and impotent.

Before Paul left that Friday, he came in to say good-bye and tell me his schedule. In the past two weeks, he had been home less and less often. When he wasn't traveling to other FIT offices, he was having late meetings with the tax lawyer. "I'm flying out to Chicago at noon today. I have back-to-back meetings straight through dinner, so I'll probably have to stay over."

"Fly the plane safely," I offered as he bent down and dropped a kiss on the top of my head.

Once Paul was gone, I got out of bed.

Lately, it had been taking me a long time to get ready in the morning. Once-ordinary acts had become sensuous moments. I noticed how the coffee smelled, how each sip tasted, how the pellets of water hit my skin in the shower, how the moisturizer glided over my body.

I dressed in my usual jeans and a sweater, but I was conscious of the coarseness of the denim material, of the seams riding my crotch, of the soft cashmere rubbing my neck and my wrists.

As I walked the twenty blocks to the institute, I felt the weight of my jacket resting on my shoulders, smelled the rose and cinnamon perfume I'd worn, and stared with wonder at the trees' drastically changing colors. The streets were littered with leaves by now, and when the wind blew, more of them fell like flashes of fire swirling to the ground. I was glad the sleepy summer was gone and the weather was changing. The crisp fall air was exhilarating. Being assailed by the sharp breeze was like getting a jump start.

During the mile walk to the institute, I'd reacquaint myself with the graduate student I'd invented that first time I read a phone sex script. Her persona helped me through every day. By the time I reached 65th Street, she and I had merged.

For the last two weeks, it had been her confidence and ease that had enabled me to open the door to the Butterfield Institute. She enabled me to walk inside, climb the stairs to the fifth floor, enter the semidark office, and practice calls with one of the institute's male therapists. It was her courage that helped me sit down with Candy so she could critique my style.

Candy's main complaint was my initial nervousness at the beginning of each call. She suggested I'd be more relaxed if instead of relying on my own initiative, I used the institute's prepared list of questions. That had helped, but I was still overwhelmed by the bluntness of what I had to say. Not just the flat-out words like *cunt* and *cock* and *fuck*, but having to describe what it felt like to have a man inside me, to have him touch me and turn me on.

When I remembered to let my imaginary graduate student take over for me, the calls were better. She wasn't afraid. She'd talked to enough men in her bed to know exactly what to say. But even she couldn't stop the panic when Candy informed me that after two weeks of practicing, I was ready to take a real call.

"What do you want your name to be?" Candy asked.

We were sitting in her office. She was sipping espresso, and I was holding my hands together so she wouldn't see them shaking.

"Does every phone therapist have a pseudonym?" I asked.

Candy said they did. "First for protection, but also because for some of us it's easier to separate and become someone else on the phone."

"Alice," I responded, surprised at how easily I had chosen the name. Alice. I could see her. Alice was my graduate student. Able to see the wonder in this new world. Alice, who was bright, brave, and just bad enough to enjoy all this.

For the next twenty minutes, Candy briefed me on my first caller. "Bill and his wife were patients here for several years," she explained. "He's an extremely large man and his wife found it painful to have intercourse with him. After many years of rejection, he developed performance problems and they turned to us. In addition to other therapies, we used phone therapy with Bill to help rebuild his confidence. He's no longer a patient, but he's become a client."

I wanted to know more about the case, but Candy said everything else was confidential unless Sam decided otherwise. "Just remember, Bill's at a stage where he likes to direct his fantasies. All you have to do is be accepting and giving. He's a special man, Julia. So relax. Everything will be fine," she said, as she set me up in the same room where I'd been practicing calls. I settled back in the big armchair with the phone in front of me. From speakers in the ceiling, gentle classical music took the edge off the silence. And then a few minutes after Candy shut the door behind her, the phone rang.

~

"Hello," I said, croaking out the word.

The man on the other end responded with his own hello.

"Bill?" I asked, trying to keep my voice from cracking.

"Yes. Is this Alice?"

And with my eyes shut and the phone in my hand, it was. "Yes, this is Alice."

"So you're new?" Bill asked.

"Uh-huh. How'd you know?"

"Candy told me about you. Are you nervous?" His voice was rich and lyrical.

I laughed. "Oh boy, am I nervous. Can't you hear my heart beating over the phone?"

"Well, you don't have to be nervous with me. You know, you have a very gentle voice."

"Thank you."

"My back was to the door when you walked in because I was

talking to another juror, so I didn't see you, but I heard you ask if this was grand jury room number two. Your voice made me turn around. I was so pleased when you took the empty seat beside me. You've never been on a grand jury before, have you?"

"No." From what I'd learned in training, he was leading me into a fantasy he'd already begun. All I had to do was pay attention and pick up his clues.

"So you didn't know that once you sat down, that would be your seat for the whole month?"

"No. But . . . when I saw you next to me, I was glad."

"Why is that?" Bill asked.

"Because . . . because of how wonderful you smelled. I kept breathing it in, hoping you wouldn't notice."

"I wish you'd told me. Is that why you stayed and talked to me during the break?" he asked.

"Yes. I wanted to get closer to that smell."

"I hope I'm not disturbing you, at home like this. I mean, it was kind of sneaky how I got your number—telling you each jury member should have another member's number in case you couldn't get through to the bailiff."

"Isn't that why you're calling? To tell me we don't have to show up for jury duty tomorrow or something?" I asked.

"No. Is it all right I called?" he asked.

"Yes."

"Your boyfriend isn't there, is he?"

"No, he's away."

"He travels often, doesn't he?"

I hesitated. "Yes." The introduction of a boyfriend confused me.

"And leaves you lonely?"

"Yes, he leaves me lonely," I answered.

"What do you do to keep yourself busy when he's away?"

"Watch a lot of old movies."

I answered before realizing that was exactly what I was doing now that Paul was traveling and working late so often.

"Do you cry at the end?" he asked.

"Always."

"If I was with you and you started to cry, I would brush away your tears with my lips," he whispered into the phone.

I was strangely moved by the image. "No one has ever done that before," I said, again telling the truth.

"Are there other things no one has ever done to you that you'd like me to do?"

Bill was taking shape in my mind. Not as a face, but as sensations, colors. He was dark blue velvet. Heavy cream. A large bird flying through a moonless sky.

"Yes. Are there things no one has done to you?" I asked.

"No, I want to know about you," he answered quickly.

I must have taken a wrong step.

"What do you want that your boyfriend doesn't give you?" He put the focus back on me.

A moment passed. I couldn't think of what to say.

"Alice?" he prompted, and she responded for me.

"He never makes love to me long enough," I answered finally.

"I will," he said. "Where should I start?"

If only he'd talk about his fantasy. This was so difficult for me to do. And then I realized this was his fantasy: to please a woman, to please me. After that, it was easier.

"We'd both be completely dressed, sitting on my couch. There'd be just one light on. And you'd kiss me. Keep on kissing me—"

"So that you could almost come from the kiss?" he asked.

"Yes," I whispered, surprised that nothing about this make-believe conversation was repulsive or frightening. I was in my head where I'd been so many times before, only now there was another voice in my fantasy.

"Alice, have you ever come from a kiss?"

"No."

"That's what I'm going to do to you now. I'm going to make you come from kissing you. Would you like that?" Bill asked.

"If you kiss me for that long, your lips will be sore."

"I don't care. I want to rub my lips on yours. Wet and slippery. And so, so soft. Can you feel it?"

"Yes," I said, and I could.

"I'm unbuttoning your blouse and pushing it off your shoulders so I can kiss your breasts. So I can suck on your nipples," he said.

"Your lips are like feathers on my skin. Bill, are you hard?"

I'd been trained to ask this question often to gauge whether the call was working; if a man wasn't hard after a few minutes, something was wrong.

"I'm very hard," he said, and I segued into the next stage of the conversation.

"Are you touching yourself, Bill?"

"Yes, I'm rubbing myself while I imagine kissing you. I want to keep on kissing you. Alice, tell me how it feels."

"Wonderful. Our lips are so wet they glide against each other."

"Uh-huh," he murmured.

"And your tongue darts out—oh—it's hard—like your cock." It was my voice, but it was Alice who was thinking up the words.

"Oh . . ." His breathing had changed.

From the tapes Candy had played for me, I was familiar with this transition. At a certain point, usually minutes from orgasm, a man's breathing changes and his responses become shorter and less coherent.

"Your tongue parts my lips and slips inside my mouth where it's warm and wet. And then just as I start to suck on your tongue, you pull back and withdraw," I said.

"But . . . you go after me . . . ," he told me.

"Yes . . . I grab on to your tongue with my teeth and draw it back into my mouth. Your tongue fills up my whole mouth."

"Suck on it . . . suck . . . on my tongue . . . ," he pleaded.

"Yes . . . I'm sucking on it, going up and down on your tongue. It's filling up my whole mouth. I let you slip almost all the way out and then suck you back inside again. God, I wish your tongue could come, right now, inside my mouth," I whispered.

"Ohh . . . God . . ."

It was the first time I'd really listened to a man come. Not seen him and felt him, but heard his release through the sounds he made.

"Was it all right?" I asked, suddenly shy.

Bill sounded content. "Yes . . . Yes, it was wonderful, but next time, I want to make you come too. All right, Alice?"

He'd thrown me off balance.

"Yeah. Okay. Good-bye, Bill." I shivered and hung up the phone.

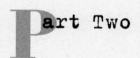

Part Two

# 9

I sat in the dimly lit cubicle, suddenly aware of the music that had been playing during my entire conversation with Bill. A complex orchestral piece that featured a piano. It soared and dipped and sounded slightly sad. Or was that what I was bringing to it?

Was Bill as lonely as he'd seemed or was I reading into the things he'd said? Had I given him solace or only made him that much more aware of the problems with his wife? Shivering again, I hugged myself and then remembered the jacket on the back of my chair. But it did nothing to warm me. The cold was inside where the words had been.

What had I done? How had I been able to dredge those words up and out of me and speak them to a stranger over the phone? To take him from one mind-set and help him arrive at another?

For so many years, I had never let anyone glimpse that passionate, perilous place where part of me hid. How could I have asked anyone to navigate there? To force them to share something I was so uncomfortable with I kept it hidden from even myself? I was afraid if I traveled too far from the life I'd created, I wouldn't get back.

Masking emotions had been something I'd learned at my father's knee.

As a child, my father always asked me how I felt. In therapy I came to understand that my answers never were as important as the fact that I would instantly open up to him. But baring my young soul took its toll and robbed me of my privacy. At some point, rather than have feelings I'd be obliged to divulge, I must have forced myself to stop having them.

Except it's not possible for a child to will herself not to have feelings. She continues to have them but represses them. Which was why, Dr. Stone had explained, I was so conflicted when I started college and why, when finally faced with freedom, I imploded.

"When you were young, you expected yourself to handle more than you could, and your adult problems are a sort of a result of that," Dr. Stone had explained. "But what might have been a brilliant adaptation for a child with the mental tools and means available to a child may not necessarily work for an adult.

"You have to learn there are other ways to protect yourself, Julia. To check reality, to determine your own fate—you couldn't do those things as a child. We have to help you gradually and carefully drop the old unconscious defense mechanisms in favor of new conscious acts of self-protection."

Unfortunately, Dr. Stone and I never finished that job. Yes, I had started to have all my feelings again and not to blame myself for the negative ones. And I had mastered how to calm my fears and ease my anxiety, but that wasn't enough. I had quit too soon. Too much of my darkness remained unexplored. Was I now finally going to uncover it and bring it out into the light?

I must have been sitting there for at least ten minutes when Candy knocked on the door and came in. Her presence startled me back to reality. I wasn't ready to go, but she asked me to follow her back to her office for her critique.

"That went extremely well, Julia, but it ran a little short. You had Bill on the phone for only twelve minutes. Clients are more satisfied when the call lasts for fifteen minutes to a half hour. Some men like to stay on even longer. But for a first call, you did great."

"Is every man that easy to please?" I asked.

"Not that easy, no. More typically a client will have less imput. And you'll have to do more work. I think you'll be surprised that most of them will want to let you take charge. Over eighty percent of our clients are professionals who spend their lives making decisions. It's titillating for them to give up that control for a while. They enjoy having the tables turned."

"What about Bill's wanting me to come? Is that typical?" I asked.

"No, but not unusual either. It's a powerful aphrodisiac for a man to know he can excite you. For Bill, it's even more important. You probably should have made an attempt."

"For real?" I asked.

"Many phone therapists do. But it's too difficult to try that here at the institute. That's one of the reasons why you'll be working from home from now on."

I nodded. "I need a cup of coffee."

Candy laughed and set about making us both espresso while she explained that once I started taking calls at home, I'd need to come in only twice a week to review my calls with her and Sam. After she handed me my coffee and took a sip of her own, she gave me a suction cup with a mike wire attached, a palm-size tape recorder, and a box of miniature tapes.

"You'll need to record your calls so we can analyze them. The suction cup goes on the handset and the wire gets plugged into the mike outlet on the recorder. The trick is to remember it's hooked up—sometimes the suction cup falls off, so be conscious of it."

I picked up the black, mushroom-shaped rubber cup and tiny tape recorder. They looked sinister.

"Isn't it illegal to tape someone?" I asked nervously.

"Only if the person isn't informed, but we forewarn all our clients."

"And it doesn't inhibit them?" I pressed the suction cup against the fleshy part of my palm and felt its pull as it adhered to my skin.

"We tell them about it during the screening process, so by the time they talk to you, they've forgotten all about it," Candy said as she opened her desk calendar. "Now, let's talk scheduling. For the next few weeks, you won't do more than a few calls, three or four times a week. What are the best hours for you?"

I tried to imagine myself in my apartment, on the phone. Paul never came home during the day, but it might be safer to take the calls at the institute.

"Don't any of the trainees do the calls from here?"

"Not usually. It's just not private enough. And it's not conducive to relaxing. We think your state of mind translates over the phone, but if you want to make an exception—"

I interrupted her. "No. Late mornings are fine. Or early afternoons." I was determined to experience this the way any other trainee would.

Downstairs, Sam's secretary waved me into his office. He was sitting at his desk surrounded by papers, but his expression was so gleeful it was hard to believe he'd been working. His glasses were on top of his head, nestled in his mane of white hair, his shirtsleeves were pushed up, his feet were up on his desk, and he was drinking out of a soda can with a straw. He motioned me to a chair across the desk from him. I sat down.

"For your first call, you did great . . ."—he paused—". . . Alice," he said with flourish.

"I—were you listening?" I wondered if he could see the heat that flushed my face.

"It's standard operating procedure with all trainees. Didn't Candy tell you?"

"Well, I knew she was listening, but I didn't know you were too." My embarrassment was turning to anger.

"I'm sorry it wasn't made clear. But what we're doing here is damn delicate. We can't put you, our patients, or our clients at risk."

"Risk? Is there something about all this that could be dangerous?" Now I was concerned.

Sam stood up, walked around the desk, and sat down in the chair next to me.

"No. The risk is one of improper therapy. We're very cautious about our procedures in every area. Clients are never given trainees' real names or phone numbers. Phone therapists never know their callers' last name."

As I listened to him assure me the only real danger was in not being careful, I was also trying to remember everything I'd said on the phone, trying to convince myself nothing about my conversation with Bill was new to Sam.

"When I heard your name, it made me smile," he said.

"Alice? Yeah, it seems appropriate, doesn't it? Down the rabbit hole and into a strange world I don't understand."

"You didn't sound confused on the phone," he said.

"Yeah, but all those things I said . . . that I didn't know I was going to say . . . I don't know where they came from." I picked up a paper clip and unbent it.

"You were able to tap into your unconscious. You know, not every trainee can do that." He leaned back and put his hands behind his head, his dark blue eyes fastened on me. "Not everyone can be as verbal and uninhibited as you were."

"In a million years, I'd never have described myself as uninhibited." I was not surprised Sam was so easy to talk to. I'd guessed as much that first night we really talked at the Botanical Garden.

"Maybe you wouldn't describe Julia Sterling that way, but how about Alice?"

"Yes, Alice was uninhibited."

"But you feel separated from Alice?" he probed.

It wasn't as warm in Sam's office as it had been upstairs and I felt goose bumps on my arms. Since the cuffs of my sweater were pushed up around my elbows, I crossed my arms and pulled both cuffs down at the same time. For a moment I could concentrate only on the sensation of the soft wool now concealing my skin.

"How do you feel right now?" Sam asked.

I laughed. "God, there you go again. What is it with all of you? Don't you know any other questions?"

"It's a serviceable question for therapists to ask patients, but I agree with you, it's a lousy question for fathers and husbands to ask of wives and daughters."

"But I'm neither your patient nor your daughter nor your wife," I said.

"You are, however, for the time being, my employee and it's my responsibility to know how you feel after your first call." He leaned all the way forward so that we were only a few inches apart and I could smell his musky scent, a pleasant combination of patchouli and lemon. I could see the network of laugh lines around his eyes and the furrows across his forehead from raising his eyebrows whenever he asked a question. His face was so open; his eyes were without judgment. So powerful was his ability to instill confidence that I actually did want to tell him how I felt and hear what he'd say about it.

"I don't know how I am. I never did anything like that before. I never said anything like what I said. I was in another dimension. It was public and private and I'm very confused."

"Good. That's what I want. As long as you don't fucking repress your responses, you'll be fine. Let's call it quits for the day. Take it in, figure out what it meant, and decide—consciously decide—if you want to continue."

"Is that what you'd ask every trainee to do?" I asked.

"Yes."

I stood up to leave but stopped at the door.

"Sam, can I ask you a question?" I asked.

He nodded yes.

"Does listening to those calls excite you?"

"Sometimes."

I didn't ask and he didn't tell me if this had been one of those times. I wasn't ready to know.

# 10

Before I went home, I stopped off at the health club I belonged to; it was on the forty-fifth floor of a hotel near the United Nations. The pool was glassed in, so while you swam you looked out at the city's skyline and the heavens above. After ten minutes, I was lost in the rhythm of the strokes and lulled by the constant movement of my body pushing through the water.

I swam harder and went faster, trying to beat my usual time. For almost an hour I heard only the sounds of my own breathing and saw only the bubbles I blew in the turquoise water. Back and forth I traveled, until I'd covered a mile in forty minutes, and then exhausted but calmed, I got out, got dressed, and went home.

In my apartment, I made a cup of tea, put a brownie on a plate, and took them both into the greenhouse. After settling down in my slipper chair, I checked my answering machine. Olivia had called, confirming weekend plans, and Jack had called.

So that I could deduct my phone calls as a business expense, our accountant insisted I have a private line. It rang only on the phone beside my bed and in the greenhouse, and I paid the bills myself from my freelance income. I was suddenly glad for the privacy it afforded.

I returned Jack's call, and while I waited for him to get on the line, I took a bite of the rich chocolate.

"How was your day?" he asked after we'd exchanged greetings.

I kicked off my shoes and curled my legs under me and licked some crumbs off my fingers. It had been an innocent question. He was simply interested the way he always was. But I didn't know what to tell him.

"Would it repulse you if I liked it?" I asked, after I'd very briefly described my first phone call.

"Nothing you could do would repulse me," he answered, without hesitation. "We don't judge each other, you and I."

Was that true? A memory scratched at my consciousness, but I couldn't get to it. Or didn't want to. "Really? I wonder if I told you my darkest fantasy, you wouldn't just give up on me."

"Try me. Tell me your darkest fantasy. Just as long as it's not about the old goat."

"Who's the old goat?" I asked.

"Your new friend and mentor, Dr. Sam Butterfield. That's how I see him. A satyr, prancing after you on his old, yellowed horny hooves."

I swallowed another bite of the brownie. "Oh, Jack, come on. He's a brilliant therapist."

"He's a man who runs a sex clinic, who takes his freelance writer out for martinis in the middle of the day, who quotes her love poems, who listens in while she has phone sex with one of his clients and then tells her what a good job she did at it . . . C'mon. I hate it when you're naïve."

"You actually hate something about me?" I teased. It was a relief to be silly.

"I hate two things. I hate it when you're naïve and when you do the god thing."

"What?" I asked.

"You know . . . you meet someone and put him or her up on a

pedestal. Elevate him or her—in this case, him —to godlike status. Then, when you eventually discover a flaw, which is inevitable, you feel betrayed. Meanwhile, the poor fool never asked to be deified in the first place."

"When have I ever done that?" I asked.

"You did it with your friend Laurie. With at least a dozen guys at school. With two teachers at grad school that I know of and probably a whole bunch of other people I don't know about. You've done it with your husband. Now you're doing it with Sam."

"What about you? Have I done it with you?"

"No, you never put me on that pedestal," Jack said.

I picked up the last of the brownie crumbs and licked them off my fingers. "Good. Then I won't have to watch you topple off and lose you as a friend."

"You couldn't if you tried."

"Jack, are you sure about this theory? If it was such a glaring pattern, wouldn't you have mentioned it before now?" I queried him.

"It's true. Believe me. I've been a Juliaphile for years. I've studied the subject. I know her by heart." There was such a sweetness to the last few words, my breath caught in my chest. "Listen, Julia," he continued. "I think I'm coming up to New York."

"When?"

"In about two weeks. The week of the twenty-fourth. Will you be around?"

"Sure, I'll be here. You know, it's been over two years since I saw you last," I said.

"Have you changed?"

I looked at my reflection in the glass window. "I guess I have a few new lines around my eyes."

"'My love came back to me / Under the November tree / Shelterless and dim. / He put his hand upon my shoulder, / He did not think me strange or older, / Nor I him.'" Jack's deep voice resonated over the phone.

"What was that?" I asked.

"A poem by Frances Cornford called 'All Souls Night.' It would be more appropriate if I were coming up in November instead of October, but we can take poetic license."

"What is going on with you? Poetry? You haven't read poetry since college."

"But I have a photographic memory, remember?"

"Actually, what I remember is that you once promised to write me a poem. It sounded so romantic. But you never did, and I was disappointed."

"I'm sorry," Jack said, as if it really mattered to him.

"So, write me a poem now."

"No, now I'm old enough to know I can't write poetry."

"But you've decided to start quoting it?" I asked.

"I can't let that old goat be the only one to impress you. I have to stay competitive."

I laughed. Jack didn't.

"So where are you staying?" I asked, to fill the sudden silence. Had there ever been silences between us before?

"At the University Club," he said.

"With all that wood paneling and those stuffed moose heads? Why don't you stay at some exotic hotel with marble bathrooms and a stunning view of the skyline?"

"I'm not a marble bathroom kind of guy. Do you think we can go to a play?"

Living in Florida, he was always starved for culture. So whenever he did come to New York, we crammed the days with activities.

"Do you want me to get tickets?" I asked.

"No. I'll take care of it. Are evening tickets all right?" he asked.

"Yeah, especially if you come at the end of the week. Paul's been spending Thursdays and Fridays traveling to other FIT offices."

"You know, I really don't think he exists."

Jack had been invited to my wedding but had been on assignment in Japan and never made it back. And in all the ensuing years, the two men had managed to never meet. In fact, Paul had somehow never even answered the phone when Jack called. It was Jack's running joke that I'd invented a phantom husband.

"Well, when we talk, he doesn't exist," I said as I suddenly became aware how much of my life Paul wasn't a part of.

"Julia, I have a confession to make," Jack said. His tone had turned serious and became more so as he continued. "I checked with some guys I know at the *New York Times*. Rumor has it the police are investigating several phone sex companies for prostitution links."

I looked at the empty plate in front of me. The fine white china was smeared with a faint impression of grease. "What are you saying? That the Butterfield Institute is one of them? That Sam is fronting a prostitution ring?"

"He might be. I haven't been able to confirm or deny that yet. But I wanted you to know. So you can be careful."

My fingers tightened around the phone receiver. "You don't trust me to take care of myself? Christ, when did you turn into Paul?"

"Hey! Slow down." Jack was insulted. "I'm just offering information, not shoving tranquilizers in your face. I'm not denying your abilities. I just asked some questions you're not in a position to ask and passed on the information. Okay?"

I was still gripping the phone too tightly. "Are you snooping around just to protect me?" I asked.

"What other reason could there be, Julia?"

I lashed out. "That you're doing the investigating for an article. Planning on one of your famous exposés."

His laugh surprised me. "Do you actually believe I would do that to you?"

"Well, aren't you the journalist who never compromises his principles?" Certain this jibe would wound him as much as his reference to my helplessness had wounded me, I waited for his response.

"Except you've forgotten one thing." There was absolutely no rancor in his voice.

"What?"

"How I treat you is as important to me as any investigation. I would never compromise you," Jack said in a way that sounded more like a man offering a prayer than one arguing his point.

His words dissipated whatever fury I still felt and I let out a long, slow sigh. A welcome moment of silence followed.

"I'm glad that's over," he said finally.

"We fight pretty good, don't we, Jack?"

"Because neither of us is trying to win. We just want to get to the place where the battle will end."

"I don't know if I'm going to take any more calls next week," I said without explaining the non sequitur.

"Because of what I've told you?" he asked.

"No. Because the call today wasn't what I imagined. It wasn't a game. Jack, do you think it's taking advantage of a man to do this to get a book out of it?"

"They're paying you to help them masturbate and you're worried you're using them?" Jack asked.

"You're picturing a disembodied voice. I was talking to a guy named Bill who didn't want me to be lonely. Who had this sadness in his voice. He got in my head, Jack."

"Oh no. No one is going to get in your head but me." This time he was laughing, so I didn't take him seriously. Not about his feelings. Or his suspicions. Not then. Not yet.

# 11

~

The next day, Saturday, Paul flew in from Chicago early in the morning and went straight from the airport to play tennis with Larry Vernon. I didn't see him until noon, when Olivia and I met both of them at a gallery in SoHo.

They were late and while we waited, Olivia and I walked around the high-ceilinged loft, examining the art on the walls. Each piece was a photo collage of three and sometimes four different images married together.

Rocks were fused with faces, ruins floated on the ocean, houses overgrown with ivy opened onto forests, the sun set inside a glass bowl, phantom lovers hovered over an empty bed that hung above a meadow.

Moving from print to print, I was lost in the strange ambiance the collages created. I didn't even notice when Paul and Larry arrived until my husband came up beside me, touched my arm, and kissed me hello. His hair was still damp from a shower, and he looked relaxed for the first time in weeks. Paul was wearing a crisp white shirt, black corduroy slacks, and a sports jacket. Two women had turned to look at him. Feeling their stares, Paul smiled back, enchanting them. I remembered that when he'd first turned that smile on me I'd been charmed too.

"Do you like these?" I asked Paul, referring to the artwork.

"The imagery is too labored."

When I disagreed, he tried to convince me. Normally, I would have made a greater attempt to understand his point of view, but that day I didn't care. Obviously annoyed, he changed the subject and asked where we were having brunch.

"I don't know. Olivia made the reservation."

"You didn't find out? What if they don't take credit cards? You should always find out in advance, Julia. You know I don't like to be blindsided."

Two months earlier, my teeth would have clenched and my stomach would have knotted at the way he was talking to me, but I was viewing him from a greater distance now and not responding the same way anymore. Since I had begun working for Sam and spent part of each day as a woman named Alice, some of the cords that bound me to Paul had been severed.

"I have cash if they don't take cards. It's no big deal," I said, and moved over to inspect another photograph.

In the background was a wide landscape of soft rolling hills. In the foreground, a calm, placid lake. Above the lake was a cloudy sky with a sliver of sun just breaking through. And flying, like a great giant bird, was a naked woman, her arms outstretched like wings. In the mirror-sharp surface of the lake, the woman's reflection was watery and slightly fragmented.

"You seem to respond to that one," Paul said.

"Yeah, I guess so."

"Would you like me to buy it for you?" he asked, as he boyishly brushed his hair back and grinned in a way that had always been so appealing. "I've been so distracted lately with the impending investigation, I'd like to make it up to you." He walked over to the desk and picked up the price list.

Coming up beside him, I took the list out of his hand and put it back on the desk. "No. Don't do that. Just tell me what's going on. Confide in me, Paul. All I want to do is help."

"That's sweet, Julia," he said, and smoothed my hair down with the flat of his hand the way a father might. "All you can do to help is not worry."

"Except not knowing is awful. The things I'm imagining are probably much worse than anything you could tell me."

"There simply is nothing to tell," he said.

Olivia and Larry came over to tell us we should go if we wanted to keep our reservation, so we left the gallery and headed uptown on West Broadway. People crowded the streets, walking, window-shopping, and stopping to buy everything from fine art books to hot dogs and sugared nuts from the street vendors.

While we waited for the light on the corner of Prince, I glanced across the street and realized I was staring at my stepson. Max and his girlfriend, Betsy, were holding hands and talking to each other, oblivious to everything around them. Nervously, I glanced over at Paul.

His icy eyes had narrowed to slits and he was frowning. He'd seen Max too, and as the light changed, he turned to Larry. "You and Olivia go ahead. We'll meet you at the restaurant."

By now, they too had seen Max and understood.

So Paul and I lingered on the corner watching Max and Betsy cross the street, unaware of what awaited them. But I knew. With Max being so independent and Paul so controlling, clashes between them were inevitable. Max was never afraid, and so I was always afraid for him when he butted up against his father's intractable will.

Wanting to stave off the oncoming confrontation, I put my hand on Paul's arm. "Don't be mad at him for not telling us he was coming into town. He just wanted to see Betsy. He must have missed her terribly. Don't you remember what it was like to be eighteen and in love?"

Paul hated to be criticized, and he turned on me. "Don't tell me how to act, Julia. Max disobeyed me. He wasn't supposed to come into the city until Thanksgiving."

"But it's not such a big thing—" I was saying, when he cut me off.

"Max!" Paul called out.

Max heard his father's voice and looked around. Finally seeing us, he smiled sheepishly. "Dad? Julia? What are you guys doing here?"

"I think you should answer that question first," Paul said in an alarmingly quiet voice.

As usual, Paul's anger was making me more anxious than it was Max. Wanting to protect my stepson from his father's rage, I stepped forward and put my arms around him to hug and say hello.

Ignoring me, Paul continued. "I thought we decided it wasn't prudent for you to come back to New York until Thanksgiving. That you were going to tough it out."

"I asked him to come in, Dr. Sterling," Betsy offered.

Keeping his eyes on his son, Paul ignored Betsy. He thought she and Max were too young to be so serious about each other. I shared Paul's concern, but that didn't alter the fact that I enjoyed Betsy. She made Max happy.

"C'mon, Betsy. You don't have to lie for me." Max smiled at her. He looked so much like Paul then. They were the same size with the same dark good looks, except Max's eyes weren't icy blue; they were hazel.

"I know what you thought I should do, Dad," Max said, "but I told you on the phone I didn't want to wait months to see Betsy."

Aware of the argument, strollers stared as they passed.

"That's irrelevant," Paul said in an even voice that occluded the depths of his anger. I chewed on my bottom lip and watched a vein throb in Paul's neck. His arms were hanging loosely by his side, but his fists were clenched.

"Maybe to you, Dad, but not to me. I thought about it and decided there just wasn't any downside to my coming in for the weekend."

"You disobeyed me."

"No, I just made up my own mind," Max responded.

It was a long moment. Paul wasn't saying anything, just glaring at Max, who was taking it and glaring right back.

"And where are you staying?" Paul finally asked.

"At Betsy's."

I touched Paul's arm again, forcing him to look at me. "Olivia and Larry are waiting for us. Let's go. It's not such a big deal. They missed each other." I indicated Max and Betsy. "Let them have their weekend—"

"Let Larry and Olivia wait." Paul's voice was as icy cold as his eyes.

Betsy, suddenly wary of Paul, took a step backward, and since she and Max were holding hands, she involuntarily pulled him with her. To Paul, it must have appeared as if Max were leaving.

"Don't you go anywhere, young man," Paul ordered. His voice was slightly elevated for the first time. "We're not finished here unless you intend on putting yourself through school."

"Dad, I'm not going anywhere, but what I did was no crime, okay? I came in for one lousy weekend. That's it." Max was upset but still holding his own.

"It's not what we agreed on," Paul insisted vehemently.

Like an emotional sponge, I was picking up their feelings and experiencing their anger and frustration for them.

"What's the big deal here, Dad? It's my life, you know?"

Paul could no longer control his voice level. "That's not the goddamn point. Having discipline is a virtue, Max. Knowing you can stick it out is a valuable lesson to learn."

"I have enough teachers at Princeton, thank you."

Father and son eyed each other. Having reached their inevitable standoff, each was sure he was right and neither was about to back off.

A minute passed and then Max broke the silence. "Oh, come on, Dad. What would you have done in my place?"

Suddenly, like a snake shedding his skin, Paul let go of his anger. "Goddamn smart aleck," he said, but he was smiling. "I should have taught you obedience instead of independence."

In the end, it was as Sam had explained: Paul forgave his son because he saw so much of himself in Max. Reaching out, he hugged Max close.

"Next time," I said as I kissed Max good-bye, "remember that Betsy isn't the only one who misses you."

"You're shaking. Are you all right?" Max asked me.

"I'm fine," I lied.

～

As we walked to the restaurant where Olivia and Larry were waiting, Paul boasted about how clever Max had been in getting himself off the hook.

"Are you concerned Max isn't adjusting to being at school?" I asked.

"Not at all."

"But I thought . . . the other night, you told me you didn't want him to come home because he was having a tough time adjusting."

"He'll be all right, Julia. He's not you." There was a nasty edge to his voice. Paul may have forgiven Max, but he was still angry at me for being critical of him.

"What the hell does that mean?" I asked.

"Maybe you don't want to acknowledge it, Julia, but you're reliving your own failed college experience through Max and projecting your fears onto him. You must stop. I don't want him to absorb your feelings and integrate them as his own."

"Why would you even bring up what happened to me at college? I wasn't talking about myself but about Max."

"On the surface you weren't, but you were doing it unconsciously."

I would have continued to disagree, but I knew any further argument would be futile. Paul had already made up his mind. Convinced he was always right, he'd just continue to insist he was the professional and never made mistakes.

But he did. After all, he was just a man.

Because Max's mother had died on horseback, Paul made the mistake of forbidding Max from ever going riding. Early on, Paul made it clear to me, to Max's school principals, and to the owners of the camps Max had gone to that his son was prohibited from going near a horse.

When Max was eight, his nightmares started. Waking up to his cries in the middle of the night, I'd go to him and find him bathed in sweat, his face wet with tears.

When I told Paul that Max refused to talk about the dreams, he said we shouldn't make Max feel self-conscious. "Every child has night terrors, Julia. He'll outgrow them."

Except he didn't.

It took me several months to convince Max to confide in me. He agreed only after I promised not to tell Paul. And then the confession burst out of him. He was desperate for some comfort.

"In every dream there are giant horses riding wild through the streets and we all get trampled. Every time, no matter how far or how fast we try to run away," he told me, "we all die."

Without betraying Max's confidence, I approached Paul and asked him to get Max help. Paul insisted his son didn't need therapy. "I know the signs of trouble, and Max isn't exhibiting them," he told me. "You're just projecting your fears onto him, Julia."

There was no arguing with him, so I called my own father and discussed the situation with him. Adopting his advice, I took Max to see the horses at New York's Claremont Stables.

As soon as Max stood beside a horse, something in him relaxed. The affinity he felt for the animals must have been in his blood; his mother had ridden all her life and his maternal grandparents still raised and raced horses.

After the nightmares abated, Max wanted to return to the stables. He'd stand near the large animals, feeding them from his hand, laying his small face on their necks and whispering to them.

One day, four years later, Max came home from school three

hours late. When I questioned him, he gave me a feeble excuse about where he'd been. After it happened twice more, I sat him down and demanded he tell me where he was going and what he was doing.

Stubbornly, he insisted it was a secret.

"Either you tell me or you tell your father, but one of us has to know where you're going."

"Okay," he said, "but you promise not to tell Dad?"

"As long as you're not breaking the law."

"I've been taking horseback riding lessons," he said proudly.

"By yourself?"

He nodded. "I've been using the money Grandma and Grandpa gave me for Christmas."

"Max, you can't keep this from your father. You have to tell him."

He refused, and we fought about it. "Dad will make me stop. And for no good reason. It's not my fault he has some phobia about horses."

"If you're old enough to make up your own mind, you're old enough to take responsibility for what you're doing. You have to tell him," I insisted.

Max didn't agree. "No, I have a right to my own private life. You and Dad always tell me that. Besides, you said you'd keep my secret as long as I wasn't breaking the law. Well, is there a law that says I can't ride horses?"

"Yes, in this house there is. You know that."

Eventually, like his father, Max wore me down. Except I didn't let Max go alone. I went with him, and together, we learned how to ride.

At first I had trouble controlling my anxiety every time we mounted the horses. The fact that I was defying Paul consumed me. Eventually I overcame my fears by concentrating on how I was helping Max explore the dark and secret things Paul had refused to let him bring to the light.

We had great times trotting through the park on those afternoons until, in time, Max became more consumed with competitive sports at school. Eventually his obsession with horses abated and only occasionally did the two of us take off an afternoon to go riding.

Paul had never discovered our secret.

~

Leaving the restaurant, Olivia and Larry and Paul and I decided to visit a few more galleries. The streets were crowded and we could only walk two abreast, so Paul took off with Larry—talking tennis—while Olivia and I trailed behind.

"Are you all right?" Olivia asked. "You were so quiet during lunch."

I shrugged. "Seeing Max upset me. I really miss him."

"Did Paul give him hell?"

"For as long as he could and then treated him like the returning prodigal son."

"So what else is new?" Olivia asked sarcastically. She knew Paul almost as well as I did.

I smiled, then felt the smile fade. "Olivia?"

"What?"

"I still haven't told Paul about the research I'm doing at the institute. It bothers me that I'm not being honest with him."

"So tell him."

"It's not that simple." I wished it could be.

"It never is. The precept of honesty is one thing; being honest is another."

We passed a mother wheeling two babies in a carriage and both of us had to step aside. "I hate lying," I said when we fell into step again. "Except I know he won't understand; he'll just insist I quit."

"Julia, he's your husband, not your jailer."

Paul and Larry had crossed the street just as the light changed. Olivia and I had to stop at the corner.

"They're not even aware we're not behind them anymore." Olivia shook her head and her curls danced.

"I'm not ready to take him on yet." I sighed, disappointed in myself.

"So, you're not ready. Don't be so hard on yourself. You try more than anyone I've ever met to be good. No one can be that good."

The light changed and we crossed the street. Halfway down the next block, Olivia stopped at a vendor's table. "Oh, look, Julia, fake Chanel buttons. They're great copies," she said, and then asked the price.

Typically, when I was with Olivia, I tried on clothes and bought accessories I never would have looked at if I were alone, but that afternoon even Olivia couldn't make the buttons exciting. After she bought two sets, we continued on. Up ahead, Larry and Paul looked back, gestured which gallery they were going into and disappeared.

"Sometimes I don't think I'm living the right life," I said.

"What do you mean?"

"I have a wonderful apartment, a child I love, a successful and handsome husband, loyal friends, but . . ."

"But something is missing," Olivia finished for me.

We'd paused again, this time in front of the gallery's large glass doors. Inside, I could see our husbands examining the art. Paul was talking and gesturing with his hands while a woman, probably the gallery owner, nodded. Considering the rapt expression on her face, I could tell she was flattered by his attention.

"Once Max and I went riding," I said to Olivia as we stood outside. "We came to a stone fence. I'd never jumped before, but Max said he could talk me through it. I was afraid, but he insisted. He said jumping was like soaring. That it was the most amazing feeling and I had to try. Part of me wanted to, but another part of me was frightened. I could only think of what might happen . . . if I missed . . . if I fell . . .

"Finally, I couldn't do it, so I rode the long way around."

"And you don't want to do that anymore," she said, as she opened the gallery door.

"No, I don't," I answered, and walked inside.

# 12

The sun shone brightly Monday morning, filling the apartment with warm light. Nervously waiting for the phone to ring, I paced back and forth from my bedroom to the greenhouse, undecided where I should take my first call. My anxiety led to concern. What if Jack's sources were right? What if the institute was involved in something more sinister than phone sex? No, they were unconfirmed rumors, I reminded myself. Angry I'd let Jack's skepticism intrude, I forced my thoughts to the upcoming call. Nothing was going to interfere with my book. This project was something I wanted to do. Needed to do.

When the phone finally rang, I was in the greenhouse, so I sat down in my slipper chair and said hello. His name was Tom and he was an ex-patient from the institute. He wanted to practice staying excited for as long as he could without coming. Using a script almost verbatim from the transcript book, I kept him on the phone for forty-five minutes before he orgasmed. For me, it was more like teaching an aerobics class than supplying an erotic experience, but Tom seemed satisfied.

About an hour later, I took my second call from a client who, in a polite and sophisticated voice, introduced himself as Arthur.

~

"Do you have a fantasy?" I asked.

"Yes," he said.

"Would you like to tell me about it?"

"Not yet. First tell me where you are. Tell me what you are wearing."

I described a boudoir setting and suggestive outfit totally unlike the leggings and oversize sweater I had on. "Are you ready to tell me your fantasy now?" I asked.

"I can't," he said. "Not yet. I don't know who you are."

"I can be anyone you want."

"Can you be my little girl?" he asked.

His request unnerved me, but I answered yes.

"No, you have the wrong voice." He was unexpectedly angry. "Who else can you be?"

A bank of clouds rolled in from the south, shrouding me in shadow. Suddenly, I was self-conscious about sitting inside the all-glass room where anyone looking out of a window could see me, and I turned away.

"Give me choices," he said.

Once again borrowing from the book of transcripts, I tried out three different scenarios until Arthur finally responded to one.

"You want me to tell you what to do?" I asked.

"Yes," he whispered, relieved. "Yes, be my master."

I held my breath and then released it. In this world, everything was new.

"All right. Stand up, Arthur. Stand right in front of me," I read off of the photocopied page.

"Yes." He was now docile.

"You're going to do exactly what I say, all right?"

The sky darkened, turning the day abruptly to night. Big rain-drops smattered on the glass above me and around me, so loudly I had to press the phone tightly to my ear to hear Arthur.

"Tell me what to do," he urged.

"I want to see you naked. Get undressed," I said.

There was a clap of thunder in the sky.

"How should I start?" he asked.

"With your shirt. Take off your shirt first. Do it."

And that was all it took.

~

The call from Arthur left me unsettled. He had been so hard to reach. I was glad for the break before my third and last call of the day. Realizing I'd forgotten to record either of my first two calls, I took out a notebook and wrote down as much as I could remember, surprised that I'd vividly imagined the men I talked to. It was my first insight into how the phone worked. Unlike movies, photographs, or videos, where you're given the visual facts, on the phone you supply them for yourself. Coming from your own unconscious, the images are more personal and ultimately more satisfying.

After eating some lunch, I called Paul's office for the second time that day, checking on his whereabouts to be sure there was no chance of his arriving home unexpectedly.

By the time my third call came through, I'd moved into the bedroom and had already attached the suction cup to the phone's handset and plugged the mike into the recorder.

My caller's name was Frank and he was an art director at an advertising agency, on a trip to Los Angeles. He was married, he told me, confessing more than either caller had before. Since his wife couldn't get into dirty chatter, he said he indulged when he was away.

Frank sounded as if he'd grown up in Brooklyn or the Bronx. There was a lot of street in his voice, a certain guttural gruffness. I imagined him as strong shades of earth colors. Wavy dark lines. A hot breeze.

He told me, as a way of getting acquainted, that a friend of his who'd gone to the institute for some help a few years ago had turned him on to phone therapists.

"What do you like the most about it?" I asked.

"Talking to so many different women."

That was all the information I needed to know where to start. "So you like meeting new women?" I asked.

"Yes."

"Frank, is there a bar in your hotel?"

"Sure."

"That's where you are now. A few other people are sitting at tables, but you're alone at the bar." It was the first time I'd invented my own story and not taken one from the transcripts, but I could see it playing out in front of me as clearly as if I were watching a film.

"Yeah, me and the bartender talking about the sports scene in sunny California." He didn't need much help stepping into the fantasy.

"I come through the doors and notice you sitting at the bar by yourself. I stand there, checking you out, and then decide to come over and see—"

"See what?" he interrupted.

"See if anything might happen between us. I ask you what you're drinking."

"Beer," he said.

"I ask for the same thing and then ask you if the seat next to you is taken."

"No, sit down," he said, sliding into the scene.

I imagined a hotel room somewhere in Los Angeles where a man lay naked on a bed, and I felt a flutter of pleasure.

"So what are you wearing?" he asked.

"A short black skirt, no stockings, black high-heeled sandals, a white silk blouse that buttons down the front. My hair is blond, up in a twist, but little curls have escaped. It's so hot out and I've been running around all day so before I came in here, I went to the ladies' room and took off my pantyhose and my bra."

"Can I tell you're not wearing underwear?" His voice had taken on a huskier tone.

"Not at first. But after we've been talking for a while, you look down and notice my nipples pushing against the fabric of my blouse."

"Can I touch them?" he asked.

"People in the restaurant might see," I protested mildly.

"I don't mind. Do you?"

"No. Go ahead; touch me through the silk."

"Like little buds," he murmured.

While Frank spoke, my hand drifted under my bra. My nipples were hard, just as he'd described.

"Hmm. That feels good. I shift in my seat to make it easier for you and my skirt rides up higher on my thighs."

"I run my hand up your leg," he said.

"Hmm. That feels good. Don't stop."

"My fingers move higher and higher."

I was doing what he was describing—trailing my fingers up my leg. The sensations were as real as if he were there doing it himself. "I move closer to you and whisper my secret in your ear: 'I'm naked under my skirt.'"

"Oh God, I want to touch you," he said.

"You're hard, aren't you?" I asked.

"Can't you see my erection pushing against my pants?"

And behind my closed eyes, I could. "You know, Frank, there's a woman over there at that table who's watching."

"I think it's exciting that other people can see how turned on we are. They're jealous," he said. "What are you doing now?"

"Touching your cock through your pants. You're so hard. Even through the fabric, you feel hot."

"I'm burning up. God, Alice, I want to fuck you. Are you wet yet?" he asked.

"Yeah," I answered, wondering if I really was. Almost afraid to find out.

"Tell me," he begged.

"Soaking wet—so wet I'm afraid if I got up, I'd leave a spot on the chair."

"On the other side of the bar there's a bowl of maraschino cherries the bartender puts in drinks. I lean over and take one. Then I part your velvety thighs and push the cherry way up high inside you," he whispered.

My insides flipped over. "While everyone's watching?" I pictured the stares of the men and the women at the tables around us.

"Yes. I have the cherry stem in my fingers and I'm tugging on it. Real gentle until the fruit pops out—all round and glistening from your juices. I put it in my mouth and suck on it."

I moaned. I was as far into the dream as Frank was.

"Do you like how it feels?" he asked.

"Yeah."

"Do you especially like it because I'm doing it in front of all these strangers?"

"Yeah. Would you like it if I went down on you in front of them?" I asked.

"Absolutely. Right here in the bar. Right now, okay?" he pleaded.

I imagined reaching out, pulling him toward me, bending down, burying my head in his lap. I imagined the stares of the people who were watching, but rather than it being inhibiting, it was liberating. I was going as far as I could and then going even further. "I unzip your pants, reach inside, and pull out your cock. It's so warm and hard with one tiny drop of semen sparkling on the tip. I bend down and lick it off with my tongue . . . so sweet."

"Oh . . . go on . . . please," he begged.

"I close my lips around the head of your cock and suck you into my mouth."

"Are they watching, Alice?"

"Yeah. One of the women has inched her chair closer and she's touching herself."

"Is she wet too? Can you tell?"

"From the expression on her face, she is."

"I want you to find out. Ask her if this is making her wet, all right?" he asked.

"She says she's dripping. She wants to fuck you, she says. She wants to feel your cock inside of her." The words were raw and rough, but it didn't matter. Saying them aloud felt pleasurable. I was so loose. So light. Skimming the rim of the crevice. About to fly away.

"She'll have to wait. I want to come inside of you. Right here, in the bar. All right?"

"I put my lips back on your cock and slide my mouth up and down the shaft of your penis. I go down so far the tip of your cock pushes against the back of my throat."

"Hmm . . ." He was lost.

"The bartender's watching too, but you don't care, do you? You just want to have your cock sucked, right?"

"You're such a good cocksucker, do you know that? It's really such a wonderful expression—*cocksucker.*"

"Can you feel the sperm starting to build? Can you feel the pressure in your balls?" I asked.

"The heat's rising up the shaft of my cock . . ."

"I'm swallowing you whole, taking all of you in my mouth—"

And then I heard the sounds that told me he was coming.

~

"Frank?"

"Hmm?"

"Are you all right?"

"Great. Thanks, Alice. That was great."

I then realized I was holding the phone with only one hand while my other hand was thrust deep down inside my leggings where I was wet.

# 13

After I hung up the phone, I lay there on my bed, aroused and frustrated and thinking about what had happened.

Frank was a stranger I'd never met, never seen, never spoken to before, and probably would never speak to again, and yet talking him through his fantasy had excited me. How could such an impersonal act have so pleasured me? I didn't have any emotional connection to him, yet I had responded completely. What did that say about me?

My thoughts returned to Frank's image of that glistening wet cherry and I touched myself. I craved the same release I'd helped Frank find, even if I had to give it to myself.

I'd masturbated before, but it had always been furtive. Hiding my needs from Paul and myself, I had done it half asleep and always in the dark. But that afternoon, I luxuriated in the light and the swells of sensation I was able to set off inside of me.

Satiated, I lay there afterward and wondered what the rules were now. Maybe there were none. Maybe that was what Sam had been trying to tell me.

The phone rang again, startling me. It was Jack, and while we talked, I listened to him as if he were one of my clients. For the first time, I felt his voice brush my skin like suede.

"The phone was busy for a long time," he said finally.

"Yeah. I was doing research."

"You're using a euphemism? With me? What's wrong?" he asked.

"Nothing."

I'd always been open with Jack, easily confessing my fears, my insecurities, and my dreams. I trusted both his instincts and his intelligence, yet I couldn't get out the words to explain what had just transpired.

"You're not embarrassed, are you?" he asked.

"Yes, I am . . . all right?"

"I don't want you to feel pressured, Julia. I'm only curious because this is something you're experiencing and I want to understand it."

Still, I couldn't tell him about the calls.

"No problem. Let's talk about something else. You know what I'd like to do?" he asked.

"What?"

"Drive over to your apartment, pick you up, and take off. Head upstate to see the trees turning. Stop just to take a long walk or because a town looks interesting. Or when we get hungry. Just chase the road."

"Like what you did when you graduated?" I asked.

"It was different then. I was too busy thinking about work. And I was alone. Half the fun is saying to someone, 'Look at that.'"

"And talking about it later. Over dinner in some old-fashioned diner," I added.

"Seeing if you both remember it the same way. Amazed when the other person saw exactly what you didn't and gives you their vision like some kind of gift," Jack said.

I could imagine the ride, the trees, the twisting roads, the inn where we'd stop to spend the night. Suddenly I didn't want to be on the phone with Jack—I wanted to be sitting beside him in his car, looking at his profile, watching his fingers move on the wheel.

"Okay, when do we leave?" I asked.

"How soon can you be ready?"

"I'm ready now."

It was a different kind of fantasy, but I'd slipped into it with the same kind of ease. And when we got off the phone, I had to remind myself he was still the same Jack Griffin whom I'd known since I was seventeen. But if he was, why did everything about him seem so different?

~

I looked at the clock. That night I was to meet Paul at a donor's house for a dinner party organized to help raise yet more money for FIT. If I was going to be on time, I had to get ready. After taking a shower and drying off, I put on a long, hunter green velvet skirt with a scarlet silk blouse, and black suede lace-up boots and then coiled my hair into a twist and stuck in some pins.

I looked in the mirror, but the image I saw didn't fit how I felt inside. Without thinking about what I was doing or what it meant, I took off my skirt, boots, pantyhose, blouse, and bra—and then put everything back on except my underwear.

The velvet skirt was silk-lined and swished against my bare skin with every step I took. The blouse lay soft against my bare breasts, and every time I breathed, I felt a caress. Like the woman I had been on the phone, I was only half dressed. And no one at the party would know. Except me.

~

In the taxi on the way downtown—the dinner was in a town house over by the East River—I shifted in my seat, feeling the fabrics brush against me. When I got out of the cab, the air wafted up my skirt and cooled off my skin.

Inside, I was welcomed by the host and a waiter who offered me champagne. Across the room, I saw Paul talking to a woman, listening intently and standing just a little too close to her. She didn't seem to mind and even put her hand on his arm to make a point and then left it there for several seconds more than was appropriate.

Paul glanced up then, saw me, and broke away to come over and greet me. No one else would have noticed, but I could see in his posture and on his face that he was slightly more relaxed now that I was there. As usual, my presence reassured him. As he reached my side, he touched my hand the way he always did—as if he were making sure I was real—and then he leaned down to kiss my cheek. I breathed in his scent and its familiarity made me aware of how separate and apart I felt from him, this place, and this night.

"You look wonderful," he said, and smiled. How could I fault him for being satisfied that everything was now as it should be? For years his approval had been exactly what I sought, exactly what gave me pleasure.

"Come with me. There are some people I want you to meet," he continued. Sipping my champagne, I followed him across the room, wondering what would happen if I put my hand out and stopped him, if I reached up and whispered my secret in his ear: *I'm not wearing any underwear.*

My deviation from the script wouldn't please him. *What's the matter, Julia? Are you feeling all right?* he'd ask, concerned. And then, when he realized I was fine, he'd be annoyed. *Don't you understand how important this dinner is? We have work to do here tonight!*

Of course I didn't tell him. The secret would stay mine.

After a half hour, the hostess announced dinner was ready and we all went into the dining room. I was seated between two men I had never met, both of whom were already at the table when I sat down. The man on my left was talking to the woman next to him, so I began a conversation with the man on my right. George Helprin, the CEO of a cosmetics and fragrance company, was a large man with close-cropped silver hair, chiseled features, and steel gray eyes, and he looked every bit the part of a corporate giant.

I was good at starting conversations—enough evenings being

Paul's hostess had given me confidence that I could engage anyone. But that night, for the first time, the dialogues were truly enjoyable.

I asked George how one went about selling something as ephemeral as perfume.

"You tap into a woman's imagination, her fantasies," he explained, and described some of the techniques his research people used to delve into the consumer's mind.

"Do you ever talk to the women yourself?" I asked.

"No, but I read most of the research," he said, and took a sip of his wine.

"Do you remember any of the women's fantasies?" I asked him.

He smiled and was quiet for a minute. "Yes, yes, I do, actually. I remember several of them." He seemed surprised, as if he'd never realized that before.

"Was there one you remembered more than the others?"

He put down his salad fork and turned to me; his eyes were far away. "Yes, there was a woman who lived in England. She was a professor at Oxford."

"What was her fantasy?" I prompted.

"She said she wore perfume for herself. It was her one extravagance and she spent more money on it than she could afford. I think she was a single mother. It was food, she said, for her soul. In the most intimate way, she described how she applied our fragrance to the back of her knees and down her cleavage. She said that each morning, when she applied the perfume, she imagined it wasn't her fingers but a man's fingers putting the scent on her skin."

If the conversation had been happening over the phone, if George Helprin had been a client, I would have used his story to move him into a fantasy. It would be his fingers on the skin of this well-educated woman whose only indulgence was perfume.

I imagined leaning closer to him and whispering an offer: *I can make you come just by talking to you, by telling you a story. Will you let me try?*

After the main course was served, I turned to the man on my left. James Romer was a venture capitalist who was quite stiff and very proper, with wire-rim glasses and a bow tie.

I was being good, chatting about the charity and what an important function it fulfilled. From the charity, it was a natural segue into fatherhood, and I asked James about his children. He reciprocated by asking about my children and I told him Max had just begun his freshman year at Princeton, which impressed him, and so I asked him where he had gone to college.

"Harvard, but before there were any women there," he said, implying that was the way it should have stayed.

"I imagine the school changed drastically once they let us women in?"

"Yes, there were traditions, fine traditions that have all but disappeared," he said.

Not wanting to get embroiled in an argument about feminism and the old guard, I steered the conversation in another direction. "Did you meet your wife when you were in college?"

"No, I didn't meet her until my first year of law school."

"So who did you take to all those college football games?" I asked.

He cocked his head and looked at me quizzically as if I had asked the oddest question, but he answered me. "Used to go out with girls from Radcliffe."

I calculated back and figured out it must have been the early fifties.

"Girls in poodle skirts and tight sweaters with shining hair."

His eyes softened.

"What was your girlfriend's name?" I asked.

"Sarah. Sarah Gould."

"Do you remember the first time you kissed her?"

He was lost in telling me his story. "There was a spot around the side of her dorm where we hid in the shadows of a big elm tree. We'd sit there for hours and neck. And then it would get late and Sarah would have to rush back to her room. There were curfews and dorm mothers back then."

If he were on the other end of the phone, I'd tempt Mr. Romer with an illicit tryst in the dark, under a tree. There'd be a fully clothed virginal girl who would do everything but go all the way. After dry-humping this ponytailed girl, he'd walk back to his dorm with aching balls and find me waiting for him. I'd tell him I'd sneaked in and bribed his roommate to bunk down the hall so I could fuck him in his single bed, in his room at Harvard, while the good girls at Radcliffe slept tight.

Later, I overheard James Romer telling Paul what a delightful wife he had. Paul looked over at me curiously, wondering what I had said to this straightlaced businessman to make him compliment me so effusively.

# 14

I swung open the door to the institute at five minutes to nine o'clock the next morning. Several patients sat in the waiting area, but this time I didn't study them. With surer steps, I walked to the receptionist's desk. By now she knew me, and after checking my name against her list of appointments, she waved me upstairs.

After I sat down, Candy poured us both coffee and asked for the tape I'd made of my telephone calls. I explained I'd forgotten to use the recorder on the first two. "I did make notes, though," I offered.

"It's important for you to use the recorder," she reproached me. "We can't work on your technique unless we can listen to your conversations. Try to remember next time."

Unlike Sam, who would have asked me why I had forgotten and then would have wanted to discuss my reasons, Candy was uninterested in anything but the task at hand. In fact, during those months I worked with her, we never had one personal conversation, never shared any information about ourselves.

"Well, let's listen to what you did tape. Then we'll go over the notes you made."

The voices came at me from the two speakers on either side of Candy's desk. Who was that saying those words? The tape machine had distorted the sound of my voice—transformed me into a stranger, an unfamiliar woman who had no inhibitions. A woman who had access to words and phrases I'd never used. It was Alice speaking. Not I.

As I listened to the intimate talk, I was suffused with the memory of my experience. The excitement. The sensations. And I was embarrassed. But Candy focused only on my approach and delivery, intent on improving my style and execution. Paring the call down, she clinically dissected the beginning, middle, and end.

Between sips of coffee, Candy pointed out areas where I could improve by either elaborating, slowing down some, or asking a question. Finally we got to my notes, but since I hadn't transcribed any explicit dialogue, these calls were difficult for her to critique. We spent the rest of the hour discussing why I'd been uncomfortable talking to the man named Arthur.

"Dominance is a popular request. Take these . . ." Candy handed me a half dozen transcripts. "Study them until you're facile with the scenarios. Okay?"

I would have preferred not taking more calls like Arthur's, but I nodded in acquiescence. I was there to learn, not to ask for special treatment.

Our session completed, Candy checked with Sam's secretary. Elaine said he was ready for me, but by the time I got downstairs, he'd been called away. She told me to wait in his office.

Without Sam to welcome me inside, I felt like I was trespassing. I sat down in the visitor's chair on the other side of the desk but was ill at ease. The room was ominously silent.

Was Jack right? Was something else going on in this place? Something dark and illegal that Sam was hiding? Was it my job as a writer to try to find out if there were any secrets?

A few seconds went by. Somewhere a phone rang. Obviously Sam had left in a hurry—his desk was covered with paperwork. Upside-down, his handwriting was illegible.

Ashamed to be prying, I looked away. Damn, Jack's suspicions had made me curious. Unable to sit still, I walked around to the window behind Sam's desk. A grand elm tree almost obscured the view, but through the rich red-brown leaves, across the street, was a well-tended brownstone. A refined and elegant woman sat at a card table, reading the paper, a cup of tea at her elbow. What does she think when she looks in here? Does she wonder about the conversations she only glimpses in pantomime?

Another moment passed. Turning away from the window, I looked back at Sam's office. From his vantage point, I surveyed his desk. My glance swept past the clock, the writing utensils, the date book, and rested on a group of several framed photographs. Patients couldn't see these from the other side of the desk. These were just for Sam's perusal.

The first was of a younger Nina half hidden behind two trees in a dense wood. The next showed a Halloween night procession. The camera had captured three very serious teenagers dressed as portentous inquisitors in black hooded robes. The last frame held a yellowed newspaper clipping—a classic shot of a 1960s protest. In the background was a police wagon filled with angry hippies. In the foreground, a cop pushed a bearded, long-haired young man to the ground. Staring defiantly at the camera . . . was Sam.

Even thirty years younger, there was no mistaking him.

What did they mean, these pieces of a man's life juxtaposed on his desk? Why had he chosen those shots to look at each day? Why not other, more pleasant memories?

My eyes drifted from the photographs back to the papers. Shamelessly, I stood there looking down, reading. It was risky. How would I explain if Sam walked in and caught me? I picked up the phone, dialed my own number and while I listened to the rings, continued to examine Sam's paperwork. It appeared to be all patient related.

On the third ring, my machine answered. My recorded voice reminded me of the tape I'd been listening to in Candy's office. Interrupting the recording, I punched in my code and heard an automated male voice announce there were two messages.

Then I noticed the side drawer of Sam's desk was open.

After punching in the code to replay the messages and while the tape rewound, I read the titles of the folders in the drawer. Most appeared to be patients' files. One was marked *Personal*. Using the tip of a pen I picked up off Sam's desk, I flipped the manila tabs forward until I reached the one I was interested in.

The first message on my answering machine was from Olivia, confirming our date for later that morning.

The first thing I saw in the file was a handwritten note.

"Sam will be just another minute." Elaine had appeared in the door.

Startled, I moved back from the desk until I felt the window ledge cut into the small of my back. "I hope it's all right," I gestured to the phone. "I needed to call my machine."

"No problem," Elaine said, drawing out the last syllable of the word.

~

The note was signed *Rita*. It was difficult to read sideways, but I deciphered certain phrases: Opportunity that no one else . . . The money has given me . . . Even if other people think its wrong and question its morality . . . Without your help . . .

~

"I'm sorry, Julia," Sam said. He was standing in the doorway looking at me. "Change in plans, I'm afraid. I hate to do this to you, but I have to cover another doctor's session. Can we reschedule?"

As I hung up the phone, my heart raced. Had Sam seen me reading his personal papers?

"Sure, that's fine." I walked around the desk toward him, stopping at the chair where I'd been sitting, and held onto its back for support.

"Any surprises?" he asked.

For one alarming moment I thought he was referring to my reading his papers, but he was only asking about my first calls from home.

"I was more nervous than I anticipated, but Candy thought I did okay."

"Leave me the tape," he said, "and I'll listen to it before our next appointment."

Fumbling in my bag, I found the tape and put it down on Sam's desk. As he followed my movements with his eyes, he noticed the disarray he'd left. His expression changed and he frowned.

Was he worried because he had something to hide or because he was a conscientious doctor concerned about jeopardizing doctor–patient privileges?

"I'm damn sorry I kept you so long for nothing," he said, as he walked over to his desk and shuffled the papers back into their folders.

"It wasn't that long. Just enough time for me to call my machine and retrieve my messages," I told him, and then left his office.

Had I been trying to assuage my guilty conscience or reassure Sam I hadn't been alone in his office long enough to see anything inappropriate?

What could I have been thinking of to spy on him?

What had I been looking for?

Evidence.

Something that would either clear Sam of Jack's insinuations or damn him. Instead I had found only more proof of Sam's professionalism. Or had I? What had that note meant?

Had I stopped trusting Sam? I wondered as I walked down the last few steps to the first floor landing.

No. I still believed in him and what he was doing. Sam's supposed sins were Jack's obsession, not mine.

Except I believed in Jack too.

I left the institute and walked out onto the street. The wind was blowing and leaves from the elm in front of Sam's window fell to the ground. From upstairs they'd seemed to glow a deep russet tinged with red, but here on the sidewalk they were just more debris under my feet.

# 15

I had made plans to meet with Olivia at eleven that morning at the health club, but because Sam had canceled our session, I arrived early. I put on my bathing suit and started without her. Before eight in the morning and after five in the afternoon, you had to wait for a lane, but late morning was usually quiet. There was no one else swimming when I dove into the cool blue water. My body hit the still surface, disturbing and displacing it, and I glided halfway to the other end before I came up for air.

After I'd been swimming for fifteen minutes, a couple came in. Both middle-aged and in fairly good shape, they walked in wonderful synchronicity, side by side, keeping pace with each other. Did they move through the rest of their lives like that too? I slowed down to watch them. When the woman paused to put on her bathing cap, the man waited for her. Noticing she'd missed a curl, he reached over to tuck it in with his forefinger.

The woman smiled at him and then, one after the other, they climbed down the ladder and, still in rhythm, began their laps. Swimming at the same speed, they reached the end of the pool at the same time, touched the wall, and turned to swim to the other side in tandem.

A few minutes later, Olivia arrived and the four of us swam comfortably in the big pool. When I'd completed my mile, I got out. Wrapping myself in one of the club's too-thin towels, I sat down on a plastic lounge chair to catch my breath and dry off. Mesmerized by the couple still doing laps, I wondered if they were married. They had to be. The ease between them, their awareness of each other's timing, and their ability to adjust to it takes years to achieve.

When Paul and I walked down a street, he was always several steps ahead of me and I invariably found myself rushing to keep up.

"I'm half a block behind you," I once called out, certain he wasn't aware how far back I was.

"My legs are much longer than yours," he answered. "You have to walk faster."

Paul is 5'11" and I'm 5'4"—not that great a difference. We didn't walk at the same speed because we'd never gotten into the same rhythm.

~

I remembered when we had taken Max up to Princeton. Had it only been two months ago? We spent the afternoon helping Max get settled and making lists of what we still needed to buy him. That night, we went to dinner with Max, his new roommate Josh Becker, and Josh's parents. Afterward, we declined the Beckers' offer of a nightcap and went back to our room at the Nassau Inn.

"Josh seems like a nice kid," I said to Paul as I got into bed. Paul wasn't really listening to me; he'd already turned on the television and was flicking through the channels, the beginning of the ritual that shut me out. Having just left Max off at his dorm room for the first time, I felt more isolated than usual that night. Rather than give in to my melancholy, I focused instead on the impersonal attributes of the hotel room and wondered who had been there before me and what they had done.

Although my own experience with Paul didn't bear out my theory, I assumed most people found hotel rooms sexy. Away from home, from kids and pets, the phone, the upstairs neighbors, and jobs that have to be done, alone together in a room filled mostly with a bed—wouldn't the majority of people make love?

Paul was lost in his pay-per-view movie, so I lay on my side, shut my eyes, and imagined what another man might do. How he'd walk across the room after getting out of the shower. How he'd lock the door and then walk to the woman waiting for him in bed. He'd sit by her side and reach out to brush the hair off her face as he'd lean forward to kiss her.

I rolled onto my side and reached out for my husband's hand. Made braver by my loneliness, I scooched closer to him and kissed him. Without taking his eyes off the television, he kissed me back. Sweetly but without any passion. Disappointed, I moved back to my side of the bed and went to sleep.

The next morning we met Max for breakfast, and over pancakes he asked us if we could skip the shopping. There was a freshman orientation he wanted to go to.

Afterward, alone with me in the car, Paul said he was pleased Max had asked us to leave. "He's such an independent kid."

"I'm not sure it's that simple. Max always hates good-byes. I think he wanted to get the leaving over with. He was practically in tears."

Paul had stopped at a red light, and we watched as students crossed the road.

"Julia, understandably it's hard for you to be up here and not re-live what you went through at college, but don't imagine your experience will be Max's. He's not you. He'll be fine. He knows how to set his own parameters."

"I thought I did too."

"Don't make this about you. Max is more stable than you were; he's better adjusted."

After so many years, those were our roles; that was our rhythm.

Olivia and I left the health club and went to Bergdorf Goodman; I was looking for a birthday present for my sister-in-law Amy, and Olivia was searching for shoes. The store was where I'd always gone shopping with my mother before she and my father had moved. She'd taken me there to get my first dressy dress at sixteen, my first high-heeled shoes, my first fur coat, and my wedding gown. Yet as familiar and comforting as Bergdorf's was to me, it was even more Olivia's domain. She claimed shopping there was better than a year of therapy. Getting lost among the extravagantly beautiful things always chased away her blues.

Taking the elevator, we started on the seventh floor, roaming through home furnishings, looking for something Amy might like. Olivia suggested luxurious bath soaps and small soft hand towels made in Paris. I considered a china tea set and a fine silver-and-gold fountain pen. But nothing seemed right until we stepped into the lingerie department and found a peach-colored silk robe. Waiting for the saleswoman to write up the charge, Olivia and I walked around examining bras, camisoles, and slips, each hanging on its own silk-covered hanger, displayed more like jewels than underwear.

My fingers ran across the lace-encrusted push-up bras and panties, the ribbons on garter belts, the satiny bodysuits—not only in blacks and midnight navys but in deep reds, golds, leopard. Everything here was more suggestive than the simple Calvin Klein cotton bras and briefs I wore. Why had I never been tempted by these confections before?

I was lusting after a buttery-soft black silk camisole when Olivia came up beside me. "Go ahead, try it on."

I looked at the price tag—sixty-five dollars. "It's outrageous."

"That's no excuse. You're working now. C'mon, treat yourself."

In the dressing room, I pulled my navy sweater over my head and slipped the camisole on over my bra.

"How does it look?" Olivia asked from the dressing room next door.

"Ridiculous," I answered. Seconds later, she was peeking in through the curtains.

She laughed. "Take your bra off."

So I took off my bra and slid the camisole back on, shivering as the material touched my skin. In college I'd gone braless to make one statement; this was another.

Half an hour later Olivia and I left the store, each carrying a shopping bag. In hers was a pair of shoes; in mine was Amy's robe and my white cotton bra wrapped in tissue paper.

Leisurely, we walked uptown toward a florist's shop on 61st Street between Park and Madison, where Olivia was to choose flowers for a party she was giving.

Every inch of the store was crammed: armoires were open to reveal shelves of antique vases and bowls; chairs were laden with bolts of extravagant fabrics used to wrap vases for parties. Old screens half hid potted palms; birdbaths were convenient places to set orchid plants; ferns sat in stone fountains; and half a dozen small tables, each with a different vase of flowers atop it, created a pleasing obstacle course.

Years before, I'd introduced Olivia to the owner, whom I'd met at an orchid show. Colette Riser had became instrumental in helping me build my collection. Plants and flowers were her whole existence; her social life consisted of arriving at parties several hours before the guests to arrange the flowers while her lover, a theatrical lighting designer, set the dimmers and spots.

Hearing the bells jangle as we shut the door behind us, Colette came out of her office. Somewhere between 35 and 50, she dressed herself as eclecticly as she did her shop. Today she was wearing a burgundy velvet beret, a white blouse with a lace collar, a long blue jean skirt, and high-heeled cowboy boots.

"Come. I'm ready for you," she said, pushing us into her workshop.

On a scarred butcher block table were two bowls of flowers. One was a bouquet of antique roses in varying shades of peach with occasional accents of violet.

In the other arrangement she'd combined tiger lilies, asters, and dark bloodred roses with yellow and orange tulips to create a flame of flowers.

One was elegant, the other audacious. Both would have looked wonderful in Olivia and Larry's loft.

"I can't choose," Olivia said, as she walked around them for the fourth time.

"The lilies and tulips would be more dramatic," I offered.

"But look at those roses." Olivia shook her head, confused.

I touched a petal, crushing it until my fingers felt moist.

Colette went to take a phone call and we continued trying to make a decision until her voice, raised in anger, distracted us.

"Listen, it was a mistake. I'm sorry, but haven't you ever made a mistake?"

When she returned, her face was flushed.

"Is something wrong?" I asked.

"I have two clients who are married to each other but who get billed separately because when he calls it's for his business and when she calls it's for their home or friends. Anyway, it seems like last week his secretary called with an order and my assistant thought it was the wife calling. So a very extravagant bouquet for the man's girlfriend got charged to the wife's account.

"And who gets blamed? Now it'll be my fault if the guy's wife figures out he's having an affair. And what's even worse is they'll probably both wind up canceling their accounts."

"That would be better than your being subpoenaed in the divorce action," Olivia said.

"Oh, that would help business," Colette said sarcastically.

"You never know. Publicity, even when it's bad, is good," I said.

Ten minutes later, we were still trying to decide between the two arrangements. Colette suggested we take both to Olivia's loft and look at them there.

"She must have some great stories," Olivia said in the cab on the way downtown.

"Do you ever think about the people who know your secrets?" I asked.

Olivia nodded, "You, Larry, my shrink."

I laughed, "No. I mean other than the people you've told?"

"Like Colette knowing something about her clients?"

"Yeah, like the phone sex operators who talk to other women's husbands and boyfriends," I mused.

"Julia, you've been so closemouthed about it. Tell me what it's like to talk to those men." She shifted in the seat so her whole body was completely turned to me.

"It's too soon. I've only taken a few calls . . . but so far it's . . . it's empowering. I don't know how else to explain it yet except that when I realize what I'm doing to a man with words . . . with my words . . . I get aroused. It's pleasurable. To say those things. To think them. God, it's all so damn seductive."

"You really like it?" She was incredulous.

Through the window, a tugboat puffed its way upriver. "Why does that surprise you?"

"I'm not surprised that someone might like it—just that you do."

"Have you ever noticed how many women we know seem asexual?" I asked her.

She looked out the window for a moment. "Yes, a lot."

"Do you think we've subjugated our sexuality so we'd be taken seriously as equals?" I asked.

"Maybe. You know as far back as I can remember—even at school—there was a prejudice against woman who were too sexy. As if that would prevent her from being a good engineer or a good architect." The indignation had brought color to Olivia's cheeks. "I went along with it. After all, I was more interested in success than sex."

"Why do we think those two things are diametrically opposed to each other in a woman but not in a man? Why don't we have any role models who've shown us otherwise? Can you think of a woman you consider really brilliant and heroic—who's also sexy?"

As the cab sped forward she tried to think of someone. "No." She paused. "Where is all this coming from, Julia?"

"The phone calls, I guess. They're changing me. It's like another part of me is slowly emerging."

Olivia frowned. "Julia, have you told Paul yet about what you're doing?"

"I keep putting it off," I confided.

She was as worried as I was at how he was going to react. "Maybe you should just write the book under a pseudonym," she joked.

"Yeah. I'll just use my phone name—Alice."

"Alice? Where'd you get Alice? Do we know an Alice?"

"From *Alice in Wonderland*."

"What, the X-rated version?" she said, and both of us laughed.

The cab driver, who had seemed oblivious to us, now stared into his rearview mirror, examining our faces. I wondered how much he'd heard.

"Listen, Olivia," I said, lowering my voice. "I need to tell you something, but you can't talk about it with anyone, not even Larry. It has to do with FIT. Paul is trying to convince me I'm overreacting by being concerned. I need you to tell me what you think—whether my fears are out of line or not."

After I explained about the IRS investigation, Olivia asked me too many questions I didn't know the answers to.

"What do you mean he won't tell you any more than that?" she asked.

"He just keeps saying he doesn't want me to worry," I said.

"Of course you should be worried. I'd be a nervous wreck if Larry was under federal investigation. Julia, you have to insist he tell you what's going on. You can't let him get away with this protective bullshit!"

"What can I do? Force him to confide in me?"

"Maybe he doesn't want you to know the truth." She looked out the window at the choppy river. "Maybe he really has screwed around with funds or something."

"You never give him a break," I said.

"Julia, you have to find out what's going on," she said, ignoring my comment. "You can't keep allowing him to treat you some fragile china doll."

Years before, Olivia and I had shared our stories with each other, the way you do when you get to know someone. She'd told me about her relationship with Larry and I'd reciprocated. Of everything, it was my husband's need to keep me dependent that had disturbed her the most. And still did.

The cab pulled off FDR Drive and turned west.

"It's part of our deal. There are things in every marriage you have to resign yourself to," I said.

"Which one of us are you trying to convince?" she asked, and when I didn't answer, she continued. "You know, maybe this book is a better idea than you know. Maybe now that you'll be earning enough to make your own living, you won't be so frightened to examine what's going on with you and Paul."

I bit my bottom lip. She was right, but I wasn't ready to admit it yet. Part of me still felt I had to defend my husband. "Can't we just drop it?"

Silence was unusual for us, so we were both relieved when the cab pulled up in front of Olivia's building on Mercer Street. Getting out, we each juggled a flower arrangement and our shopping bags.

~

As soon as we got upstairs and put the flowers down it was obvious the more vibrant arrangement looked better in Olivia's gray, black, and silver loft.

The decision made, Olivia insisted I stay for cappuccino. I think she wanted to ensure I wasn't still angry. When it was time for me to leave, she gave me the roses to take home.

As the driver turned the cab onto the FDR Drive, I buried my face in the peach roses and remained in that miniature garden all the way uptown, trying to forget the things Olivia had said about Paul.

When the cab hit a bump, I held tight to the glass vase, but some water splashed out and wet my jeans. Even that was scented. Colette had once told me she submerged crushed gardenias beneath the other flowers, hiding them in the water for the heady fragrance they added to her bouquets.

The flowers couldn't distract me from thinking about Paul. Was it right for us to have so many secrets from each other? What would happen if . . . my stomach cramped up with nerves. The anxiety, ever coiled in my chest, stirred—ready to spring.

Okay, what would be the worst thing that would happen if all my secrets were exposed?

The cab drove down my block. Up ahead, the construction site loomed. Soon, upstairs in my greenhouse, that building's shadow would do irrevocable damage to my orchids.

What would be the worst thing that would happen if Paul discovered what I'd been keeping from him?

I paid the driver with a ten-dollar bill and got out, holding the roses carefully, close to my body.

What was the worst thing that would happen?

Every scenario I could think of was truly terrible.

# 16

"**I** call you from the airport to tell you I've arrived and give you the address of the hotel. I want to know how soon you can meet me." the man on the other end of the phone said.

I settled back against the pillows on my bed and stretched out, readjusting my camisole. "As soon as I can get out of my next meeting," I answered.

"Knowing we had plans, did you dress for me?"

"Of course. I put on a low-cut black bra and tiny black lace panties and then covered it all up with the most proper business suit I owned. I wanted to sit through all my meetings knowing no one would ever guess how decadent my underwear was."

"Did you tell anyone?" he asked.

His name was Charles and I'd talked to him once before the previous week, so I knew what to expect. Even though it was only three in the afternoon, I'd drawn the bedroom blinds and turned off the lights; I didn't want to be distracted by my surroundings.

"I thought about telling them all so I could see their reactions, but I didn't. I kept my secret."

"And now all the meetings are over?"

"Yes, so I go downstairs and hail a cab. When I give the driver the hotel's address, he looks at me in his rearview mirror as if he suspects why I'm going there," I said.

"Tell me why you're coming here. I like to hear you talk." His voice surged like waves on a warm azure sea, sweeping me forward with my story.

"I'm going to a hotel room to meet my lover so I can fuck his brains out."

"Are you excited?" he asked.

"Yeah. I'm already wet. And my nipples are hard. All in anticipation of seeing you. Of having you touch me. Of being able to touch you. The driver takes a turn too quickly and my insides lurch. The sensation reminds me of what you'll be doing to me soon."

I wasn't inventing this—it was true: I'd been looking forward to this call all day.

"Do you touch yourself in the cab?"

"No, I'm waiting for you to touch me," I said. This too was true. One hand was holding the phone; the other was chastely by my side.

"And when you get to the hotel . . ." he led me on.

"The lobby is so elegant and everyone is so refined, I want to shock them all—to say to everyone I pass, 'I'm here to fuck someone.'"

"Do you?"

"No, I hurry up the marble steps and over to the elevator bank, where I wait with two businessmen who look me over, the way strangers do. I smile at them, wondering if they know, if they've caught the scent of a woman in heat. And then the doors open and we all get in the elevator together."

"And do you think about letting the men touch you?" he asked.

I hadn't, until he suggested it. "Maybe . . . maybe I'll let them both put one finger up me to feel how wet I am, but then the elevator stops and they get off. Now I'm alone. I lean back and watch the numbers light up as I ride up to meet you."

"I hear the knock on the door. I've been waiting for you for over a half hour," Charles said.

"You come to the door fully dressed," I continued. "You kiss me lightly, but just touching you overwhelms me. My lips are electrified. I sway and you hold me. I cling to you for a second, actually afraid I might faint. I'm standing so close to you . . . breathing you in."

"And then we separate," Charles said. "I've ordered from room service . . . cold white wine, caviar. I've already opened the wine and have poured myself a glass. Do you want some?"

"I want to share yours. So you dip your fingers in your glass and hold them out for me. I put my lips around your fingers and suck off the wine."

I shut my eyes as I listened to Charles describe how much he enjoyed having me suck his fingers. I was seeing him not in detail but as sensuous colors, and I was feeling him, not his skin or his hair but as sensations pulsing inside me. He was as real to me then as if I'd met him and seen him and had known him for months.

"You offer me more wine. You love looking at my lips when they're wet, don't you?" I asked.

"Yes, do you know why?" he asked.

"Because you like to imagine they're wet with your come?"

"Yes," I could hear the throaty pleasure in his voice, and that too aroused me. "Now, I want to watch you get undressed. Slowly. I want you to strip for me."

"Turning my back to you, I take off my jacket, unzip my skirt, and drop them on the floor, and when I turn around—" I let the camisole straps slip off my shoulders. "I'm only wearing my black bra, bikini, and black hose that end at the top of my thighs," I said, as I pulled the camisole off and tossed it on the floor. For the first time on the phone, I was naked.

"You're thrusting your little cunt out at me," he whispered. "Are you that horny?"

"Yes, I'm aching to have you touch me there."

"You're going to have to wait. I want you to want me so badly you're willing to beg. Now, take off your bra."

"I unsnap the hooks and let it fall. My breasts are pointing out to you. My nipples are so hard," I said, knowing even without looking down or touching myself that it was true.

"Would you like me to wet my finger with the wine and rub your nipples?"

"Yes, would you?" I asked.

"And now, should I lick the wine off your nipples?"

"Please."

"I circle each nipple with my tongue until I've licked them clean and there's no trace of wine left," he said. "Now, would you like me to do the same thing to your cunt?"

"Yes," I murmured.

"I don't think so. Not yet. You have to wait longer."

"Then can I undress you now? I want to see your penis."

"Yes, slowly. Very slowly," he cautioned.

As I described taking off his clothes, I listened to his breathing quicken. From the last call, I'd learned Charles wanted a woman who craved sex and luxuriated in the idea of being touched and of touching as much as he did, who liked to speak as much as to listen and would share the seduction with him.

I wondered if his wife knew that about him and why she couldn't accommodate him. All he wanted was a reciprocal arrangement. After our first call, he'd been quick to make another appointment with me. He said he knew I'd enjoyed the call and hadn't just been pretending to in order to get him excited. In the last few weeks, I'd talked to thirteen other men; only Bill, my first caller, had been as turned on as Charles was by turning me on.

"Oh, look how hard your cock is . . . I want it in my mouth."

"No, you have to wait. All you can do now is look."

"Then walk around the room for me," I said. "Show off your erection. I love how it sticks out so far in front of you."

"Do you really?"

"Yeah. I just wish you'd let me touch you," I pleaded.

"Not yet. First, tell me, Alice—does your cunt taste as sweet as your breasts?" he asked.

My hand fluttered between my legs and before I answered him—for the first time during a call—I pulled the suction cup off the phone's handset. "Why don't you tell me?" I said.

"I get down on my knees and position you so you're standing over me in those wonderful little lace things you have on. I slide the crotch aside and tease you with my tongue. Do you know how wet you are?"

"Yes, listen," I said, and did something else I'd never done before, though it was something Candy had suggested: I grabbed a candle out of the candelabra on my nightstand, rested the phone on my thigh, slipped the candle into my vagina, and then slowly pulled it out and pushed it back so Charles could hear it moving in the slick I'd worked up.

"Keep doing that. Tell me how it feels," I heard him whisper as I put the phone back to my ear.

"I'm feeling your cock in me . . . long and thick . . ." I said into the phone, and I was. "You're so hard and I'm so wet. Do you want to come now?" I asked.

"Not yet," he said. "First, I want to watch you make yourself come. Will you masturbate for me?"

"I've never done that before." I was telling Charles the truth. "I've never let a man watch me masturbate."

"But you'll let me, won't you?"

"Will you be masturbating at the same time?" I asked.

"Yes. Watch me touching myself while you touch yourself. Are you doing that?"

"Yes, I'm rubbing myself." I was completely entrenched in the fantasy, completely absorbed by the make-believe rendezvous.

"Are you watching me, Alice?"

"I'm watching your hand going up and down on your cock, then circling the head. You know just how to do it, don't you?"

"Yes, I know exactly where to touch myself, and I can see from watching that you have a lot of practice making yourself come, too."

"Yeah," I said.

"Is that because you like to come so much? Tell me."

"Yes, I love to come. But I want to come with your penis in my mouth. With your mouth on my cunt," I whispered.

"Yes, imagine that, imagine my cock filling your mouth, my tongue licking your clit, my teeth tugging on it. Does it feel good? Tell me." His voice was so low I had to strain to hear him.

"You're so big . . ." By now I was breathless too and only half-conscious of what we were saying.

"I don't know . . . how much longer I can watch . . . without coming," he said between breaths.

"Will you come on my face? I want to feel your sperm shooting out. I want to rub it into my skin."

"Not until I've made you come with my mouth. You're grinding your pussy into my face and I'm sucking on your sweet cunt lips while you're sucking on my dick. Are you ready?"

"Yes, I want to come so badly . . . it's been so long since I've come."

Was it the truth? A lie? Was any of this real? Certainly our voices were creating a reality of heightened sensations, of exquisite tensions about to explode.

"I can feel the sperm building up," his voice was taut.

"It's going to be burning hot, shooting out . . . I want to feel it on my cheeks, on my eyes, shooting against my lips . . ."

"Yes. Yes . . ." As he let go he moaned, a long pleasured animal sound I half heard, half felt as I crossed over, becoming, like my caller, a stranger seeking sexual release with a voice on the other end of a phone.

# 17

All that afternoon, the conversation I'd had with Charles interrupted my thoughts. I'd stop what I was doing and allow it to wash over me like a summer ocean swell. And then I'd float there, remembering what I'd said and done, being alternately embarrassed and thrilled. Finally, I went into the greenhouse and made notes, reliving it all, but this time for a purpose.

Jack called to confirm out plans to meet the following week, and after we got off the phone, I reread my notes.

On paper I always referred to myself as Alice. She had already changed me and brought me out of hibernation. What was next? The longer I worked on the book, the more control she gained. How willingly would Alice disappear when I decided she'd served her purpose?

When I finally looked at my watch, it was after seven. Paul hadn't yet called to tell me if he was coming home for dinner. Before Max had gone to Princeton, Paul had always called to let me know his plans, but back then we'd had a routine.

Getting up, I walked toward my bedroom, stopping in the doorway to Max's room. It was darker and colder than anywhere else in the apartment. Was it the emptiness?

If Max were home, he'd be eating a predinner snack, telling me about a history class or an English paper. It had been ten weeks since he'd left and four weeks until he'd be home, and I missed him. Our brief reunion in SoHo hadn't been like seeing him at all.

A breeze blew cold against my face. Where was it coming from? I raised the blinds and checked—yes—one of the windows was open. The housekeeper must have been airing out the room and forgotten to shut it. I closed the window tightly and then switched on Max's bedside table lamp, letting its warm orange glow chase away the gloom.

Not wanting to leave, I read the titles in his bookcase: most of Shakespeare's plays, most of Arthur Miller's, some science books, psychology books, Dickens, Melville, Updike, Vonnegut. Which were Max's choice? Which were required reading? Which had Paul given him?

Sandwiched in among the books was the model of a cross-section of the Earth's layers I'd helped Max build when I'd filled up my afternoons with his projects instead of my own.

I glanced at my watch again, almost seven-thirty. There wasn't much of a chance he'd be in, but I picked up the phone by the bed and called his dorm room in Princeton.

"Hello?" he answered.

Hearing his voice, I smiled. "Hi, Max."

"Julia! I can't believe it. I was just thinking about you."

"Because it's dinnertime and you're hungry?"

"That too, but because I was just in the library. When you and Dad come down, I have to take you there. You'll go crazy. They have all these old botany books with the greatest drawings of leaves and flowers."

"I can't wait to see them," I said sincerely.

"How're the flowers?" he asked.

"There's some leaf damage I can't figure out."

"Did you try filtered water?" Once before, Max had discovered the problem was in the water that came up through the building's pipes.

"I tried but had no luck."

"What about the temperature? Isn't it getting colder?" he asked.

"Yeah, but gradually, and I'm compensating for it. Nothing's happened to do this kind of damage."

"What about the light? How's the building going?" he asked.

"They've gotten up to only the eighth floor, so we're still all right."

"But maybe the flowers know their hours of sunlight are numbered and they're nervous."

"I wouldn't be surprised if you're right. So tell me, how are you doing?"

"Great, but boy, is there a lot of work," he complained.

"Too much?"

"Too much for me to see Betsy as much as I'd like."

"Well, your father will be pleased to hear that. How is Betsy?"

"Sometimes it seems like she's so far away. But I guess that's okay—the distance, I mean. Julia, I don't want to see other people. Do you think that's wrong?"

"Your father would say so."

"Yeah, I know, but I'm your son too. I want to know what you think."

I hesitated long enough to swallow the lump in my throat. "I think you should just go slow."

"Listen, will you do me a favor? Go to the vault for me and get my mother's watch. Not the fancy gold one—the plain one, with the black leather strap. Betsy's going to be eighteen the day before Thanksgiving and I want to give it to her."

"Have you really thought this out, Max? It's a big thing to give away a piece of your mother's jewelry."

"That's the point. I want to give Betsy something that really matters, you know? So will you get it for me?"

"Sure," I said.

"And do you think Betsy could come to the farm with us for Thanksgiving?"

Every year we spent that holiday with Max's maternal grandparents. "You'll have to call your grandparents and ask them."

"Maybe we'll even have time to ride." He sounded excited.

"Max, I want you to think about telling your father you're riding. It's wrong to keep such a big secret from someone you love."

"Boy, it's been a long time since you brought that up," he said.

I was silent, reflecting on what he'd said. Outside the wind blew against the windows, but this time there was no draft.

"Yeah, I guess it has been," I said.

"Julia?"

"What?"

"Is something wrong? You suddenly sound far away, you know?" he asked.

"I'm fine, Max. Just working too hard, like you."

"Yeah? Doing what?"

"Research for a book I may write."

"About time! What's the subject?"

"Well . . . it's about therapy," I said. "A new kind of sex therapy," I added.

"What kind of sex therapy?" he asked.

"It's a new technique that uses role-playing to help people overcome their problems." I hoped he wouldn't ask me any more questions, but he was curious.

"What kind of role-playing?"

"Maybe when I'm done I'll let you read the book, okay?"

He laughed. "Okay. But I think it's great that you're writing. I'm really proud of you, Julia" Although Max was growing up, he hadn't grown afraid to express what was in his heart. "How's Dad reacting?"

"Let's say he's not as enthusiastic as you are. Actually, he's asked me not to do it. I think he's worried about the subject matter, afraid it might offend certain donors and interfere with his raising money for FIT." In my lap, my hands clenched tightly together. Explaining the situation to Max had brought my anger to the surface.

"That doesn't surprise me. Dad doesn't always think about you," he said.

When had Max learned so much about the dynamics of my relationship with his father? But there was no time to discuss it further because I heard the front door open and shut.

"I'm talking to Max," I called out, and Paul came in, taking the phone from me.

When Paul and I spoke over the telephone, he was gruff and eager to get off. At home, he let the machine screen his calls. Only for a few people did he make the effort to talk: important donors, members of the FIT board, and always Max.

As I left the room, Paul was describing a basketball game he'd seen a few nights before.

In the kitchen, I unwrapped some leftover chicken and put it on plates. I was ripping up lettuce for a salad when Paul came in. "Do you want some?" he asked.

I looked up to see he had uncorked a bottle of red wine. "Not red, no. You know that."

Watching the muscles in his neck tense, I knew I shouldn't have refused his offer. I should have just accepted the wine, but it irked me he'd chosen red when he knew I didn't like it.

"Then I'll open some white for you," he said, as if it would take great effort.

"No, make me a drink instead. I'd like vodka."

"You can't drink hard liquor with the pills you're taking," he said.

"Actually, I haven't been taking those pills for the last few weeks," I lied. I hadn't been taking them for years.

"Don't you know better than to take yourself off medication, Julia?"

"Are you going to make me a drink or lecture me?" I asked, expressing the anger I'd been feeling since I'd mentioned the book to Max.

Paul left the kitchen, and while he was gone, I thought maybe I'd tell him about the book when he came back. Say it in a way that would make it clear my mind was set.

"Max sounds good, doesn't he?" Paul said, as he handed me a crystal tumbler. I took a long sip while he continued. "You were worried about him for nothing, Julia. I told you he'd be all right. But I don't want you to call him too often. It might undermine his self-confidence."

I took another icy sip of the alcohol and instead of saying what I'd planned, I started arguing. "Not call him? Come on, he needs some support. It's not an easy transition for any kid, no matter how resilient they are."

"But he is fine, Julia. Don't you understand, he's not you?"

"I'm not me either," I said, rage embedded in each word.

"What does that mean?"

"That I'm sick of your trying to keep me an invalid." Using a paring knife, I sliced a tomato for the salad.

"Great. Just great. I have a difficult day and then come home to your neurosis."

I looked up. "Why was your day difficult?"

Paul finished the wine in his glass and then poured himself more. "I shouldn't have said anything. The last thing I want to do is upset you." He was using his most professional tone, trying to dilute my anger by suggesting what I was really feeling was apprehension that something was seriously wrong at FIT.

"Stop it, Paul. Just stop," I was yelling. "You keep putting up these damn barriers between us. Don't you see I'm not a little girl anymore? You don't have to protect me."

"Where is this coming from?" he asked calmly. "What is this about?" He stood on the other side of the island, about two feet away from me—it was as physically close as we'd been in weeks.

"Paul, you and I are in trouble. We can't keep ignoring it."

"That's misplaced anxiety talking. Most likely you're upset about Max's being gone and the agency's being investigated. I said only that I had a difficult day. There's nothing to worry about. Now, tell me, where are those pills?"

"I'm not taking any more fucking pills. I want to talk to you. Isn't that what a good patient does, talk things out with her doctor—"

"I'm not your doctor, I'm your husband."

"Are you sure about that?" I was almost shrieking.

In the stillness that followed, neither of us spoke or moved. I didn't even breathe. I'd intended only to tell him the truth, not to antagonize him.

Always the indefatigable therapist, Paul was able to twist around what I'd said to fit his agenda. "Obviously, this is a tougher time for you than you want to admit. All the more reason you shouldn't fight me on this. Let me get your pills."

He seemed composed as he reached for the wine, but he knocked the bottle over and it hit the salad bowl, sending it spinning to the floor, where it shattered.

We both stood there looking down at the green lettuce leaves, slices of bloodred tomato and shards of glass lying haphazardly on the black and white tiles.

There is a fallacy about therapists, that because they're in the business of helping others put their lives together, their own lives are in order. It's wishful thinking on the part of the patient, who needs to believe someone has worked out his life—and if not a therapist, then who?

I pulled a broom and dustbin out of the pantry closet and started sweeping the soggy mess up off the floor. Paul watched me for a few seconds and then took his glass of wine and walked out of the kitchen.

Until recently, we'd rarely fought. Not because there weren't things to fight about but because I knew how to avoid conflict. I never argued a point just to prove I was right, never reminded Paul of his shortcomings, and never corrected him. I'd played peace-keeper even if it made me a pretender.

After I finished cleaning up the remains of the salad, I sat down at the kitchen table, sipped my drink, and realized I couldn't play that role anymore either. Which left—what?

Paul sauntered back into the kitchen, making a show of rinsing out his empty wineglass. "Would you like to go out? We could take a walk and get something to eat," he suggested, as if nothing untoward had occurred.

"Yeah, I'd like to," I said sadly. Why had I slipped back instead of going forward? Why hadn't I confronted the issues instead of retreating from them? Why was I such a coward?

~

We walked up Madison Avenue to a French bistro I liked but Paul usually avoided because it was crowded and the tables were close together. It was getting late and a window table looked available. Once the captain seated us and gave us menus, he sent a waiter to take our drink order.

For the second time that night, Paul chose a bottle of red wine without conferring with me. This time I remained silent. Ordinarily he had only a glass or two of wine, but that night he drank steadily. "So, you want to know about the investigation?" he asked after the waiter had taken our orders and refilled his glass.

I was surprised he'd heard anything I'd said. Maybe we had made some kind of breakthrough after all. "Yes," I answered.

"The IRS wants to see all FIT's expenses, including my expense account. They won't find a thing, though. I may have a large budget for entertaining, but it's necessary. The fifty thousand dollars I spent last year brought in over six million."

He stopped, not to get my opinion but to take another swallow of his wine. "And we only use fifteen percent of what we take in on operating costs. Do you realize how low that is? It puts us in a very good position."

He wasn't talking to me, not really. He was quoting the facts and figures he and the lawyers had developed. The recitation was interrupted when the waiter brought my onion soup and Paul's roasted chicken. When I broke the thick, cheesy crust with my spoon, steam wafted up. Paul speared a roasted potato. "If everything is so aboveboard, why are they investigating you at all?" I asked.

"The board has made it completely clear they're behind me," he said, ignoring my question completely. Then he drank more wine; the food on his plate was almost untouched.

"Why wouldn't they be behind you?" I queried.

"That's not the point. The point is, I've talked to each of them personally and I have their unanimous support."

I put my soup spoon down. "Paul, it's clear you're not telling me everything."

"There's nothing I haven't told you," he insisted.

"Well, I don't believe you."

He glared at me. Then went back to his wine. "Remember, Julia, I do not want you to discuss this with Max."

"I won't, but I think you should."

"Not until we have turned over our numbers to the auditor sometime around Thanksgiving. It won't make it into the press until then, so there's no use distracting him now."

"But what if it leaks out? Won't it be worse if Max hears about it from someone else?" I asked.

"After Thanksgiving, Julia. That's it," he said.

During the rest of our dinner, we fell back on the kind of conversations we'd always had—about Max, Paul's work, and upcoming FIT activities. After what seemed like a long time, Paul signaled the waiter that we were done.

I ordered decaf cappuccino; Paul ordered espresso. After we finished our coffee, he paid the check and we walked home. The evening's earlier argument was far behind us.

We had never once talked about me.

Arriving home, I went into the bedroom to get undressed and Paul went into his study, but he didn't stay there. By the time I came out of the bathroom, he was already in bed, scanning channels with the television remote.

I lay against the pillows and shut my eyes, determined not to complain about the noise and start another quarrel. Suddenly, I felt Paul's breath on my cheek as he leaned over me to unbutton my nightshirt.

I groped for the TV remote but couldn't find it and was afraid to ask Paul to shut it off. Disappointed by my lack of courage, immersed in my old role, I was taking whatever was being offered—willing to make do with the noise in exchange for any attention.

Knowing my nipples were the most sensitive part of my body, Paul took advantage of the shortcut, exciting me as quickly as he could, and then immediately entered me. There was no lingering, no exploration, no making love, no enthusiasm; our coupling was an empty ritual performed that night to keep the pretense of our marriage intact.

Paul was on top, but he politely rested his weight on his arms to spare me, and I lay there, equally accommodating. I ached for more intimate contact. I wanted his hands rubbing my skin raw, his tongue licking me into a frenzy. I wanted to sweat and shout and get lost in the things two bodies could do on their way to oblivion.

Keeping my eyes shut, I focused on the physical sensations. Then I heard Charles's voice penetrating my consciousness. Finally, my body loosened up and I let go, thrusting up to meet the pressure between my legs. Except I made the mistake of opening my eyes. When I saw my husband's face, I lost my orgasm. Paul exhibited no pleasure, not even the satisfied look I'd glimpsed through my half-shut eyes on those mornings I'd secretly watched him masturbate.

I let him finish, and when he rolled off me, I turned my back to him and listened to his breathing slow while tears dripped down my face. "Paul?"

"Hmm?"

"When we first met, what attracted you to me?" I asked.

For a moment, he didn't say anything, and I thought maybe he had fallen asleep, but finally he answered me in a sleep-thickened voice. "How much you needed me," he mumbled.

It was then, at midnight, after such a long day, that I decided I had to finally tell Paul about he book. I didn't care if I risked whatever little was left of our union. "Paul?"

But this time he was asleep, and so the book would remain a secret for a while longer. How many were there between us now? Secrets of regret, of disappointment, some too old to excavate, some forgotten, some still fresh, like wounds.

~

When I fell asleep, I dreamed of Alice. Wearing a filmy yellow chiffon dress that was almost see-through, she flitted in and out of a large group of people at a party held on a terrace high above the city. I followed her, a shadow watching my more vibrant self having a wonderful time, engaging in conversation, laughing, flirting.

She was drinking a flute of champagne when a man came up to her, kissed her deeply, put his arm around her waist, and then pulled her beside him on the terrace ledge. Heads bowed, they whispered and touched. I tried to tell her it was a dangerous place to sit, but no matter how loudly I yelled and how frantically I waved my hands in front of her face, she ignored me.

Giving up on Alice, I tried to get the man's attention, but he was intent on her. If only I could see his face, I thought in my sleep, then I would know his name and could call out to him and he would look up.

Suddenly, I was swimming toward him in chilly, turbulent waters surrounded by fog. Sensing he was just up ahead, I kept going. But my endless strokes led me nowhere. Obscured by my unconscious, the man remained out of reach.

# 18

Half a dozen calls and several days later, I waited for Jack at two on Thursday afternoon in front of the Museum of Modern Art at 53rd Street between Fifth Avenue and Avenue of the Americas. It was the first really cold day that fall and although I'd worn a camel overcoat, black trousers, and a black turtleneck sweater, I wished I'd brought gloves. Seeing a tall figure coming up the block, I wondered if it was him. Watching, I waited for the man to get closer. No, it wasn't Jack.

"Hello, Julia." I heard the deep, familiar voice behind me and swung around.

He was so much taller than me; I'd forgotten that. "You've grown," I said, and he laughed as he leaned down. I barely felt his lips brush me in a quick friendly kiss.

Used to living in Florida, Jack was dressed in the wrong clothes for the season: chinos, an open-neck, white cotton shirt, a worn leather jacket. His golden brown hair was still falling in his eyes and he was as thin as always, but there was a strength about him I didn't recognize. It had been so long, I was awkward, as if I were with a stranger, not the man I talked to almost every day.

"It's so cold. Aren't you cold?" I asked.

"We're talking about the weather?" he said, smiling. I'd forgotten that too, the lopsided smile. The way his mouth only lifted in one corner. It was the smile of a cynic.

"Forget it. I was only being thoughtful. I hope you are cold. I hope you freeze."

"That's better. So how the hell are you?" he asked.

We went inside the museum and spent almost two hours looking at a special exhibit of abstract expressionism, winding up arguing about whether Jackson Pollock was a genius who knew what he was doing or an alcoholic who fell into a sublime accident of time and place. As we wandered around the museum, facing the paintings rather than each other, I relaxed. It was easier to talk to Jack without looking at him. That way he was a man I was used to—the intellectual, the aesthete, the observer—the disembodied voice.

Outside once again, we walked east, and when we stopped at the corner, I studied his profile. With his aquiline nose, high cheekbones, and definite chin, he'd be all angles if it weren't for his long eyelashes and full lips. His hair was blonder near his temples and was long enough to curl over his collar. Where his shirt was open his skin was tanned and I fought a sudden desire to touch it and see if it was as warm as it looked.

Despite his height, he walked slowly enough for me to keep up.

"Where are we going?" I asked.

"I have some research to do—"

"I thought you did all that this morning," I said, interrupting.

Jack was frowning. "No, something else came up." He was being unusually cryptic. "I didn't get everything done. Do you mind?"

"No. I didn't make any plans. What kind of research?"

"I thought I'd take a look at some of the places the detective described, okay?" he explained.

Jack had come to the city to conduct an interview for a story he was writing about an ex–New York City detective who'd been done in by a conniving socialite and was now on the lam in Florida.

"Yeah, God's in the details, right? You told me that back in school when you made me rewrite my first story," I said.

"Well, you hadn't done any of your research yourself. It was all secondhand stuff," he laughed.

"No one can accuse me of that anymore," I said with a smile, but Jack didn't return my smile. "I drove two hours to go to that dinky bar the next day," I complained. "Interviewed everyone there and spent half the night rewriting. When I finally turned in that story, you never even told me if you liked it."

"I printed it, didn't I?"

"You always acted as if you expected me to be the best," I said.

"I did, and I was always so surprised you needed to be praised."

"Why?"

He shrugged. "Because it was so clear to me how wonderful you were."

We had reached the St. Regis Hotel. As we walked up the steps, I was aware of Jack beside me, moving with an economy of motion, a manly grace. Just inside the doors, he stopped, took a small notebook out of his pants pocket, and wrote in it. I noticed how his pocket retained the outline of the notebook. *He must always carry it there,* I thought.

Inside, we walked through the quiet lobby scented with rubrum lilies and, along with several other people, stepped on the elevator.

"I was here with Paul recently for a fund-raiser," I said.

"Really? Helen Mallory brought Detective Dacuk here for a fund-raiser too. She wanted to impress him so he'd believe her story."

As the cage soared upward, I felt the ascent in my chest. Jack was so close to me, the hem of my coat touched his trousers. I was surprised at my physical response to him. We knew each other so well. Why was I feeling as if I were with someone I'd just met? What had changed? Again, I wanted to reach out and touch him. Instead,

I stared at the spot where we were connected until the doors opened up on the penthouse.

"At night," I said, moving over to one of the tall windows that flanked the entrance area, "all these windows look out on the city. It's quite beautiful."

But he wasn't looking out the window, he was staring at me, holding me with his eyes. Behind me, the sun streamed in, warming me. In front of me, Jack's eyes were making me shiver. I didn't move until he walked away to examine the large banquet hall and take more notes.

"Julia, how many people were here the night you were?"

Was I the only one affected by the obvious tension between us? Well, if Jack could be pragmatic, I thought, so could I. "About twenty tables, ten people at each table," I answered.

"Was there somewhere you had drinks first? Detective Dacuk described a kind of reception area."

"Yeah, out here," I said, and led him toward the ballroom.

The ceilings were painted with trompe l'oeil blue skies and clouds and cherubic angels peeking out through faux cupolas covered with ivy and garlands of flowers. Small gold-leafed chairs were placed around cocktail tables. More oversize windows looked south at the downtown skyline.

I heard shuffling noises and turned to see a maintenance man arrive with a box of lightbulbs and a ladder, which he set up under the chandelier that spread six feet in every direction. The crystal shuddered as he replaced the first burned-out bulb. I was watching him when Jack came up behind me.

"All right, let's go. I got it."

I turned. He was closer to me than I'd realized and my coat sleeve brushed his jacket, but he didn't seem to notice. How could he be so blasé while inside I was churning?

Searching for the elevator, he took a wrong turn, and we wound up in a dimly lit hallway flanked by a long metal coatrack.

We were alone then. And many things were suddenly possible between us there in the dark. *But he's not feeling the way I am,* I reminded myself.

"This must be where they check the coats," Jack said so awkwardly that if I hadn't been so tense, I would have laughed. Instead I just nodded.

My eyes adjusted to the darkness and I was staring, just trying to get used to the flesh and blood of him, when he came over and stood close to me. We were being tentative. Careful. Like new lovers.

"I never forget the color of your hair," he whispered as he finally leaned forward. I thought he was going to kiss me and my heart skidded, but he didn't touch me. He just shut his eyes and inhaled. "Or how you smell. God, Julia, that smell. I once got onto a crowded elevator in some giant office building in Atlanta and thought I smelled you. I even turned around and searched for you. Obviously, the woman behind me wasn't you, but I still wanted to follow her, just so I could keep smelling her."

"Did you?" I asked.

"No, I just kept on inhaling until the elevator stopped and wound up with an incredible erection." He laughed softly and reached out to brush my hair off my face, letting his fingers linger on my cheek.

Suddenly unsteady, I let out a long breath and leaned back against the wall. He was only inches away from me and could have easily stepped forward, or I could have. But neither of us did. And then someone—probably the same maintenance man—came whistling by.

"Let's go," Jack said, and I followed him as he retraced his steps. This time he immediately found the elevator. Once the elevator arrived and doors shut, we were alone again. I willed Jack to make a move, but he remained immobile, and by the time we reached the lobby, I was angry at him for holding back, for letting the moment slip by.

Seething and silent, I followed him outside. It had been years since I experienced that conflict; a painful desire to fight for what I wanted, mixed with an acute warning that I shouldn't, that instead, I should strive to do the right thing and be good.

On the steps, under the gilt awning, Jack asked me what was wrong.

"Nothing." I shook my head as if I were shaking off the feelings he'd evoked in me.

"No, I know you. What is it?"

"If you knew me so goddamn well, you wouldn't have to ask what it was. You'd know, wouldn't you?" I snapped.

We were at school. I could smell the newsprint and the scotch and remember the crazy hours and my crazier mind. It was almost four in the morning and Jack and I were driving back from the newspaper plant in his beat-up white Oldsmobile listening to Buffalo Springfield on the campus radio station. It was always cold in Ithaca, and the heater in his car didn't work. I could see my breath when I talked—or was that smoke from one of my endless chain of cigarettes?

Having just put the paper to bed, we were both exhausted but had decided to stop at the all-night doughnut shop. Snow was falling fast around us and it was freezing, and something in me snapped. I was so tired of Jack's being impervious to me. So sick of wanting him. Getting out of the car, I slammed the door shut and a piece of aluminum trim fell deep into the snow. When Jack came over to help me find it, I grabbed him by the arm.

"Why don't you like me?" I yelled at him.

"I adore you, Julia. What are you talking about? You're one of my best friends. One of the best writers on the paper. What the hell is the matter?"

"Why don't you find me attractive?" I hissed.

He shrugged and then smiled. It was that smile, so smug and self-contained that made me even angrier. "You're too easy," he said.

I wanted to slap him. Instead I shouted, "I hate you, Jack Griffin," and shoved myself at him, kissing him on the mouth, forcing his lips open, pushing my tongue inside him. Rather than fight me, he pulled me into his arms and we stood there leaning against his dirty white car, kissing each other for a very long time.

We forgot about the doughnuts and got back in the car. Racing to get back to my dorm room so we could be together, Jack drove much too fast on the icy roads, but the car's old tires held out. After parking the car in front of my building, he leaned over and kissed me once more. With his lips pressing against mine, he breathed in my breath and held my face in his hands.

When we separated, the predawn weak winter light was rising through the clouds and shining in Jack's eyes as he smiled at me so sweetly I felt it like another kiss. And then his expression changed. The intensity of his scrutiny scared me.

"Don't say anything heavy, Jack, I can't handle it."

"I have to understand." A muscle in his cheek twitched.

"Okay . . ." I said, hesitantly.

"I need to know about all these guys you see, Julia. Before we start anything. I need to know why you do it."

"Boy, are you fucked up!" I yelled. "What kind of moralistic crap are you laying on me? If you don't like me the way I am, forget it. I won't change. Not for you. Not for anyone." I was shouting, pushing him away and pleading with him to understand all at the same time.

But he couldn't understand. No one could have. I was right up against the edge by then, not even capable of understanding myself.

We sat in the cold car for a few more minutes without either of us saying anything. I waited for him to make it all right and he waited for me to do the same thing. Finally, frustrated and angry, I opened the door and stomped out, my feet crunching in the fresh snow.

Upstairs in my room, I wandered over to the window and looked down as I undressed. Jack was still sitting in his car where I'd left him, only now, his head was thrown back against the seat and he was staring up at my window. I put an arm across my bare chest and stepped back, frightened by the look of pain on his face. I'd destroyed something I hadn't even known I had.

Three weeks later, I crashed. A combination of a troubled psyche, late hours, trying to keep up my straight-A average, too little food, too many men, and some very dangerous drugs.

When I didn't show up at the newspaper or answer my phone for two days, Jack came to see what was wrong and found me under my desk, weeping. After sitting with me for a few hours without being able to make any sense of what I was saying, he picked me up and carried me down to his car and then drove me home. When we arrived in Manhattan, five hours later, I was still crying.

Jack had a list of stops, the last one being the old Scribner's bookstore that, sadly, had been turned into a clothing store. He just stared into the windows for a few minutes, shook his head, and we walked on. At six-thirty, we stopped at Béllini, an Italian restaurant near the theater. Inside, the lights were peach-colored and the room was lively with other pretheater diners. The atmosphere was conducive to conversation between friends.

I had a salad and grilled salmon showered with paper-thin rounds of lightly fried zucchini. Jack had the same salad and the restaurant's signature risotto dish. We were back to being buddies, and Jack happily answered all my questions about the story he was tracking down.

"I'm sorry we didn't get uptown," he said, suddenly changing the subject. "I was hoping you'd take me to the institute and introduce me to the Butterfields," he said.

I swallowed. "You would have met only Sam. Nina's in Boston, teaching at Harvard for the semester."

"So Sam's all alone in New York?" Jack paused, then took a sip of the white wine we'd ordered. "Well, he's really the one I wanted to meet anyway."

"Why's that?" I asked.

"To take the measure of the man."

"Why's that?" I repeated.

"Don't be coy, Julia; it doesn't become you. You know exactly why. Because he's changed you somehow. I don't know how to describe it. Maybe it's as simple as he's been the one to inspire you to take the next step in your career." Another long pause, another long stare. "No, it's more than that; he's opened your eyes."

I stared down at my plate of food. I'd hardly eaten any of my fish. "Well," I said, trying to keep my voice even, "he'd probably love it if you told him that."

"So what do you see, Julia, now that your eyes are open?"

I was embarrassed because for the first time that day, I realized what I'd seen was Jack. Really seen him. Not remembered him in some sophomoric haze or heard him over a phone wire but watched him move through space. Seen him look at me. Observed his energy. Memorized his words. Noticed how his hand held a pen. How his fingers looked, reaching to stroke my cheek.

When I didn't answer, he laughed and drank more of his wine. "Just don't get fooled by him, Julia. Everyone has an agenda. Stay skeptical." He was quiet for a minute.

I shook my head. "That's how you get through life, isn't it? Staying skeptical? It's sad."

"If I don't expect miracles, I'm not disappointed when I don't find them. And if by chance I happen across a small wonder, I'm awestruck, " he said.

"And when was the last time you were awestruck? I'm having trouble with this concept—Jack Griffin awestruck." I laughed.

"A few hours ago in a dark hallway, breathing you in."

He said this in the most matter-of-fact voice, but it left me speechless.

When he said those things to me over the phone, they affected me, but not the same way they did in this bright restaurant in the midst of so many other people. Over the phone, I hadn't been able to see the dead seriousness in his eyes or the way his mouth was set in such earnest. Neither of us could eat anymore. After the waiter cleared our plates, we ordered cappuccinos and returned to discussing Jack's article.

"Is what you're doing dangerous?" I asked.

"How so?"

"Well, the detective's a felon. He's hiding out and you know his name and where he lives."

"I know Dacuk isn't his real name. And he never takes off his sunglasses or his hat when he meets me. I don't even know where he lives. I get in touch with him through his lawyer and only meet him at restaurants. He's hidden inside layers of disguises."

"Why do you sound so angry all of a sudden?" I asked, but Jack just kept looking at me. I tasted something bitter. Was it the coffee? "What's going on?" I asked.

"You're swathed in disguises too: Max's mother, Paul's wife, devoted daughter, good friend, Upper East Side lady, part-time journalist. Each one is a separate identity," Jack was spewing out the words as if he'd kept them inside for much too long. "Look at you, up to your neck in clothes. There's no skin showing, Julia. Where are your shoulders, your wrists, your neck? What are you hiding? And what about this phone sex stuff? That's separate and apart from everything else too. So separate, you can't even talk to me about it. How do you think it makes me feel that you can talk to all those strangers but not to me?"

My eyes welled up with tears, but when I reached for my napkin, Jack held my hand down on the table so that the tears rolled down my cheek. Then as quickly as he'd taken my hand, he released it. "God, I'm sorry. I swore to myself that I wasn't going to do this. But I can't stomach what you're doing."

Anger had replaced my tears. "I'm doing research for a book, Jack."

"I'm not just talking about the calls. I can't stand how you just blithely believe whatever Sam Butterfield tells you. You're a journalist, for Christ's sake. Why aren't you questioning what's going on over there? Or at least trying to find out if there is anything to the rumors I heard?"

"Because I'm not looking for dirt. I'm not trying to destroy anyone." That hurt Jack. I could see it in the way he tried to deflect my comment with his body. But I continued, "I was hired to do a specific job. And that's the job I'm doing. It's important to me."

He was nodding, trying to understand it from my point of view. "I care more about you than about being right, so I promise I won't mention it again. It's simply that I can't help but be——"

"Skeptical," I said interrupting. And I laughed.

"Am I forgiven?" he implored, the look in his eyes more serious than his jocular tone of voice.

"Yeah, but it's getting late. We'd better go." Realizing we had only a few more hours left to our day, I was suddenly saddened. I almost reached out for him, to hold him there beside me. Instead, I stood up and led the way out of the restaurant.

As powerful and amazing as the play was, I couldn't concentrate. While the actors on the stage recited their lines and made their moves, I sat in the darkened theater ignoring the Pulitzer Prize—winning words so that I could try to understand what Jack had said to me. Yes, I hid. I split myself off and kept my selves separate. Could I merge them? Did I finally want to try? A year ago, I'd been at peace with myself, with the life Paul and Max and I were living. But Max was gone now. All that seemed to be holding Paul and me together was the past.

After the last curtain call, Jack suggested we go across the street to Sardi's. Inside, it was crowded and we only found one seat at the bar, so I sat and Jack stood, towering above me. We both ordered Dewar's on the rocks, our college drink, and I bought a pack of cigarettes from the bartender, partly out of nervous energy but also because smoking was something I wasn't supposed to do.

While we waited for our drinks, we analyzed the play and discussed the acting.

"Do you think actors sometimes believe they are their characters?" I asked.

He took a gulp of his scotch and his Adam's apple moved. "Yes, the good ones do."

Maybe this was how I could explain it, I thought. "Jack, that's how it is on the phone. What I do . . . it's like acting." I raised my glass to my mouth. The smell was familiar and foreign. Like Jack. Like the night. "It's exciting," I whispered into the glass. I drank more scotch. "It's exhilarating to verbalize your imagination. To speak words that are usually only thoughts. To slide into another reality. Talk a fantasy out loud."

I stopped to take another drink. He was silent. Just watching me. "Jack, what do you fantasize about?"

"You," he said. He was looking down at me and his eyes were shining.

Although I'd asked the question, hearing his answer made me suddenly afraid. "Don't say that. It will ruin everything between us. We're not strangers. We know each other too well. We can't cross the lines and be exposed and then go back again."

He didn't say anything for a minute. "That's what you're concerned with? Not that you're married and you love your husband and you shouldn't be having a conversation like this with anyone but him?"

What had I admitted? Why wasn't I protesting? Explaining how much I valued my marriage? I drained my drink. When the ice hit my lips, it burned.

With a nod to the bartender, Jack ordered more drinks, and as soon as the new glass was put in front of me, I took a sip and lit a fresh cigarette. A few more plays had let out and the bar was crowded. Jack edged closer to me, his legs pressed lightly against mine. Aware of the sensation where our bodies touched, I attempted to ignore it.

Then suddenly brave, I wanted to show off for him. "Tell me about the woman in your article. What's she like? What's her relationship to the detective?"

Finished with his description, he expressed his doubts. "Somehow Helen bamboozled Dacuk into breaking the law, but I can't get him to talk about how she did it."

"Tell me about him. What's his background?"

"Italian, stocky, dark curly hair, worked his way up through the department, married, a few grown kids, Catholic."

How would a woman turn an upstanding detective into a criminal? I drank more of the scotch. How would I seduce a righteous, repressed detective?

"I've done things I'm really ashamed of . . ." I kept my eyes down demurely. "Things that were wrong. Sins. God, I wish I was good like you." I looked up at him.

Jack didn't take his eyes off me.

"If you could help me, I might be able to make some restitution. If you could just guide me." Putting my hand on his arm, I implored him, "Give me advice, please." I touched his wrist, slipping my fingers up under his cuff, feeling the fine hairs on his arm. "Maybe you could help me figure out how to do the right thing." I gripped his wrist tightly.

From behind me, a man leaned across the bar and shouted at the bartender. "How am I gonna get a drink? Will you tell me? How am I gonna get a drink?"

Jack and I were both startled back into ourselves.

"That's how it works on the phone, Jack. I just disappear into another role."

"Wow." Jack shook his head in disbelief.

I looked down at my glass—when had I emptied it? My wristwatch read half past eleven. Had we been there that long?

Jack threw some money on the bar and we walked outside. As a cab cruised by, Jack's arm shot out to hail it.

He opened the door for me and I slid in, but instead of closing it, he held it open. Then, although the University Club was within walking distance, Jack got in beside me and gave the driver my address.

I don't know which of us moved first, but by the time the cab had driven off, we were kissing. We moved with the gyrations of the taxi as it sped down the half-empty streets. Eyes closed, I floated in a daze that was part alcohol, part lust, and part something else. Jack and I were not reliving some old ritual—we were inventing a new language with each other. I couldn't even feel the separation between our lips as his tongue darted into my mouth.

It was almost forty blocks from Sardi's to my apartment, but we didn't speak once during the ride. There would be time enough for words when we wouldn't have anything else to give each other. When the taxi finally did stop, I opened my eyes and saw Jack's swollen lips and heavy-lidded eyes—in a face suffused with want. In the background was my building's canopy.

"So I guess this is where you get out," he said.

"No, let's go back downtown. I'll drop you at your club. That will give us a few more minutes. Then I'll take the cab back uptown by myself."

Jack gave the driver the address of the University Club. The man shrugged, muttered something in Arabic, then put his foot back on the gas and took off down Fifth Avenue. In the back of the cab, Jack and I exchanged another kiss that lasted for two miles.

Jack's hands were big enough so that my whole face rested in his palms. Enclosed by him, penetrated by his tongue, only tasting him, only smelling him, I couldn't think. I was living on the edge of my lips. Somewhere I knew our legs were intertwined and I was aware of his erection, hot and urgent, imprinting my skin. I'd described a kiss almost like this to the first man I'd talked to on the phone. Except this one was real: a kiss that could make you come if you gave yourself over to it.

And then the cab came to its second stop. With difficulty, Jack and I pulled apart and opened our eyes.

"Will Paul be there when you get home?" Jack asked.

"I don't know."

"If he's not there, call me. Call me and we can talk over the phone," he whispered. "We can fall asleep listening to each other's voice."

Without waiting for me to respond, he got out of the cab, shut the door, and then stuck his head back in the window.

"Back at school, I was wrong to ask you to explain yourself to me," he said.

"You made me feel as if I were bad." My words were barely audible.

"I'll never make that mistake again, no matter what you do. You understand?"

All I could do was nod.

Jack looked at the meter, which already read fifteen dollars. "Here," he said handing me twenty dollars. "You'll call me?"

"If I can, yes."

"Are you all right, Julia?"

"No, I don't think so. But I don't think I should be all right, do you?" A scared laugh escaped.

"I guess not." He smiled and left.

I watched him walk up on the sidewalk toward the entrance of the club with long strides. He was moving much faster than he'd walked when I was by his side. I realized he must have slowed down for me. Then the doorman opened the doors and Jack was gone.

Leaning back against the seat, I asked the driver to take me home.

~

The apartment was empty; Paul hadn't yet returned from his trip. In the bathroom, I studied my face. Smeared makeup, disheveled hair. I touched my lips and shuddered, they were so tender.

In bed in the dark, the scotch rocked me back and forth. My hand found the phone and I held on to it without lifting it up out of its cradle.

With my eyes shut I could still summon the sensation of Jack kissing me. What was he doing now? I pictured him undressed. His shirt and pants were thrown over a chair and he was waiting for me to call. He stopped pacing to stand in front of the window and look uptown, trying to find the outline of my building against the sky-line. The soft lamplight gleamed across the expanse of his naked back.

He'd meant what he'd said, but would he really be able to accept who I'd become? What I wanted?

Would anyone?

I reached out as if to touch his skin . . . and then I don't remember anything else.

# 19

When I woke up, it was past eight, and from the suitcase on the floor, I knew Paul had come home sometime during the night. I called his name, but there was no response. He was out running.

Before I even got out of bed, I picked up the phone and called the University Club. My mouth was dry and my head hurt, but I had to talk to Jack. To make sure everything was still the same between us. Listening to the phone ringing in his room, I whispered, *Please be there, please*. But the line kept ringing.

Finally the operator got back on.

"Could you check and see if Mr. Griffin has checked out?" I asked, and my heart raced while I waited for her response.

"Yes, at eight this morning. I'm sorry," she said.

I'd just missed him. I hung up, and suddenly I was freezing. I pulled the blanket up around me, and lifting the quilt off the floor, I wrapped that around me too.

When Paul came back, he found me shivering in bed. "Are you all right?" he asked from the doorway.

"No, I don't feel well."

Paul came to the door and stood there in his T-shirt and running shorts, the sweat glistening on his face and running down his neck. He was always at his best ministering to the sick who needed his help.

He sat beside me. I laid my head on his shoulder and smelled the dampness of his T-shirt and the cold air on his skin. "What's wrong?" he asked.

"I don't know. I woke up and just didn't feel right."

"It was probably a bad dream. Can you remember any of it?"

"No." I didn't have to try to remember. I knew it wasn't a dream.

He extracted himself, went to the bathroom, and came back with some water and two pills, which he put beside me. Ignoring the pills, I drank the water, surprised I was so thirsty.

By the time I finished, Paul was down on the floor doing sit-ups. "How was the play?" he asked as he raised his torso up.

What a relief to be having a normal conversation with him. I hadn't even thought he'd remembered where I'd been. "As amazing as everyone says," I answered.

"And Jack?"

"It was good seeing him," I answered, holding back sudden tears and wondering if my voice was giving away my emotions.

"I'm glad. With my being gone so much, you should get out more. What time did you get home? You were fast asleep when I got in."

"What time was that?"

"About twelve-thirty. The plane was late."

"I don't know—I probably got home about ten-thirty. Maybe eleven," I told him.

Why had I lied? Paul certainly wasn't jealous. He wouldn't have cared that we'd gone out drinking after the play. What would have happened if my being out had worried him? If he were jealous that I'd been with a man? If he'd just stopped doing his damn sit-ups and noticed that I wasn't quite myself anymore?

Except he didn't. When he finished his exercises, he got up and walked into the bathroom to take a shower without even looking back.

Where there should have been guilt, I felt none. Its absence told me more than its presence would have. I had even more secrets now. They were all around me, circling my head, perching on my shoulders, settling on my hands. Yet rather than weaken me, they were making me strong—strong enough to see how great a difference there was between what I wanted and what I had. Between who I was and who I could be.

~

When the phone rang an hour later, it jarred me. Having missed Jack at his hotel, I hoped it was him calling from the airport. I was disappointed to discover it was a client named Steven. Trying not to sound as if I were making an effort, I began enthusiastically. But Steven was reserved and it took me a while to get him to relax. We wound up talking about his other interests for a while.

"So you're a history buff? Do you have a favorite period?" I asked.

"Right now? Yes. Right now, it's nineteenth-century England."

My mask collection was reflected in the mirror opposite my bed; two masks, both framed behind glass because they were made of paper, dated back to the 1850s. Both had been part of elaborate costumes at one of the many balls that were popular then. Suddenly, I was drifting back in time with the man on the other end of the phone.

"We are at a fancy dress ball in Winchester, England, sometime around 1860. Around us are other men and women in costumes, all wearing masks, strangers suddenly free to pursue dangers and delights. Everywhere you look is an odd couple dancing the waltz: an Indian princess with a sailor, a fortune-teller twirling in the arms of a pirate, a Harlequin leading a witch. And there are other couples, also in costume, not dancing but hiding in the shadowy alcoves off the main hall. They are embracing."

"Are you a member of the aristocracy?" he asked.

"Yes. Above reproach," I said, as I switched the phone from one ear to the other, lay back on my bed, closed my eyes, and shut out my bedroom and my thoughts of Jack. I pictured the great ball, tasted the wine, smelled the wax mixed with the heavy fragrances people wore to cover the scent of their sweat.

"Who are you masquerading as?" Steve asked.

"Madame du Barry. My hair is up off my bare shoulders in a pompadour and I have a moue—a beauty mark—painted to the left of my lips to draw more attention to them."

"What color are your lips? What shape?" his voice was heavy and slow.

"My lips are full, my bottom lip pouts out a little, and they are stained a deep crimson." I licked them with my tongue.

"And your dress?" he asked.

"It's the color of pale pink rose petals and fits tight to the waist, then fans out wide from my hips and falls to the floor over hoops. The bodice is cut so low and square across my chest that my breasts are almost completely exposed—"

"Can I see your nipples?" he asked.

"No, but if I were to take a deep breath, they might escape, and then you could see them."

"Who am I disguised as?" He was asking me to do all the work, but that was his prerogative. Besides, I didn't mind. The scene was now so clear, I could almost hear the sounds of the orchestra and feel the sensation of the silk against my skin.

"You're Satan dressed in a dark red tunic and black tights. You have a cape of even deeper red satin swirling around your shoulders. Your evil mask hides your face well, and sticking up in your hair are pointy black horns.

"The material of your costume clings to you, so even from across the room, I'm aware of your body, of the strong muscles in your legs, of your broad chest."

It happened so easily now. Once within the fantasy, the adventure flowed from me, taking shape as I said each word. Exciting these men excited me. As I led them through exotic adventures, I was creating my own pleasure too.

"You're staring at me quite openly for a refined lady, aren't you?" he asked.

"Wearing this mask gives me certain freedoms. I can take liberties I otherwise couldn't enjoy. But you, sir, are being just as brazen, aren't you? I can feel your eyes lingering on my pale breasts for much longer than would ordinarily be proper in mixed society."

"Are we just going to stare at each other across the hall?" he was slightly impatient and I quickened my pace.

"I come to you across the crowded dance floor and hold out my arms. You step forward and take me, and we dance. It's very exciting because I don't know who you are and you don't know who I am. Protected by our disguises, we can be as daring as we like."

"Yes, tell me . . ." he urged.

"Just the way you're holding me so tightly and close to your body. You'd never dare press that hard against a lady."

His breath quickened. "Do you like what you feel?"

"Yes, I like how my breasts are crushed against your chest and how the muscles in your back feel against my hands. It's quite dark here, so no one notices when, after we have been dancing for a few minutes, I reach down and feel between your legs to see if you have an erection."

He laughed. "I've had one since you walked across the room."

"It's so thick and hot against my hand. Should I leave my hand there while we continue to dance?"

"Yes." His breathing became audible.

I, too, was lost in the dream, dancing in the great hall with a stranger who was dressed like the devil. Holding his penis in my hand, I was attracted and slightly shocked by what I was about to do to him.

"Oh," I cried.

"What?" he asked.

"The way you just twirled me—look—my nipples have popped out. You reach down and scoop my breasts out of the tight fitting dress, completely exposing them."

"Oh yes . . ." he said. "I touch them, rub them. I can feel your nipples harden until they are just as hard as my penis."

"Your penis is getting harder and hotter."

"Keep your hand there. Stroke me," he pleaded.

"Back and forth, up and down the length of you. Your tights are so thin, you feel naked. I can make out all the ridges and veins. God, you're huge, like a horse."

"I want to be inside of you," he said.

"Here on the dance floor?" I asked

"Yes, fuck me here." His words were part moan, and they throbbed inside me.

"I guide your hand to the slit in my dress and you draw my skirts apart, exposing my naked thighs. Can you feel how wet I am?"

"Hmm."

"Your costume is designed the same way, so I reach through the split in your tights and pull out your penis. Look how it glistens in the candlelight," I said.

"There's another man watching what you're doing," he suggested.

Another man? I tried to see him in the shadowy alcoves ringing the dance floor. Who was he? What part was he going to play in all this? I took a deep breath and then slowly let it out. How would it be with two men?

"Yes, I see him. He's dressed in a ship captain's uniform. He's standing near us, watching me rubbing your cock."

"Watching me rubbing your pussy. He wants you too. Would you mind? Would you let us both have you at the same time?"

"If that's what you want," I said, and in this curious world of words, I meant it. By now, the idea of having two men had become incredibly erotic.

"I want to see you put your mouth around another man's cock. I want to watch him suck on you and get you hot," he was panting.

"What will you do to me while he's sucking on me?"

"I'll be kissing your breasts. You'll have two men suckling you. Would you like that?" he asked.

"Oh yes. Do you want to watch him put his cock in me too?" My hands were no longer holding the phone.

"Yes, I'll allow him to enter you but only to prepare you for me. He can't come in you."

"No, when you're ready to burst and can't tolerate waiting anymore, you'll just nod to me and I'll push him off and you'll enter me."

"And he'll be left standing there with a big fucking erection all wet from having been inside you," he said.

The phone had slipped and I had to put it back up to my ear, but I was too far gone for mechanics to distract me.

"He'll be so crazy watching us fuck that he'll come just standing there." Steven sounded intoxicated. "Does that excite you? That a man can come just from looking at your pussy?"

"Yeah. I'm so hot," I whispered.

"And wet?"

"Yeah, so wet. He made me so wet you can just slide in. Are you ready?" I asked him.

"Yes," he said.

"I wrap my thighs around your waist, holding you so tightly you can't get away. Inside, I'm clenching my muscles around your cock . . . releasing and clenching . . ."

"Oh . . . I want to feel that . . ."

"You're still growing inside me. Expanding to fill up all my space." I was panting now too.

"I want to come," he groaned.

"Yeah, fuck me hard. While he watches. Come on, harder. I want him to see your cock disappear all the way inside me."

"Yes. Now. Now!" he yelled, and then was quiet.

~

After the call, I took a long shower. What would Jack have thought of that? Could he tolerate knowing that I had just come without having any emotion or attachment to the man on the other end of the phone? Would he be disgusted to know how exciting it had been to imagine being exposed in public, to have two men wanting me and touching me and fucking me? He'd claimed he would never question anything about me. But could he accept how perverse my fantasies were? Could he tolerate them? No, more than that— could he share them?

With the hot water streaming over me, I shut my eyes and summoned the feeling of being with Jack in the back of that cab and my skin goose-bumped.

Did I want Jack?

Or did I just want to make every man want me?

# 20

The following Monday morning when I arrived at the institute for my session, Candy and I discussed the calls I'd taken the week before. "You have to pay more attention to the tape recorder, Julia. At least three of your calls were cut off halfway through."

"Yeah, I noticed that." I hoped it didn't sound like a lie.

"Try using tape on the suction cup—see if that doesn't help," she suggested.

Before I left, she handed me an envelope. Inside was a check for two thousand dollars.

"What's this?" I asked her.

"It's payday. That's the money you've earned taking calls."

"I'm not supposed to get paid. The calls are research for the book," I told her, and put the check down on the desk.

"Julia, your name is on my payroll along with the name of every other phone therapist who works here. If you want to give the money back, you'd better talk to Sam."

Fifteen minutes later, in Sam's office, I put the check down in front of him. He was wearing a gray shirt, almost the same shade as his hair, which was pulled back in a ponytail. I noticed for the first time that he was wearing a tiny emerald in his ear. Rather than make him appear effeminate, it exaggerated his masculinity; he looked like a wild gypsy.

"I can't take this," I said.

Picking up the envelope, he glanced inside. "Why the hell not?"

"Because what I'm doing is research; I'm not working for the institute."

"You're doing both."

"No. When you get paid to write a book, the research is included in the price," I explained.

"All I know is you clocked over thirty hours of calls—work any other therapist would have gotten paid for." Sam put the envelope back down on the table.

"I just can't take it."

"Why? What does it mean to you?"

I looked away from the envelope, away from his eyes, out the window. "Don't be my therapist, Sam. Please, just take the money back. Donate it to Paul's charity," I offered.

"Hell, you can do that as easily as I can," he said.

"No, if I take it . . . I'd feel . . ." I stopped.

"Have you had lunch?" he asked.

"No, I've been upstairs meeting with Candy."

Sam folded the envelope and put it in his pocket. "C'mon. Let's take a walk. I'll buy you a hot dog and a soda."

We left the building, walked west to Fifth Avenue, and then into Central Park. It was the first week in November and by now, all the leaves had turned. Everywhere I looked was ablaze with crazy colors. The maples had turned a shocking shade of red. The crab apples were burning gold. Even the trunk of a tall evergreen spruce was wrapped with crimson ivy vines.

Lying on the ground, the leaves covered the pathways like a thick carpet whose colored patterns rearranged with each of our steps. The rustling and crumpling of leaves beneath our feet accompanied us as Sam led the way up a small hill.

"So how are you feeling about the calls?" Sam asked. Behind him, the breeze blew past a locust tree and hundreds of tiny leaves drifted down like saffron rain.

"I'm still nervous when I start a new call. I don't really relax until I figure out what that particular man wants, but then I'm fine."

"How do you feel when a call is successful?" he asked me as we continued walking.

So far, Olivia was the only person I'd truly confided in, but if Sam and I were going to collaborate, he'd find out eventually. "I guess I feel powerful when I hear a man moan on the other end of the phone because of something I've said to him."

Ruby leaves swirled around our feet like small tornadoes. "But that's all I'm saying. I'm not falling into one of your traps."

"What trap is that?" he asked innocently.

"You want me to tell you I feel repulsed. Or perverted or something. You want me to say that I think there's something wrong with me because of how I'm responding."

"Why would I want you to say those things?"

I sighed. "Shit, I fell right into that, didn't I?"

"Julia, this isn't a game. I have this conversation with each therapist the institute employs. Every one of them goes through certain difficulties during training. At times, they're all disturbed or frightened by what they uncover about themselves."

"What do some of them find out?" I kicked some of the overripe leaves with the toe of my shoe.

"Well, one therapist kept creating scenarios with a third partner, exposing bisexual tendencies she didn't know she had or had repressed. A male therapist discovered the phone enabled him to hold off ejaculating for hours at a time and have orgasms so intense they could last as long as fifteen minutes. But rather than enjoying it, he couldn't tolerate the loss of control he felt during those fifteen minutes."

We'd arrived at the great iron gates leading into the new Central

Park Zoo. This wasn't the traditional caged zoo I remembered from my childhood but a park with wide open spaces where animals had more freedom—except that the absence of bars was only an illusion. The animals were still as much prisoners as they'd ever been, only now their cells looked and smelled more like their natural habitat. Was it easier before, without the pretense of freedom?

Stopping at the round pool—one of the few things that hadn't changed—we watched the seals dive, surface, clap, and bark for fish.

"What do you think I'm afraid of finding out, Sam?"

"You tell me."

"I don't know."

"The hell you don't. On some level, the knowledge is there, even if you're not ready to accept it. Don't push yourself. Just remember, you're completely in control and can stop any damn time you want."

I nodded.

"I never knew it would be so easy," I whispered.

He turned to me. "The calls?" he asked.

"My responses. They scare me. They're so disconnected from anything I ever knew. Christ, I've never even met these men, but they make me feel . . ." I'd already revealed much more than I had intended.

Sam waited for me to continue talking; when I didn't, he put his hands in his pockets and looked around. "C'mon. Watching these guys is making me hungry. Let's go," he said, and led me over to a food cart where he bought us both Cokes and hot dogs with everything on them. Sitting on green wooden benches, we stopped talking long enough to start eating.

Halfway through my hot dog I turned to Sam. "Have you been listening to my calls?"

"Yes. Have you thought about my listening?" he asked.

"Once or twice."

"There's nothing atypical about my listening, Julia. It's my responsibility to make sure you're doing the job our clients are paying for, as well as to make sure you can handle it."

I took another bite, chewed, and then swallowed before I asked my next question. "So everything about the way you're dealing with me is typical? You take all your therapists to lunch in the park?"

"Only the ones that have so much trouble talking in a therapist's office." Even though I wasn't looking at him, I heard his smile.

"And is this also typical of the way you collaborate with other writers?" I asked.

"I've never collaborated with a writer before." He sucked up some soda through his straw. "What are you trying to get me to say? That this is unusual behavior for me? Just ask me, Julia. I'll tell you."

I felt as if I'd been stung by some king of insect. "All right. Is everything about the way you're treating me typical?"

"No."

"So why are you treating me differently?" I asked.

"Because you interest me."

"As a patient?" I asked.

"No. As a person. Since the night I saw you with your husband at that fund-raiser, I've wondered why a fabulous woman like you would remain with a man who's so self-involved."

"It's no different than a lot of marriages," I said with a shrug.

He laughed sardonically. "That makes it okay? To be one of the multitudes who do no more than pay lip service to the idea of partnership?"

"As opposed to your marriage with Nina?" I asked.

"I sure as shit hope so. Nina and I may have our faults, but we don't shut down. We fight and we fuck—"

"But not always with each other?" I said sarcastically.

"Good—get mad at me."

I drank what was left of my soda and then wiped my mouth with the paper napkin. "Taking that check would make me feel like a prostitute," I blurted out. I'd said it because it was true, but as soon as the words had left my lips, I realized I'd wanted to broach this subject since Jack had first mentioned his suspicions. I glanced at Sam to gauge his reaction. If I was looking for some telltale sign that Jack's sources were right, I didn't find it.

"All the more reason for you to cash it. The whole point of your becoming a phone therapist was to understand it firsthand. All of it—not just the good parts—but the uncomfortable parts too." He took the envelope out of his pocket and put it between us on the bench.

Hesitating, I kept my hands in my lap.

"What does being a prostitute represent to you?" he asked.

"Being a worthless woman. Pathetic. Cheap. Degraded."

"Is that what you think, or are you just spouting the prevailing moralistic crap?"

"I don't know, Sam." It was true. I'd never examined the issue before. "What do you think of prostitution?"

"That it's no more dishonest a profession for some women than being a wife. That it should be legalized. That the goddamn government should get out of the bedroom unless someone is being hurt.

"Prostitutes—good ones—are multitalented women. Part shrink. Part mother. Part lover. Many are fulfilled by their jobs. Take pride in their success. And why shouldn't they? They offer a valuable service, satisfy a difficult need, and get paid well for it. What the hell is wrong with that?" He slammed his first down in the palm of his other hand.

Was Sam merely philosophizing, or was he defending his business? Considering his principles, either was possible.

"When you put it that way, it doesn't sound that different than phone sex. Do you know a prostitute I could talk to? It might help me with the book," I asked.

He swerved around my question. "Don't fucking do that. Don't hide behind 'the writer' to avoid the issues you've raised about yourself. It's not wrong to be fascinated with people and their sexuality, Julia." Was he too avoiding an issue or just being the ever-alert therapist? "I'm fascinated and I'm not ashamed of it. You don't have to be ashamed of it, either. It's healthy to want to experience your sexuality and understand it all, even the parts of it you think are repulsive." Sam stood up, dropping crumbs on the ground where pigeons were already waiting. "C'mon. Let's walk."

I stood up to and took a step to follow him. And then I turned back. The envelope was still on the bench. A dull brown leaf fell from a chestnut tree and landed beside it. "Wait. I'm still confused." I said.

"There's only thing you need to understand. You can't get to the end before you get through the middle. Do me a favor: don't judge me and don't judge yourself until you've gotten to know Alice a little better." Without waiting, he started to walk farther into the zoo.

I picked up the check, put it in my bag, and followed him.

"Aren't there any areas of sexual behavior where you make moral judgments?" I asked when I'd caught up.

"Judgments are too limiting. We have to explore our souls and each other's souls. Sometimes that also means exploring their bodies—not as if it were a dirty perversion but as if it were a celebration. You can't learn about everyone as half of a couple across a dinner table."

Having reached the polar bears, both of us stood in awe and watched the giant white animals roar as they pawed the air.

"Some discoveries between people lead to sex; some don't," Sam continued. "But I think you'll find getting into someone's head can be every bit as erotic as having sex with them. You'll talk to men over the phone for half an hour whom you'll know better than their wives know them—because they're sharing their secrets with you."

He'd moved the conversation in yet another direction, but it didn't matter to me anymore. He had been right—I *was* fascinated. I wanted to understand everything he was saying. It seemed to have so much to do with me, with everything that had been happening to me for the last few weeks. "Does that mean they're being unfaithful?" I asked.

"Those terms are too confining. Christ, you can fuck someone with your voice, with your eyes, with one touch of a finger on a wrist. Is all of that being unfaithful?" He'd answered my question with one of his own.

"I don't know; perhaps it is." I was looking at him, not the bears. He was making such an effort to reach me, I could feel his energy pouring out.

"You can't take sex out of living no matter how hard you try. You can only dam it up. And that has repercussions. Besides, people relate to each other sexually whether they want to or not, whether they ever admit it or not," he said.

~

We left the bears and headed out of the zoo. "Sam, Paul still doesn't know about the research." As he examined my face, I continued, trying to explain it to myself as well as to him. "I've tried to find the right time to tell him, but he's going through this thing at work."

"The investigation?"

"How do you know?" I asked.

"Mike Menken and I are old friends from way back. How is Paul doing?

"He says he's fine, but I don't think he's telling me the truth. He's very tense and stressed out. Argumentative. That's why I haven't told him."

"That's the only reason?" Sam asked.

"No, you know it's not. I'm afraid, well . . . I don't think Paul will be able to be objective. He won't understand. Won't see any of this as a discovery. He'll just try to convince me I'm having another breakdown."

"He'll deny you your feelings?" Sam asked, already knowing the answer and once more surprising me with his uncanny insight.

"Yeah."

"All the more reason you need to tell him what you're telling me."

"I know."

"No matter how you handle this," he said, "you're going to have trouble with Paul when he finds out."

"Yeah, I know."

"He's a man who treasures being in control. He'll see everything you've done as a threat and try to regain his dominance any way he can."

I was going to ask Sam how he knew those things about my husband, but all that mattered was that he was right. By now we were deep in the park, far away from the traffic coursing through its mid-section, far away from the more populated paths. I looked around me, at the vivid molting trees, the leaf-strewn roads, but I didn't recognize any mileposts. I didn't know where we'd wandered.

"Julia, are you aware I'm attracted to you?"

All I could do was nod. His words had both thrilled me and made me uncomfortable. Did I want to be with Sam that way?

"But I think it's more important for you and me to channel the energy between us into the book. It would be best served there—for me, but more important, for you."

"Why do you think so?" I asked, suddenly full of Alice's bravado.

"'A pretty game, my girl / to play with me so long; / Until this other lover / Comes dancing to thy song, / And my affair is over.' It's called 'The Flirt,' by W. H. Davies." Sam said.

"I haven't been flirting with you," I insisted.

"Bullshit! You're flirting with every man you meet now, and that's fine. You're discovering your sexuality, experimenting with it."

"The last time I did that, I flipped out."

"Was your sexuality actually the cause of your breakdown?"

He was talking to me as if I were another therapist. "No, I was using sex to avoid my real problems. But I was way out of control with the sex."

"Julia, the same thing can't happen again. You're not out of touch with your feelings anymore. And if you ever do get into trouble again, you'll recognize the signs and ask for help."

"I just don't want her to surface again." My bravado had disappeared, I was frightened now.

"Who? Alice?" he asked.

I had already told him so much, a little more couldn't matter. "No, not Alice. The bad Julia—that's what I used to call her."

"What you thought of as the bad Julia was just a parade of young men who disappointed you. You're so quick to connect to people . . . it's a gift, but it's one you have to use judiciously. You couldn't have understood that back then. Probably what happened was by the time these boys disappointed you, you were already aroused and the evening was too far gone, so you went to bed with them and, yes, enjoyed it. For what it was. But then you felt bad about yourself afterward because unbeknownst to you, the disappointments had begun to manifest before you took off your shirt."

"But I've been hiding this part of myself for years."

"So don't hide it anymore. Explore it. Explore yourself."

"But not with you?" I knew why part of me wanted it to be with him—he was a therapist—if he was guiding me, he'd there to catch me if I fell. With anyone else, I'd have to take risks.

"Yes, with me, but as my collaborator," he responded.

"You're saying writing the book with you would be some kind of exploration for me?"

"Hasn't it been one already?"

"Yeah, and some kind of therapy too." I smiled.

Up ahead was a green field studded with lemon and vermilion leaves; it looked like an abstract painter had been let loose in the park. Nature wasn't quiet or calm anymore. The riot of fall colors had completely changed the park's atmosphere.

"Most discovery is therapeutic. That's why you don't have to fear it. I know Freud said sexual desires and differences were based on neurosis, but I don't believe that. My hypothesis—and boy, have I received shit for it—is that left to our own devices, our sexual natures would help, not hinder us. The freer people are sexually, the more creative they become. Repression is what leads to neurosis."

We were surrounded by a grove of tall evergreens. Shafts of afternoon sun filtered through the trees and somewhere in the distance, a dog barked.

"You know, you've managed to do exactly what I was trying to prevent you from doing: analyzing me," I said.

"Maybe I am just being your friend. Why don't you try not to assign definitions or make judgments for a while? Just open yourself up to the discoveries you're making and see where they lead."

We'd left the circle of trees and came out on a path I recognized.

Suddenly I knew where we were. The 84th Street exit was just up ahead. "I get off here."

"Think about what I said, Julia."

I looked at Sam's leathery face. "I don't think I'll be able to do much else."

He smiled. I saw a friend. And a collaborator. And a lover I'd never know. If I felt a pang of regret, it was quickly replaced by a sense of excitement. If this was an adventure, Sam was proving to be a formidable guide.

After we said good-bye and parted, I kept walking. Just before I crossed the road toward the exit, I looked back, but Sam had vanished.

I focused on the layers of dried-out leaves beneath my feet, getting drunk on the colors. Even though the reds and oranges and yellows meant the leaves were dying and winter was coming, I didn't mind. Another new season would alter the landscape yet again. In the snow, it would be even easier to lose sight of the old landmarks, and for some reason that idea thrilled me.

# Part Three

# 21

~

It was late and I had to rush home to make my three o'clock call. I'd just finished attaching the suction cup and putting a new tape in the recorder when the phone rang; it was Arthur. During our last call, he'd asked me to hurt him. I anticipated this one would be just as difficult. After today, I thought, I'd ask Candy to give his calls to someone else.

Until I'd realized who was calling, I'd been sorry I hadn't had time to get out of my jeans and sweater, but now I was glad. Instead of taking the call on the bed, I pulled the phone over to the easy chair by the window where the afternoon sun was shining in.

As I did with every client, I asked Arthur if there was a fantasy he wanted to pursue. Fully expecting him to play his pathetic game with me, I was startled with his response.

~

"Do you think I know you well enough by now to tell you what I really want, Alice?"

At that moment a plane must have passed, casting a flickering shadow across the sun. I looked right into the harsh white light and was temporarily blinded.

"Yeah, you know me well enough. You can tell me."

"And you'll do it? Whatever I ask?"

What more could he ask than what he had already asked for during our last call, when he'd ordered me to pull him by the testicles? "Yes," I answered, trying not to let him hear the apprehension I felt.

"Are you such a whore?" he asked.

I'd forgotten how frightening his cultured, sophisticated voice could sound when it turned nasty. "Is that what you want, Arthur? For me to be the whore this time?" No one had asked that of me, yet after the conversation I'd just had with Sam, it seemed almost appropriate. "I can do that. Sashay up to you in your parked car and offer myself to you—twenty bucks for a blow job; fifty if you want to come inside me."

"No." His voice lost its edge. "I want you to help me."

I switched the phone to my other ear. "Of course I'll help you. What do you want me to do to make you come?"

"You don't understand!" His voice became razor sharp once again. The swift shift actually caused me more alarm than his tone of voice.

Why was I being so patient? Obviously he was a disturbed man. I should just get off the phone. Someone as inexperienced as I never should have been handling him in the first place. He needed a real therapist. But he was already on the phone. I'd try just once more time. "Arthur, do you want me to force you to get undressed?"

"You can't help me like that. Not with your cunt voice . . ."

Was he asking me to pretend we were actually together instead of talking over the phone? "We're here in my room. The lights are low. We're lying together on this huge king-size bed and—"

"That's not what I want!" he yelled, interrupting me.

"All right, then tell me what you want, or else I'm going to get off the phone."

How different everything would have been if I had just quietly replaced the receiver in its cradle and disconnected Arthur.

"If I tell you, will you promise to do exactly what I ask?" he was whispering now, but the softness of his voice was much more sinister than his shouting had been.

"Yes."

He took a deep breath and then let the words out in one long rush. "I want you to hurt me."

"I know, and I will—"

"No!" The suddenness of his shout terrified me. "Not over the phone, Alice. You can't do it saying blood and bone words, saying pain words. I need to feel. Need to feel the bad. I need to scream. Just the way she—" He stopped himself.

I nestled the phone between my shoulder and neck and wrapped my arms around my chest. "Why would you want anyone to hurt you?"

I was nervous and my words were halting, unsure. I didn't yet understand what he was asking for.

"Hurting me . . . it's the only way to make the monster in me stop." Half sobbing, half muttering, he was barely coherent. "The monster has to stop. Cease. Desist. Finish. Do you get it yet?"

"Stop what?" I shut my eyes, as if that would deflect what he was about to say.

"Did it. Again. Yesterday. Didn't want to, but couldn't help myself. So you have to hurt me, now. The way I hurt her. Once the monster feels the pain, then he will stop."

I was straining to understand each word.

"I don't want to hurt her. You understand that? I don't want to hurt her." His voice was building up to a hysterical pitch.

I didn't want to be his confessor, but his slick voice had already pulled me into his black dread. Just because we were connected by a fiberoptic wire, just because I knew what turned him on and had heard him come, I didn't have to endure this. I could hang up.

"Can't stop," he was still explaining, "unless you help. You won't care. Won't bother you. You are just a voice. A cunt. Nothing can hurt you. You see?"

"Who are you hurting?" I asked, even though I was certain I didn't want to hear the answer.

"My stepdaughter. She . . . she's . . . fourteen. I do things to her. Things no one should do. Not even the monster. Pain and flesh things. Now do you see? Now, unless you're a monster too, you'll help me."

My throat tightened and I pressed my hand up to my mouth, shoving my knuckles between my lips, trying not to gag as the image of a fourteen-year-old girl burned into my consciousness. "Arthur, exactly how can I help you?"

"Meet me somewhere and do it to me. Do to me what I do to her."

"I can't." As far as I was concerned, there was no possibility I could do what he was asking.

"Please, please!" He was whimpering now. "I'll pay you whatever you want. Just don't say no." He was begging.

"What about seeing a psychiatrist?"

"No. Only this way. I have to feel the pain. To get on the other side of the pain. Can't you understand?"

I didn't know what to do. Keep him talking? Go along with his plan? Or just hang up?

But how could I abandon the girl now that I knew about her? Her terrorized image kept me on the phone talking to Arthur long after I wanted to get off. I felt responsible for getting him to come into the institute for real help, but my insistence only infuriated him.

"I knew you wouldn't do it. You let me down. Like every other bitch. All of you bitches."

"Don't say that. I want to help. Let me try to figure something out." I was talked out and sick to my stomach. "Give me your phone number, Arthur. I promise I'll think about what I can do and call you back."

He recited his number in a numb voice and then hung up. I was left with a slip of paper trembling in my hand.

# 22

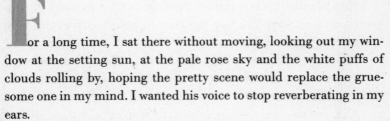

For a long time, I sat there without moving, looking out my window at the setting sun, at the pale rose sky and the white puffs of clouds rolling by, hoping the pretty scene would replace the gruesome one in my mind. I wanted his voice to stop reverberating in my ears.

Arthur was obviously ill and suffering, but my pity was for his stepdaughter, a prisoner in her own home, jailed by the man who should have been her protector. When I finally stood up, the suction cup I'd attached to the phone at the start of the call fell to the ground. At some point it must have come loose. How much of the conversation had been recorded? I pressed the rewind button, then the play button, but as soon as I heard Arthur's voice I was so repulsed I shut the machine off. Turning the volume down so I heard only noise instead of words, I tried again. The first five minutes of the call had been recorded. There was nothing after that.

In the kitchen, I stood at the sink drinking glass after glass of ice water so quickly the liquid spilled out of my mouth and slid down my chin and neck. Leaving the glass in the sink, I took handfuls of water and splashed it on my face, not caring how cold it was and only stopping when my hair was half drenched and my sweater soaked.

*I should call Sam,* I suddenly thought, then dialed his number from the kitchen phone. His secretary told me he'd left for a conference in New Orleans and that he'd be gone for the next 48 hours. I left a message saying he should get in touch with me as soon as possible.

There was only one other person I wanted to talk to—Jack. Since he'd left New York, all our conversations had been awkward, but I called him anyway.

As soon as he heard me out, he reassured me I'd done all the right things. Then he suggested I call the police.

"Before I talk to Sam? I can't. What if Arthur is an ex-patient?" I asked.

"Legally, the doctor–patient privilege is void in cases of suspected child molestation. Sam has an obligation to report this even if Arthur is a patient."

"Well, then I'm sure he will. But I can't. I have to wait for him."

"Does this man have your home number?" For the first time, Jack sounded worried.

"No, just the institute's number. The men call there and the operator patches the calls through to me—or something like that."

"So there's no way he can contact you directly or find you?"

"No, but it's not me I'm worried about—"

Jack interrupted me. "But it is you *I'm* worried about. Is Paul on his way home?"

"No, I'm supposed to meet him . . . why?" I was suddenly confused to hear Jack talking about my husband.

"Well, don't you think you should call him and tell him what's happened?"

For the second time that day, I found myself explaining why Paul still didn't know anything about what I'd been doing for the last six weeks. On the other end of the phone, Jack was silent until I'd finished.

"We can talk about that later. Right now you need to keep trying to get hold of Sam. And Julia . . ."—his voice held me—"please, be careful."

"I will," I said, and when I got off the phone I called Sam's secretary back. Elaine said he hadn't called in and was probably on the plane by now. She gave me the hotel's phone number and said he should be there by nine.

By nine, I was supposed to be with Paul at a dinner party the Wilcoxes were hosting to celebrate the tenth anniversary of FIT. How could I go? I had to stay by the phone and wait for Sam.

Paul's secretary was reluctant to interrupt him while he was in conference, but I insisted.

"What is it, Julia?" He sounded rushed.

"Listen, I'm sorry to bother you, but I've come down with some kind of bug. I just don't think I can make it to the party tonight."

"Oh no, not tonight. Take something, Julia. I need you there. By my side. I need you looking as if you don't have a trouble in the world. We're down to the wire with this investigation. I don't want to raise any suspicions."

"That's nuts! What would be suspicious about my being sick?"

"I'll explain it to you later. I have to get back to my meeting now. Please Julia, take something. All right?"

My husband didn't want to hear the panic in my voice. My distress was inconvenient. Jack had only heard me say hello and had cleared his office. No, I wouldn't start comparing them. The phone rang and I jumped. My first thought was that Paul was calling me back to apologize. Or maybe it was Sam.

"Hello?" I said.

"Julia, what's the matter. You sound weird, you know?" It was Max.

"Nothing, sweetheart. I just had a fight with one of those efficient telephone marketing people. What's up?"

Max wanted to know if we'd mind if, after spending the Thursday of Thanksgiving with us, he took Betsy to visit a friend of his who lived in Connecticut.

I tried not to let him hear the disappointment in my voice as I told him he should double-check with his father but that it was fine with me. Except it wouldn't be. I'd been holding my breath waiting for him to come back, thinking—at least for a while—that our old life would be restored. With him home, I wouldn't be as aware of how little Paul and I had to say to each other. I'd planned four days of things we'd do together. Now we'd only have one day and night and then Max would be gone again.

I must have done a good job pretending, because after a few minutes of filling me in on his latest tests and papers and after asking about my flowers, Max got off the phone to go have dinner.

Before abandoning the phone, I called Sam's hotel in New Orleans. Although I knew he couldn't have arrived yet, I wanted to leave a message.

I got undressed and went into the bathroom, startled by the image that greeted me in the mirror. My skin was a sickly pale color and my eyes were haunted. If I couldn't do something about how I looked, I really would raise suspicions at the party. So I soaked a face towel with lavender and took it back to my bed.

Lying there, I was overwhelmed by images of Arthur hurting his stepdaughter. Horrors flashed through my mind no matter how hard I tried to bar them, until finally, I gave up and went to take a shower.

Once I'd dried my hair and put on fresh makeup, I still had almost two hours before it was time to leave. Wearing a robe, I went into the kitchen, opened the freezer, took out one of the brownies I kept stashed there, and put it in the microwave to defrost. But when I bit into it—back in my bedroom sitting on my bed—it was still icy and hurt my teeth. I ate it anyway while I watched the phone, willing it to ring. Finally, in desperation, I turned on the television hoping to find some distraction in the six, the six-thirty, and then the seven o'clock news.

When I eventually got dressed, nothing looked right. What I

picked was either too summery or too wintry. I settled on a sage green round-necked, long-sleeved jacket and wide-legged pants. I slipped on black suede pumps and picked a black alligator bag. In some kind of trance, I brushed my hair, sprayed on perfume, undid my small gold hoop earrings, and screwed in emerald drops my mother had given me, saying the green made my eyes look bluer.

Before I left, I called the hotel in New Orleans once more. My message was still waiting.

It was much colder outside than I'd anticipated and the thin coat I'd worn wasn't keeping me warm. The Wilcoxes were on Park, only ten blocks downtown, so I'd planned on walking, but after only two blocks, my teeth were chattering. I searched for a cab, but there were none, so I trudged on, somehow missing every light. It took me twice as long as it should have to get there, and when I did arrive, I had tears in my eyes. My cheeks stung from the wind and my hair was disheveled.

Although I was only fifteen minutes late, Paul looked visibly relieved when I walked in. He made his way over to me and kissed me hello. "Are you all right?" he asked. "You do look pale." He touched my hand as if he was taking my pulse.

"I'll be fine," I said. "Let me go to the ladies' room and straighten up."

When I came back, I made the rounds: saying hello, kissing cheeks, and making small talk. When I finally made it to the bar, I asked for a vodka on the rocks.

Once I had the drink in my hand and had taken a few sips, I asked Lanni if I could use the phone, and she led me to their den.

"You all right, kiddo?" she asked. "You look worried."

⁓

I called Sam's hotel and this time left a new message saying I wasn't home but I'd call back every half hour. I asked him to please stay in his room until I called back.

While I tried to make small talk, I wondered if Arthur had gotten home yet. Would this be one of the nights he'd lose his battle with himself and abuse his stepdaughter, or would he be able to control his perversions?

I chatted away another half hour, doing what I had become so efficient at—asking about other people's jobs and children and summer homes and apartments and renovations and decorations and health and hobbies.

No one realized my mind was in a stranger's apartment, holding a vigil for a fourteen-year-old girl. I was sitting beside her on her bed, watching the clock move ahead, waiting for the door to open and see Arthur's shadow precede him.

When I left the living room a half hour later to go back to the den, Paul followed me with his eyes but he didn't come after me. After shutting the door, I sat on the couch and dialed the New Orleans number I now knew by heart. Sam still hadn't checked into his room. What was taking so long? I called the airport and was told his flight had been delayed an hour.

In the dining room, Lanni was seating her guests. Paul and I were across from one another, and as I sat down, he looked over, trying to read my face. Avoiding my husband, I turned to the man on my right.

I don't remember what we talked about or anything that was served or how I kept up my side of the conversation. I was aware only that the dinner was taking too long and that I wanted it to end because I couldn't get up to call Sam again until after the coffee was served.

No matter what words the people on either side of me spoke, I heard only Arthur's sad, halting confession. If only I could help him . . . stop him from tormenting his stepdaughter . . . stop his voice from repeating inside my head . . . stop the unending misery he must be causing that young girl. Was he doing it now? What was she feeling? Forcing myself back to what was going on around me, I entered a conversation in the middle and managed to stay with it until coffee was served.

The hotel operator told me that Dr. Butterfield had checked in, but when she rang his room for me, there was no answer. As the conference's keynote speaker, Sam had obligations. But damn it, I'd asked him to stay only until I called back.

There was nothing left for me to do. The energy had drained out of my body and I had to drag myself back to the dining room. My head was pounding and I felt nauseated. How was I going to get through the last hour of postprandial conversation?

When Paul and I finally left at eleven-fifteen, another board member offered to drop us off, so Paul and I weren't alone until we got upstairs and into the apartment.

It was time to confess. To sit my husband down and tell him the whole story—explain everything that had gone on. But first I had to go to the greenhouse and check my machine to see if Sam had called. In the dark, the red message light pulsed on and off. I had just depressed the play button when I heard Paul behind me. "Julia, come out here, I want to ask you something."

I couldn't play the messages now. What if Sam had called and Paul heard him talking on my tape? So, leaving the machine until later, I walked out into the kitchen. Was Paul finally going to ask me why I had acted so strangely at dinner? Why I seemed so distracted and distant? It would be an easy segue from there to the truth.

"What did you hear at the Wilcoxes'?" he asked.

"Nothing out of the ordinary. Why?"

"Did anyone say anything to you about the investigation?" he asked as he poured himself a glass of wine.

"No." I crossed the room. He followed me down the hall and into our bedroom.

"What were you and Bruce Travis talking about?" he asked.

Bruce, one of the most influential people on the board, had been sitting on my right. "Mostly about his kids. About his older daughter's anorexia," I added, surprised I had remembered anything about our conversation. I sat down on the bed and Paul sat on the arm of the chair by the window where I had talked to Arthur— was it only hours ago?

"I helped her get into Todd's program at Duke. Did he tell you that?"

"Yeah, he did. Actually, he seemed quite grateful," I offered.

"Why didn't you mention that before?" Paul asked.

"I did just now."

I started undressing. I was so tired, all I wanted to do was crawl into my bed and shut my eyes. I just hoped I'd be able to sleep without Arthur's voice or his stepdaughter's image haunting me.

"Don't make me pull the information out of you. It's very important to me, Julia. Very important. Bruce has the ear of every member of the board. If he sticks by me, everyone will. Now think—is there anything else he said?"

Too exhausted to fight, I sat down naked on the edge of the bed and tried to recount additional details from the evening's conversations. By the time I finished, Paul seemed relieved.

"So that's it?" he asked.

"Paul, I'm beat. I didn't feel well to begin with and—"

"I know, sweetheart, but I need to know. Did anyone say anything else?"

I got up, went to the closet, pulled on my nightshirt, and then got under the covers. "All right, Paul. Sarah Thompson said her son had written an article for his school newspaper about the charity. Scott Garver said he thought there were too many people on the fund-raising committee. Frank Hardy told me he was hoping to get more publicity about the basketball connection. Oh, Tom Warren's wife said that she wished board meetings were on any other night but Thursday because they wanted to go away for more long weekends to Aspen and Southampton, but—let me see if I can remember her exact words—'the damn board meetings get in the way.'"

"You don't have to be sarcastic. This could affect my future." He paused, then corrected himself. "Our future."

"No, you were right the first time. It's your future."

"What exactly does that mean?" His voice had dropped into the dead zone where he spoke without inflection.

"I don't know. It's just how I feel. You're the therapist; you deal with people's feelings. This is my feeling. That it's your future and has very little to do with me. I'm important to you only as a social appendage. I'm something you're supposed to have—a supportive wife, smart and pretty and clever enough to make you look good."

Paul, who was still in his business suit, opened his mouth to say something, but I cut him off. "Don't tell me you love me and you love Max and we are your family and that's why you're doing all this, because the truth is, you're doing it for yourself. If I didn't exist, would you be doing anything any differently?"

Paul looked at me with concern, the doctor examining his patient. "I'm sorry. You are tired. Why don't you go to sleep?"

"No, not now that we've started talking. There are other things I have to tell you."

He stared at me across the expanse of the white lace bedspread. "I don't want you to get upset. I think you should go to bed, Julia. We'll talk in the morning," he said, and disappeared into the bathroom.

I had planned on lying there until he got into bed and fell asleep and then going to check my messages, but Paul didn't come to bed. When he left the bathroom, he went into his den.

I shut my eyes and listened to the sound effects from the movie he was watching, as I had done for so many nights of our life together—noise coming from a room down the hall, muffled shouts and screams.

If Paul was sitting on the couch facing the television, he'd see me if I walked by to go to the greenhouse. Besides, even if Sam had left a message, I couldn't call him now; there'd be nothing either of us could do about Arthur until morning.

It was past midnight. Was Arthur asleep? And what about his stepdaughter? Was she sleeping? Or waiting for her stepfather to come into her bedroom to torture her again?

# 23

I slept fitfully, dreaming, then waking, then falling asleep again. I finally woke up for good at about 7 A.M. Through half-closed eyes, I watched my husband put on his running clothes. As soon as I heard the front door shut, I went into the greenhouse and listened to my message. It was from Sam, apologizing for not being able to wait for my call and asking me to call him before eight this morning.

I dialed the number of the hotel in New Orleans.

At last, Sam was in his room.

"What's wrong, Julia? I got all these messages."

After I'd explained what had happened and answered his questions, I asked if he was going to call the police.

"Not yet, Julia. The phone line is part of my practice; every client is promised confidentiality. Especially if Arthur is an ex-patient."

"None of that matters if a child is being abused."

"It does if he's an ex-patient and he has a history of suffering from delusions."

"Let me call the police," I pleaded.

"Absolutely not. You work for me, Julia. You don't call the shots; I do. And this can wait until I get back." It was the first time I'd ever heard him this angry.

I was wearing my thin white cotton nightshirt, and while I talked to Sam, I was pacing. At some point, I looked out the window and saw the construction workers sitting on their scaffolding, drinking their morning coffee, eating their buttered rolls and staring right at me. I turned my back on them.

"Why are you assuming he's an ex-patient? He may be some guy who just called up blind," I said.

"You may be right, but until we know for sure, we can't do anything. Did you get the call on tape?"

"Some of it, yeah. But I must have knocked the suction cup off—I didn't get everything. I'm sorry, Sam; I didn't record the part where he admits he's hurting his stepdaughter."

"Don't worry about it. I'll be back tonight. Meet me at the office tomorrow morning and bring the tape with you. We'll figure out where to go from there," he said.

My head started to ache, a dull, unrelenting pounding. I pressed my fingers to my temples. "But he might be with her right now. Or again tonight. Can't you call Candy from there and at least find out if Arthur's a patient, and then if he's not, let me call the police?"

"Julia, you're assuming what this man told you was the truth. Few people actually act out what they fantasize about. That's why they're satisfied using the phone."

"But what if this time, this man is telling the truth?" I asked.

"Can you play me the tape now, over the phone?" He was humoring me, but I didn't care. Maybe when he heard the desperation in Arthur's voice, he'd realize how urgent the situation was.

"Yes, all right. Hold on," I put down the phone, went into the bedroom, got the tape recorder from my nightstand drawer, returned to the greenhouse, switched on the machine, and played the tape into the mouthpiece.

The recording was so loud I didn't hear Paul's key in the door or his shout that he was home, so it wasn't until the tape abruptly cut off and I heard noises in the bathroom that I realized my husband was back.

"I'll call Candy," Sam was saying, "but my instincts are that this guy is just acting out. I'll see you in the morning, Julia. I know how upset you are, but don't be overly concerned. All right?"

As soon as I hung up the phone, I panicked. What had Paul heard? Nervous with anticipation, I went into the bedroom, busying myself making the bed and straightening up, waiting for Paul to come out of the bathroom.

He had a towel wrapped around his waist and drops of water glistened on his shoulders. "You know, sometimes you surprise me," he said.

My heart smashed into my rib cage and then I felt a kind of relief. Now I'd have to tell him what had been going on. No hiding anymore. No more postponements.

"What did you hear?" I asked.

"Since when have you been interested in such violent TV?" he asked.

TV? Had he thought the noises he'd heard had come from the TV?

"I wasn't watching television . . ."

Paul had turned away and walked over to his closet. He hung the towel on a hook and started to get dressed. His body was so toned, so tight, there was no softness; not a single muscle was relaxed.

"I was just switching channels, looking for the news," I lied.

He'd stepped into his shorts and was pulling on a starched white dress shirt. "Too bad. Maybe it'll be on again tonight. It sounded like my kind of movie," he mused as he buttoned a cuff.

"Want me to turn it on in here?" To me, my voice sounded hypertense, but Paul didn't seem to notice. I busied myself rearranging perfume bottles on my dressing table.

"No, I'm almost late for a meeting now," he said, as he knotted a red tie.

All morning I tried to block out the sounds of Arthur begging me to help him. Finally I called Olivia, and she agreed to meet me at the health club, where we did a mile's worth of laps. Even underwater I heard him. After we'd dried off and dressed, we went downstairs to a coffee shop and I told her what had happened.

~

"You have to call the police," she insisted, after I finished explaining. "Regardless of what Sam says. And you've got to tell Paul."

I took a deep breath and smelled the chlorine again. "Don't you think I know that? I just can't do it yet."

My friend looked at me and shook her head, "Oh Julia, what are you doing?"

"I know things aren't right between Paul and me, but as bad as it is, it's what I know. Can't you understand?"

"You're crazy! You're throwing away your whole life. For what? Something safe? But he's not even safe. Don't you see? He might have jeopardized your whole future with God knows what crazy schemes he's pulled with FIT. The IRS doesn't investigate for no reason. Don't you know that? And what about this phone shit?" She was yelling so loud other patrons were turning around to stare at us. "Why are you really doing it? Isn't it so he'll catch you and fight with you? So he'll finally pay some attention to you?!"

"Why are you screaming at me?" I asked.

"Because I don't know how else to make you listen."

"Well, I've listened to you. But I don't think you know what the hell you're talking about." I got up and left her sitting there.

~

I walked all the way home even though it was over three miles. I knew what Olivia had said was true—I had to tell Paul what was going on. But that wasn't what mattered now. There was a young girl in trouble somewhere and I couldn't do anything to help her.

Christ, how did he hurt her?

Was he going to do it again tonight?

And why wasn't she telling anyone about it?

~

By five o'clock that evening I was halfway to being crazy, so despite Sam's admonitions, I called the police department.

It took several tries to finally find out that I needed to talk to someone in the sex crimes division, but when I reached them, the man who answered the phone said someone would have to get back to me.

"Can I have your name?"

"Alice," I said automatically.

"Alice," he repeated. "And your last name?" he asked.

I hung up.

# 24

I didn't even try to sleep that night. By six o'clock, I couldn't bear lying in bed anymore. Paul was still sleeping when I got up, pulled on sweats and sneakers, crept out of the apartment, and headed straight to the phone on the corner of Fifth and 84th. The silver frame of the phone was streaked with dirt, the shelf was cracked, shards of broken glass littered the ground, but none of it mattered. I picked up the handset.

The quarter clanged through the slot and I dialed the number of the police department. An officer answered. "Nineteenth Precinct. Can I help you?"

"I want to report a child abuse case," I whispered.

"I'm sorry—I can't hear you too well. Can you speak up?"

I repeated what I'd said and then he asked me for my name. It was the same routine as it had been last night.

"Do I have to give you my name?"

"No ma'am, but it would expedite things quite a bit."

I hesitated.

"Ma'am?"

"Yes?"

"Why don't you tell me the child's name?"

But I didn't know the girl's first name; Arthur had never mentioned it. I didn't even know her last name.

"I'm sorry," I said into the phone, and hung up. I had no choice but to wait until I could see Sam.

～

It was a gray day, but there were still plenty of joggers out for their daily run around the reservoir. Joining the throng, I entered the park and was immediately assaulted by the stale smell of urine and the scattered garbage the city's rats had dragged out during the night. There were even fewer leaves on the trees than there had been a few days ago, and the gnarled branches looked naked. Heavy clouds occluded the sun and the water in the reservoir didn't sparkle. I don't like running, but that morning, it absorbed me the way swimming wouldn't have. Languid strokes and soothing currents would have given my mind space to drift back to Arthur, but on the track I had to put one foot in front of the other and consciously push myself forward. My knees ached and my lungs hurt and I started to sweat. Clammy and cold, I kept going, doing the loop until I had no breath left.

As I came up to our apartment building, Paul was leaving with an overnight bag. "You went running?" he asked me as he raised his hand to hail a cab.

I shrugged. "I felt like sweating. When will you be home?"

He opened the cab door and threw his suitcase in. "Not till Friday. I have to go to Boston, Philly, and Washington." He shut the door and the cab took off. He'd been so preoccupied, he'd left without even saying good-bye.

Upstairs, I made myself coffee, but it was bitter. I tried to eat some cereal, but it tasted like cardboard.

Too anxious to stay home, I arrived at the institute before Sam and had to wait for him. My stomach was cramped either in anticipation of our meeting or from the awful coffee I'd gulped down.

When he showed up a few minutes past nine and I saw his concerned face, I finally felt a reprieve; Sam would take care of everything now. Soon this ordeal would be over. The girl would be safe.

"You look like hell," Sam said as he ushered me into his office. "Haven't you slept at all?"

"No," I shook my head. "I keep imaging them together, wondering how he's hurting her. God, she's only fourteen. Did I tell you that?"

"Yes, now . . ." He picked up the phone. "Let's see what Candy's found out." While he listened to her, he scribbled notes.

"Well," he reported to me, "His last name is Lindt. Candy gave me his American Express card number, driver's license number, and his office phone number and told me he has never been a patient. Under 'referred by' on his card it says 'advertisement.'" Sam paused. "He's not an ex-patient, but goddamn it, he is a client. Before we do anything else, I'd like you to call him back and tell him you've thought over his request and he'd be better served seeing a more experienced therapist."

"I've already done that, Sam. He wasn't interested in therapy."

"I want you to try again," Sam insisted.

"What he wants me to do is meet him," I argued. "He wants me to hurt him. I spoke to him—I know."

"And I want you to fucking try again, all right?" Sam's face lost some of its roundness as his anger sharpened his features and narrowed his lips. "It's two days later. If he was engaged in a fantasy, he may have disassociated from it by now. If he wasn't, he may be more responsive because you're making an effort."

My stomach churned. I didn't want to hear Arthur's voice. I didn't want him to take advantage of having me on the phone and confide anything more to me. Meanwhile, Sam punched his number into the phone. When it started to ring, he nodded to me, indicating I should pick up the extension. The plastic was slippery in my hand.

"I've been thinking about you," I told Arthur Lindt when he came on the line. "And I don't think I can help you, but I'm sure a real therapist could. I have the name of one to give you."

"Forget it, I've been. Discussed my childhood ad nauseam and let the guy scope out my head." Arthur switched to a pseudo-European accent: "So you killed small bugs, you hurt tiny animals. How did it feel to tear their arms out? To twist their little necks?" His voice returned to the sophisticated cadence I was used to. "The guy was more of a sadist than I was. Oh no, Alice, please don't insult me. Don't talk to me about therapists. They can't stop me from wanting to hurt her. She is just fourteen . . . can't you help me?"

"Maybe the therapist you tried wasn't the right one for you," I suggested.

"What's going on—are you pimping for some shrink now?"

I recoiled from his sudden hostility and looked over at Sam, who was listening intently. He nodded at me, encouraging me, and I continued. "No, I just want to help you." My voice broke into a sob. I couldn't get the image of that girl out of my mind. "I just think—"

Lindt interrupted me. "Will you meet me or won't you?" he sounded jumpy.

"My boss just walked in. It's against the rules for me to talk to anyone who isn't paying. I'll try to call you back later when no one's around. Okay?"

I hung up and sat there, waiting for Sam to speak, to tell me what we were going to do, to take charge. But all he did was sigh, stand, and, rubbing the bristles on his chin, walk over to the window and stare out at the street.

"Christ, I didn't want to bring the fucking police in on this," he said, more to himself than to me.

Why was he so reluctant to make the call? "Don't you have a legal obligation?" I asked.

"Fucking rules! I hate the system. I've fought it my whole life." He was still looking out the window.

Was there a more sinister reason he didn't want to call the police? "I don't understand. You heard him." I said, hoping Sam would justify his hesitation so I could stop doubting him.

"The police have too much fucking power in areas that shouldn't be any of their damn business."

Sam turned around looked over at me. I looked right back at him. Defying him. The resolve and the anger in his eyes dissolved into resignation. He picked up the phone. It took him several minutes, but finally he was connected to the Special Crimes Division of the New York City Police Department.

"Some detective named Fontenella will get back to us in a few minutes," Sam told me after he hung up. Do you want some coffee?" he asked.

"Sure."

~

Only moments after Sam returned with two mugs of coffee, the detective called back. I listened as Sam described the situation and answered questions. "Yeah, all right," I heard him say. "But I don't want anyone coming over here in uniform. I don't want my patients to be alarmed." He nodded as the detective on the other end of the phone continued speaking.

"The detective's name is Toni Fontenella. She's on her way," he told me after the call ended. "I'm sorry you have to be involved in this, Julia, but she wants you to stick around so she can talk to you too," he added.

Sam had a patient, so while I waited, I went upstairs to the library and looked through the card catalogue for books on child abuse. Finding many more titles than I expected, I chose the first book that seemed pertinent. The case histories were repugnant, and rather than give me any insight, they crystallized the fragmented nightmares I'd already envisioned. Despite myself, I kept reading, fascinated yet horrified, much the same way people are drawn to stories about the Holocaust even though it was an atrocity.

Finally, Sam's secretary called to ask me to return to his office.

~

Sitting at the table with Sam was a tall, patrician-looking woman with dark hair and a strong Roman nose. She seemed about my age and spoke with a tough Brooklyn accent.

Sam introduced us. "Alice Carroll, this is Detective Fontenella." Sam's use of my phone name caught me off guard, so I hesitated before I shook the detective's hand.

"First, I'd like to hear the tape," she announced.

To my ears, the recording was too loud. It echoed. Certain words reverberated. Arthur sounded like an angry, malevolent man and Alice sounded like a tease. If only I could hear the words as senseless noise, to block out their meaning and make the tape nothing more than atonal music.

After we'd been talking to the detective for a few minutes, I realized there was a marked difference in the respectful way she talked to Sam and the disdainful way she treated me.

"How long have you been a phone sex operator?" she asked.

"Slightly more than a month," I answered.

"Do you take the calls here?"

"No, at my home."

"And where is that?" She had a Bic pen poised over a notebook. I hesitated.

"Is that necessary, Detective?" Sam asked.

"Is it a secret where you live?" She'd directed her question to me, but Sam answered.

"No, but we like to protect the people who work with us. So if it's not critical to have Alice's address, I'd just as soon you used the institute's."

"That's fine." The detective clipped her words. For a few seconds, she occupied herself writing something down. "Now tell me, Miss Carroll—when did you turn the tape recorder on?"

"As soon as we started talking."

"What about the conversation you had before you turned on the tape, when you both talked about what kind of fantasy he wanted?"

"There wasn't any other conversation," I said.

"C'mon, Miss Carroll—I know how these calls go. Didn't Mr. Lindt instruct you in exactly what kind of role-playing he wanted to do?"

"No, I already said he didn't." Why was she putting me on the defensive? Did she think I was lying?

"What's the real reason you shut off the tape?" she asked.

"Don't you understand? I didn't shut off the tape. The suction cup is a flimsy little thing—it came unstuck."

"You mean you've never shut off the tape when you were doing a call? You never got so hot and horny you wanted privacy?"

Her knowing this truth—which no one else had even guessed—bewildered me. "What exactly are you asking?"

I must have sounded upset because Sam intervened. "Is it necessary to fucking interrogate my employee?" He was having a hard time controlling his temper. "She came forward; she agreed to talk to you. Why would she be holding anything back?"

The detective capped her pen, shut her notebook, and took my tape recorder off the desk. "If you don't have any objection, I'd like to take this," she told Sam.

"Fine."

"We'll do whatever we can but it's a long shot. No laws have been broken. Phone sex isn't illegal—yet—so all we can do is send an officer to interview the stepdaughter and see if she wants to make a formal complaint."

"Won't she be worried about getting in trouble with Lindt if she does that?" I asked.

"We do know how to do our job, Miss Carroll. We're not stupid. We have ways to carry on these investigations so the child feels protected."

I didn't know what I'd done to Detective Fontenella, but she obviously found me objectionable.

"You'll let us know as soon as you know something, Detective?" Sam asked.

"Yes," she said.

"Today?" I asked.

She looked as if she was deciding whether I deserved an answer. "We'll attempt to contact the girl this afternoon," she said to Sam. Then using only the minimum eye contact necessary to let me know she was addressing me, she asked, "Do you expect him to call you back?"

"No, I'm supposed to call him back."

"You think you can refrain from doing that for the next twenty-four hours?" she asked archly.

"Detective, are you having a problem with something I said? Because—"

"No," she said, interrupting me with a contempt-filled glance, and then she turned away, making it clear there *was* a problem, just not one she wanted to share.

⌣

Before I left the institute, I asked Candy to cancel my calls for the rest of the week and then took a cab home.

I spent the afternoon trying to organize some of my notes, but all I was capable of doing was making piles and then rearranging them. Somewhere, a policeman or policewoman was with Arthur's stepdaughter, and until I knew the outcome of that meeting, I couldn't function.

At five-thirty, Sam called. "No luck, Julia. The detective said she was with Lindt's stepdaughter herself but the kid denied anything was wrong. She described a good, solid relationship. She thinks Lindt was either playing out a fantasy with you or using sympathy to try to get you to meet him."

"And what do you think, Sam?" I asked.

"I agree with Fontenella. Lindt was probably playing some kind of game with you."

"I sure hope so," I said. "I certainly don't want that sick story Arthur told me to be true . . . except . . . Sam, tell me—isn't it possible the girl could have been too frightened of the police to tell the truth? Or scared that if she turned Arthur in, he'd eventually hurt her worse?"

"Yes, all that's possible. But there's nothing you and I can do about it anymore. You understand that, don't you?"

"Yeah," I said. And I meant it. Until we hung up and I was still thinking about Arthur Lindt and his stepdaughter.

Maybe Sam was wrong. Maybe there was something I could do.

# 25

Everything began to unravel after I got off the phone with Sam. For the next three days, the forces I'd set in motion buffeted me back and forth from despair and despondency and finally into action.

It started that Wednesday night with two calls I received, the first from Olivia.

"What happened with the detective?" she asked.

"The child didn't admit anything."

"I'm sorry," she said, and then continued. "I'm sorry about what happened the other morning too. Before this turns into some monumental argument, with both of us getting caught up in being right, why don't we meet for lunch tomorrow?"

I didn't want to talk about Paul anymore, but I agreed. Like Olivia, I didn't want our anger to fester and grow. I knew only too well how emotions that we don't confront can take on gigantic proportions.

The second call that night was from Jack. Our conversation was fine, so long as we were talking about Lindt.

"The police really do have ways of talking to sexual abuse victims to put them at ease," he said, trying to convince me.

"Since when do you have faith in the police? You're a cynic, remember?"

"In a situation like this, you have no alternative but to believe they know what they're doing."

"Great. So what am I supposed to do now?" I asked.

"Nothing. Forget about it. You're not in a position to do anything."

"Jack, what if I agreed to meet him so I could get him to confess and—"

"Absolutely not," he said interrupting. "Are you crazy? What if he's some kind of lunatic? You could get yourself killed!"

"I can't just walk away. I keep thinking about that girl and imagining what she's going through."

"Julia, the police don't believe there's anything going on. Trust them."

I was silent.

"What does Sam think?" Jack asked.

"I thought you didn't approve of Sam," I countered.

"I don't disapprove of him. Let's say I'm wary of him and I'm jealous of him," Jack said.

"Well, I know why you're wary, but why are you jealous? Because he flirts with me?"

"No, because you flirt back."

Our dialogue came to a standstill. The night Jack had spent in New York was now an obstacle between us.

"Jack, was that flirting in the cab?" I asked.

"What do you think?"

For a few seconds neither of us said anything, and then I rushed to fill in the silence. "It's not what you think with Sam. It's just that his life is about sexual function and dysfunction, so it's impossible to be around him and not think about sex. But when I close my eyes and imagine being with someone, it's never Sam."

"Who is it?" he asked.

"Besides, the last person I need in my life is another thera-pist . . . ," I rambled. "You know, I've never not lived with a thera-pist, except for the one year I was at college. The year I had a nervous breakdown. On second thought . . ." I was joking, so we both laughed, but it was forced. When it died, another silence remained.

"You didn't answer my question," Jack reminded me.

"What question was that?"

"Never mind. Julia, why didn't you call me back that night when you got home? Was Paul there?"

I thought about how much easier it would be to just lie and say Paul had been home, but I'd always told Jack the truth—it was part of the fabric of our relationship. "No, he wasn't there."

"So, why didn't you call?" he demanded.

"I was afraid of what might happen." I felt the dull pain of an-other headache reaching out and gripping me.

"But you weren't afraid in the cab."

How could I explain when I didn't even understand? "We'd both had too much to drink."

"Don't . . ." His confusion had turned to anger and I knew then I'd made a mistake suggesting what had gone on could be so easily dismissed. But I didn't know how to make reparations. Nervously, I started to ramble again. "At least you don't have to worry about Sam's running a prostitution ring anymore."

"Why's that?" he asked.

"Well, he never would have been willing to meet with the police if he were doing anything wrong. He certainly wouldn't have let them come to the institute."

"Not necessarily. If he's convinced himself that what he's doing isn't wrong, he could pull off a meeting like that without any prob-lem."

"You always have an answer, don't you?" I couldn't keep the edge out of my voice.

"No, I always have a question."

We'd come to another dead end in the conversation. "How's your article going?" I asked, to fill in this silence.

"It's going swimmingly." His flippancy was as annoying as my headache.

"And how's your garden?"

"Full of fruit. How are your orchids?" He continued the meaningless banter.

"The flowers are fine, but today they finished enclosing the ninth floor of that new building down the block. Soon my sun will be completely cut off and I'll have to invest in an entirely artificial light system."

"That's really a shame," he said sarcastically.

"Jack, what are we doing?" I finally asked.

"Are you sure you want to hear my answer? You might not like what I have to say." He sounded far away.

"Then I don't want to hear it. Not tonight."

"Good night, then," he said, as if it didn't matter anyway, and abruptly ended the call.

As soon as I had hung up, I wanted to call him back, to listen to whatever he had to say, but I didn't. Those repulsive images of Arthur Lindt and his stepdaughter had returned and I couldn't shake them.

Since Paul was away and I wasn't hungry, there was no reason for me to make dinner. I tried to read but kept getting up to prowl my own apartment, sucked in by what sounded like sighs, what seemed to be shadows: all tricks of my unconscious. Finally I got into bed. I lay there, trying to fall asleep, counting the hours until morning when the dangerous time would be over and I thought Arthur would go to work and his stepdaughter went to school. How was he hurting her? *Stop*, I admonished myself. But I couldn't. The questions were as pervasive and constant as drums beating out a warning.

The next morning I was anxious and distracted. I drank too much coffee and continually checked the time. Olivia's secretary called and gave me the address where we were meeting for our reconciliation lunch. The restaurant was near Paul's and my bank, and I had promised Max to retrieve his mother's watch from the vault so he could give it to Betsy for her birthday. Even if the errand kept my mind off Lindt and his stepdaughter for only a half hour, it would be a welcome respite.

I gave the cab driver the bank's address on 55th Street and Avenue of the Americas, but because the traffic was so snarled, I got out on Fifth and walked west through the flood of office workers on their lunch break.

Because of the hour, the bank was jammed. Annoyed I'd picked such a busy time, I thought about leaving, but I was so rarely in that part of town. It was worth waiting rather than making another trip another day. *Maybe I shouldn't be getting the watch at all*, I thought, *at least not without asking Paul.* But Anne's things belonged to Max, didn't they? Shouldn't I respect Max's right to make up his own mind? Shouldn't Paul respect mine?

I was finally ushered into the bowels of the bank by Mr. Troy, the bank officer who, as usual, checked my signature, took my key, and then preceded me into the vault. After extracting my box, he set me up in a small square cubicle furnished with only a desk, a chair, and a fluorescent light. He left after asking if there was anything I needed, shutting the door behind him.

The artificially circulated air was too cold and I left my coat on. It made me clumsy as I opened the gray metal box. I pushed aside the various manila envelopes inside the box before unearthing the silk pouch I was looking for. Spilling Anne Sterling's abundant jewelry on the leather desktop, I sifted through the jumble of tangled chains, pearls, rings, bracelets, and pins—all cool to my touch—until I found the simple watch Max had asked for. Still fairly new, its alligator band was stiff, its gold-rimmed rectangular face unscratched. I slipped the watch into my bag, put the rest of the jewelry back in the pouch, and then put the pouch back in the box. I was ready to shut the box's lid when I noticed one of the manila envelopes was opened.

*Birthday bonds* it said in my loopy handwriting. Inside were the bearer bonds my parents still sent me every May 16th. When I lifted it up, the envelope felt light, so I reached inside and pulled out the engraved certificates. There should have been thirty. Thirty one thousand–dollar bonds. Instead, there were five.

Besides me, Paul was the only other person with access to the vault. But he wouldn't have done anything with my bonds. I must have put them in the wrong envelope. So I took out every envelope in the box and systematically examined each one. Still, I couldn't find the bonds.

Despite the cold air inside the room, sweat dripped down my back. I opened the door and called over the bank officer.

"Are you done, Mrs. Sterling?" Mr. Troy inquired.

"Do you keep a record of who takes out this box?" I asked.

"Yes, it's all on file. Would you like to see it?"

My visit that day had already been recorded in Mr. Troy's precise handwriting. On the line above that—dated three weeks earlier—was a similar notation, indicating Paul had been there. Was it possible Paul had done something with my bonds?

Bearer bonds aren't registered. Whoever has possession of them can cash them in. Could Paul have taken them and cashed them in?

The bank officer was standing, waiting. A few blocks away, Olivia was in a restaurant, also waiting.

"Do you have a phone I could use?" I asked. Mr. Troy showed me to his office and left me alone once again. When Paul's secretary answered, she told me he was in Boston. I took down the number of the Boston office and then called there. The woman who answered the phone said Paul was in a meeting. I insisted she interrupt him.

"Is it an emergency?" she asked.

I told her it was. Thirty seconds later, Paul was on the phone.

"Julia, what's wrong? Is it Max?" His voice was strained.

"No, Max is fine. But I'm at the bank—and almost all my bonds are missing."

"That's why you called? I thought it was an emergency. I thought there was an accident." Mixed in with his relief was impatience.

"It is an emergency. I'm missing twenty-five thousand dollars in bonds."

"This isn't a good time, Julia. I'm in the midst of a meeting. I'll call you when—"

"Paul, did you cash my bonds?"

His voice remained steady and calm, probably for the benefit of everyone in his office. "I should be getting back to my hotel by about seven or eight tonight; I'll speak to you then."

"No. Tell me now. Did you take them?" I was shouting.

He must have turned away from everyone for some privacy because his voice was lower and harder to hear when he answered. "I didn't think I had to discuss every trivial financial decision I make with you."

"It's my goddamn money. How could you just take it without asking me?" I slammed my hand down on the desk and heard a crack. I'd split a papier-mâché paperweight probably made by Mr. Troy's child for him. The sight of the broken gift only infuriated me more. "You don't have the fucking right to take what belongs to me! You don't own me, you son of a bitch!"

"Julia, you're getting hysterical. I want you to calm down. We'll discuss this tonight," he said, and hung up before I could respond.

～

Olivia had picked a restaurant chic enough to be busy but quiet enough so we could talk.

"Hey, what's the matter?" she asked when I sat down.

We were supposed to be there to repair a rift that revolved around Paul. How could I tell her what I'd just discovered?

"I know you, sweetie." She searched my face. "Something awful has happened. What is it?"

I'd lost my bearings. Only Olivia, sitting opposite me, talking to me, kept me at all centered. "What is it, Julia?" she asked again. And because I could see her heart in her eyes, I confided in her.

"What are you going to do?" she asked when I was done explaining and had regained some of my equilibrium.

"That's why you're my friend—you didn't ask me how I feel."

"I already know that from looking at you," she said.

I drank some of the wine that Olivia must have ordered for me without my being aware of it. "He acted as if I were the one who'd done something wrong. He's angry at me for expecting him to discuss every financial decision with me. Christ! He is so good at twisting the truth around. And I'm so damn sick and tired of it."

When the food arrived, I just moved my salad around on the plate. While Olivia ate, she apologized for riding me so hard the other day, and I laughed sardonically. "But you were right after all to warn me, weren't you? If Paul has stolen my money, God knows what else he's done. He very well might have put me in jeopardy."

"I don't want to be right."

"Oh, I know." I drank some more of my wine. "He didn't do this alone, though. I allowed him to treat me this way by willingly playing along with him, by being the obedient patient, the good wife, the fragile convalescent, by making up excuses for his emotional failures and believing my own inventions."

"Oh no. You're not going to take responsibility for what he's done." She was adamant. "That's exactly what he wants you to do."

I ached for all the time I'd crumpled up and tossed away.

As Olivia and I drank coffee, she tried to bolster me. A persistent image of a female child curled up on her bed, arms wrapped around her chest as she tried to protect herself, interfered with Olivia's pep talk.

It was me and it was Arthur Lindt's stepdaughter merged into one symbol of acquiescence. There was little she could do to alter her fate; she was only a child. But I wasn't.

"Come on. Let me go home with you," Olivia said, as she paid the check.

"No, I'm not going home; I want to go talk to the police."

"The police?" She was shocked.

I laughed, realizing the conclusion she'd reached. "No, not about Paul. But imagine that? Imagine my charging him with theft. How'd he like that to hit the papers right in the middle of his investigation? No, I want to go back and talk to that detective and see if I can't convince her to try just one more thing with Lindt."

~

The precinct house was on 65th Street halfway between Lexington and Third Avenues, sandwiched between a firehouse and a Russian Orthodox church. I climbed up worn stone steps, opened the door, and walked into a building that was at least fifty years old. Inside, there was a certain comfort to the beat-up wood floors and old-fashioned windows and benches. Policemen and -women moved through the main room with bustling efficiency, and it took several minutes to find anyone to direct me to Detective Fontenella's office.

She saw me right away but was curt. "What can I do for you . . . Miss Carroll, wasn't it?" She was suspicious of everything about me, including my name.

Her office was a small, cramped space cluttered with papers. There wasn't a bare inch of space on her desk. Several child's drawings were tacked up on the wall. Tucked into the corner of a framed diploma was a photograph of a ten-year-old little girl with her mother's strong features and dark coloring.

"I can't stop thinking that maybe Arthur Lindt's stepdaughter was too frightened to tell you the truth."

"If she was hiding something, I would have noticed."

"I'm sure you would have." I took a breath. "But isn't it possible even an expert might be fooled if the girl was hiding something because it was a matter of her survival?" I asked. *I'd* done it, hadn't I? I'd hid so much from my parents to get their approval and then done the same with Paul. They were therapists, yet they'd never guessed.

"My professional experience proves otherwise," Toni Fontenella said with disdain, and moved one pile of papers on top of another. "It's unfortunate you heard this man's false confession, but I suppose that's your job. Now, if you don't mind, I have work to do."

"Do you think my job is that disgusting?" I demanded.

"Yes, I do. Every time you pick up the phone and talk dirty chatter to some john, you degrade women."

"Because I listen to lonely men who finally have an opportunity to work out their fantasies, to connect without fear of disease, without hurting anyone?" I was surprised how much I sounded like Sam.

"You might be able to justify what you do, but don't ask me to."

"I would have thought that working with people in trouble would make you more sympathetic." I spat the words out as if they tasted bad.

"I'm sympathetic to real victims, Miss Carroll. Not to women or men who set themselves up to be victims. Selling sex is your prerogative. Mine is to think that the system you're perpetuating stinks. You're reinforcing a stereotype and catering to the lowest common denominator."

"I'm on the other end of a phone, Detective."

She was no longer trying to control her anger. "Is there really any difference between that and strutting down Eleventh Avenue, picking up guys in cars?"

"None of this is the point. It doesn't matter whether you understand what I do. Just let me help you catch this guy. I can meet him at some hotel and you can set up video cameras or whatever it is you use and film him confessing. Show that to his stepdaughter. Maybe if she knows he's told someone else, she'll be less frightened to tell someone herself."

"That's not police procedure."

"But it's not illegal, is it? It can't be entrapment when he asked *me* to meet him. He even offered to pay me. And you're not going to use the tape as evidence in court—just show it to his stepdaughter."

"I don't need you—" She was close to losing her temper.

"What do you have to lose?" I interrupted. "What if this one time your instincts were wrong? What if she was just too damn frightened to tell you the truth?"

"We appreciate your interest. Thank you for coming down here." As far as she was concerned, she'd dismissed me and was free to return to the paperwork on her desk.

I started to walk out and then stopped.

"Detective Fontenella, let me ask you something. If she was your daughter, wouldn't you want someone to make the extra effort, regardless of the goddamn procedure?"

She picked up her head, and for one moment, our eyes met. That's when I left.

~

In the cab on the way home, I noticed the city was getting ready for the onslaught of the approaching holidays. Red and green decorations were appearing in window displays and lights were strung through the limbs of the trees in front of the expensive boutiques on Madison Avenue.

Thanksgiving was only three weeks away. For the rest of the ride, I tried to concentrate on Max's homecoming instead of on a fourteen-year-old girl I didn't know and would never meet.

# 26

For the rest of that day I sat in my greenhouse, incapable of action. I ignored my notes, my flowers, and the phone, even when I knew it was Paul calling. I listened to him leave a message that he'd be home the following evening, but he made no reference to our earlier conversation.

That night I was still jumpy, waiting for . . . I don't know what, exactly, but my anxiety level was so high everything made me uncomfortable. The air was too thick now that heat was being blasted from the radiators, so I opened all the windows. Then the rooms were freezing. Unable to warm up, I piled on sweat clothes and then, still shivering, climbed into my bed and tried to go to sleep. But the questions were there, waiting for me.

Was Lindt with his stepdaughter now? And if he was, was he hurting her?

And nothing I could do—not turning on the television or playing soothing music—chased them away.

In the morning, I looked out the window in the greenhouse and was eye level with workers covering the steel skeleton with concrete. I examined the darkness that filled my apartment instead of sun. It wasn't just the encroaching winter or the loss of light due to the construction. I wasn't seeing the light

Alice Carroll might be sexually alive, an explorer, a woman empowered by her own capabilities, but I wasn't and I was jealous of her. Alice would have been able to convince Detective Fontenella to do something. She would have known what to say to Paul and how to give Jack what he wanted without risking what we'd been on the verge of discovering about each other.

Walking by a mirror, I stared at my face. My eyes looked tired and dull. And when I touched my skin, I was surprised at how dry it was. Like all those dead leaves in the park. I ran a bath, poured in bath oil, then soaked in the hot water. I even scrubbed my skin with a loofah and rubbed on body lotion. Nothing helped.

When Jack called, he asked me what was wrong. I blamed the apartment building going up across the street. I told him I was worried the orchids would suffer from the lack of direct light, that I was disheartened by the coming winter and distracted by not being able to help Lindt's stepdaughter.

"You're losing something, Julia. You're slipping backward."

I only nodded at the phone, afraid to say anything, afraid to talk to him too long lest I start to remember too much—the touch of his mouth, the smell of scotch and cotton in the back of the taxi, and the clenching deep in my stomach when he whispered against my neck.

Around three that afternoon I went to the library, where I pulled out gardening books and stepped into the photographs of foliage and flowers. I walked through secret gardens of Venice and pocket parks in Paris, but my escape was over as soon as the library closed.

Outside, it was raining and windy. Since I didn't have an umbrella, I wrapped my scarf around my head and ran the five blocks home, but I was still soaking and chilled when I got there.

Opening the front door to my apartment, I found all the lights on and Paul's suitcase in the foyer.

I followed the sound of his voice into the kitchen where he stood, a can of Coke in one hand, a glass of ice in the other.

"You have the right number"—he was on the phone—"but the wrong party. There's no one with that name living here." He hung up.

"Hello," I said.

He turned. "Hi." He didn't smile. "Where were you? Why are you wet? You could catch cold like that."

"I was at the library. I walked home."

"It's dark out, not safe."

"I carry a perfume atomizer so if anyone approaches me I can just spray them in the face. It's supposed to sting like hell and give me some time to get away."

"That's ridiculous, Julia. If anyone came up behind you, you wouldn't have the strength to fight them off. Just give them whatever they want. Don't try to be brave."

How ironic. With him, I'd been anything but brave. "Paul, why did you cash my bonds?"

"If I knew you were going to be so irrational—"

"Don't you dare turn this around. I'm not being irrational, over-wrought, overemotional, or inappropriate. You stole twenty-five thousand dollars from me."

He poured the rest of the soda in the glass and drank half of it in one gulp. "I'm your husband. What we have, we share. Have I ever questioned you about how you spend the money I earn?"

"We're talking about twenty-five thousand dollars. What did you take it for? Why did you need it?"

But Paul didn't answer me. Instead, he took another drink and inspected me with his clinical gaze.

Enraged, I grabbed the soda can off the counter and flung it across the room. After smashing into the wall, it fell to the floor and rolled under a cabinet. "Tell me what you did with the money!" I screamed.

"Over the last few years I've had to borrow money from FIT to supplement our income: to rent the summer house, to send Max to school, and to pay dues at the club. Our lawyers felt it would be wise to pay off the loan before we turn our numbers over to the IRS," he said, and slammed his glass down so hard on the countertop I thought it was going to break. "Now if the inquisition is over, I'm going to make some calls in my office," he said, and walked out.

I stood in my kitchen for a few minutes, trying to calm down. It was done. The money was spent. What did it matter? Paul taking my bonds without asking me wasn't that significant. It wasn't indicative of how we lived our lives together.

But of course it was. How could I pretend otherwise? How could I fool myself into believing I was being too sensitive again? Hands shaking, I made myself a cup of peppermint tea and was throwing away the tea bag when the phone rang.

"Hello," I said. My throat was sore and my voice was slightly hoarse from screaming.

"Is this Alice Carroll?" It was a woman's voice.

"What? Yes," I said, confused because the call hadn't come in on my private line.

"This is Detective Fontenella. Sam Butterfield gave me this number, but when I called a few minutes ago, the man who answered the phone didn't know anyone by your name."

Sam must have inadvertently given the detective our home number instead of my private number. Perhaps it was a fortuitous mistake. The lies had multiplied and had grown so large they were suffocating me. I'd had enough. It was time for the truth. "That's because Alice Carroll isn't my real name. Dr. Butterfield gave you the name I use with clients in order to protect me."

"From whom?" she asked.

"My husband. That's who answered the phone. My real name is Julia Sterling."

"Your husband doesn't know about the work you're doing with Dr. Butterfield?"

"That really isn't any of your business, is it, Detective?"

"No. I'm sorry. I called because you . . . were so upset yesterday I went back through my interview with Lindt's stepdaughter." For the first time, she no longer sounded arrogant. "And I wanted to tell you everything checked out. There really doesn't seem to be any reason to pursue this case. Except we can never be too careful. So if you're still willing to go ahead, I'd like to talk to you about your idea."

"All that matters is that you help the girl."

After we made plans to meet at her office the next morning, I hung up. When I turned around, I found Paul standing in the doorway staring at me.

"Why were you talking to the police?" He looked frightened. Had he, like Olivia, jumped to the wrong conclusion? For one sick moment, I contemplated telling him I'd reported the theft and turned him in.

"Don't worry, Paul; it had nothing to do with you."

He relaxed. "You know, a detective called here before you got home, but she was looking for someone named Carol. No, it was Alice Carroll. She insisted she had the right number. Was it the same detective?"

"Yeah." I nodded.

"Do you know someone named Alice Carroll?"

So this was how he was going to find out, standing in our kitchen, having overheard a few words of a telephone conversation. I felt oddly peaceful as I explained all that had happened since that night at the Botanical Garden almost two months before.

At some point, Paul sat down on a kitchen stool, but I remained standing as if making a presentation. When I finished, he asked me the kinds of questions a doctor would ask a patient.

"How did it feel to make the calls? How did it feel to get paid? Were you aware you were acting out your inhibitions? How did it feel to consciously go against your husband's wishes?" he finally asked, referring to himself in the third person. The quintessential shrink, he revealed no anger, no rage. The only sign of his distress was a pale blue vein throbbing in his neck.

After he'd asked his questions and I'd given my answers, Paul sat there, still and silent for a few moments, while I waited.

"Julia," he began in the same calm voice, "you understand you can't write this book anymore. And you certainly can't go forward with this plan to help the police get a confession out of this man's stepdaughter. Especially now that the detective knows your real name. I simply can't afford to be linked to any kind of scandal at this time. I thought I'd explained all this to you weeks ago, but obviously you chose to ignore me. You can't ignore me any longer. Do you understand? You must call this detective back and tell her you've changed your mind. Then call Sam Butterfield and tell him you've changed your mind about writing the book with him. And then go rip up every single one of your notes."

I'd been given only half an ultimatum. Obviously, he expected me to obey, to be the agreeable wife and excellent patient he'd always counted on.

"No fucking way!" I shouted.

He was stunned. "Don't you understand? You're my wife. You can't want to subject me to—"

"This has nothing to do with you," I shouted, interrupting.

"If you expect us to have a marriage, you have to show me you're worthy of my trust. You have to do what I'm asking." Paul stood up, took the phone off the receiver, and held it out to me. "Call the detective, Julia."

But I didn't take the phone.

So this was how our marriage would end.

I'd always known the end would come, but I'd never been able to imagine how it would happen. I'd never envisioned myself having the courage to tell Paul it was over or taking the first steps to dissolve it. I'd never imagined it would be as simple as keeping my hands by my sides.

"I won't call the detective, Paul. A child may be in danger. I can't turn my back on her because you're worried it might reflect badly on your reputation. That's ridiculous. What harm could you suffer if anyone knew I'd helped the police expose a child abuser?"

"You're being naïve." He was no longer the therapist but a man who was discovering he'd lost all his control over his wife. "There are thousands of children being abused every minute; you can't do anything about them. You can't solve the world's problems. All you can do is screw things up for me."

"What a hypocrite you are. The noble humanitarian, Dr. Paul Sterling. What the fuck did you become a therapist for if you didn't believe you could help people solve their problems?"

I took a step to leave, but Paul reached out and grabbed me, his fingers digging into my wrist.

"Where did you take those calls, Julia? Here in my home? In my bed?" He was snarling, his lips curled back in a grotesque grimace.

"Yes."

"You need help. You desperately need help." His voice was riddled with disgust.

Pulling me closer to him, he shoved me in front of the phone. "For Christ's sake, Julia, call that detective. Call her and tell her you've changed your mind. Don't do this to me. I forbid you to meet that man. You're only deluding yourself that you can help."

I wrested free and ran out, past Max's room, through our bedroom, and into the bathroom, where I locked the door and slumped down on the cold tile floor. Leaning against the wall, I stared up at the white ceiling and listened. I was waiting to see if he'd followed me. To see if he was going to pound at the door and scream at me to let him in. To do any of the things I would have expected a man to do.

We'd both lied to each other about so many things. Of all the lies, the worst was the one I'd told over and over, through all the years we'd been together. I had pretended to be someone I wasn't. I had paid lip service, as Sam had said, to being the kind of wife Paul wanted. I'd thought that by keeping the nether parts of myself hidden, they'd cease to exist. How wrong I'd been.

When I finally left the bathroom, the bedroom was dark and empty, and from down the hall came the violent sounds of another brutal television movie. After shutting the door, I crawled into bed.

And then I did make a phone call—not to the detective canceling our meeting but to Sam.

He was surprised I had decided to help the police, but he was supportive. "Have you told Paul?" he finally asked.

"Let's say he isn't exactly encouraging me."

"Fucking asshole," Sam muttered. "If you don't mind," he continued, "I'd like to go with you tomorrow, all right?"

~

That night, for the first time all week, I was able to fall asleep without worrying about a child I'd never met.

Accompanied by Sam, I went to Detective Fontenella's office at eleven that Saturday. Paul went to play tennis.

Sam had more at stake than Paul if the institute's name were linked to the investigation, but if he was concerned, he didn't show it. During the entire hour and a half we spent with Detective Fontenella, Sam was interested only in what the police would be doing to protect me and subdue Lindt if it became necessary.

According to the plan the detective and her staff had worked out, I was supposed to call Mr. Lindt the following Monday morning and tell him I'd decided to help him. I was supposed to suggest a hotel and offer to lay out the money for the room so he wouldn't have to put the charge on his card. With my controlling where and when we'd meet, the police could choose the hotel and set up the rooms: one for Arthur and me, another for them and their video equipment. We all discussed what I should do if Arthur hedged about my making so many of the decisions. Sam said if the man was indeed troubled, he probably wouldn't focus on the specifics.

I listened to everyone finesse the details, but I didn't ask any questions. Alice Carroll didn't need my intervention.

Finally, at the end of the meeting, Detective Fontenella turned to me. "Julia, we're going to be there if he threatens you, but short of that, you're on your own. Can you handle it?"

I didn't know. It wouldn't be as safe as talking on the phone. There would be no separation between us. I'd hear his voice and see his face. He was going to have a scent and solidity. He was going to be a real man whom I might have to touch.

As Sam and I left the police station, I faltered on the top step and put my hand on the iron balustrade, which was so cold it stung my skin.

"Sam, what makes someone want to hurt a child?"

"We don't completely understand why people need to hurt other people. Too often, all we can do is use behavior modification to make the act less exciting," Sam explained.

"Where is the girl's mother when Arthur's with her?"

"In many of these situations, the mother acts as the enabler, ignoring all the signals. It fits her agenda to remain uninvolved, to keep her husband occupied."

"Is that why the girl hasn't told her mother?" I asked.

"That, plus the girl may love Arthur. Even though he hurts her, he's probably wonderful to her in other ways, confusing her so she can't separate all the different feelings she has for him."

"Sam, I don't know anything about pain," I said.

"You must know an awful lot about it or you wouldn't be doing this," he said.

We started toward the corner. "No, I know about keeping secrets. About not being yourself because you're frightened of the consequences. But not about the kind of pain I might have to inflict."

"It's all right if you're scared."

I laughed. "Scared? No, this is much more than just some free-floating anxiety. It's more than going to that hotel room too. Paul basically ordered me not to come here today. Not to write the book."

"Why don't you wait until all this is over before you decide about the book," Sam suggested.

"No, giving up the book would be as bad as abandoning Lindt's stepdaughter."

"I'm proud of you," he said, and smiled.

"Sam, it's going to be horrible in that room, isn't it?" I asked him.

All he could do was nod his head yes.

# 27

The bar was in a quietly respectable business hotel in Midtown. I saw his tentative approach in the mirror above the multiple shelves of bottles and glasses. He was a big man with slightly hunched shoulders and a paunch. In the dim lights, he looked about fifty. Hesitating, he ran his hand through his curly reddish hair as he looked up and down the bar and then took a step in my direction. There was a sheen of perspiration on his pale, freckled skin.

"Alice?"

I recognized his voice as it surged through me like a jolt of electricity. I jerked around on the bar stool. "Yes," I answered.

"I'm Arthur Lindt." He was so ordinary looking. Just a middle-level executive carrying a briefcase, about to have a drink with a heavily made-up blonde in a black skirt, black silk shirt, and high-heeled boots.

Or was he also in disguise?

"Why don't you sit down and have a drink." I indicated the seat to my right. I watched him in the mirror, clasping my hands in my lap so he wouldn't see them trembling.

"That's a good idea. A drink." He signaled the bartender and ordered a scotch on the rocks and then turned to me. His eyes were a washed-out green, slightly bloodshot. "So . . ." He pulled a red-and-white box of Marlboro cigarettes out of his jacket and, using a silver lighter with a Mexican design on the case, lit the first of many cigarettes that would be lit that evening.

Sam had suggested I give myself some time with Lindt in a public place before going up to the room. "Be clear with him about what you want, Julia. Tell him to have a drink, to sit on your right, not your left, that you're not ready to go upstairs, or that you are. Just assert your will. Make sure he understands you have one. You don't know what he might ask you to do once you get upstairs. You need to be able to say no and have him know you fucking mean it."

Arthur Lindt took a large gulp of his drink and inhaled his cigarette.

"Can I have one of those?" I asked.

"You smoke? You don't have a smoker's voice." Was he always this suspicious?

"I'm not a chain smoker, if that's what you mean, but every once in a while I like one. "

He opened the box, offered it to me, and then rolled his thumb along the bar of his lighter and extended the flame. As I looked up, our eyes met. Was there a message there, or just a man's pale green eyes fringed by long red lashes?

"I have to admit I was surprised you agreed to help me," he said, as he tapped an inch of gray ash into a china ashtray emblazoned with the hotel's insignia.

"Yeah. To tell you the truth, I was surprised too. I've never done anything like this." I'd decided to be as honest with him as I could so he wouldn't be suspicious of my extreme nervousness.

He assessed me. "No?"

I shook my head and took a drag off the cigarette.

"You talk to men on the phone all day. No one's ever asked you to meet them before?"

"Yeah, sure, men have asked, but I've always said no."

"You're not what I thought you'd be." He was staring at my hands. I'd taken off the wide wedding ring and the gold watch I usually wore and my fingers and wrist looked bare. Rather than curl my hands up and draw even more attention to them, I lifted my glass and brought it to my mouth.

"What did you think I'd be like?" I asked.

"Not so delicate. Taller. Broader. Big hair. Big tits." He crushed his cigarette out so violently I flinched, but he didn't notice. He was already lighting another.

Was I in trouble here? Had it been a mistake to come? "That's what's so great about using the phone—you can imagine anyone you want into existence." I willed myself to sound blasé.

He shrugged. "What I wish is that I could imagine someone out of existence."

As it got closer to six o'clock, the bar filled up with more men and women who had Arthur's worn-out and weary end-of-another-day look. It was five fifty-five. The police had been upstairs in room 530 since four that afternoon. I'd gone there first with Detective Fontenella, who had introduced me to a plainclothes policeman and policewoman. I had looked through the video camera into room 532 and seen the bed and the chair next to it through the lens.

Arthur drained his drink and put it down on the bar. The noise of the ice cubes hitting the glass made me shiver. *This too shall pass*, I thought, calling upon my old mantra for the first of many times that afternoon. It didn't help.

"You want 'nother?" the bartender asked Arthur, but I answered for both of us. "No, we'll take a check."

I let Arthur pay and then preceded him out of the bar, leading him across the small lobby, and then we waited with three other people for the elevator. When the doors opened, I procrastinated and got on last. Once several of us had pressed the buttons for our respective floors, the doors slid shut.

The small box was stifling and I was having a hard time getting enough air in my lungs. Afraid my rising anxiety would spiral, I tried to take a deep breath without attracting too much attention. Meanwhile Arthur looked down at his shoes.

I'd almost hoped the elevator would skip five or that somehow the fifth floor would magically disappear, but it didn't. When the doors opened, I got off first and Arthur followed me.

The elevator shut behind us. We were alone in the hall and the quiet intimidated me. What would happen if I was wrong, if Arthur did try to hurt me? Or worse, tried to have sex with me? *Relax*, I said to myself. *The police will be next door; only seconds away. Nothing will go wrong.*

Approaching the room, I fished in my bag for the key. The metal key hitting the plastic disc embossed with the hotel's name was the only sound in the long, lonely hallway.

On the floor, in front of 534, was a room-service tray with a half-eaten piece of chocolate cake, an empty cup, a china tea set, and a rose in a silver bud vase. Just the ordinary remnants of a snack. Walking by, I wished I could exchange places with whoever was behind that door, probably doing something as unexciting as napping.

Twisting the key in the lock, I opened the door, felt for the switch, and turned on the lights. The room spread out before us. To the right, against the wall, loomed a king-size bed. By comparison, the other furniture—a desk, a bureau, an easy chair—was insignificant.

Arthur walked directly to the floor-to-ceiling windows and fixated on the view.

"I'm kind of nervous . . . ," I said as I dropped my bag on the bureau. "I told you, didn't I? I've never met anyone I talked to on the phone before. But you really sounded like you needed help."

"Yeah," he said, as he took another cigarette and lit it.

I was leaning against the bathroom door. He'd moved over to the desk to use the ashtray. "Can we get the money out of the way?" he asked.

"What?" For a moment, I'd forgotten I was supposed to be getting paid.

"Money. The two hundred. And the money for the room. Don't you want it?"

"Sure. Yeah," I told him.

He put the cigarette back up to his lips, inhaled, exhaled, rested it in the ashtray, took a white bank envelope from his breast pocket, and handed it to me. Did he expect me to check that it was all there? I flipped through the bills, nodded, and dropped the envelope in my bag.

Twilight had turned the sky a bruised, purplish gray. Clouds moved swiftly above the office building facing the hotel. Hundreds of yellow squares stared at us like unblinking eyes. After searching for the cord, Arthur pulled the drapes closed and the sound of the fabric fanning out whooshed through me like a sharp wind.

"What do you want me to do?" I was still standing, leaning up against the wall. My legs were shaking so badly I didn't think I could remain upright without support.

"What I do to her," he said, as he walked toward the bed and switched on the reading light.

"Who is she?" I asked.

Detective Fontenella had emphasized the need for him to identify the child on tape.

"My stepdaughter. I already told you that."

I watched Lindt put his cigarettes and lighter on the nightstand, take off his jacket, drop it on the recliner, untie his tie, drop that on top of his jacket, then do the same with his shirt, his pants, shoes, and socks. He'd left on only his shorts. Lindt had undressed as if he were alone, as if I weren't really there. The only other person in the room with him was his stepdaughter.

Maybe after all, he had been truthful about why he wanted to meet me. He certainly wasn't acting as if he'd lured me there for sexual pleasure. Lindt was behaving like a condemned man about to face sentencing.

But then, almost naked, he twisted around to face me, grimaced like a sick clown, and obscenely clutched his crotch.

My disgust was so overwhelming I thought I was going to

scream. I felt the sound of it fill my chest. I felt the vomit rise in my throat. I'd been crazy to come here. Lindt was deranged and I was in danger. How quickly could a man hurt a woman? Kill her with his hands? Faster than it would take the police to run through a door?

He'd turned away from me and was pulling down the bedspread. Then he lay down on top of the blanket. "Shut off that light and come here," he directed.

Without the bright light, the ordinary room became even more ominous. Shadows leaped up from the corners and the large man on the bed lurked like a forbidding giant. Forcing myself to go to him, I moved in some kind of torturously slow motion.

"Sit down," he said, indicating a spot on the edge of the bed, "where I sit with her." He, too, sounded nervous.

I sat down beside him. The flesh of his body was as pallid and freckled as the skin on his face. His legs, arms, and chest were covered with fine red hair. Under his shorts, he was not erect.

The air smelled suddenly putrid as the combined odors of stale tobacco and liquor rushed at me and my stomach heaved again. I didn't want to breathe.

"All right, what should I do?" I tried to speak normally, hoping he wouldn't notice my voice was quavering.

He turned on his stomach but twisted his head around to the right so he could instruct me. "I sit by the side of her bed and rub her back until she's really relaxed." Lindt shut his eyes and waited.

Some small part of me relaxed as I realized he wasn't going to ask me to get undressed. I don't know if I would have been able to have done that and been naked on the video.

"Rub your back?" I asked, stalling.

"Yes," he was impatient. "Everything I tell you I do to her, you do to me."

How was I going to touch his pasty skin? I put my hand halfway out and then gagged. This time I had a hard time swallowing what had come up.

"What's the matter, Alice? Afraid to touch the man?" His voice had taken on that odd, twisted tone he'd used over the phone when he was fully engaged in his fantasy.

Yes—Alice—I'd forgotten. I could make her take over for me. Alice would do what had to be done.

It was Alice's hand that reached out and her fingers that stroked Arthur Lindt's back. I focused on his stepdaughter, imagining the little girl being forced into bed with him. Picturing him rubbing her, lulling her, preparing her for what was to come, I regained some of my courage.

"Rub her whole back," Lindt said.

So together, Alice and I massaged all of his blanched, rubbery skin.

In hell, time does not pass. The nightmare repeats itself endlessly until you're just about to lose your mind. Oblivion would be too kind.

It seemed like fifteen or twenty minutes, but now I know it was only five minutes until he issued his next instruction. "I kiss her back. Up near her shoulders. She has a ticklish spot there and she likes how it feels. It excites her, even though she doesn't want to let it."

I shuddered. It was one thing to touch him with my fingers but not with my lips. How was I going to do what he was asking? I tried to convince myself this was not Arthur Lindt but one of those men I'd known in college whose last names I couldn't remember anymore. *It's just another one of them,* I repeated. *Just another one.*

"Alice, why have you stopped? The man is waiting. You don't want to make him angry, do you?"

The panic helped me force Alice to lean down and kiss his skin, this stranger's skin. Somehow I did it without vomiting all over him.

"I light a cigarette about now," he said.

It seemed such a harmless request, such a reprieve. With great relief, I lit the cigarette. God, it tasted good. Blowing the smoke out into the air, I watched the blue spiral dissipate.

"Okay, put the cigarette down. In that ashtray. Don't put it out—let it burn. Now that she's relaxed, I reach between her thighs and excite her until she starts to come."

He turned over on his back and was watching my face, so I tried not to react, but I was horrified. Somehow, I had convinced myself this was not going to be about sex—only pain.

"Once she starts coming," he continued, "I take the cigarette and press it against all that pretty pink flesh."

Recoiling, I moved away from him. "No. Oh no. I can't," I blurted out.

"You have to do it, Alice. Please," he said, halfway between a plea and a sob.

"What is your stepdaughter's name?" My voice was audibly shaking by now, but he didn't seem to care.

"Celia," he groaned.

With a name, I could give her a face, a voice, eyes full of horror, a mouth twisted in agony. I focused on her terrified face and didn't taste the bile in my mouth or feel my heart trying to burst through my ribs.

"Excite me, Alice. Make me hard. Then give me the pain. Give it to the monster. So the monster stops giving it to her. Will you?"

I agreed to his request. "Yes, all right." I was buying time, trying to figure out if he'd already admitted enough on the tape so I could quit.

"Alice? What's wrong?" He raised himself up on one elbow. "Aren't you going to make me come?"

"Yes. Yes, I will—"

Arthur Lindt interrupted me. "Okay," he said. The muscles in his face had tightened, his skin didn't seem as slack, and the madness in his eyes was replaced with calm conviction. Suddenly, he exuded a power he'd lacked before. Was it knowing that he was finally going to get what he wanted?

"Okay," he repeated, "that's it. I have a case. Julia Sterling, you're under arrest for engaging in prostitution," said the almost-naked man sitting on the bed beside me.

# 28

Like a kaleidoscope turning, all was chaos. The colors had lost their individuality in a blur and the pieces rearranged themselves, settling into a new pattern. I didn't know what I was looking at. Nothing made any sense.

How did Arthur Lindt know my real name? What game was he playing? When had the scenario shifted course? Before I even had a chance to react, he leaned down and reached under the bed. Almost simultaneously a streak of silver flashed in front of me and Lindt gripped my hands. I tried to wrest free, but he had me in a tight hold.

The metal clanged as it locked tight, cold steel encircling my wrists. I'd been handcuffed.

Why was he playing with this obscene toy?

Where were the police?

Why weren't they rushing in to protect me from this lunatic and the bizarre fantasy he was forcing me to act out?

"Are you nuts? Unlock these things. Help!" I must have been

yelling, because later that night, I would find that my throat was sore. "Help!" I shouted out again.

It's odd the things that stick in your mind. What I remember is the cigarette still smoldering in the ashtray and the bitter scent of a burning filter.

"Stop yelling in my ear, Mrs. Sterling. No one's coming to rescue you. I'm Detective Jim Luther, Nineteenth Precinct, badge number 443556. And you are under arrest."

I was still trying to absorb what he was saying when the two officers who'd been in the room next door entered—but they weren't rushing. Their guns weren't drawn. And instead of grabbing Lindt and protecting me from him, they flanked me.

Arthur Lindt stood up—he was still Arthur Lindt to me—and began to get dressed in the clothes he'd taken off only a short time before.

"Aren't you going to stop him? He's crazy!" I implored the policewoman.

"He's not crazy, Mrs. Sterling. *You* are under arrest. We're taking you down to the stationhouse," she said.

"Why? What's going on?" I turned to Arthur, who was buttoning his shirt. "What about the girl?"

"Let's go," was his only response.

*This too shall pass,* I mouthed silently, saying the words over and over, hoping they would at least clear my head so I could think logically. But the words didn't help.

Arthur—or rather Detective Luther—took my arm and ushered me out of the room. The two officers followed. In the hallway, we passed by the same tray of dessert remnants, still on the floor.

My hands were locked together in a clumsy embrace. And because the cuffs were cumbersome and threw my balance off, walking was awkward.

Waiting for the elevator, I leaned against the wall. Until the detective's arms lifted me up, I hadn't realized I'd slid to the floor. Forced to help me into the elevator, the same elevator we'd been in just a half hour before, Luther half pulled, half dragged me along with him. We were so close I could smell that nauseating combination of stale tobacco and liquor that clung to his skin and clothes.

Once the doors shut and I had a new wall to support me, Luther thankfully let go of me. Reaching into his pocket, he pulled out another pair of handcuffs and snapped them on his own wrists.

It seemed an insane act. Could I be hallucinating? Could the cigarette I had smoked have been laced with acid? In college, drugs had sent me over the edge of my imagination more than once.

"What are you doing?" I asked.

He hesitated, not sure if he should answer me. Shrugging—as if it didn't matter anymore—he explained: "You might have been followed here."

Like everything else that had happened, I didn't understand that either. "Who would have followed me? What are you talking about?"

"No more questions. From here on in, we ask the questions," Luther said, putting an end to any further conversation.

Instead of leaving through the main lobby, the policeman led us through the kitchen, where various chefs, waiters, and busboys stopped what they were doing to watch our progression. Now I understood why prisoners being transported are always photographed with their heads lowered—it's to avoid the heartless stares of strangers. People who know better have the nerve to gawk unmercifully when a supposed criminal is in their midst.

Our little troupe exited on the avenue about thirty feet down from the hotel's main entrance and moved en masse toward the curb where a police car waited. The policeman unlocked and opened the back door and pushed Luther inside.

I was next.

Bending to get in, I turned sideways and was able to see the hotel's façade. Detective Luther had been right. Someone *had* followed me. Sam was standing there. Right next to the hotel. Watching.

I froze. Maybe I could break free and run to Sam. He'd clear this up. The police would unlock my handcuffs and let me go.

Sam could see what was happening. So why wasn't he running over to help?

"C'mon, get in," the policeman ordered, and I slid into the seat.

Why hadn't Sam come to my aid? What was going on? I struggled to stop myself from screaming. I was Alice again and I'd fallen down the rabbit hole, landing in a place where nothing made sense.

During the ten minutes it took to get to the precinct house, I kept sane by repeating Jack's phone number to myself. *305-555-2323.* As soon as I got to the police station I would call him. He would get me a lawyer. I could trust him. *305-555-2323.* Was I crazy? I should be calling my husband. But I didn't want to talk to Paul. Not yet. I needed Jack. *305-555-2323.* I would call Jack. It would be more work for him to get me a New York lawyer, but he wouldn't mind.

What did it mean that I wasn't turning to my husband?

I couldn't think about that. *305-555-2323.* I was going to call Jack. Jack would know what to do.

But I didn't get a chance to make a phone call. As soon as we got to the stationhouse, the female cop took me right to a small, windowless room that contained four chairs and a scarred table littered with dirty coffee cups. In the corner was a cardboard box—opened and empty. Beside the box, old newspapers were stacked a foot high.

She told me to have a seat. There was a clock on the wall. How could it be ten to seven? Had only an hour passed since I'd met Lindt in the bar?

The door opened and a stranger walked in. He was medium height and balding and was wearing silver-rimmed glasses and street clothes. Detective Fontenella followed behind him and acknowledged me with a nod. In the last week, she'd ignored me, then treated me contemptuously, and then acted as if I were a coconspirator.

As she sat down opposite me, I couldn't yet tell how she was going to treat me now.

The man introduced himself and then sat down. "I'm Rob Hayley, assistant district attorney. You already know Detective Fontenella, I believe."

"I want to make a call. I need to get a lawyer," I demanded.

"Of course. You certainly are entitled to representation, but first, why don't you just sit back and listen. Allow us to explain what's going on," Hayley said.

I hesitated. Wasn't I supposed to have a lawyer no matter what? Didn't I need to protect myself?

"We're not going to ask you a single question. You don't have to say a word, Julia," Detective Fontenella said as she leaned forward toward me. Now I knew she was going to treat me like a friend. "I know how freaked out you must be, but if you'll just let us explain, we can clear everything up in a few minutes."

Taking my lack of response as acquiescence, Hayley began talking. "Although Detective Luther has arrested you for prostitution, our intent here is not to book you or to prosecute you."

"That's good, because I am certainly not a prostitute," I snapped. I focused on Detective Fontenella. "You know that. You helped me set this up so we could get Arthur to confess what he was doing. You helped me tape it. You were going to show the tape to his stepdaughter in hopes she'd finally admit what was going on, so you could arrest him. So you could protect her from him." I didn't care that I was rambling; I desperately wanted to understand.

"Julia, listen to me," Detective Fontenella said softly. "There is no stepdaughter. There is no Arthur Lindt." She waited to give me a moment to absorb this. In my head, I was rewinding my conversations with Arthur, from the first call I'd taken—when he'd wanted to be dominated—to what we had talked about in the hotel room before he'd asked me to masturbate him.

"Are you saying it was all a setup from the beginning?" I asked.

"Yes," she said firmly. "From the beginning, Detective Luther has been posing as Arthur Lindt." She took another pause. "We were lucky you were the one who took Arthur's first call. You were so sympathetic to his sickness, you made it easy for him."

My cheeks were burning. They'd all made a fool of me. "How

could you do that?" I screamed. "Why would you do that?" Forgetting I was restrained, I tried to gesticulate, but the cuffs cut into my skin and I winced.

"Officer Martin, please remove Mrs. Sterling's handcuffs," Rob Hayley ordered.

The locks opened with the same clicks I'd heard when Jim Luther had slapped them shut. Bringing my hands up, I clasped them together in my lap. My wrists were sore and I couldn't stop touching the places where the metal bracelets had been.

Rob Hayley continued the explanation. "Our intention was never to malign or mistreat you, Mrs. Sterling. But we needed assistance. The kind of assistance only you could supply.

"You have two choices. It's up to you which way we proceed. We can take you round the horn—" He could tell I had no idea what he was talking about, so he translated in layman's terms: "We can print you, book you, and take you down to the courthouse at 100 Centre Street for arraignment—or we can let you go.

"Which will it be? Do you want to walk out the back door— through court after you post bail—or walk out of our front door of the precinct house? Right now?"

While Hayley spoke, Detective Fontenella kept her eyes on me. I looked back and forth between them but kept silent. What were they saying? What did they want me to do?

"Don't you want to walk out of the front door, Julia?" Fontenella asked.

"I can't believe this! You really do things like this? You set people up and scare the fuck out of them to get them to help you?" I shouted.

Ignoring my outburst, Hayley addressed his next sentence to Fontenella. "Detective, spell out what we want Mrs. Sterling to do for us."

"Julia, we know that for the last three, three and a half years, Sam Butterfield has been running a prostitution ring out of the institute. But we need better evidence than we've been able to collect so far. All we want is for you to help us get inside so we can do our job."

I started to protest, to defend Sam, but Detective Fontenella interrupted me. "Think about what I'm saying, Julia. You have so much compassion for the underdog. Think of all the under-dogs he's taken advantage of. All the women—women like you—who he's convinced to risk their health, their dignity, and their self-esteem. Think of all the men he's fooled into believing that what he's offering is not only legal, but rehabilitating and recupera-tive."

"You want me to turn on him?" Despite what she'd said, Sam was still the same man who had, as Jack had put it, opened my eyes.

"All we're asking is for you to agree to make an introduction for us. Tell Sam about a woman you know, a friend of yours, who needs work and wants to train at the institute. That's it. She's undercover. We just need to get her inside. She'll do the rest," Fontenella con-cluded.

"I could never do it. Sam would know I set him up," I worried out loud.

"If it ever came to that, you could claim you were taken in by her too. But Sam is going to jail, Julia. You'll be the least of his prob-lems."

"Why can't this woman just apply for the job herself?" I asked.

"If it were that simple, we'd be in already."

"But Sam saw me leaving the hotel in handcuffs. Won't he be suspicious?" I asked.

"We prepared for that possibility, Julia. That's why the man Sam thinks is Lindt left the hotel in handcuffs too. You'll be able to explain everything."

I was trying to understand, but there was too much information to grasp all at once. Sam was guilty? Jack had been right? No. I trusted Sam. I'd listened to his philosophy, understood it, embraced it. And had been changed by it. Its precepts were neither corrupt nor lawless.

Detective Fontenella moved her chair forward so we were even closer. "If you help us, no one will ever find out what happened to-day. Not in the hotel. Not here. We haven't yet filed the criminal report, and if you help us, we won't file it. Without that report, there's no way the press can get hold of the story. There won't be a single news item on television. No scandals in the tabloids."

"There will be absolutely no leaks to the press alluding to your arrest for solicitation. Nothing at all to publicly embarrass you . . ."—Rob Hayley paused for emphasis—". . . or your husband."

What a scheme they had concocted. Once I gave Detective Fontenella my real name, she must have done her homework. When she found out I was married to a prominent man whose reputation was crucial to the job he did, she must have done a jig around her office. It gave them such a good bargaining tool. Either I cooperated or my husband would be disgraced and his stellar reputation besmirched. It was not even a veiled threat.

But that wasn't what impelled me to help them. It was the thought of Max that convinced me. I couldn't humiliate him. I wouldn't embarrass him. I had to protect him. Wasn't that why I'd committed the real crime of staying with his father all these years?

Once I'd agreed, the rest was simple. Detective Fontenella and I discussed what I would tell Sam about my experience in the hotel room, and she wrote down the name of the "friend" she wanted me to introduce to him.

Then she walked me down the hall.

"You've had a rough time, Julia," she said at the front doors. "I'm sorry we had to put you through this, but there was no other way. We truly appreciate your willingness to cooperate." She offered her hand, but I wouldn't shake it.

It was a frosty night and the bitter wind battered me as I walked down the station's stone steps to the street below. It didn't matter that I was shivering—the cold was refreshing, and I took big gulps of the air into my lungs as if it could wake me up from the inside out. But I still felt numb.

Despite the dark, I didn't hail a cab. I wanted to walk. I needed to walk and to think. So, shoving my bare hands into my coat pockets, I headed north on Lexington Avenue. I passed people on their way home from work and on their way out to dinner. A few feet ahead of me, a couple argued about whether to go to a Chinese or Italian restaurant. I envied their normalcy.

As I continued uptown, I rehashed everything that had been said at the police station. But I still couldn't accept that Sam was guilty.

Detective Fontenella had never offered me proof. All I knew for sure was that the institute allowed a man named Arthur Lindt to set up an account to talk to a therapist over the phone.

Neither Fontenella or Hayley had explained how they knew a prostitution ring was being run from the institute. But then, they didn't have to prove anything to me; they had all the leverage.

As I stepped off the curb at the next intersection, a black Mercedes ran the light. It sped by so fast I was surprised I'd recognized the car's insignia.

If I had stepped out a second sooner . . . but I hadn't.

If Sam had come to my defense when he saw me being led away in handcuffs . . . but he hadn't.

There was one other explanation for Sam's not coming to my rescue. Didn't he have a problem with the police? There was that photograph on his desk: Sam being pushed to the ground by a cop with a club. Maybe he panicked when he saw what was happening to me. Had a flashback. Maybe he wasn't a hero. But that didn't make him a pimp.

~

Upstairs, the apartment was empty. I ran for the sanctuary of my greenhouse and noticed there were several messages on my machine. The first was from Paul telling me he was going to a basketball game with Bob and a few other people and he'd be home after eleven. His cavalier tone broke through my daze. A bracing wave of anger shook me out of my benumbed state and I seethed. Just that morning—which now seemed like many, many days ago—I'd told him where I was going and what I'd planned on doing. He had chosen to deal with this situation the way he'd dealt with so many others— with denial.

The next message was from Olivia, who asked me to call back as soon as I got home. There were two messages from Jack, the first leaving a number where I could reach him, the second saying he was getting on a plane to do an interview, but would I please call his machine and just tell him I was all right.

I called Jack's machine first, glad to hear his voice on his message tape. I left word that it was all over and everything was fine and that I'd call the next morning. Anything else would have been too complicated.

Calling Olivia next, I repeated as much as I could bear to.

"Can I do anything?" she asked when I finished. "Can I come over and sit with you until you fall asleep or take you to dinner or get you drunk or something?"

"No, but thanks. I think I'm okay now that I'm home. I wish the club wasn't closed, though; I'd like to go swimming."

"Why don't I meet you there in the morning?" she asked.

"Yes, early, okay?"

After we hung up, I took a shower. I made the water as hot as I could tolerate and used up half a bar of soap trying to get rid of the feeling I had of being soiled. If only this water could wash away time and I could step out of this shower and start everything all over again. How far back would I have to go?

To the first day I lied to Paul about the little white pills. To the first night I lay beside him pretending I didn't know anything was wrong between us. Years. I'd have to go back years.

Wrapped in my terry cloth robe, I padded into the living room and poured a snifter of brandy. My father's drink. Should I call him in Arizona and ask him to soothe me? Why bother? Like Paul, he'd offer expert advice instead of compassion. Taking the first burning sip of the liquor, I knew it was time to admit none of those old ways worked any magic.

But perhaps love could. Was that thought the reason, when the phone rang a moment later, I assumed it was Jack and answered so eagerly?

It was Sam.

For a moment, I panicked. I wasn't prepared. What was I supposed to say? I couldn't remember.

"Julia, I've been so fucking worried. Why haven't you called? Are you all right?"

*It's going to be fine,* I told myself. *He'll explain about freaking out when he saw the cops. He'll redeem himself.*

"I tried to get over to the hotel, but I got stuck with a patient. I'm sorry. Tell me, Julia, what happened? Where have you been?"

So Sam didn't know I had seen him standing outside the hotel.

Nor did he know that with one lie he had sealed his fate.

After a lifetime of telling lies, to my husband and myself, it was easy to tell another. I repeated the story Detective Fontenella had concocted to explain why I'd left the hotel in handcuffs. "It was a mess. Arthur got carried away and tried to hurt me. The police had to break in. They arrested Arthur and then to protect their case against him, they faked arresting me for solicitation and took us both to the station. Then they let me go."

"Fucking asshole! Did he hurt you?" Sam asked.

Was it my imagination, or did he sound relieved?

"No . . ." *Arthur Lindt didn't*—I wanted to scream into the phone—*but you're hurting me now by continuing this charade!* Instead, I continued the ruse and told Sam the police were holding Lindt overnight until they could get to his stepdaughter. "Detective Fontenella said she'd call you in the morning as soon as she finds out anything."

"Good. Why don't you come over and wait for her call with me in my office? We can talk more about what happened. And how you feel. I can only imagine how fucking stressful this must have been for you."

He was suddenly so smooth, so loquacious; he was giving himself away.

When we finally got off the phone, I drained what was left of the brandy, not caring how much it stung my throat. Leaving the glass next to my bed, I crawled under the covers and turned on the television, praying that between the liquor and the mindless show, I would fall asleep before Paul got home, so I wouldn't have to retell the saga all over.

# 29

The shrill ringing of a telephone shocked me awake, and still half asleep, I reached out for the receiver. "Hello?" my voice was tense, but there was no one on the other end. I heard only a flat, dead dial tone. Had I been dreaming or had the phone really rung? My heart was pounding the way it does when you're awakened suddenly, and as I lay in bed, waiting to calm down, I heard sounds coming from the television in Paul's study.

When had he come home? Had he stood in the door to check in on me or had he walked right by the bedroom, still in denial there was any reason for concern?

I realized I was lying there waiting. For what? For him to come to me? To fall asleep? Remembering a childhood game, I started counting. If I was still awake when I reached one hundred, I'd get up and go inside to confront my husband.

It was time to let go of the image of Paul I'd been holding on to for so long. I hadn't married him but an idea of him. How unfair I'd been to Paul Sterling, choosing him for what he had not been. It was his lack of passion that had attracted me, his inability to be intimate that I'd craved. I hadn't been ready for anything else back then.

The winds were coming off the park and blowing against the window, rattling the glass. I listened to the traffic below us, a few late-night buses and cars zooming down the mostly deserted avenue. Across the street, rats ran in circles looking for food and people who, with no other place to go, used the park's hard benches as beds. Disordered flashbacks from earlier in the evening flickered through my mind: the hotel room drapes swinging shut, Arthur Lindt's red hair, the design on his cigarette lighter, the mass of freckles on his back, the oversize bed, the china ashtray filled with ashes and butts, Lindt's voice instructing me on what to do, my hand holding a cigarette, the tinkling ice in a glass of scotch, Arthur lighting my cigarette in the bar, my lighting that last one in the room, the flash and feel of the handcuffs.

I began to shake. This was no fantasy I'd invented to tantalize a man over the phone but an ugly scene involving the police, nasty threats, betrayal, and criminal activities.

I'd counted past one hundred and hadn't fallen asleep—and Paul hadn't come to me. Had I really thought he would? I got up, pulled on a robe, walked into Paul's den, and stood in the doorway.

"We have to talk," I said to my husband, who was lying on his couch wearing gray sweats and drinking a glass of red wine.

Paul looked away from the television and over to me without bothering to hide his exasperation. "Not tonight, Julia. I'm beat. Let's wait till morning. I can't even think straight. I spent all day answering questions about our numbers and all night trying to get blood from stones with potential donors."

Instead of leaving, I walked in and dragged his desk chair over to the couch so that I was sitting closer to him. His eyes didn't move from the TV screen where a rerun of the movie *Patriot Games* was playing. For a few seconds, I watched along as Harrison Ford sped his vehicle down the expressway, frantically trying to call his wife on her car phone. Having seen the movie before, I knew what was coming. So did Paul, but he remained riveted.

"Paul, I met with Arthur Lindt today and was videotaped with him so the police could show the tape to his stepdaughter. Well, that's what I thought. But it was all a setup."

Paul turned to me, his face paler than it had been a moment ago. "I thought we'd decided you weren't going to meet him—wait—a setup? What exactly are you saying?"

"The police set me up. Arthur Lindt was an undercover cop. He arrested me. Threatened to charge me with prostitution unless I agreed to help."

"Help who? You're not making sense. Help the police?"

"Yeah," I said. "Help the police set up Sam Butterfield so they can finally get him for running a prostitution ring out of the institute."

For one weird second Paul turned back to the TV.

"Detective Fontenella promised neither my name nor my part in their investigation will ever be released to the press."

When he twisted around again, I could see how much difficulty he was having controlling his rage. "Why would you do exactly what I asked you not to do? What were you thinking?" His voice was so damn authoritative.

"I was thinking about a girl who was being abused."

"A girl who was no one to us," he said.

"I couldn't just abandon her because of your fear of publicity."

"You should have let someone else take care of it. Someone who had nothing to lose." He still hadn't raised his voice.

"I couldn't let someone else take care of it—no one else could have done what I did. I thought a child needed help. Surely you can understand what it's like when someone needs your help?"

"This has nothing to do with someone's needing you. I needed you to do the right thing. You disregarded that. Did you even consider how this could affect my position?"

"What are we arguing about, Paul? There was no girl. There won't be any story in the paper. This won't affect you. Or Max."

"Won't affect me? My charity and I are being investigated by the IRS. What is going to happen when it comes out that one of my major donors is a criminal? That the police flipped my own wife to help expose him? That she was working as a phone sex operator?"

"Nothing like that will happen. None of this will be linked to either of us."

"Oh God . . ." Paul dropped his head in his hands and sat there without moving for almost a full minute. When he finally lifted his head, he reached out and touched my fingers with his. It was the same thing Max did when he was hurt or sick.

"I gave you my professional advice, Julia. Why did you ignore it? Why did you put yourself in a dangerous situation where you were completely vulnerable? What if this man had been for real? What if he had hurt you? You're fragile, Julia. You're supposed to be taking care of yourself. I'm responsible for you and I've failed. I didn't realize how much help you still needed."

I ignored the psychoanalytic jargon he was spouting. "You're not responsible for me." My voice came out like a great growl. Paul was going to get all the anger I'd kept from everyone else: from Arthur Lindt, Detective Fontenella, the assistant D.A., and Sam. Especially from Sam. "I am fucking damned responsible for myself. Can you understand that?"

On the television, Harrison Ford, now in the hospital, was bending over his battered wife, his face about to crumple into grief.

"You're overwrought," Paul said, in a professionally calming tone.

"I'm not overwrought. Once and for all, listen to me! There's nothing wrong with my reasoning. My goddamn cognitive powers are intact. I went to that hotel room knowing you warned me not to. I did it anyway."

"What do you want from me, Julia? Histrionics? Chest beating? You want me to get as upset as you are? What will that accomplish? You're home now. You're safe. It's over. I'll take care of everything as long as you promise you'll start taking your medication and never disobey me again. All right?"

"Who the hell do you think you are?" I yelled. "How can you ask that of me?"

"I warned you to stay away from such an explosive situation, but you chose to walk right into it."

I leaned forward as if my presence would elicit some different kind of response. But it didn't. Why had I moved closer to him when I knew I could no longer reach him? I looked up at my husband's concerned face, into his professionally objective, ice blue eyes, and knew I could never go back to the way it had been with Paul being Max's protector and mine. Neither of us were any longer his wards. Paul couldn't steer us away from the dangerous paths and the unsafe harbors anymore. What had ever been so damn attractive about the constrictive comfort he'd provided anyway?

If, instead of offering a psychoanalytic diagnosis, Paul had said all the right things that night, it wouldn't have mattered. I wasn't trying to salvage our marriage anymore. I just wanted Paul to acknowledge who I'd become. To see me, not the distorted image of me he still held on to. I was going to leave, but I wanted him to know exactly who was leaving. So, with my face only inches from his, I began to blurt out details of the evening, desperately trying to engage him in my drama.

"Julia, I don't want to listen to this," he said dispassionately.

"Don't you listen to your patients? Pretend I'm a patient. You do that all the time anyway. Let me tell you how awful it was, Paul. And in another way, amazing. Empowering. I went there frightened out of my mind, but I didn't freak, I didn't panic."

Gently, he pushed me away from him so that we were about a foot apart. "You have to calm down, Julia."

On the television, Harrison Ford found out his daughter would live and then decided he had to rejoin the CIA so he could find and destroy the monster who had done so much damage to his family.

"Why don't you let me put you to bed, Julia? We'll talk in the morning."

"No, it will be worse in the morning. You will have had that much more time to convince yourself I'm having some kind of psychotic breakdown."

"But that's exactly what this is."

For so long my psychosis had been our only common ground.

"No, I'm not. I'm strong now, Paul, and I won't let you try to convince me of weaknesses I've overcome."

"I'm not trying to convince you that you're weak. I'm merely pointing out that you have lost your sense of appropriate behavior."

"No. No. Nothing I've done was inappropriate!" I yelled.

"I know you think that, but you're too upset to see clearly now."

I knew what I'd done and why I'd done it, and the one thing I didn't need was a therapist to help me understand it.

"C'mon—go to bed. I'll call Mike and get the name of a good criminal lawyer. You were almost arrested tonight—or have you forgotten? You need counsel. We need to know how to proceed." He paused for a moment to think and then looked at me curiously. "Julia, why didn't you call me when the police took you in? My service knew where I was all night. I could have been there in minutes. I would have gotten you a lawyer. What were you thinking?"

There was only one reason I hadn't called. After so very long, the time had come to finally admit it out loud. "Paul, I want a divorce." My voice was as flat and emotionless as his had been.

"I don't think you mean that. You're simply under too much stress to even realize what you're saying. We'll talk about it tomorrow, after you've had a chance to rest."

I didn't bother to argue with him after that. What more was there to say?

～

I left Paul sitting in his study with the television lights flickering over his face, but I didn't go back to the empty bedroom. I wandered through my apartment like a sleepwalker, studying the night terrain, touching objects, feeling fabrics.

I opened the door to Max's bedroom and sat down on my stepson's bed, smoothing out the pillows and the comforter. How was I going to tell Max his father and I were separating? How tough would it be for him to deal with so much upheaval in his freshman year? How would I explain that I wasn't leaving him? And that I never would. I shut my eyes and saw him, small and vulnerable, lying in this bed, bathed in sweat and screaming about the giant horses coming to take us away. But that was years ago. He was taller than me now and he'd healed.

We both had.

# 30

I settled down in my greenhouse, staring at the inky green plants, and woke up there in the morning, a dark shadow across my face. Turning east, I looked out. The tenth floor of the building across the way had been completely enclosed. All my direct sun was now blocked. And that, after everything that had happened, was what made me cry. The sun had been stolen from my magical room.

Sometime later, I heard Paul get up and go running. While he was gone, I made myself some coffee, got dressed, and was ready to leave to meet Olivia when he came back.

Sipping from a cup of take-out coffee, he stood in the hallway stretching his legs. He was sweating and his skin was red from the cold. "Good morning," he said, giving me a charming but studied smile.

Some people's faces are open and inviting—when you look at them you sense their souls. But my husband's face was always closed off, impenetrable despite the expression he'd pasted on.

"I'm going to the club," I told him.

"Swimming will be good for you, but before you go, I'd like you to call an attorney Mike recommended and set up a meeting with him. And don't forget, we have dinner plans tonight with Mike and his wife. You need to confirm our reservation—"

I interrupted him. "Are you crazy? Cancel it. We're not having dinner with anyone!"

He looked perplexed. "Cancel dinner with Mike? How can I, Julia? He's chairman of our board. I acknowledge you're going through a bad time. I know it's tough. But once you start taking your medication again, things will get easier."

He was the one who was troubled. It was as if the day and the night before had never happened. As if nothing had changed—but it had. I'd tried to help someone I didn't even know and wound up being coerced into betraying someone who mattered to me very much. My head hurt; my stomach cramped. My legs and arms and neck ached from having been curled up in my armchair overnight.

I didn't continue arguing. I didn't even say good-bye. I just turned and walked out our front door.

~

Olivia was already in the pool when I got in. She waved midstroke and continued doing laps. The water soothed me and I swam on and on, looking out at the clear blue sky. A mile is eighty laps, and it usually took just under an hour. After the first fifteen minutes, I was in rhythm with my strokes, no longer thinking but being part of the water, feeling the coolness breaking against my skin. Beneath my goggles, I watched the turquoise bubbles rise and float up to the purplish blue surface.

What would it be like to swim in the ocean every morning the way Jack did? He said it started out very cold, but once your body cooled down to meet the temperature of the water, you felt as if you and the salt water were in sync.

Maybe I'd go and see him after all this was over. After Thanksgiving. And I'd swim in his ocean with him.

Random thoughts continued to float along with me; a plan was taking shape. I was finally thinking of what would come next.

In the women's locker room, Olivia and I took showers. We talked over the thin metal partitions as we scrubbed the chlorine off our skin and out of our hair. Then, each wrapped in a towel, we stood in front of the mirrors, putting on makeup and drying our hair.

"Look at how pale my skin is," I said to her.

"Indoor skin," she said.

"This is what will happen to the orchids now. They'll change their hue; some of their luster will fade."

"Can't you offset it by the artificial light you're going to install?" she asked as she applied a thin line of black to her eyelids.

I shut off the drier and brushed my hair. "There's still a difference between natural and manufactured light." I paused. "Olivia, do you ever wonder what it would be like to live where the sun could always get to you? To have the sun warm your body all the time?"

"Yeah. You need to have the air-conditioning on all the time," she said.

In the mirror, our eyes met. "You're going to be fine. No matter what Paul says or does. You know that now, don't you, sweetie?" she asked.

"Yeah." I smiled at her. "I know, but do me a favor—keep reminding me, all right?"

Over by my locker, I rubbed myself one last time with a dry towel. I felt the roughness of the terry on my skin like a man's calloused hands.

Who had calloused hands?

A gardener.

Did I know a gardener? Had I seen someone's hands roughed up with calluses? For the first time, I realized that when I'd masturbated on the phone, while I touched myself, I'd imagined a man's calloused hands were touching me.

I looked at myself again in the mirror. When I was eighteen, my face had no definition; I was pretty in a typically teenage way. Now there were slight shadows under my eyes, my bones were stronger, the vagueness in my face was gone. I let the towel drop and looked at my body—how would a man see me?

Once we were both dressed, Olivia waited for me in the lounge while I used the pay phone to call Jack.

When I reached him, Jack insisted on hearing the story then and there. After I finished, there were a few beats of silence. When he finally spoke, his voice was harsh with anger. "Christ, you shouldn't have had to go through that! How dare they set you up! Violate your rights! Julia, you know, if you want to pursue this—"

"Paul's already contacted an attorney, but all I want is to get this whole goddamn mess behind me."

"I should have been there . . . or found out more . . ." Now regret echoed in his voice.

"I asked you not to, remember? It would have made me furious if you hadn't honored my request."

Behind me, one of the maintenance men dropped a piece of pool equipment and it crashed on the tile floor. "Where the hell are you?" Jack asked.

"I'm at the health club. With Olivia. I've been swimming. I had to get out of the apartment, away from Paul."

"What does that mean?"

"Oh Jack, he tried to turn everything around and convince me I'm falling back into old destructive patterns of behavior."

"By sticking your neck out? Your husband needs to get a life away from his couch."

"So do I," I said.

"Is that what you're thinking?"

"Yeah, but listen, Olivia's waiting for me and I have to go over to the institute and pretend I'm going crazy not knowing what's happened with the detective and the girl. I'll call you later. When I get home."

"Julia?" The way he'd said my name pulled at my insides.

"Yes?"

He hesitated. "Just be careful. Crossing the street. Going up the elevator. Walking down the stairs. Just take care of yourself, all right?" His words wrapped around me, held me tight.

"Yes, all right. Jack?"

"What?"

"Do you have calluses on your hands?"

"From all the yard work, sure. Why?"

"I was wondering, that's all. I'll talk to you later," I said, and hung up.

~

Olivia and I had breakfast in the coffee shop downstairs. Actually, *she* ate breakfast; *I* drank two cups of coffee. By the time I got to the institute, Detective Fontenella had already called Sam.

He rose from his desk when I walked through his door.

"When they showed Lindt's stepdaughter the videotape of the two of you, she broke down and admitted he's been abusing her for over two years. Julia, you did a wonderful thing—you freed that child."

As I stood in the middle of Sam's office, the tension of the last few days pulled even tighter around me. I'd expected to be incensed by Sam—I hadn't counted on being saddened. I wished I wasn't there doing what I was about to do.

Excusing myself, I went into the bathroom and, for the second time that morning, stared at my face. This time I wondered at the silvery tracks of tears on my cheeks. I hadn't known until then that I was crying.

Shutting my eyes, I took a deep breath and a strange longing came over me. If only I could go back to the way it had been between Paul and me when Max was little—when I wanted to be taken care of and Paul had taken care of me so very, very well. *No,* said the voice who had been hidden away back then. *No.* I was no longer dependent on him. There were decisions to make now, and I could make them on my own. I wasn't afraid anymore. And when I opened my eyes and looked back in the mirror, I wasn't crying anymore.

## 31

Sam wanted to take me out to lunch. "To acknowledge what you've done," he said.

How could I sit across a table from him and not give myself away? Yet how could I refuse his offer? He was giving me exactly the opportunity I needed to get this whole business over with. So we made plans to meet two hours later.

To kill time, I went window-shopping on Madison Avenue. But I saw nothing. Winding up at Barney's department store on 61st Street, I wandered through the aisles touching soft leather bags, feeling silk scarves, and sniffing exotic perfumes. Preoccupied with what lay ahead, I found the different kinds of merchandise indistinguishable. Finally, I took the escalator downstairs to the pay phones and called the lawyer Mike Menken had recommended.

Chuck Laird sounded like a nice man. Falling into a habit I'd developed since starting with the institute, I tried to imagine him. Buff colors. Suede. Sandy beaches.

It turned out Paul had already called and briefed him. "So when would you like to come in, Mrs. Sterling?" he asked.

"First, let me ask you a question. Is what the police did to me entrapment?"

"If they were to try to prosecute you, yes, it would be entrapment. But the NYPD has no desire to take you to court. They are using you to get to Sam Butterfield. Plain and simple. It's unpleasant and ethically questionable, but it happens a few times a day in this city."

"So if I just do what the police have asked, will that be the end of all this?" I shifted my weight from one foot to the other.

"In a word, yes. Make the introduction for them and then just walk away. But you do have several other options, which I should outline for you." He explained my rights and then my alternatives, each of which required taking further legal actions.

"I appreciate what you're saying, but all I want to do is end this as soon as possible."

"That's why the police use this technique so often. They have a lot of success with it."

"Is there a downside to my simply cooperating?" I asked.

Nothing he said gave me any reason to cancel my lunch.

Sam was already waiting when I arrived at the same restaurant where we'd had drinks months earlier. Inside, several of the patrons were speaking French and one woman had a poodle at her feet. I wished I were in the right mood to appreciate that I'd stepped off a New York street and into a Parisian bistro on the Left Bank.

I'd been nervous meeting Arthur Lindt, but at least I'd had Alice's persona to hide behind. Sam was expecting Julia and I wasn't sure I was a good enough actress to play myself.

The owner rushed up and greeted Sam effusively. Then he showed us to a corner table far away from the front door.

After asking if I'd drink wine, Sam ordered a bottle of rosé and the waiter scurried off to get it. A busboy put down a basket of hard crusty rolls, a pot of butter, and two glasses of ice water. Hoping my shaking hands wouldn't give me away, I took a long sip from my glass.

"I think I've done enough research—" I started, but I was interrupted by Sam's brash laughter.

"I'd sure as shit say so!" he added.

I laughed along with him.

"So you're ready to get started on the book?" he asked.

In the craziness of the last twenty-four hours, I had forgotten about the book. For months, it had been my talisman and my destination, and until that moment, I hadn't realized it was no longer possible. I felt sick.

"Yes," I said fervently.

"Regardless of the consequences to your marriage?"

"That isn't an issue anymore."

He nodded and handed me all the tapes of my phone conversations. "Then you are going to need these." He smiled.

At that moment, the waiter arrived with the wine and poured some for Sam to taste. After receiving Sam's approving nod, he filled our glasses with the rose-colored liquid.

Lifting his glass toward me, Sam made a toast. "To the book, then, and all the fantasies it will make come true." Reaching across the table, he clinked his glass with mine, and then we both drank. In my lap, I dug my fingernails into the flesh of my thigh to stop myself from feeling anything. How I wished the toast could come true. How I wished Sam hadn't betrayed me.

But he had.

Sam had stood outside that hotel and watched the police take me away. He had not stepped forward. Had not interceded. He had stayed hidden in the shadows of the hotel's façade and seen exactly what had happened and then lied to me about it.

The wine was cold and slightly fruity. It should have been delicious, but it wasn't.

"You're so fucking quiet. What's going on?" he asked.

*If I could go to Lindt's hotel room*, I told myself, *I can do this too. I can pretend. I can talk to Sam the way I always have.* I took another sip of wine.

As our discussion continued, I almost did forget what I'd discovered about Sam and the institute. For a little while, our conversation, like so many we'd had in the past, completely absorbed and engaged me.

"Last night, Paul told me he thinks I'm having a breakdown . . ." Approaching dangerous ground, I fell silent and let Sam pick up the conversation.

"He needs to believe that. It's a rationalization he can live with," Sam offered.

We both drank more wine, and the waiter appeared to refill our glasses and then take our order.

"Well, anyway, for what it's worth, I think you're fine. More than ready for the next stage," Sam continued after the waiter left.

"What stage is that?" I asked.

"To merge all those Julias into one and see who she is. You might actually be pleased with her if you could just refrain from judging her too fucking harshly."

"What does this Julia do?"

"She lives in the world, not outside of it. She doesn't back away from experiences just because they frighten her. And she takes chances," he finished.

Tears threatened, but I blinked them away.

"It's been a long siege," Sam said. "Maybe you should take some time off. Why don't you postpone starting the book until after the first of the year."

Behind my eyes, the answers were all there, but in the shadows. I could make out their shapes, but not their details. "After the first of the year . . . yes, maybe. Maybe I should wait."

Our food arrived. I'd ordered a niçoise salad and Sam had ordered salmon tartar, which he proceeded to mix with an enormous amount of mustard and Tabasco. While he ate and I pushed food around on my plate, we talked about a schedule for the book. "Well, first I'll need to transpose all my tapes to notes." I was spinning the fantasy and continuing the charade. "Then using those along with your notes, I'll prepare a detailed chapter-by-chapter outline. It will take about six weeks, and then I can begin the actual writing."

Sam never suspected it was all a fabrication. I never stopped wishing it wasn't.

The lunch was almost over. The waiter had arrived with our espressos. I was so anxious, I drank mine too soon and burned my tongue. Staring into the offending brew, I began tentatively: "Sam, there's a favor I have to ask." Picking up my head, I looked across the table at him.

"Anything. How can I help?" His expression was so receptive, his tone so sincere. The green emerald sparkled in his ear. He wasn't a criminal, I thought. He was an iconoclast. Someone who conscientiously broke the rules because he didn't believe in them. No, that was romanticizing him. He was a pimp. I took another sip of the coffee. It was cooler now and easier to swallow.

"A friend of mine is getting divorced and she needs to earn some money. She's not trained for any kind of office work, but I think she'd make a good phone therapist. Will you meet her?"

## 32

For the next few days I waited. Never far from a television or radio tuned to the news, I listened for any mention of Sam Butterfield or his institute. Restless, never hungry, I developed insomnia and was prone to crying jags. A therapist might have done some good, but I was sick of the profession. Besides, I knew the signs. It was a depression and, like quicksand, no matter how hard I fought it, it was sucking me under.

And why not? I wasn't only dealing with Sam's betrayal and facing the end of my marriage—I was mourning the loss of my book.

I obsessed on how to craft a book that could never be written. Despondent, I took out the tapes I'd made in the last six weeks. My intention was to throw them away, but instead I logged them into a notebook and then started listening to them. Initially, I was embarrassed to hear my own voice seducing those strangers, but soon I heard beyond the words, to the men's needs, their fears, their loneliness, and their desperate attempts to find the eroticism missing from their lives.

There were times I laughed out loud, times I cringed. Other times I was nervous, angry, and heartbroken. Often I was aroused, sometimes so much I turned off the tape and made myself come. But mostly I was amazed as I listened to the transformation of a thirty-eight-year-old woman as she discovered the pleasure and power of her sexuality for the first time.

During those days, Paul was waiting too. He circled around me, living in some kind of limbo. Whenever I broached the subject of our separation, he equivocated. Finally, I agreed to postpone making any plans until after Max came home for the holidays and the IRS investigation into FIT's finances was concluded.

It was the Tuesday before Thanksgiving. I was in the greenhouse listening to the last of the tapes when the phone rang. It was Jack. After we said hello, he asked me what I was doing and I told him.

"You know, of everything that's happened, I'm the most upset about losing the book. Goddamn it, Jack. I wanted to write that book."

"So write it."

"I can't. You know that." I was annoyed.

"No, all I know is you can't do the book Sam hired you to do. But there is another book you can write. A much more important book about you and Sam and the training—"

Interrupting him, I finished his thought. "And Arthur Lindt and the police setting me up— Wait, before I get too excited—can I do this, Jack? Can I really write about what happened? Can I expose them all?"

There was nothing in the shadows anymore. I could see so clearly now. I just couldn't say the words fast enough. "Oh God, Jack. I want to try. Will you help me? You know what's weird? If I pull this off, I will have written the exposé I accused you of wanting to write when you started snooping around."

It was a relief to laugh. To know I was going to be able to write the book after all and Jack would be there to help me.

"Julia, now that we've figured out what you're going to do with all those tapes, maybe it's time for you to play one for me," he said.

"Are you crazy? I can't play you any of those tapes."

"Then send me one," he suggested.

"I can't." I turned away from the window, away from the building, and looked at my plants.

"Why?" he asked.

I hesitated.

"Because they're confidential?" he asked.

"Yeah," I answered. Thankful for the convenient excuse he'd supplied.

"But that's not the only reason, is it, Julia?" He was pushing.

"No, it's not, all right? I can't let you hear them because I would be embarrassed, because it would be awkward—what would you think of me?"

"Nothing I haven't already thought before."

"What does that mean?" I asked.

"That you're not only smart but you're sexy too. That you're creative and sensual and inventive and—"

"Now I am embarrassed," I interrupted, half joking. Reaching out, I moved a pot around so the purple flower faced me. One drop of water glistened on a petal.

"Julia, don't be embarrassed. Not with me. Not anymore. Not unless you want to go backward. Let it go. Listen to me—I've never stopped wanting you since the first time I saw you standing in my kitchen, fresh out of my roommate's bed."

"I didn't love him," I said, and shut my eyes.

"But you didn't love me either," he said regretfully.

"No, I didn't, not then . . ." The rest of the words remained unsaid.

"Go on, finish. What were you going to say?" he encouraged.

"Not yet, Jack. Not so fast."

He laughed out loud. "Not so fast? Julia, I've been waiting for you since I was nineteen."

I didn't know what to say, but it didn't seem to matter to Jack. "Tell me something, Julia—have you and Paul talked yet? Have you decided what you're doing?"

I opened my eyes and looked out the window at the tall new building. "I'm leaving him." It was surprisingly easy to say.

"So you and I are both going to be free at the same time."

Again, I couldn't say anything even though in my mind all the words were there, waiting to be spoken. "I'm going to have to move."

"Come down here. Come live with me. Or live near me. Just don't disappear, not now," he said.

"Leave New York? I have to think—"

"No, you don't. You have to act. You've been doing too much thinking for too long. Julia?"

"Yes?"

"What are you wearing?" he asked in a deep whisper.

"Jack, I told you—"

He didn't let me speak. "You and I have been so good at pretending there was nothing between us all these years except friendship. We had no choice. But we can be ourselves now. C'mon, Julia—talk to me. Now, over the phone, the way you did with those men."

"I can't." I stood up and paced the length of the greenhouse.

"Why the hell not?" he asked.

"Because you're Jack. And with you, I'm Julia. I wasn't me with those men—I was Alice Carroll. Shit, I can't explain it. Why is this suddenly so damn important to you?"

He laughed sarcastically. "You don't know?"

"No."

"Okay, then, do something else. Tell me about our kiss in the cab. Tell me what it felt like."

"Why are you pushing me so hard?" I was shouting, but I didn't care.

"Because you talked to all those strangers. You shared their fantasies and made them hard and made them come and you won't even describe what it felt like to kiss me? I'm so fucking jealous I'm going crazy. Don't you see that?" Now he was yelling too.

"I can't do what you're asking. Can't you understand that?"

"No. I can't. I don't want to. Because if I do, I'll have to face that nothing between us has changed. Don't you know I want all of you? Not just the sweet, smart Julia, but the sexy one too, the one that gets turned on and has fantasies. I want to know what those fantasies are. I want you to know about mine. Fuck it, Julia, if you don't understand what I'm talking about, you might as well stay with Paul. Good-bye." He slammed the phone down.

I sat down in my slipper chair, holding the receiver in my lap until a mechanical voice broke through the static buzz. "If you'd like to make a call, please hang up and dial again . . ." And as the voice droned on, I put the phone back in its cradle.

# 33

~

Early Thursday morning, Max came home. Using his key, he let himself in. I didn't even hear him until he called out my name and then his father's. I rushed out into the foyer. My arms barely reached around his back and he was so strong he was crushing me, but I didn't pull away. I just breathed him in, feeling the rough wool of his sweater on my cheek and smelling the crisp cold scent of winter.

"I've really missed you," I said. "How'd you get here so soon?"

"I got a ride. But I didn't get to eat breakfast. I'm starving. Can you make me some French toast?"

Ever since he was a little boy, over the weekends or on holidays, when there was enough time, he'd asked for French toast. It was the one breakfast Paul didn't like.

"Only if you come inside and sit with me while I make it," I answered.

In the kitchen, Max poured himself some juice and leaned on the island watching me work. "Did you remember to get my mother's watch?"

Max was wiping the watch clean when Paul came back from running. The greeting he gave his son was more formal than I had given him but no less heartfelt. When he noticed Anne's watch, Paul's eyes narrowed and his lips disappeared into a thin line. He stiffened as if ready to deflect a blow. He didn't say a word, but Max knew Paul was waiting for an explanation.

"I'm giving it to Betsy. Her birthday was yesterday."

"I don't think you should. It was your mother's."

"I know." He shrugged. "That's why I want Betsy to have it." Paul's expression remained stern.

"Sorry, Dad," Max said, "but it is mine, isn't it?" When Paul didn't answer, Max slipped the watch into his pocket and out of his father's sight and turned to me. "Julia, do you have a box I could put this in?"

As I slid the egg-soaked bread into a frying pan, I told him I'd look after breakfast. Before either Paul or his son had a chance to start another conversation, the doorbell rang and Max ran off to get it, yelling as he went that it was Betsy.

Paul turned his back to me as he poured himself a cup of coffee. "Is that why you went to the vault? To get Anne's watch?" he asked.

"Yes." I flipped the bread with the spatula.

"Why didn't you ask me if that was a good idea?"

"Because Max is over eighteen and Anne's things belong to him now."

Max brought Betsy into the kitchen where we all sat down. Max and I ate French toast; Betsy and Paul drank coffee. Paul was uncomfortable watching his son with his girlfriend. Whenever Max leaned over to kiss her or squeeze her hand—it had been over a month since they'd seen each other—Paul turned away. Eventually, he used the shower as an excuse to leave the three of us alone.

After Max finished eating, he wanted to go look at the greenhouse. Outside, the sun was shining, but in the glass-enclosed room the flowers were in shadow.

Max stood transfixed, staring out the window at the monstrous building across the way. "So it finally happened, huh?"

"Yeah," I answered. "But we knew it would. As soon as they put up the scaffolding."

"I kept thinking something would stop them, you know?" Max said with a sad smile.

Betsy, who'd been examining the orchids, looked up. "What happened?"

"That building—it was never there before." Max pointed. "It's changed everything in here."

"All of my light is gone," I continued to explain, wondering if Max sensed I was talking about more than the sunlight in the greenhouse.

He seemed to, because he turned to me then and very tenderly asked, "Julia, what are you going to do now?"

"I don't know, Max."

"You're really bummed about this, aren't you?"

About the building. About Paul and me. About how I was ever going to tell Max I was leaving his father. I raised my hands up and then let them fall to my sides. "Hey, at least now we know what's the worst that can happen."

He leaned over and kissed me on the cheek. "I love you." He'd said it so easily, so simply. Where had he learned to be so generous with his emotions? Certainly not from his father. And not from seeing Paul and me together.

~

That afternoon we took our annual drive out of the city to Max's maternal grandparents' horse farm in Duchess County, New York. Max and Betsy sat in the backseat, wrapped in each other, while he pointed out the signposts he'd used as a kid to judge how much longer the trip was going to take. "It's only an hour drive, but when I was a kid, it seemed like forever."

In the front seat, Paul and I barely spoke. To camouflage our silence, I played tapes: vintage Beatles, Simon and Garfunkle, and then Phil Collins and Bonnie Raitt.

Paul was tense in the car. Spending Thanksgiving with Max's grandparents had become a tradition long before I came into the family, but it was one Paul didn't like. The farm was where Anne had died and he hated being there, making the concession to go only once a year for the holiday dinner. The rest of the holidays, we invited the Drabbles to visit Max in the city, and often during the summer, they took Max on vacation with them. Wonderful people who'd never gotten over the loss of their daughter, they were conscious of not overwhelming their grandson with their surfeit of love.

The Drabbles had never treated me as a surrogate daughter and I'd never expected them to, but over the years we had become dear friends and I was more comfortable with them than Paul had ever been. He never stopped trying to compete with their genteel ways and old money. Around them, he name-dropped and bragged about his latest success, never realizing all that mattered to the Drabbles was that he be a good father to their grandson.

~

We pulled through the gates at about five and then it was a two-mile drive up to the stone house that sat on the edge of the two-hundred-acre farm. Jane Drabble, a white-haired, soft-cheeked woman who favored pastel button-down shirts with khaki pants, came running out of the front door, followed by her husband, Brian. He was wearing a cashmere sweater with patches on the elbows, well-rubbed corduroys, and Docksiders. They sailed in the summer and rode horses all year long. Both of them had skin burned by the sun and beaten by the wind.

They threw their arms around Max and then Max introduced them to Betsy. After greeting Paul and me, they ushered us inside where it was warm and smelled invitingly of roasted chestnuts and pine cones. In the living room, other members of the family were sitting and standing around the six-foot-high hearth where a fire roared.

Sipping spiked apple cider and nibbling popcorn, we got caught up with the Drabbles' son, Peter, and his wife, Susan. We talked to their two children, Scott and Christopher, the old twin aunts, other cousins, and their kids. As I murmured about what a good year it had been, I wondered what would happen if I just told everyone the truth about my book, the research I'd done, and Arthur Lindt in the hotel room. How would they respond? Surprisingly, I didn't imagine anyone—even here in this enclave of respectability—would be as aghast as Paul had been.

At six-thirty, Winifred, the elderly housekeeper who'd been with the family for as long as anyone could remember, announced that dinner was ready. We took our seats in the dining room around the long banquet table, which was set with the Drabbles' best china and silver.

Dinner was a boisterous affair, especially because the twin aunts were both quite deaf. As usual, Max and his cousin Scott made a point to have long conversations with the sisters, who thoroughly enjoyed the boys' attention. The din that night was also exacerbated by a political argument that started with Peter and his father. Soon, everyone was involved, including the two deaf aunts, who kept shouting, "What are they saying?" to Max or Scott, both of whom took delight in loudly repeating the last polemic uttered.

My husband talked to everyone there except me. Watching him from my new vantage point, I wondered why more people didn't notice how forced he was, how he kept all but his son at arm's length. Oh, Paul listened and responded, but he wasn't engaged. He was ever the therapist. It was in the set of his shoulders, the way he sat back in his chair, the angle of his head as he listened and nodded, encouraging confessions.

Max and Betsy, who were sitting next to each other, couldn't keep their hands off each other, even when they were eating. At some point during the day, they'd gone off alone and Max had given Betsy the watch, because all during dinner, she kept looking down at her wrist, checking to see that Max's gift was still there. Whenever Paul saw her do it, his face clouded over and he turned away.

I was sitting between Peter and one of his sons, but this wasn't one of Paul's FIT dinner parties where I had to make sure the conversation flowed. Thanksgiving at the Drabbles' was a free-for-all, a warm embrace I always looked forward to. For the last fourteen years, there'd been no question where I'd spend Thanksgiving. By this time next year, my book would be finished and the investigation long since settled, and I—would I still be here?

After coffee and dessert were served, everyone drifted into the living room or the library or down to the billiard room to play pool. Restless, I grabbed one of the heavy jackets that hung from the brass hooks in the mudroom and slipped outside.

It was nine o'clock and a half-moon shone brightly on the frosted ground. An infinite number of stars studded the sky. The temperature had dropped and was well below freezing. In the distance, a horse whinnied and another answered. Crossing the lawn, I took the pathway down to the old stone wall bordering the woods, where a herd of deer lived. Sometimes, if you stood still long enough and stared into the trees you could see them, camouflaged by the branches.

After a few minutes, I heard something behind me and turned around to catch sight of Max and Betsy walking arm in arm toward the stable. Leaning against the stones, I watched their single merged form move in a slow dance across the nighttime landscape. They were lost in each other in that way I imagined happens only when you're eighteen and in love for the first time.

Or can it happen like that when you're older? Can you fall in love with the same intensity and passion at thirty-five or forty or fifty? Can someone still come along and make an imprint on your body and your mind and irrevocably shake you awake? I was thinking of my cab ride with Jack, but I brushed it aside. I hadn't talked to him since our argument. Every day I'd wanted to call him back, but I wouldn't until I knew how to explain why I couldn't give him what he wanted.

As Max and Betsy disappeared into the barn, I heard creaking and looked back to the house as Paul and Brian stepped outside. Each was smoking a cigar. Paul didn't often smoke, but once a year he shared this ritual with his former father-in-law.

They sat down on the wide stone steps and their voices broke the stillness. Then laughter sounded—a boy's and a girl's—and then the steady clip-clop of horses' hooves.

My husband looked toward the barn, alerted by the combination of sounds. So did Brian Drabble. I understood before they did what was happening and watched Max and Betsy—who had no idea there were any witnesses to their nighttime ride—come out of the stable on horseback.

It was an enchanting moonlit scene: two beautiful kids gracefully loping across a winter field on the backs of sleek, elegant animals. Until Paul let out a frightened cry and took off, running after them.

Neither Max nor Betsy heard him over the sound of their galloping horses.

Finally, realizing he couldn't outrun the horses, Paul gave up and started jogging back toward the house. From opposite directions, Brian and I ran toward him, and we all met by the stable.

"Brian!" I'd never seen Paul so frantic. "You've got to go after them. Max has never been on a horse before—he'll hurt himself!" Paul was out of breath and out of control. His heart had left his chest and was riding with his son on the back of that big black horse.

Before Brian could take a step, I stopped him. "No, don't go, Brian. It's all right. Max knows how to ride."

Paul stared at me as if I'd been talking gibberish. "What do you mean?"

"He's been riding since he was twelve," I explained.

"He's been riding since he was twelve?" he repeated.

I nodded.

"And you knew about it?" His face twisted into an angry snarl; only his eyes still registered fear.

"Don't you remember when he was a little boy and had those terrible nightmares? I took him to see the horses then, so he wouldn't be so scared of them. He fell in love with the animals. Years later, he wanted to take riding lessons and I went with him."

"But I forbade him ever to get near a horse!" Paul was putting it all together, adding up all the betrayals.

"Your protection was suffocating him. Besides, he desperately needed to know his mother, and the horses were part of her."

Beside me, Brian Drabble stepped forward and put his hand on my arm. There were tears in his eyes. He nodded at me and something passed between us. I felt almost as if I'd been blessed.

Then he turned back to Paul. "You don't need me here," he said, and headed back to the house.

Paul walked over to the stable door and pounded it with his fist. "How could you have lied to me like that?" He hit the wood again and the hollow sound echoed in the silence. Then, looking out in the direction his son had taken, he said, "I don't know if I can forgive you for this."

Taking a step closer to him, I slid on a patch of ice. Paul saw me skid but didn't reach out to steady me. Instead, I found my own balance. "I don't expect you to forgive me, Paul. I didn't do anything wrong. I am your wife, not your patient. I'm Max's stepmother, not his baby-sitter. I made the best decisions I could and I stand by them."

"Then stand by them alone." He was still searching the darkness, scanning the space stretched out before us for some sign of his son, listening for the sound of the returning hoofbeats.

"Regardless of how you feel about me, I don't want you to be angry with Max. Paul, Max needed to know about the horses. Can't you remember those nightmares? You said he'd outgrow them, but he didn't. He wouldn't tell you because he knew even better than I did how much you still mourned Anne, and he thought he'd make you sad. But he told me that in his dreams giant horses came and tried to take us all away. He tried to fight them off alone. They were snorting and foaming at the mouth. They reared up on their hind legs and overpowered him. So I used live horses to chase away the phantom ones. You're the therapist. You can understand that, can't you?"

Paul's gaze steadfastly searched the horizon for some sign of movement. If it hadn't been for Max, I would have gone back inside the house, called a taxi, gone to the redbrick train station in town, and boarded the first train back to . . . but I couldn't abandon Max. Not yet. Not until I knew that everything would be all right between Paul and him.

So I stood in the freezing cold beside the man who'd been my husband for the last fourteen years. But we did not say another word to each other. While we waited, it started to snow, the air filling with flakes, falling like stars out of the sky. Swirling around our heads, the snow made it even more difficult to see out into the night. Finally we heard a far-off echo. As it grew louder, my heartbeat grew louder too, in anticipation.

Max's face was flushed with the cold and snow dusted his hair, but his eyes glittered and he smiled in greeting until he realized his father was seeing him on a horse for the first time. His eyes slid over and examined mine. I shrugged, trying to warn him and calm him at the same time.

Dismounting, Max stood beside his horse and held the reins while, behind him, Betsy also dismounted. She stayed back. I tried to give her some signal everything would be all right, but she never took her eyes off Max.

"Dad, before you say anything—" Max started, but Paul interrupted.

"Take the horse inside, son. Tie him up. Put a blanket on him. He'll catch cold out here all sweated up like that."

"Let me explain—"

"I said take the horse inside," Paul said sternly.

Max turned around to Betsy and handed her the reins to his horse. She led both animals into the stable.

"If you want to yell at someone, yell at me," I said to Paul. "I encouraged Max to think it was all right to have secrets from you. I was wrong—for Max; for me too. We both should have stood up to you and confronted you. We should have fought it out."

Paul ignored me as he spoke to his son. "I forbade you to ever ride horses, didn't I? Yet you rode," Paul accused Max. "You lied. You betrayed me."

"You were intractable, Dad. And you made it clear there was no discussion. You never wanted to hear how frightened I was. Julia did, and she helped me.

"I got up on my first horse sweating bullets, but I got on. And I don't care if you're furious, because it wasn't about what you wanted—it was about what I needed."

"Your mother died on a horse!" Paul shouted, and then shook his head as if to shake off the memory that had invaded his tirade. "The point is, I forbade you."

"Yeah, with words, but they were just words, you know. The same kind of words you used to tell me not to be sad anymore that Mom was gone. Or not to worry about my nightmares, but those words didn't work. The nightmares always came back."

"You should have been in therapy if it was that bad, not on the back of some animal," Paul said to Max, and then swung around and attacked me with more words. "If you'd been thinking straight, you would have found a way to tell me and I would have taken him to a good child psychologist and we would have worked out his dreams in a controlled environment."

I was ready to answer. I knew exactly what I wanted to say, but before I could answer, Max answered for me. Although he used his own phrases, he expressed exactly what I would have. Was that really so strange? We were both the children of men who got results by going so deep inside the psyche they lost sight of the soul.

"Therapy can do a lot, Dad, but it can't do everything. You have to live too. You have to make mistakes and try things sometimes, you know?"

"Even if you're risking your life?" Paul screamed.

Max took a step closer to his father. "Yes."

Paul was forcing himself to stay in control. He couldn't let go, not even with his son. But Max let go for him. He was, after all, a son who loved his father, who understood him and forgave him in a way that I never could.

"Dad, I understand why you ordered me not to ride. You were scared for me, and that's why I didn't tell you. Just like you were scared by how much I missed Mom. Or how much you did.

"But sometimes you need to feel all those things, you know? Even if they're bad. Even if your stomach does flips and your heart skips a beat—at least you know you're alive. Sometimes talking doesn't work and you just have to feel things and do things, you know?"

I wasn't sure Paul knew, but I did.

"It's late," Paul said, and turned away from the stable. "And it's cold." He started to walk past Max up to the house, but Max stepped in front of him and Paul was forced to stop. For a second, they just looked at each other. I wondered if Paul were really seeing his son or just a reflection of himself. It didn't matter. In the end, Paul threw his arm around Max's shoulder and pulled his son close. "C'mon. Let's go inside," Paul said quietly.

Max glanced back at me.

"It's okay," I said. "I'll wait for Betsy. You go with your father."

They walked off together, arms around each other, but at the door, Max said something to Paul, who went inside by himself.

Max came back to where I was standing. When he reached me, I put my arms around him. Behind me, I heard Betsy come out of the barn, and I could feel her waiting. "Listen," Max said. "I'm sorry about all that. It really was my fault."

"No, we share that honor."

"It will be okay for me. Somehow or other Dad and I always work things out. What about you? Will it be okay with the two of you?"

"I'm not sure anymore, Max."

He cocked his head the way he always had when he was a little boy trying to understand something.

"You know I'll never be far away, Max." I reached up and stroked his cheek. How soft it had been then; how scratchy it was now.

"I do know that. And whatever you do, it will be all right with me. I guess I've known things weren't good between you two for a long time."

Betsy came up to him then and he took her hand and pulled her close, tucking her into his side. His long arm wrapped completely around her back and she looked up at him with so much adoration I shut my eyes, worried for her that she found such grace in his protection. It was something I didn't want anymore—to be protected by a man.

# Epilogue

~

It is midnight. I haven't turned on the lights in the greenhouse so I can't see the tall building out my window. For several hours, I've just been sitting here surrounded by the plants I've spent so much time growing.

It's been almost three weeks since Jack called and then hung up so abruptly, so angrily. We haven't talked since.

~

I'm well into a chapter outline on my book, now that I know how it will end. The story broke two weeks ago on the eleven o'clock nightly news. On the basis of evidence the district attorney's office presented, Sam Butterfield had been indicted by the grand jury. Sam, his hair in a ponytail and his earring twinkling, stood in front of his institute and railed against the system. He defended his renegade philosophy and denied he'd done anything wrong. The station had to bleep out all the *fuck*'s.

Watching his image on the screen, I first wished him ill, then luck, and finally, wished he just wound up with whatever he deserves.

~

Five days ago, the IRS closed their investigation into my husband's charity. Paul fared better than Sam. The story, which was buried on the metro page of the *Times,* stated that only a few minor infractions had been discovered. The agency would retain its nonprofit status. My husband's reputation remains intact; as does his position with the board. The only stipulation the IRS made was that the agency could no longer pay for the director's apartment. Paul will have to take back a few private patients in order to pay the rent.

~

It's been three days since Paul and I decided, without recriminations or arguments, to live apart. There was no passion in our leaving each other, just as there had been none in our coming together.

The next morning, we drove up to Princeton and told Max about our separation. He seemed to take it in stride, insisting he'd be okay if this meant both of us were going to be happier. I knew we were hurting him, but there was nothing I could do to protect him. I took solace in knowing he'd get through it; he's that strong.

~

And so am I.

Now there's just one thing left for me to do. I pick up the phone and dial Jack's long-distance number, not caring that it's late and I might be waking him up.

~

"Hello." His voice is groggy with sleep.

"Hello."

"Julia," he says, and his sleepy smile comes across the line.

My heart is thudding in my ears. I'd always been nervous when I'd talked to a client, but this is far more difficult. This time, I have something to lose and something to gain. This time, it's not just some sexual game I'm playing. And this time, I can't ask Alice Carroll to come to my rescue.

~

"Are you busy?" I ask.

"Sort of. I was sleeping."

I lay back in my chair picturing his body, tasting his lips, feeling his calloused hands on my skin. I'm so anxious, I have to wait and catch my breath.

"So you're in bed?"

"Yes, I am."

"What are you wearing?" I whisper.

I hear him sigh, a delighted sigh.